CYBERPUNK

Stories of Hardware, Software, Wetware, Evolution and Revolution

EDITED BY VICTORIA BLAKE

underland press

TABLE OF CONTENTS

INTRODUCTION

By Victoria Blake

"As American SF lies in a reptilian torpor, its small, squishy cousin, Fantasy, creeps gecko-like across the bookstands," Bruce Sterling wrote in the first issue of *Cheap Truth*, a one-page, double-sided bright coal of a fan-zine first published in 1983. "Dreaming of dragon-hood, Fantasy has puffed itself up with air like a Mojave chuckwalla. SF's collapse ha[s] formed a vacuum that forces Fantasy into a painful and explosive bloat . . . Short stories, crippled with the bends, expand into whole hideous trilogies as hollow as nickel gumballs."

These were fighting words, aimed directly at the bulls-eye of publishers, editors, critics, authors, and readers in the "smokestack" publishing-industrial complex. There was, Sterling wrote in *Cheap Truth* issue five, "a crying need to re-think, re-tool, and adapt to the modern era. SF has one critical advantage: it is still a pop industry that is close to its audience. It is not yet wheezing in the iron lung of English departments or begging for government Medicare through arts grants. . . . SF has always preached the inevitability of change. Physician, heal thyself."

The physician, in this case, was the collection of early 80s writers that *Cheap Truth* showcased as carriers of the flame—Lewis Shiner, Rudy Rucker, William Gibson, et al—and the challenge was to find a new voice for a new kind of reader in a new kind of world. "This year's Nebula Ballot looked like a list of stuff that Mom and Dad said it was okay to read," a pseudonymous Lewis Shiner wrote in *Cheap Truth*. "I mean, this is the kind of writing that Mom and Dad grew up on, full of 'Golly's' and blushes and grins. And aren't those dolphins cute? . . . They'd rather hear that somebody 'muttered an oath' or came out with some made-up word like 'Ifni!' than be told that they really said 'shit' or 'shove it up your ass, motherfucker.'"

Nobody had ever read anything like what the cyberpunks were writing—stories and novels that were the bastard child of science fiction, with a common-man perspective, a love of tech and drugs, and an affinity for street culture. That most cyberpunk was written by white males didn't seem to ruffle any feathers. Cyberpunk was new, it was vital, it was irreverent. Most importantly, cyberpunk *rocked*.

When Sterling and his gang of pranksters shuttered *Cheap Truth* in 1985, a mere eighteen issues after launch, he declared that the movement was over, it had become too big, and that much of the "original freedom" was lost. "People know who I am," he wrote, "and they get all hot and bothered by personalities, instead of ideas and issues. CT can no longer claim the 'honesty of complete desperation.' That first fine flower of red-hot hysteria is simply gone." In other words, The Movement had been changed by its acceptance into the smokestack machine. (*Cheap Truth* had been mentioned in an issue of *Rolling Stone*, evidence of it being swallowed whole.) When, in 1986, Sterling published *Mirrorshades*, the first and some say only true cyberpunk anthology, the movement was consolidated into a particular table of contents, a closed club whose membership was limited to the original cyberpunk writers. In 1991, Lewis Shiner renounced cyberpunk in a *New York Times* op-ed. When *Time* ran a cover story about cyberpunks, the cyberpunks themselves were outraged. Counter culture had been embraced by culture. "I hereby declare the revolution over," Sterling wrote in the final issue of *Cheap Truth*. "Long live the provisional government."

Thirty years later, cyberpunk is both very much dead and very much alive. It is dead in the sense that the Reagan years are over, the Cold War is done, straight video has been replaced by CGI, and the achievement of the Xerox machine, once the very pinnacle of technological advancement available to the masses, is being outdone by 3-D printers. But it is very much alive in that cyberpunk was never really about a specific technology or a specific moment in time. It was, and it is, an aesthetic position as much as a collection of themes, an attitude toward mass culture and pop culture, an identity, a way of living, breathing, and grokking our weird and wired world.

Anthology editing is a tricky business. On the one hand, the anthology editor must revere, must even do a little bit of worshipping at the foot of the statue. On the other hand, the editor must be removed enough to see the subject with clear eyes, and to offer an unimpassioned editorial read. But she must also bring just enough of herself to the selection to make the anthology as a whole useful, interesting, unique, timeless, and, hopefully, fun.

In putting together this collection, I have tried to do four things. The first—spurred by the worshipper within me—is to pay homage to cyberpunk beginnings. To that end, this collection contains reprints of cyberpunk gems that are now difficult to find—"Mozart in Mirrorshades" by Bruce Sterling and Lewis Shiner is one of my personal favorites—and it showcases stories by the founding or first-generation cyberpunk authors—Rudy Rucker, John Shirley, Greg Bear, and Paul Di Filippo among them—that weren't in the original collections.

Second, the critic in me wanted to offer an as-complete-as-possible look at cyberpunk themes and topics. Some of my favorites include the low-life of the Low Teks in William Gibson's "Johnny Mnemonic," the imbedded digital brains of David Marusek's "Getting to Know You," the drugs and outlaws of Gwyneth Jones's "Blue Clay Blues," the multi-mind madness of John Shirley's "Wolves of the Plateau," the body augmentation of James Patrick Kelly's "Mr. Boy," and the environmental meltdown of Paul Di Filippo's "Life in the Anthropocene."

One story from this group deserves a special explanation: "Down and Out in the Year 2000," by Kim Stanley Robinson, occupies a unique position in the cyberpunk cannon as perhaps the solitary story to critique the cyberpunk reverence for "the street." "I was living in Washington DC in the summer of 1985," Robinson wrote me in an email, after I requested some information about the genesis of the story, "hanging out in Dupont Circle park and the smaller park outside our apartment. Watching the people there, I began to think that the cyberpunks were white middle-class people like me, and they had no idea; 'street smart' was just a trendy phrase, a literary or Hollywood idea. So I wrote the story to express that feeling."

Third, the iconoclast in me wanted to move past traditional cyberpunk, and beyond the cast of known cyberpunk characters, to take a look at how the movement has developed since the end of the Cold War, and to pull the veil back on what the future might hold. Cory Doctorow, arguably the new Chairman of Tech, ends the collection by celebrating the heroic sysadmins, a rarely lauded group. Cat Rambo, not usually associated with cyberpunk, beautifully describes how relationships are changed by technology. New-comer Benjamin Parzybok, author of the novel Couch, contributed an original story notable for its authentic re-imagining of low life in the slums, a different kind of low life entirely from that described by the 80s cyberpunk. Jonathan Lethem's

"Interview with the Crab" thrilled me when I read it the first time, and it continues to astound me with its craft. I've never heard Lethem described as a cyberpunk, but my favorite of his novels, *Gun, with Occasional Music*, uses the hardboiled tone common to cyberpunk, and is populated by state-sponsored druggies, external memory devices, a virtual monetary system, and genetically altered animals who speak, love, have sex, and die like humans. The story included here takes up the themes of pop culture and fame, getting deeper into both by using a crustacean, the titular crab, as the prototypical hard-living, idiosyncratic celebrity.

And finally, in compiling this collection, the writer in me wanted to look at the craft of cyberpunk, and the interesting, innovate forms some of the cyberpunk stories take. The prose of Pat Cadigan's "Rock On" has a vitality that makes my heart beat faster. Two stories—Bruce Sterling's "User-Centric" and Paul Tremblay's "Blog at the End of the World"—co-op new kinds of communication, email and blogging, to weave their tales. Daniel H. Wilson writes what could be called a cyberpunk fairytale, and Mark Teppo pokes at an acronym-heavy future, all while telling a story in the very language he's lampooning.

I was five years old when the first issue of *Cheap Truth* came out, and only eight when The Movement was declared dead. In 1991, when Lewis Shiner renounced his cyberpunk membership, I was wearing neon hair bands, plastic shoes, and bopping my head to Cyndi Lauper. I wasn't in any way punk, and I'm probably still not. But when you're holding a hammer, everything starts to look like a nail, and when you're editing cyberpunk, you realize you're living in a cyberpunk world.

To wit, last week, the week of Thanksgiving, 2012, as the final edits were being made on this collection, the following items caught my eye: On the radio to the airport, I heard a commentator remarking on Project Glass, the Google initiative focusing on wearable computers; also on the radio, I heard about a scientist who had discovered that jellyfish can reverse the aging process, and that jellyfish stem cells might possess the secret to immortality. The talk around the pre-Thanksgiving dinner table was about California legalizing self-driving cars, and about how the rich/poor income gap in America is wider than it's been since 1967. Gawker posted a story about a man on family vacation in Florida who found anonymous sex in a theme-park bathroom with the help of an iPhone app. And on Thanksgiving itself, my second cousin told me all about a nonprofit he was starting with a group of like-minded retirees to help spread information about two things, the first being the 911 conspiracy, and the second being a government-operated data-center, Big Brother style, outside Salt Lake City.

The world seems to keep getting weirder and weirder, with no end in sight.

Thank you to everybody who helped with story suggestions, with author suggestions, and with new ways to look at the subject. But thank you especially to the authors in this collection, and to the authors who have written and continue to write cyberpunk, knowingly or not. You have given us a new view on the world, and a new voice to the great tech experiment that defines our age. I can't wait to see what happens next.

JOHNNY MNEMONIC

By William Gibson

I put the shotgun in an Adidas bag and padded it out with four pairs of tennis socks, not my style at all, but that was what I was aiming for: If they think you're crude, go technical; if they think you're technical, go crude. I'm a very technical boy. So I decided to get as crude as possible. These days, though, you have to be pretty technical before you can even aspire to crudeness. I'd had to turn both those twelve-gauge shells from brass stock on the lathe, and then load them myself; I'd had to dig up an old microfiche with instructions for hand-loading cartridges; I'd had to build a lever-action press to seat the primers—all very tricky. But I knew they'd work.

The meet was set for the Drome at 2300, but I rode the tube three stops past the closest platform and walked back. Immaculate procedure.

I checked myself out in the chrome siding of a coffee kiosk, your basic sharp-faced Caucasoid with a ruff of stiff, dark hair. The girls at Under the Knife were big on Sony Mao, and it was getting harder to keep them from adding the chic suggestion of epicanthic folds. It probably wouldn't fool Ralfi Face, but it might get me next to his table.

The Drome is a single narrow space with a bar down one side and tables along the other, thick with pimps and handlers and an arcane array of dealers. The Magnetic Dog Sisters were on the door that night, and I didn't relish trying to get out past them if things didn't work out. They were two meters tall and thin as greyhounds. One was black and the other white, but aside from that they were as nearly identical as cosmetic surgery could make them. They'd been lovers for years and were bad news in the tussle. I was never quite sure which one had originally been male.

Ralfi was sitting at his usual table. Owing me a lot of money. I had hundreds of megabytes stashed in my head on an idiot/savant basis—information I had no conscious access to. Ralfi had left it there. He hadn't, however, come back for it. Only Ralfi could retrieve the data, with a code phrase of his own invention. I'm not cheap to begin with, but my overtime on storage is astronomical. And Ralfi had been very scarce.

Then I'd heard that Ralfi Face wanted to put out a contract on me. So I'd arranged to meet him in the Drome, but I'd arranged it as Edward Bax, clandestine importer, late of Rio and Peking.

The Drome stank of biz, a metallic tang of nervous tension. Muscle-boys scattered through the crowd were flexing stock parts at one another and trying on thin, cold grins, some of them so lost under superstructures of muscle graft that their outlines weren't really human.

Pardon me. Pardon me, friends. Just Eddie Bax here, Fast Eddie the Importer, with his professionally nondescript gym bag, and please ignore this slit, just wide enough to admit his right hand.

Ralfi wasn't alone. Eighty kilos of blond California beef perched alertly in the chair next to his, martial arts written all over him.

Fast Eddie Bax was in the chair opposite them before the beef's hands were off the table. "You black belt?" I asked eagerly. He nodded, blue eyes running an automatic scanning pattern between my eyes and my hands. "Me too," I said. "Got mine here in the bag." And I shoved my hand through the slit and thumbed the safety off. Click. "Double twelve-gauge with the triggers wired together."

"That's a gun," Ralfi said, putting a plump, restraining hand on his boy's taut blue nylon chest. "Johnny has an antique firearm in his bag." So much for Edward Bax.

I guess he'd always been Ralfi Something or Other, but he owed his acquired surname to a singular vanity. Built something like an overripe pear, he'd worn the once-famous face of Christian White for twenty years—Christian White of the Aryan Reggae Band, Sony Mao to his generation, and final champion of race rocks. I'm a whiz at trivia.

Christian White: classic pop face with a singer's high-definition muscles, chiseled cheekbones. Angelic in one light, handsomely depraved in another. But Ralfi's eyes lived behind that face, and they were small and cold and black.

"Please," he said, "let's work this out like businessmen." His voice was marked by a horrible prehensile sincerity, and the corners of his beautiful Christian White mouth were always wet. "Lewis here," nodding in the beefboy's direction, "is a meatball." Lewis took this impassively, looking like something built from a kit. "You aren't a meatball, Johnny."

"Sure I am, Ralfi, a nice meatball chock-full of implants where you can store your dirty laundry while you go off shopping for people to kill me. From my end of this bag, Ralfi, it looks like you've got some explaining to do."

"It's this last batch of product, Johnny." He sighed deeply. "In my role as broker—"

"Fence," I corrected.

"As broker, I'm usually very careful as to sources."

"You buy only from those who steal the best. Got it."

He sighed again. "I try," he said wearily, "not to buy from fools. This time, I'm afraid, I've done that." Third sigh was the cue for Lewis to trigger the neural disruptor they'd taped under my side of the table.

I put everything I had into curling the index finger of my right hand, but I no longer seemed to be connected to it. I could feel the metal of the gun and the foam-padded tape I'd wrapped around the stubby grip, but my hands were cool wax, distant and inert. I was hoping Lewis was a true meatball, thick enough to go for the gym bag and snag my rigid trigger finger, but he wasn't.

"We've been very worried about you, Johnny. Very worried. You see, that's Yakuza property you have there. A fool took it from them, Johnny. A dead fool."

Lewis giggled.

It all made sense then, an ugly kind of sense, like bags of wet sand settling around my head. Killing wasn't Ralfi's style. Lewis wasn't even Ralfi's style. But he'd got himself stuck between the Sons of the Neon Chrysanthemum and something that belonged to them—or, more likely, something of theirs that belonged to someone else. Ralfi, of course, could use the code phrase to throw me into idiot/savant, and I'd spill their hot program without remembering a single quarter tone. For a fence like Ralfi, that would ordinarily have been enough. But not for the Yakuza. The Yakuza would know about Squids, for one thing, and they wouldn't want to worry about one lifting those dim and permanent traces of their program out of my head. I didn't know very much about Squids, but I'd heard stories, and I made it a point never to repeat them to my clients. No, the Yakuza wouldn't like that; it looked too much like evidence. They hadn't got where they were by leaving evidence around. Or alive.

Lewis was grinning. I think he was visualizing a point just behind my forehead and imagining how he could get there the hard way.

"Hey," said a low voice, feminine, from somewhere behind my right shoulder, "you cowboys sure aren't having too lively a time."

"Pack it, bitch," Lewis said, his tanned face very still. Ralfi looked blank.

"Lighten up. You want to buy some good free base?" She pulled up a chair and quickly sat before either of them could stop her. She was barely inside my fixed field of vision, a thin girl with mirrored glasses, her dark hair cut in a rough shag. She wore black leather, open over a T-shirt slashed diagonally with stripes of red and black. "Eight thou a gram weight."

Lewis snorted his exasperation and tried to slap her out of the chair. Somehow he didn't quite connect, and her hand came up and seemed to brush his wrist as it passed. Bright blood sprayed the table. He was clutching his wrist white-knuckle tight, blood trickling from between his fingers.

But hadn't her hand been empty?

He was going to need a tendon stapler. He stood up carefully, without bothering to push his chair back. The chair toppled backward, and he stepped out of my line of sight without a word.

"He better get a medic to look at that," she said. "That's a nasty cut."

"You have no idea," said Ralfi, suddenly sounding very tired, "the depths of shit you have just gotten yourself into."

"No kidding? Mystery. I get real excited by mysteries. Like why your friend here's so quiet. Frozen, like. Or what this thing here is for," and she held up the little control unit that she'd somehow taken from Lewis. Ralfi looked ill.

"You, ah, want maybe a quarter-million to give me that and take a walk?" A fat hand came up to stroke his pale, lean face nervously.

"What I want," she said, snapping her fingers so that the unit spun and glittered, "is work. A job. Your boy hurt his wrist. But a quarter'll do for a retainer."

Ralfi let his breath out explosively and began to laugh, exposing teeth that hadn't been kept up to the Christian White standard. Then she turned the disruptor off.

"Two million," I said.

"My kind of man," she said, and laughed. "What's in the bag?"

"A shotgun."

"Crude." It might have been a compliment.

Ralfi said nothing at all.

"Name's Millions. Molly Millions. You want to get out of here, boss? People are starting to stare." She stood up. She was wearing leather jeans the color of dried blood.

And I saw for the first time that the mirrored lenses were surgical inlays, the silver rising smoothly from her high cheekbones, sealing her eyes in their sockets. I saw my new face twinned there.

"I'm Johnny," I said. "We're taking Mr. Face with us."

He was outside, waiting. Looking like your standard tourist tech, in plastic zoris and a silly Hawaiian shirt printed with blowups of his firm's most popular microprocessor; a mild little guy, the kind most likely to wind up drunk on sake in a bar that puts out miniature rice crackers with seaweed garnish. He looked like the kind who sing the corporate anthem and cry, who shake hands endlessly with the bartender. And the pimps and the dealers would leave him alone, pegging him as innately conservative. Not up for much, and careful with his credit when he was.

The way I figured it later, they must have amputated part of his left thumb, somewhere behind the first joint, replacing it with a prosthetic tip, and cored the stump, fitting it with a spool and socket molded from one of the Ono-Sendai diamond analogs. Then they'd carefully wound the spool with three meters of monomolecular filament.

Molly got into some kind of exchange with the Magnetic Dog Sisters, giving me a chance to usher Ralfi through the door with the gym bag pressed lightly against the base of his spine. She seemed to know them. I heard the black one laugh.

I glanced up, out of some passing reflex, maybe because I've never got used to it, to the soaring arcs of light and the shadows of the geodesics above them. Maybe that saved me.

Ralfi kept walking, but I don't think he was trying to escape. I think he'd already given up. Probably he already had an idea of what we were up against.

I looked back down in time to see him explode.

Playback on full recall shows Ralfi stepping forward as the little tech sidles out of nowhere, smiling. Just a suggestion of a bow, and his left thumb falls off. It's a conjuring trick. The thumb hangs suspended. Mirrors? Wires? And

Ralfi stops, his back to us, dark crescents of sweat under the armpits of his pale summer suit. He knows. He must have known. And then the joke-shop thumb tip, heavy as lead, arcs out in a lighting yo-yo trick, and the invisible thread connecting it to the killer's hand passes laterally through Ralfi's skull, just above his eyebrows, whips up, and descends, slicing the pear-shaped torso diagonally from shoulder to rib cage. Cuts so fine that no blood flows until synapses misfire and the first tremors surrender the body to gravity.

Ralfi tumbled apart in a pink cloud of fluids, the three mismatched sections rolling forward onto the tiled pavement. In total silence.

I brought the gym bag up, and my hand convulsed. The recoil nearly broke my wrist.

It must have been raining; ribbons of water cascaded from a ruptured geodesic and spattered on the tile behind us. We crouched in the narrow gap between a surgical boutique and an antique shop. She'd just edged one mirrored eye around the corner to report a single Volks module in front of the Drome, red lights flashing. They were sweeping Ralfi up. Asking questions.

I was covered in scorched white fluff. The tennis socks. The gym bag was a ragged plastic cuff around my wrist. "I don't see how the hell I missed him."

"'Cause he's fast, so fast." She hugged her knees and rocked back and forth on her bootheels. "His nervous system's jacked up. He's factory custom." She grinned and gave a little squeal of delight. "I'm gonna get that boy. Tonight. He's the best, number one, top dollar, state of the art."

"What you're going to get, for this boy's two million, is my ass out of here. Your boyfriend back there was mostly grown in a vat in Chiba City. He's a Yakuza assassin."

"Chiba. Yeah. See, Molly's been Chiba, too." And she showed me her hands, fingers slightly spread. Her fingers were slender, tapered, very white against the polished burgundy nails. Ten blades snicked straight out from their recesses beneath her nails, each one a narrow, double-edged scalpel in pale blue steel.

I'd never spent much time in Nighttown. Nobody there had anything to pay me to remember, and most of them had a lot they paid regularly to forget.

Generations of sharpshooters had clipped away at the neon until the maintenance crews gave up. Even at noon the arcs were soot-black against faintest pearl.

Where do you go when the world's wealthiest criminal order is feeling for you with calm, distant fingers? Where do you hide from the Yakuza, so powerful that it owns comsats and at least three shuttles? The Yakuza is a true multinational, like ITT and Ono-Sendai. Fifty years before I was born, the Yakuza had already absorbed the Triads, the Mafia, the Union Corse.

Molly had an answer: you hide in the Pit, in the lowest circle, where any outside influence generates swift, concentric ripples of raw menace. You hide in Nighttown. Better yet, you hide *above* Nighttown, because the Pit's inverted, and the bottom of its bowl touches the sky, the sky that Nighttown never sees, sweating under its own firmament of acrylic resin, up where the Lo Teks crouch in the dark like gargoyles, black-market cigarettes dangling from their lips.

She had another answer, too.

"So you're locked up good and tight, Johnny-san? No way to get that program without the password?" She led me into the shadows that waited beyond the bright tube platform. The concrete walls were overlaid with graffiti, years of them twisting into a single metascrawl of rage and frustration.

"The stored data are fed in through a modified series of microsurgical contraautism prostheses." I reeled off a numb version of my standard sales pitch. "Client's code is stored in a special chip; barring Squids, which we in the trade don't like to talk about, there's no way to recover your phrase. Can't drug it out, cut it out, torture it. I don't *know* it, never did."

"Squids? Crawly things with arms?" We emerged into a deserted street market. Shadowy figures watched us from across a makeshift square littered with fish heads and rotting fruit.

"Superconducting quantum interference detectors. Used them in the war to find submarines, suss out enemy cyber systems."

"Yeah? Navy stuff? From the war? Squid'll read that chip of yours?" She'd stopped walking, and I felt her eyes on me behind those twin mirrors.

"Even the primitive models could measure a magnetic field a billionth the strength of geomagnetic force; it's like pulling a whisper out of a cheering stadium."

"Cops can do that already, with parabolic microphones and lasers."

"But your data's still secure." Pride in profession. "No government'll let their cops have Squids, not even the security heavies. Too much chance of interdepartmental funnies; they're too likely to Watergate you."

"Navy stuff," she said, and her grin gleamed in the shadows. "Navy stuff. I got a friend down here who was in the navy, name's Jones. I think you'd better meet him. He's a junkie, though. So we'll have to take him something."

"A junkie?"

"A dolphin."

He was more than a dolphin, but from another dolphin's point of view he might have seemed like something less. I watched him swirling sluggishly in his galvanized tank. Water slopped over the side, wetting my shoes. He was surplus from the last war. A cyborg.

He rose out of the water, showing us the crusted plates along his sides, a kind of visual pun, his grace nearly lost under articulated armor, clumsy and prehistoric. Twin deformities on either side of his skull had been engineered to house sensor units. Silver lesions gleamed on exposed sections of his gray-white hide.

Molly whistled. Jones thrashed his tail, and more water cascaded down the side of the tank.

"What is this place?" I peered at vague shapes in the dark, rusting chainlink and things under tarps. Above the tank hung a clumsy wooden framework, crossed and recrossed by rows of dusty Christmas lights.

"Funland. Zoo and carnival rides. 'Talk with the War Whale.' All that. Some whale Jones is . . ."

Jones reared again and fixed me with a sad and ancient eye.

"How's he talk?" Suddenly I was anxious to go.

"That's the catch. Say 'Hi,' Jones."

And all the bulbs lit simultaneously. They were flashing red, white, and blue.

RWBRWBRWB
RWBRWBRWB

RWBRWBRWB
RWBRWBRWB
RWBRWBRWB

"Good with symbols, see, but the code's restricted. In the navy they had him wired into an audiovisual display." She drew the narrow package from a jacket pocket. "Pure shit, Jones. Want it?" He froze in the water and started to sink. I felt a strange panic, remembering that he wasn't a fish that he could drown. "We want the key to Johnny's bank, Jones. We want it fast."

The lights flickered, died.

"Go for it, Jones!"

B
BBBBBBBBB
B
B
B

Blue bulbs, cruciform.
Darkness.
"Pure! It's *clean*. Come on, Jones."

WWWWWWWWW
WWWWWWWWW
WWWWWWWWW
WWWWWWWWW
WWWWWWWWW

White sodium glare washed her features, stark monochrome, shadows cleaving from her cheekbones.

R RRRRR

R R

RRRRRRRR
R R

RRRRR R

The arms of the red swastika were twisted in her silver glasses. "Give it to him," I said. "We've got it."

Ralfi Face. No imagination.

Jones heaved half his armored bulk over the edge of his tank, and I thought the metal would give way. Molly stabbed him overhand with the Syrette, driving the needle between two plates. Propellant hissed. Patterns of light exploded, spasming across the frame and then fading to black.

We left him drifting, rolling languorously in the dark water. Maybe he was dreaming of his war in the Pacific, of the cyber mines he'd swept, nosing gently into their circuitry with the Squid he'd used to pick Ralfi's pathetic password from the chip buried in my head.

"I can see them slipping up when he was demobbed, letting him out of the navy with that gear intact, but how does a cybernetic dolphin get wired to smack?"

"The war," she said. "They all were. Navy did it. How else you get 'em working for you?"

"I'm not sure this profiles as good business," the pirate said, angling for better money. "Target specs on a comsat that isn't in the book—"

"Waste my time and you won't profile at all," said Molly, leaning across his scarred plastic desk to prod him with her forefinger.

"So maybe you want to buy your microwaves somewhere else?" He was a tough kid, behind his Mao-job. A Nighttowner by birth, probably.

Her hand blurred down the front of his jacket, completely severing a lapel without even rumpling the fabric.

"So we got a deal or not?"

"Deal," he said staring at his ruined lapel with what he must have hoped was only polite interest. "Deal."

While I checked the two records we'd bought, she extracted the slip of paper I'd given her from the zippered wrist pocket of her jacket. She unfolded it and read silently, moving her lips. She shrugged. "This is it?"

"Shoot," I said, punching the RECORD studs of the two desks simultaneously.

"Christian White," she recited, "and his Aryan Reggae Band."

Faithful Ralfi, a fan to his dying day.

Transition to idiot/savant mode is always less abrupt than I expect it to be. The pirate broadcaster's front was a failing travel agency in a pastel cube that boasted a desk, three chairs, and a faded poster of a Swiss orbital spa. A pair of toy birds with blown-glass bodies and tin legs were sipping monotonously from a Styrofoam cup of water on the ledge beside Molly's shoulder. As I phased into mode, they accelerated gradually until their Day-Glo-feathered crowns became solid arcs of color. The LEDs that told seconds on the plastic wall clock had become meaningless pulsing grids, and Molly and the Mao-faced boy grew hazy, their arms blurring occasionally in insect-quick ghosts of gesture. And then it all faded to cool gray static and an endless tone poem in the artificial language.

I sat and sang dead Ralfi's stolen program for three hours.

The mall runs forty kilometers from end to end, a ragged overlap of Fuller domes roofing what was once a suburban artery. If they turn off the arcs on a clean day, a gray approximation of sunlight filters through layers of acrylic, a view like the prison sketches of Giovanni Piranesi. The three southernmost kilometers roof Nighttown. Nighttown pays no taxes, no utilities. The neon arcs are dead, and the geodesics have been smoked black by decades of cooking fires. In the nearly total darkness of a Nighttown noon, who notices a few dozen mad children lost in the rafters?

We'd been climbing for two hours, up concrete stairs and steel ladders with perforated rungs, past abandoned gantries and dust-covered tools. We'd started in what looked like a disused maintenance yard, stacked with triangular roofing segments. Everything there had been covered with that same uniform layer of spraybomb graffiti: gang names, initials, dates back to the turn of the century. The graffiti followed us up, gradually thinning until a single name was repeated at intervals. LO TEK. In dripping black capitals.

"Who's Lo Tek?"

"Not us, boss." She climbed a shivering aluminum ladder and vanished through a hole in a sheet of corrugated plastic. "'Low technique, low technology.'" The plastic muffled her voice. I followed her up, nursing an aching wrist. "Lo Teks, they'd think that shotgun trick of yours was effete."

An hour later I dragged myself up through another hole, this one sawed crookedly in a sagging sheet of plywood, and met my first Lo Tek.

"'S okay," Molly said, her hand brushing my shoulder. "It's just Dog. Hey, Dog."

In the narrow beam of her taped flash, he regarded us with his one eye and slowly extruded a thick length of grayish tongue, licking huge canines. I wondered how they wrote off tooth-bud transplants from Dobermans as low technology. Immunosuppressives don't exactly grow on trees.

"Moll." Dental augmentation impeded his speech. A string of saliva dangled from the twisted lower lip. "Heard ya comin'. Long time." He might have been fifteen, but the fangs and the bright mosaic of scars combined with the gaping socket to present a mask of total bestiality. It had taken time and a certain kind of creativity to assemble that face, and his posture told me he enjoyed living behind it. He wore a pair of decaying jeans, black with grime and shiny along the creases. His chest and feet were bare. He did something with his mouth that approximated a grin. "Bein' followed, you."

Far off, in Nighttown, a water vendor cried his trade.

"Strings jumping, Dog?" She swung her flash to the side, and I saw thin cords tied to eyebolts, cords that ran to the edge and vanished.

"Kill the fuckin' light!"

She snapped it off.

"How come the one who's followin' you's got no light?"

"Doesn't need it. That one's bad news, Dog. Your sentries give him a tumble, they'll come home in easy-to-carry sections."

"This a *friend* friend, Moll?" He sounded uneasy. I heard his feet shift on the worn plywood.

"No. But he's mine. And this one," slapping my shoulders, "he's a friend. Got that?"

"Sure," he said, without much enthusiasm, padding to the platform's edge, where the eyebolts were. He began to pluck out some kind of message on the taut cords.

Nighttown spread beneath us like a toy village for rats; tiny windows showed candlelight, with only a few harsh, bright squares lit by battery lanterns and carbide lamps. I imagined the old men at their endless games of dominoes, under warm, fat drops of water that fell from wet wash hung out on poles between the plywood shanties. Then I tried to imagine him climbing patiently up through the darkness in his zoris and ugly tourist shirt, bland and unhurried. How was he tracking us?

"Good," said Molly. "He smells us."

"Smoke?" Dog dragged a crumpled pack from his pocket and prized out a flattened cigarette. I squinted at the trademark while he lit it for me with a kitchen match. Yiheyuan filters. Beijing Cigarette Factory. I decided that the Lo Teks were black marketeers. Dog and Molly went back to their argument, which seemed to revolve around Molly's desire to use some particular piece of Lo Tek real estate.

"I've done you a lot of favors, man. I want that floor. And I want the music."

"You're not Lo Tek . . ."

This must have been going on for the better part of a twisted kilometer, Dog leading us along swaying catwalks and up rope ladders. The Lo Teks leech their webs and huddling places to the city's fabric with thick gobs of epoxy and sleep above the abyss in mesh hammocks. Their country is so attenuated that in places it consists of little more than holds and feet, sawed into geodesic struts.

The Killing Floor, she called it. Scrambling after her, my new Eddie Bax shoes slipping on worn metal and damp plywood, I wondered how it could be any more lethal than the rest of the territory. At the same time I sensed that Dog's protests were ritual and that she already expected to get whatever it was she wanted.

Somewhere beneath us, Jones would be circling his tank, feeling the first twinges of junk sickness. The police would be boring the Drome regulars with questions about Ralfi. What did he do? Who was he with before he stepped outside? And the Yakuza would be settling its ghostly bulk over the city's data banks, probing for faint images of me reflected in numbered accounts, securities transactions, bills for utilities. We're an information economy. They teach you that in school. What they don't tell you is that it's impossible to move, to live, to operate at any level without leaving traces, bits, seemingly meaningless fragments of personal information. Fragments that can be retrieved, amplified . . .

But by now the pirate would have shuttled our message into line for blackbox transmissions to the Yakuza comsat. A simple message: call off the dogs or we wideband your program.

The program. I had no idea what it contained. I still don't. I only sing the song, with zero comprehension. It was probably research data, the Yakuza being given to advanced forms of industrial espionage. A genteel business, stealing from Ono-Sendai as a matter of course and politely holding their data for ransom, threatening to blunt the conglomerate's research edge by making the product public.

But why couldn't any number play? Wouldn't they be happier with something to sell back to Ono-Sendai, happier than they'd be with one dead Johnny from Memory Lane?

Their program was on its way to an address in Sydney, to a place that held letters for clients and didn't ask questions once you'd paid a small retainer. Fourth-class surface mail. I'd erased most of the other copy and recorded our message in the resulting gap, leaving just enough of the program to identify it as the real thing.

My wrist hurt. I wanted to stop, to lie down, to sleep. I knew that I'd lose my grip and fall soon, knew that the sharp black shoes I'd bought for my evening as Eddie Bax would lose their purchase and carry me down to Nighttown. But he rose in my mind like a cheap religious hologram, glowing, the enlarged chip in his Hawaiian shirt looming like a reconnaissance shot of some doomed urban nucleus.

So I followed Dog and Molly through Lo Tek heaven, jury-rigged and jerry-built from scraps that even Nighttown didn't want.

The Killing Floor was eight meters on a side. A giant had threaded steel cable back and forth through a junkyard and drawn it all taut. It creaked when it moved, and it moved constantly, swaying and bucking as the gathering Lo Teks arranged themselves on the shelf of plywood surrounding it. The wood was silver with age, polished with long use, and deeply etched with initials, threats, declarations of passion. This was suspended from a separate set of cables, which lost themselves in darkness beyond the raw white glare of the two ancient floods suspended above the Floor.

A girl with teeth like Dog's hit the Floor on all fours. Her breasts were tattooed with indigo spirals. Then she was across the Floor, laughing, grappling with a boy who was drinking dark liquid from a liter flask.

Lo Tek fashion ran to scars and tattoos. And teeth. The electricity they were tapping to light the Killing Floor seemed to be an exception to their overall aesthetic, made in the name of . . . ritual, sport, art? I didn't know, but I could see that the Floor was something special. It had the look of having been assembled over generations.

I held the useless shotgun under my jacket. Its hardness and heft were comforting, even though I had no more shells. And it came to me that I had no idea at all of what was really happening, or of what was supposed to happen. And that was the nature of my game, because I'd spent most of my life as a blind receptacle to be filled with other people's knowledge and then drained, spouting synthetic languages I'd never understand. A very technical boy. Sure.

And then I noticed just how quiet the Lo Teks had become.

He was there, at the edge of the light, taking in the Killing Floor and the gallery of silent Lo Teks with a tourist's calm. And as our eyes met for the first time with mutual recognition, a memory clicked into place for me, of Paris, and the long Mercedes electrics gliding through the rain to Notre Dame; mobile greenhouses, Japanese faces behind the glass, and a hundred Nikons rising in blind phototropism, flowers of steel and crystal. Behind his eyes, as they found me, those same shutters whirring.

I looked for Molly Millions, but she was gone.

The Lo Teks parted to let him step up onto the bench. He bowed, smiling, and stepped smoothly out of his sandals, leaving them side by side, perfectly aligned, and then he stepped down onto the Killing Floor. He came for me, across that shifting trampoline of scrap, as easily as any tourist padding across synthetic pile in any featureless hotel.

Molly hit the Floor, moving.

The Floor screamed.

It was miked and amplified, with pickups riding the four fat coil springs at the corners and contact mikes taped at random to rusting machine fragments.

Somewhere the Lo Teks had an amp and a synthesizer, and now I made out the shapes of speakers overhead, above the cruel white floods.

A drumbeat began, electronic, like an amplified heart, steady as a metronome.

She'd removed her leather jacket and boots; her T-shirt was sleeveless, faint telltales of Chiba City circuitry traced along her thin arms. Her leather jeans gleamed under the floods. She began to dance.

She flexed her knees, white feet tensed on a flattened gas tank, and the Killing Floor began to heave in response. The sound it made was like a world ending, like the wires that hold heaven snapping and coiling across the sky.

He rode with it, for a few heartbeats, and then he moved, judging the movement of the Floor perfectly, like a man stepping from one flat stone to another in an ornamental garden.

He pulled the tip from his thumb with the grace of a man at ease with social gesture and flung it at her. Under the floods, the filament was a refracting thread of rainbow. She threw herself flat and rolled, jackknifing up as the molecule whipped past, steel claws snapping into the light in what must have been an automatic rictus of defense. The drum pulse quickened, and she bounced with it, her dark hair wild around the blank silver lenses, her mouth thin, lips taut with concentration. The Killing Floor boomed and roared, and the Lo Teks were screaming their excitement.

He retracted the filament to a whirling meter-wide circle of ghostly polychrome and spun it in front of him, thumbless hand held level with his sternum. A shield.

And Molly seemed to let something go, something inside, and that was the real start of her mad-dog dance. She jumped, twisting, lunging sideways, landing with both feet on an alloy engine block wired directly to one of the coil springs. I cupped my hands over my ears and knelt in a vertigo of sound, thinking Floor and benches were on their way down, down to Nighttown, and I saw us tearing through the shanties, the wet wash, exploding on the tiles like rotten fruit. But the cables held, and the Killing Floor rose and fell like a crazy metal sea. And Molly danced on it.

And at the end, just before he made his final cast with the filament, I saw in his face, an expression that didn't seem to belong there. It wasn't fear and it wasn't anger. I think it was disbelief, stunned incomprehension mingled with pure aesthetic revulsion at what he was seeing, hearing—at what was happening to him. He retracted the whirling filament, the ghost disk shrinking to the size of a dinner plate as he whipped his arm above his head and brought it down, the thumb tip curving out for Molly like a live thing.

The Floor carried her down, the molecule passing just above her head; the Floor whiplashed, lifting him into the path of the taut molecule. It should have passed harmlessly over his head and been withdrawn into its diamond-hard socket. It took his hand off just behind the wrist. There was a gap in the Floor in front of him, and he went through it like a diver, with a strange deliberate grace, a defeated kamikaze on his way down to Nighttown. Partly, I think, he took that dive to buy himself a few seconds of the dignity of silence. She'd killed him with culture shock.

The Lo Teks roared, but someone shut the amplifier off, and Molly rode the Killing Floor into silence, hanging on now, her face white and blank, until the pitching slowed and there was only a faint pinging of tortured metal and the grating of rust on rust.

We searched the Floor for the severed hand, but we never found it. All we found was a graceful curve in one piece of rusted steel, where the molecule went through. Its edge was bright as new chrome.

We never learned whether the Yakuza had accepted our terms, or even whether they got our message. As far as I know, their program is still waiting for Eddie Bax on a shelf in the back room of a gift shop on the third level of Sydney Central-5. Probably they sold the original back to Ono-Sendai months ago. But maybe they did get the pirate's broadcast, because nobody's come looking for me yet, and it's been nearly a year. If they do come, they'll have a long climb up through the dark, past Dog's sentries, and I don't look much like Eddie Bax these days. I let Molly take care of that, with a local anesthetic. And my new teeth have almost grown in.

I decided to stay up here. When I looked out across the Killing Floor, before he came, I saw how hollow I was. And I knew I was sick of being a bucket. So now I climb down and visit Jones, almost every night.

We're partners now, Jones and I, and Molly Millions, too. Molly handles our business in the Drome. Jones is still in Funland, but he has a bigger tank, with fresh seawater trucked in once a week. And he has his junk, when he needs it. He still talks to the kids with his frame of lights, but he talks to me on a new display unit in a shed that I rent there, a better unit than the one he used in the navy.

And we're all making good money, better money than I made before, because Jones's Squid can read the traces of anything that anyone ever stored in me, and he gives it to me on the display unit in languages I can understand. So we're learning a lot about all my former clients. And one day I'll have a surgeon dig all the silicon out of my amygdala, and I'll live with my own memories and nobody else's, the way other people do. But not for a while.

In the meantime it's really okay up here, way up in the dark, smoking a Chinese filtertip and listening to the condensation that drips from the geodesics. Real quiet up here—unless a pair of Lo Teks decide to dance on the Killing Floor.

It's educational, too. With Jones to help me figure things out, I'm getting to be the most technical boy in town.

MOZART IN MIRRORSHADES

By Bruce Sterling and Lewis Shiner

From the hill north of the city, Rice saw eighteenth-century Salzburg spread out below him like a half-eaten lunch.

Huge cracking towers and swollen, bulbous storage tanks dwarfed the ruins of the St. Rupert Cathedral. Thick white smoke billowed from the refinery's stacks. Rice could taste the familiar petrochemical tang from where he sat, under the leaves of a wilting oak.

The sheer spectacle of it delighted him. You didn't sign up for a time-travel project, he thought, unless you had a taste for incongruity. Like the phallic pumping station lurking in the central square of the convent, or the ruler-straight elevated pipelines ripping through Salzburg's maze of cobbled streets. A bit tough on the city, maybe, but that was hardly Rice's fault. The temporal beam had focused randomly in the bedrock below Salzburg, forming an expandable bubble connecting this world to Rice's own time.

This was the first time he'd seen the complex from outside its high chain-link fences. For two years, he'd been up to his neck getting the refinery operational. He'd directed teams all over the planet, as they caulked up Nantucket whalers to serve as tankers, or trained local pipefitters to lay down line as far away as the Sinai and the Gulf of Mexico.

Now, finally, he was outside. Sutherland, the company's political liaison, had warned him against going into the city. But Rice had no patience with her attitude. The smallest thing seemed to set Sutherland off. She lost sleep over the most trivial local complaints. She spent hours haranguing the "gate people," the locals who waited day and night outside the square-mile complex, begging for radios, nylons, a jab of penicillin.

To hell with her, Rice thought. The plant was up and breaking design records, and Rice was due for a little R and R. The way he saw it, anyone who couldn't find some action in the Year of Our Lord 1775 had to be dead between the ears. He stood up, dusting windblown soot from his hands with a cambric handkerchief.

A moped sputtered up the hill toward him, wobbling crazily. The rider couldn't seem to keep his high-heeled, buckled pumps on the pedals while carrying a huge portable stereo in the crook of his right arm. The moped lurched to a stop at a respectful distance, and Rice recognized the music from the tape player: Symphony No. 40 in G Minor.

The boy turned the volume down as Rice walked toward him. "Good evening, Mr. Plant Manager, sir. I am not interrupting?"

"No, that's okay." Rice glanced at the bristling hedgehog cut that had replaced the boy's outmoded wig. He'd seen the kid around the gates; he was one of the regulars. But the music had made something else fall into place. "You're Mozart, aren't you?"

"Wolfgang Amadeus Mozart, your servant."

"I'll be goddamned. Do you know what that tape is?"

"It has my name on it."

"Yeah. You wrote it. Or would have, I guess I should say. About fifteen years from now."

Mozart nodded. "It is so beautiful. I have not the English to say how it is to hear it."

By this time most of the other gate people would have been well into some kind of pitch. Rice was impressed by the boy's tact, not to mention his command of English. The standard native vocabulary didn't go much beyond *radio*, *drugs*, and *fuck*. "Are you headed back toward town?" Rice asked.

"Yes, Mr. Plant Manager, sir."

Something about the kid appealed to Rice. The enthusiasm, the gleam in the eyes. And, of course, he did happen to be one of the greatest composers of all time.

"Forget the titles," Rice said. "Where does a guy go for some fun around here?"

At first Sutherland hadn't wanted Rice at the meeting with Jefferson. But Rice knew a little temporal physics, and Jefferson had been pestering the American personnel with questions about time holes and parallel worlds.

Rice, for his part, was thrilled at the chance to meet Thomas Jefferson, the first president of the United States. He'd never liked George Washington, was glad the man's Masonic connections had made him refuse to join the company's "godless" American government.

Rice squirmed in his Dacron double knits as he and Sutherland waited in the newly air-conditioned boardroom of the Hohensalzburg Castle. "I forgot how greasy these suits feel," he said.

"At least," Sutherland said, "you didn't wear that goddamned hat today." The VTOL jet from America was late, and she kept looking at her watch.

"My tricorne?" Rice said. "You don't like it?"

"It's a Masonista hat, for Christ's sake. It's a symbol of anti-modern reaction." The Freemason Liberation Front was another of Sutherland's nightmares, a local politico-religious group that had made a few pathetic attacks on the pipeline.

"Oh, loosen up, will you, Sutherland? Some groupie of Mozart's gave me the hat. Theresa Maria Angela something-or-other, some broken-down aristocrat. They all hang out together in this music dive downtown. I just liked the way it looked."

"Mozart? You've been fraternizing with him? Don't you think we should just let him be? After everything we've done to him?"

"Bullshit," Rice said. "I'm entitled. I spent two years on startup while you were playing touch football with Robespierre and Thomas Paine. I make a few night spots with Wolfgang and you're all over me. What about Parker? I don't hear you bitching about him playing rock and roll on his late show every night. You can hear it blasting out of every cheap transistor in town."

"He's propaganda officer. Believe me, if I could stop him I would, but Parker's a special case. He's got connections all over the place back in Realtime." She rubbed her cheek. "Let's drop it, okay? Just try to be polite to President Jefferson. He's had a hard time of it lately."

Sutherland's secretary, a former Hapsburg lady-in-waiting, stepped in to announce the plane's arrival. Jefferson pushed angrily past her. He was tall for a local, with a mane of blazing red hair and the shiftiest eyes Rice had ever seen. "Sit down, Mr. President." Sutherland waved at the far side of the table. "Would you like some coffee or tea?"

Jefferson scowled. "Perhaps some Madeira," he said. "If you have it."

Sutherland nodded to her secretary, who stared for a moment in incomprehension, then hurried off. "How was the flight?" Sutherland asked.

"Your engines are most impressive," Jefferson said, "as you well know." Rice saw the subtle trembling of the man's hands; he hadn't taken well to jet flight. "I only wish your political sensitivities were as advanced."

"You know I can't speak for my employers," Sutherland said. "For myself, I deeply regret the darker aspects of our operations. Florida will be missed."

Irritated, Rice leaned forward. "You're not really here to discuss sensibilities, are you?"

"Freedom, sir," Jefferson said. "Freedom is the issue." The secretary returned with a dust-caked bottle of sherry and a stack of clear plastic cups. Jefferson, his hands visibly shaking now, poured a glass and tossed it back. Color returned to his face. He said, "You made certain promises when we joined forces. You guaranteed us liberty and equality and the freedom to pursue our own happiness. Instead we find your machinery on all sides, your cheap manufactured goods seducing the people of our great country, our minerals and works of art disappearing into your fortresses, never to reappear!" The last line brought Jefferson to his feet.

Sutherland shrank back into her chair. "The common good requires a certain period of, uh, adjustment—"

"Oh, come on, Tom," Rice broke in. "We didn't 'join forces,' that's a lot of crap. We kicked the Brits out and you in, and you had damn-all to do with it. Second, if we drill for oil and carry off a few paintings, it doesn't have a goddamned thing to do with your liberty. We don't care. Do whatever you like, just stay out of our way. Right? If we wanted a lot of backtalk we could have left the damn British in power."

Jefferson sat down. Sutherland meekly poured him another glass, which he drank off at once. "I cannot understand you," he said. "You claim you come from the future, yet you seem bent on destroying your own past."

"But we're not," Rice said. "It's this way. History is like a tree, okay? When you go back and mess with the past, another branch of history splits off from the main trunk. Well, this world is just one of those branches."

"So," Jefferson said. "This world—my world—does not lead to your future."

"Right," Rice said.

"Leaving you free to rape and pillage here at will! While your own world is untouched and secure!" Jefferson was on his feet again. "I find the idea monstrous beyond belief, intolerable! How can you be party to such despotism? Have you no human feelings?"

"Oh, for God's sake," Rice said. "Of course we do. What about the radios and the magazines and the medicine we hand out? Personally I think you've got a lot of nerve, coming in here with your smallpox scars and your unwashed shirt and all those slaves of yours back home, lecturing us on humanity."

"Rice?" Sutherland said.

Rice locked eyes with Jefferson. Slowly, Jefferson sat down. "Look," Rice said, relenting. "We don't mean to be unreasonable. Maybe things aren't working out just the way you pictured them, but hey, that's life, you know? What do you want, *really?* Cars? Movies? Telephones? Birth control? Just say the word and they're yours."

Jefferson pressed his thumbs into the corners of his eyes. "Your words mean nothing to me, sir. I only want . . . I want only to return to my home. To Monticello. And as soon as possible."

"Is it one of your migraines, Mr. President?" Sutherland asked. "I had these made up for you." She pushed a vial of pills across the table toward him.

"What are these?"

Sutherland shrugged. "You'll feel better."

After Jefferson left, Rice half expected a reprimand. Instead, Sutherland said, "You seem to have a tremendous faith in the project."

"Oh, cheer up," Rice said. "You've been spending too much time with these politicals. Believe me, this is a simple time, with simple people. Sure, Jefferson was a little ticked off, but he'll come around. Relax!"

Rice found Mozart clearing tables in the main dining hall of the Hohensalzburg Castle. In his faded jeans, camo jacket, and mirrored sunglasses, he might almost have passed for a teenager from Rice's time.

"Wolfgang!" Rice called to him. "How's the new job?"

Mozart set a stack of dishes aside and ran his hands over his short-cropped hair. "Wolf," he said. "Call me Wolf, okay? Sounds more . . . modern, you know? But yes, I really want to thank you for everything you have done for me. The tapes, the history books, this job—it is so wonderful just to be around here."

His English, Rice noticed, had improved remarkably in the last three weeks. "You still living in the city?"

"Yes, but I have my own place now. You are coming to the gig tonight?"

"Sure," Rice said. "Why don't you finish up around here, I'll go change, and then we can go out for some sachertorte, okay? We'll make a night of it."

Rice dressed carefully, wearing mesh body armor under his velvet coat and knee britches. He crammed his pockets with giveaway consumer goods, then met Mozart by a rear door.

Security had been stepped up around the castle, and floodlights swept the sky. Rice sensed a new tension in the festive abandon of the crowds downtown.

Like everyone else from his time, he towered over the locals; even incognito he felt dangerously conspicuous.

Within the club Rice faded into the darkness and relaxed. The place had been converted from the lower half of some young aristo's townhouse; protruding bricks still marked the lines of the old walls. The patrons were locals, mostly, dressed in any Realtime garments they could scavenge. Rice even saw one kid wearing a pair of beige silk panties on his head.

Mozart took the stage. Minuet-like guitar arpeggios screamed over sequenced choral motifs. Stacks of amps blasted synthesizer riffs lifted from a tape of K-Tel pop hits. The howling audience showered Mozart with confetti stripped from the club's hand-painted wallpaper.

Afterward Mozart smoked a joint of Turkish hash and asked Rice about the future.

"Mine, you mean?" Rice said. "You wouldn't believe it. Six billion people, and nobody has to work if they don't want to. Five-hundred-channel TV in every house. Cars, helicopters, clothes that would knock your eyes out. Plenty of easy sex. You want music? You could have your own recording studio. It'd make your gear on stage look like a goddamned clavichord."

"Really? I would give anything to see that. I can't understand why you would leave."

Rice shrugged. "So I'm giving up maybe fifteen years. When I get back, it's the best of everything. Anything I want."

"Fifteen years?"

"Yeah. You got to understand how the portal works. Right now it's as big around as you are tall, just big enough for a phone cable and a pipeline full of oil, maybe the odd bag of mail, heading for Realtime. To make it any bigger, like to move people or equipment through, is expensive as hell. So expensive they only do it twice, at the beginning and the end of the project. So, yeah, I guess we're stuck here."

Rice coughed harshly and drank off his glass. That Ottoman Empire hash had untied his mental shoelaces. Here he was opening up to Mozart, making the kid want to emigrate, and there was no way in hell Rice could get him a Green Card. Not with all the millions that wanted a free ride into the future—billions, if you counted the other projects, like the Roman Empire or New Kingdom Egypt.

"But I'm really *glad* to be here," Rice said. "It's like . . . like shuffling the deck of history. You never know what'll come up next." Rice passed the joint to one of Mozart's groupies, Antonia something-or-other. "This is a great time to be alive. Look at you. You're doing okay, aren't you?" He leaned across the table, in the grip of a sudden sincerity. "I mean, it's okay, right? It's not like you hate all of us for fucking up your world or anything?"

"Are you making a joke? You are looking at the hero of Salzburg. In fact, your Mr. Parker is supposed to make a tape of my last set tonight. Soon all of Europe will know of me!" Someone shouted at Mozart, in German, from across the club. Mozart glanced up and gestured cryptically. "Be cool, man." He turned back to Rice. "You can see that I am doing fine."

"Sutherland, she worries about stuff like all those symphonies you're never going to write."

"Bullshit! I don't want to write symphonies. I can listen to them any time I want! Who is this Sutherland? Is she your girlfriend?"

"No. She goes for the locals. Danton, Robespierre, like that. How about you? You got anybody?"

"Nobody special. Not since I was a kid."

"Oh, yeah?"

"Well, when I was about six I was at Maria Theresa's court. I used to play with her daughter—Maria Antonia. Marie Antoinette she calls herself now. The most beautiful girl of the age. We used to play duets. We made a joke that we would be married, but she went off to France with that swine, Louis."

"Goddamn," Rice said. "This is really amazing. You know, she's practically a legend where I come from. They cut her head off in the French Revolution for throwing too many parties."

"No they didn't . . ."

"That was *our* French Revolution," Rice said. "Yours was a lot less messy."

"You should go see her, if you're that interested. Surely she owes you a favor for saving her life."

Before Rice could answer, Parker arrived at their table, surrounded by ex-ladies-in-waiting in spandex capris and sequined tube tops. "Hey, Rice!" Parker shouted, serenely anachronistic in a glitter T-shirt and black leather jeans. "Where did you get those unhip threads? Come on, let's party!"

Rice watched as the girls crowded around the table and gnawed the corks out of a crate of champagne. As short, fat, and repulsive as Parker might be, they would gladly knife one another for a chance to sleep in his clean sheets and raid his medicine cabinet.

"No, thanks," Rice said, untangling himself from the miles of wire connected to Parker's recording gear.

The image of Marie Antoinette had seized him and would not let go.

Rice sat naked on the edge of the canopied bed, shivering a little in the air conditioning. Past the jutting window unit, through clouded panes of eighteenth-century glass, he saw a lush, green landscape sprinkled with tiny waterfalls.

At ground level, a garden crew of former aristos in blue denim overalls trimmed weeds under the bored supervision of a peasant guard. The guard, clothed head to foot in camouflage except for a tricolor cockade on his fatigue cap, chewed gum and toyed with the strap of his cheap plastic machine gun. The gardens of Petit Trianon, like Versailles itself, were treasures deserving the best of care. They belonged to the Nation, since they were too large to be crammed through a time portal.

Marie Antoinette sprawled across the bed's expanse of pink satin, wearing a scrap of black-lace underwear and leafing through an issue of *Vogue*. The bedroom's walls were crowded with Boucher canvases: acres of pert silky rumps, pink haunches, knowingly pursed lips. Rice looked dazedly from the portrait of Louise O'Morphy, kittenishly sprawled on a divan, to the sleek, creamy expanse of Toinette's back and thighs. He took a deep, exhausted breath. "Man," he said, "that guy could really paint."

Toinette cracked off a square of Hershey's chocolate and pointed to the magazine. "I want the leather bikini," she said. "Always, when I am a girl, my goddamn mother, she keep me in the goddamn corsets. She think my what-you-call, my shoulder blade sticks out too much."

Rice leaned back across her solid thighs and patted her bottom reassuringly. He felt wonderfully stupid; a week and a half of obsessive carnality had reduced him to a euphoric animal "Forget your mother, baby. You're with me now. You want ze goddamn leather bikini, I get it for you."

Toinette licked chocolate from her fingertips. "Tomorrow we go out to the cottage, okay, man? We dress up like the peasants and make love in the hedges like noble savages."

Rice hesitated. His weekend furlough to Paris had stretched into a week and a half; by now security would be looking for him. To hell with them, he thought. "Great," he said. "I'll phone us up a picnic lunch. Foie gras and truffles, maybe some terrapin—" Toinette pouted. "I want the modem food. The pizza and burritos and the chicken fried." When Rice shrugged, she threw her arms around his neck. "You love me, Rice?"

"Love you? Baby, I love the very *idea* of you." He was drunk on history out of control, careening under him like some great black motorcycle of the imagination. When he thought of Paris, take-out quiche-to-go stores springing up where guillotines might have been, a six-year-old Napoleon munching Dubble Bubble in Corsica, he felt like the archangel Michael on speed.

Megalomania, he knew, was an occupational hazard. But he'd get back to work soon enough, in just a few more days . . .

The phone rang. Rice burrowed into a plush house robe formerly owned by Louis XVI. Louis wouldn't mind; he was now a happily divorced locksmith in Nice.

Mozart's face appeared on the phone's tiny screen. "Hey, man, where are you?"

"France," Rice said vaguely. "What's up?"

"Trouble, man. Sutherland flipped out, and they've got her sedated. At least six key people have gone over the hill, counting you." Mozart's voice had only the faintest trace of accent left.

"Hey, I'm not over the hill. I'll be back in just a couple days. We've got, what, thirty other people in Northern Europe? If you're worried about the quotas—"

"Fuck the quotas. This is serious. There's uprisings. Comanches raising hell on the rigs in Texas. Labor strikes in London and Vienna. Realtime is pissed. They're talking about pulling us out."

"What?" Now he was alarmed.

"Yeah. Word came down the line today. They say you guys let this whole operation get sloppy. Too much contamination, too much fraternization. Sutherland made a lot of trouble with the locals before she got found out. She was organizing the Masonistas for some kind of passive resistance and God knows what else."

"Shit." The fucking politicals had screwed it up again. It wasn't enough that he'd busted ass getting the plant up and online; now he had to clean up after Sutherland. He glared at Mozart. "Speaking of fraternization, what's all this *we* stuff? What the hell are you doing calling me?"

Mozart paled. "Just trying to help. I got a job in communications now."

"That takes a Green Card. Where the hell did you get that?"

"Uh, listen, man, I got to go. Get back here, will you? We need you." Mozart's eyes flickered, looking past Rice's shoulder. "You can bring your little time-bunny along if you want. But hurry."

"I . . . oh, shit, okay," Rice said.

Rice's hovercar huffed along at a steady 80 kph, blasting clouds of dust from the deeply rutted highway. They were near the Bavarian border. Ragged Alps jutted into the sky over radiant green meadows, tiny picturesque farmhouses, and clear, vivid streams of melted snow.

They'd just had their first argument. Toinette had asked for a Green Card, and Rice had told her he couldn't do it. He offered her a Gray Card instead, that would get her from one branch of time to another without letting her visit Realtime. He knew he'd be reassigned if the project pulled out, and he wanted to take her with him. He wanted to do the decent thing, not leave her behind in a world without Hersheys and *Vogues*.

But she wasn't having any of it. After a few kilometers of weighty silence she started to squirm. "I have to pee," she said finally. "Pull over by the goddamn trees."

"Okay," Rice said. "Okay."

He cut the fans and whirred to a stop. A herd of brindled cattle spooked off with a clank of cowbells. The road was deserted.

Rice got out and stretched, watching Toinette climb a wooden stile and walk toward a stand of trees.

"What's the deal?" Rice yelled. "There's nobody around. Get on with it!"

A dozen men burst up from the cover of a ditch and rushed him. In an instant they'd surrounded him, leveling flintlock pistols. They wore tricornes and wigs and lace-cuffed highwayman's coats; black domino masks hid their faces. "What the fuck is this?" Rice asked, amazed. "Mardi Gras?"

The leader ripped off his mask and bowed ironically. His handsome Teutonic features were powdered, his lips rouged. "I am Count Axel Ferson. Servant, sir."

Rice knew the name; Ferson had been Toinette's lover before the revolution. "Look, Count, maybe you're a little upset about Toinette, but I'm sure we can make a deal. Wouldn't you really rather have a color TV?"

"Spare us your satanic blandishments, sir!" Ferson roared. "I would not soil my hands on the collaborationist cow. We are the Freemason Liberation Front!"

"Christ," Rice said. "You can't possibly be serious. Are you taking on the project with these popguns?"

"We are aware of your advantage in armaments, sir. This is why we have made you our hostage." He spoke to the others in German. They tied Rice's hands and hustled him into the back of a horse-drawn wagon that had clopped out of the woods.

"Can't we at least take the car?" Rice asked. Glancing back, he saw Toinette sitting dejectedly in the road by the hovercraft.

"We reject your machines," Ferson said. "They are one more facet of your godlessness. Soon we will drive you back to hell, from whence you came!"

"With what? Broomsticks?" Rice sat up in the back of the wagon, ignoring the stink of manure and rotting hay. "Don't mistake our kindness for weakness. If they send the Gray Card Army through that portal, there won't be enough left of you to fill an ashtray."

"We are prepared to sacrifice! Each day thousands flock to our worldwide movement, under the banner of the All-Seeing Eye! We shall reclaim our destiny! The destiny you have stolen from us!"

"Your *destiny?*" Rice was aghast. "Listen, Count, you ever hear of guillotines?"

"I wish to hear no more of your machines." Ferson gestured to a subordinate. "Gag him."

They hauled Rice to a farmhouse outside Salzburg. During fifteen bone-jarring hours in the wagon he thought of nothing but Toinette's betrayal. If he'd promised her the Green Card, would she still have led him into the ambush? That card was the only thing she wanted, but how could the Masonistas get her one?

Rice's guards paced restlessly in front of the windows, their boots squeaking on the loosely pegged floorboards. From their constant references to Salzburg he gathered that some kind of siege was in progress.

Nobody had shown up to negotiate Rice's release, and the Masonistas were getting nervous. If he could just gnaw through his gag, Rice was sure he'd be able to talk some sense into them.

He heard a distant drone, building slowly to a roar. Four of the men ran outside, leaving a single guard at the open door. Rice squirmed in his bonds and tried to sit up.

Suddenly the clapboards above his head were blasted to splinters by heavy machine-gun fire. Grenades whumped in front of the house, and the windows exploded in a gush of black smoke. A choking Masonista lifted his flintlock at Rice. Before he could pull the trigger a burst of gunfire threw the terrorist against the wall.

A short, heavyset man in flak jacket and leather pants stalked into the room. He stripped goggles from his smoke-blackened face, revealing Oriental eyes. A pair of greased braids hung down his back. He cradled an assault rifle in the crook of one arm and wore two bandoliers of grenades. "Good," he grunted. "The last of them." He tore the gag from Rice's mouth. He smelled of sweat and smoke and badly cured leather. "You are Rice?"

Rice could only nod and gasp for breath.

His rescuer hauled him to his feet and cut his ropes with a bayonet. "I am Jebe Noyon. Trans-Temporal Army." He forced a leather flask of rancid mare's milk into Rice's hands. The smell made Rice want to vomit. "Drink!" Jebe insisted. "Is *koumiss*, is good for you! Drink, Jebe Noyon tells you!"

Rice took a sip, which curdled his tongue and brought bile to his throat. "You're the Gray Cards, right?" he said weakly.

"Gray Card Army, yes," Jebe said. "Baddest-ass warriors of all times and places! Only five guards here, I kill them all! I, Jebe Noyon, was chief general to Genghis Khan, terror of the earth, okay, man?" He stared at Rice with great, sad eyes. "You have not heard of me. "

"Sorry, Jebe, no."

"The earth turned black in the footprints of my horse."

"I'm sure it did, man."

"You will mount up behind me," he said, dragging Rice toward the door. "You will watch the earth turn black in the tire prints of my Harley, man, okay?"

From the hills above Salzburg they looked down on anachronism gone wild.

Local soldiers in waistcoats and gaiters lay in bloody heaps by the gates of the refinery. Another battalion marched forward in formation, muskets at the ready. A handful of Huns and Mongols, deployed at the gates, cut them up with orange tracer fire and watched the survivors scatter.

Jebe Noyon laughed hugely. "Is like siege of Cambaluc! Only no stacking up heads or even taking ears any more, man, now we are civilized, okay? Later maybe we call in, like, grunts, choppers from 'Nam, napalm the son-of-a-bitches, far out, man."

"You can't do that, Jebe," Rice said sternly. "The poor bastards don't have a chance. No point in exterminating them."

Jebe shrugged. "I forget sometimes, okay? Always thinking to conquer the world." He revved the cycle and scowled. Rice grabbed the Mongol's stinking flak jacket as they roared downhill. Jebe took his disappointment out on the enemy, tearing through the streets in high gear, deliberately running down a group of Brunswick grenadiers. Only panic strength saved Rice from falling off as legs and torsos thumped and crunched beneath their tires.

Jebe skidded to a stop inside the gates of the complex. A jabbering horde of Mongols in ammo belts and combat fatigues surrounded them at once. Rice pushed through them, his kidneys aching.

Ionizing radiation smeared the evening sky around the Hohensalzburg Castle. They were kicking the portal up to the high-energy maximum, running cars full of Gray Cards in and sending the same cars back loaded to the ceiling with art and jewelry.

Over the rattling of gunfire Rice could hear the whine of VTOL jets bringing in the evacuees from the US and Africa. Roman centurions, wrapped in mesh body armor and carrying shoulder-launched rockets, herded Realtime personnel into the tunnels that led to the portal.

Mozart was in the crowd, waving enthusiastically to Rice. "We're pulling out, man! Fantastic, huh? Back to Realtime!"

Rice looked at the clustered towers of pumps, coolers, and catalytic cracking units. "It's a goddamned shame," he said. "All that work, shot to hell."

"We were losing too many people, man. Forget it. There's plenty of eighteenth centuries."

The guards, sniping at the crowds outside, suddenly leaped aside as Rice's hovercar burst through the gates. Half a dozen Masonic fanatics still clung to the doors and pounded on the windscreen. Jebe's Mongols yanked the invaders free and axed them while a Roman flamethrower unit gushed fire across the gates.

Marie Antoinette leaped out of the hovercar. Jebe grabbed for her, but her sleeve came off in his hand. She spotted Mozart and ran for him, Jebe only a few steps behind.

"Wolf, you bastard!" she shouted. "You leave me behind! What about your promises, you *merde*, you pig-dog!"

Mozart whipped off his mirrorshades. He turned to Rice. "Who is this woman?"

"The Green Card, Wolf! You say I sell Rice to the Masonistas, you get me the card!" She stopped for breath and Jebe caught her by one arm. When she whirled on him, he cracked her across the jaw, and she dropped to the tarmac.

The Mongol focused his smoldering eyes on Mozart. "Was you, eh? You, the traitor?" With the speed of a striking cobra he pulled his machine pistol and jammed the muzzle against Mozart's nose. "I put my gun on rock and roll, there nothing left of you but ears, man."

A single shot echoed across the courtyard. Jebe's head rocked back, and he fell in a heap.

Rice spun to his right. Parker, the DJ, stood in the doorway of an equipment shed. He held a Walther PPK. "Take it easy, Rice," Parker said, walking toward him. "He's just a grunt, expendable."

"You *killed* him!"

"So what?" Parker said, throwing one arm around Mozart's frail shoulders. "This here's my boy! I transmitted a couple of his new tunes up the line a month ago. You know what? The kid's number five on the *Billboard* charts! Number five!" Parker shoved the gun into his belt. "With a bullet!"

"You gave him the Green Card, Parker?"

"No," Mozart said. "It was Sutherland."

"What did you do to her?"

"Nothing! I swear to you, man! Well, maybe I kind of lived up to what she wanted to see. A broken man, you know, his music stolen from him, his very soul?" Mozart rolled his eyes upward. "She gave me the Green Card, but that still wasn't enough. She couldn't handle the guilt. You know the rest."

"And when she got caught, you were afraid we wouldn't pull out. So you decided to drag *me* into it! You got Toinette to turn me over to the Masons. That was *your* doing!"

As if hearing her name, Toinette moaned softly from the tarmac. Rice didn't care about the bruises, the dirt, the rips in her leopard-skin jeans. She was still the most gorgeous creature he'd ever seen.

Mozart shrugged. "I was a Freemason once. Look, man, they're very uncool. I mean, all I did was drop a few hints, and look what happened." He waved casually at the carnage all around them. "I knew you'd get away from them somehow."

"You can't just *use* people like that!"

"Bullshit, Rice! You do it all the time! I *needed* this siege so Realtime would haul us out! For Christ's sake, I can't wait fifteen years to go up the line. History says I'm going to be *dead* in fifteen years! I don't want to die in this dump! I want that car and that recording studio!"

"Forget it, pal," Rice said. "When they hear back in Realtime how you screwed things up here—"

Parker laughed. "Shove off, Rice. We're talking Top of the Pops, here. Not some penny-ante refinery." He took Mozart's arm protectively. "Listen, Wolf, baby, let's get into those tunnels. I got some papers for you to sign as soon as we hit the future."

The sun had set, but a muzzle-loading cannon lit the night, pumping shells into the city. For a moment Rice stood stunned as cannonballs clanged harmlessly off the storage tanks. Then, finally, he shook his head. Salzburg's time had run out.

Hoisting Toinette over one shoulder, he ran toward the safety of the tunnels.

INTERVIEW WITH THE CRAB

By Jonathan Lethem

The door to the crab's faux-Georgian Tallahassee mansion was opened by a male housekeeper with a trim red mustache, razor-cut orange hair showing white at the temples, and the disapproving air of a Mormon or Scientologist functionary. He was dressed, though, not in Western garb, nor that of a houseboy or cook, but instead in Chinese robes, so he resembled the token occidental opponent in a martial arts film—the type who lurks at the side of the primary Asian villain, and is dispatched by the hero penultimately and with great effort, as a kind of respectful nod to the Western viewer. I wondered if he might be the same person I'd negotiated with on the telephone, so protractedly, in seeking my interview with his employer. If so, he said nothing to confirm my suspicion, and spoke only deferentially now that I'd been granted access to the house. The foyer and entrance hallway of the crab's home were two stories high, with round-topped cathedral windows that flooded midday illumination on the mute, carpeted surfaces of floor and stairway, on the beige walls and tastefully framed black-and-white photographs, many of which, I noted at a glance, contained images of the crab with grinning visitors to the set of his old television program, *Crab House Days*. The housekeeper closed the door behind me and we stood together dwarfed in pillars of high light and suffocated, it seemed to me, by the Floridian summer heat and the faint odor of proteinous seashore rot that permeated the unconditioned air of the apparently immaculate house.

"He'll see you by the pool, Mr. Lethem."

I wasn't a fan of *Crab House Days* during its original run. The sitcom's five-season heyday as ABC's leading Wednesday night comedy program began during my second year of college, the years when I was least likely to care or even know what was on television or on the covers of supermarket magazines—a condition which actually persisted well into my thirties, when I got cable for the first time, largely in order to keep my eye on my favorite baseball team, the Mets. *Crab House Days* was by then well into its life as a late-night rerun, nobody's idea of hot news. And the crab's brief, unsavory resurgence in the form of the late-night cable reality show *Crab Sex Dorm* was still a few years off then, in the mid-nineties, when I increasingly began to linger, in my channel surfing, over episodes of the now-classic show. I watched *Crab House Days* idly at first, but soon I found myself entranced by the melancholic longueurs which would from time to time open up within the antic behaviors of the giant, housebound crab and his bawdy, ingenuous human family, the Foorcums.

So many evenings *Crab House Days*, ostensibly a laugh-riot, seemed to end on a wistful note. Pansy Foorcum, the abrasive sexpot daughter who was nonetheless the crab's only reliable confidante, would make herself ready for a date, talking to the crab through the shared wall of their bedrooms as she dressed and applied makeup for a night out, and then go, leaving the crab time and time again to scuttle and fiddle alone in his room. Pansy in many ways played the role of the crustacean's advocate and mediator among the other Foorcums: Sternwood, the crab's loutish father; Grania, the crab's befuddled and mawkish mother; and, of course, the crab's and Pansy's younger sibling, the scene-stealing punk-Libertarian brat Feary Foorcum. Squabbling would cease as all four of the others contemplated Pansy's departure from the house. The other family members seemed saddened, their energies dampened, as though the pleasure in baiting and insulting the giant crab were diminished past any value once Pansy was no longer present to stick up for him. For the crab's part, his passive-aggressive ripostes and mordant asides were seemingly lost on their actual targets, Sternwood and Grania and Feary; rather, they were meant for Pansy's ears, and with her departure the crab typically fell to an irate and wounded silence.

Now I allowed myself to be led through the foyer, past a vast, apparently unused dining room, its chairs and table covered with sheets, and through to the back patio. The housekeeper and I stepped through the frame of a sliding glass door. Lawn and gardens extended to high walls of vine-covered brick, fronted with a row of palm trees, and scattered between the house and the limits of the yard were well-tended circular plantings of midget palms and ferns, around an unusually large rectangular pool lipped with a wide margin of peach-colored tile. On the pool's tile, between three slatted wooden deck chairs and a low matching table, squatted the crab, wide and round as a golf cart, yet no higher than my knee.

His armor's sheen wasn't what it had seemed fifteen years before, on television, or even in the low-resolution video of *Crab Sex Dorm*, a scant three years ago. Perhaps his burnished forest green and fawn brown color scheme had always been an illusion created by makeup artists. I didn't know and couldn't—wouldn't—ask. Today his mottling was more irregular, his colors black-to-puce, with nothing of the chestnut shine and richness that had always seemed his badge, his pride, no matter how grim the burden of crabdom in a human realm. Otherwise, though, he seemed unchanged. The crab's fragmentary leg, famously amputated in a botched Halloween prank attempted, in a rare instance of filial accord, by Sternwood and Feary, in the show's fourth season, still looked as freshly wounded as ever. The static nature of the crab's injury, and his unwillingness to disguise the rather undelectable gooeyness of the stump, was often given partial credit for the erosion of the show's ratings by the end of that fourth season.

"Will you and Mr. Lethem be needing anything, sir?"

The crab didn't speak, only turned slightly, rattling claws on tile. I'd been warned of his recalcitrance, his hot and cold moods.

"Very good, sir." The housekeeper departed the lawn, leaving me there. No breeze stirred, and apart from my own breathing, and the swim of the sun's pinpoint reflections in the blue of the pool's surface, we might have been captured in the humid noon as in a block of Lucite.

"May I sit?"

Again the crab only scuttled. What the housekeeper had taken as a *no* I took as a *yes*, and found my way to one of the slatted chairs, one facing the crab but not, I hoped, so near as to make him feel intruded upon.

"I don't use a tape recorder, so I hope you don't mind my taking notes."

This drew no response.

"I want you to know, first of all, that I'm a fan. I came to your work quite embarrassingly late, but it's touched me in ways I'm not sure I can describe. But then you've touched so many lives."

The crab now began to issue a sound like a lizard's cry, or perhaps it was the high whine of a distant vacuum cleaner. Without wanting to stare too intently, I searched for signs of a listening attitude in amongst his eyestalks and feelers.

"I don't mean to suggest I have any special insights that would surprise or enlighten an artist of your stature. Think of me merely as a humble representative of an audience that hasn't forgotten you. If anything, the work grows more resonant over the years."

The sound that signaled the end of the hiss or whine was like a barely detectable yawn. The crab raised one leg, too, as if finger-testing the windless air, or calling an invisible class to order with a single, authoritative gesture—one which also evoked, inevitably, a massive hand flipping the bird to the sky, issuing a fuck-you proclamation to the world at large.

"As the more unimportant local and temporal elements of your show recede into time—I mean, all the dated jokes about long-forgotten current events, and the generic vulgar badinage which is only so typical of network comedy of that era—the singularity of your presence becomes more evident, more timeless and pure. You take part in a continuum of rather desultory figures who stand in symbolic protest against the crassness of the contemporary world, running back through Abe Vigoda and Bob Newhart and Imogene Coca, and pointing all the way, really, to Buster Keaton."

"I've heard that before," said the crab in his loud, gravelly, immensely familiar voice. It startled me almost out of my chair, but I tried to disguise my reaction. "People used to write that all the time, but it's a flat-out lie. I wasn't influenced by Buster Keaton in any way."

"I didn't mean—"

"Nobody has any idea how hard it was for me coming up. It's taken for granted now, kids like you come around, they grew up loving the crab and they figure everybody always loved the crab, the crab must have been some kind of overnight success. Sure, right, but that overnight lasted ten years, no more, no less. Ten years slugging it out on the circuit, little clubs, appearances at lodge dinners and state fairs, riding in the undercarriage of tour buses. I paid my dues a dozen times over and I still feel it right here." The crab reared up, propping on his huge, closed claws, and tapped two legs assertively on his lower shell, as if miming a gut check. "Then you guys come around here talking about Buster Fucking Keaton. Like it was some kind of party for me, this fershlugginer career. 'Hmmm, why, I think I'll just allude to Buster Keaton, that ought to make the eggheads cream their panties.' Tell you the truth, I never saw Buster Keaton when I was coming up because I was too busy busting my chops trying to entertain you people. Never saw Buster Keaton until a couple of years ago and then when I did I didn't see anything I thought was all that great."

"I didn't mean to suggest that your work was in any way derivative—"

"Keaton ever do a show about a crab living in a human family?"

I was silent.

"I'm asking you because I want to know. You seem familiar with Keaton's work, so I'm putting the question to you in great sincerity. Anything with a crab?"

"No."

"Right, that's what I figured. My material is entirely my own. I came to it the same way maybe your precious Keaton or Vigoda came by their own— pure suffering, forged into something of value to others, like crushing a coal into a diamond, at great cost of effort and personal sacrifice, a process you wouldn't know too much about since everything to you is just a big pile of slippery postmodern allusions and references with no soul to speak of, not even any notion that it might be missing one, that there might be something to mourn the loss of—a soul, I mean."

I knew it was not my place to defend myself, here—to point out that it was precisely that essence of existential suffering, or *soul*, if he preferred that term, which had drawn me to his work, made me seek for a description for how such an uncanny and timeless thing had broken out in the vacuous, tinselly environs of network situation comedy. Even as he berated me he was inviting me inside, it appeared to me. My task was to selflessly accept that invitation.

"You say your material is entirely your own. That suffering and sacrifice you speak of lies so close to the surface of your humor. How close were the Foorcums to a portrait of your own family?"

"What are you, like the one guy in the United States with no Google?"

"I'm sorry?"

"I've said a thousand times if I've said it once: I haven't spoken about—or to—my family in over forty years. What makes you think I'm about to sing for you? What was your name, Lehman?"

"Lethem."

"Mr. Lethem, with all respect, go fart on a Wheat Thin. What makes you think today's the day some kid sashays in here and I'm just suddenly in the mood to break my silence for you on a whim, when I wouldn't even sing for that fucker Larry King? Even if I wanted to, my lawyers wouldn't let me. Every single person who ever knew me in that shitheel town has tried to sue me at some point, let alone the members of my beloved goddamn family. Rule one: We speak of the Foorcums as the Foorcums alone, or this is O-V-E-R."

"The Foorcums, then. Are you in touch with Richard Drimpet and Joan Cranewood-Freehan, who played your on-screen parents?"

"These are your questions?" The crab scratched with a single leg against the tile in one direction repeatedly, away from his body, as if trying to strike a match or dislodge something stuck to a foot. His claws, though, lay totally inert, draped before him. "Drimpet and I were off speaking terms by season three, another item you could've peeled off a fan site. Joan used to call me from time to time. She tried to get me to do a guest appearance on that *Snowbirds* show, kept pestering me to come on. But what am I going to say to a bunch of old ladies in a mobile home, you know? 'Follow the sun, chickadees! You haven't got that long to live!'"

"Was it difficult between you and Reg Loud? His embodiment of Feary Foorcum was so memorable, but the two of you were pitted against one another continuously throughout the show. And his behavior after the cancellation was rather bitter." I hoped the crab could follow my leads without having to take offense. Reg Loud had, of course, been jailed for narcotics possession several times after his difficult child-stardom found its nadir in the years following *Crab House Days*. For the crab, I could only assume the ferocity of the character's portrayal of his brother, combined with the young actor's very public woes, resonated deeply with ancient, real-life traumas. I was still circling what seemed to me the main, and perhaps tenderest subject, of Delia Watertree, who'd played Pansy Foorcum.

"Difficult? The opposite. Sometimes in this crazy fucked-up world of show business you meet someone with a real beating heart, someone who matters to you, who knows what it's all worth. Rarer than you might think, unfortunately. Reg is the only thing that kept me going on that show as long as I did."

"I'm surprised to hear you say that. Because his character was usually seen as the crab's tormentor."

"I've taken my licks. That's the business, that's the character. Don't confuse show business for real life, Lethem. Compared to some licks I've taken, that show was all cake and candy and ice cream."

"He flooded your room with sulfur oxide in an attempt to cause you to molt six months early," I said.

"Heh heh. Yeah, that was a good one. One hundred percent the kid's idea, too. Good head on his shoulders. You know, a lot of the best bits came from him and me working together, batting stuff to the writers, free of charge. We'd improv in rehearsals—he was always cutting up, making me pee my pants. Talk about bitter, Loud never got credit for any of that stuff. Head writer walked off with two Emmys. Reg deserved better, much better."

"It's an incredible story. Does he know how you feel about it?" I couldn't recall the last turns in Reg Loud's quite miserable tabloid spiral, except that five or six years earlier he'd resurfaced in a brief stint as a local morning talk show host, spewing right-wing survivalist bilge over the airwaves of some medium-sized Midwestern city, Indianapolis or Cedar Rapids.

"Fuck you trying to imply? Of course he does."

"No offense. I'm glad to hear it."

"None taken."

"I wonder if I could get a chance to talk with him for my story. Do you know how I could get in touch with him?"

The crab fell momentarily silent, but cinched the glistening stump of his amputated leg deep under his lower shell, as if he'd now been involuntarily made to recall some particular hurt.

"He wouldn't care to talk about *Crab House Days*," said the crab. "He's moved on."

"What about Delia Watertree?"

"That bitch."

Delia Watertree, launched to fame as the coarse but irresistible Pansy Foorcum, was the only member of the cast who'd ascended to greater heights since the show's cancellation. The entirety of her subsequent career seemed a kind of long renunciation of the broad and overtly sexual appeal of the Pansy Foorcum character; in her stage and screen roles (she'd never glanced back at television work) she relentlessly played against her natural, peaches-and-cream beauty, favoring roles in glasses or bruise makeup or pants suits or buckskin, playing lawyers, frontier settlers, sexual-assault victims, suicidal writers, vanished aviators, and the like. Nevertheless, a measure of Pansy Foorcum's innocent lustiness thrived almost subliminally within the shell of her prestigious career, confirmed by its apparent absence, as though she and her audience were together rising above prurient thoughts in rewarding her with Oscar and Tony nominations for her nobler roles. Too, her quiet, reflective mannerisms still recalled the poignancy she'd evoked in spells of gentleness toward her sitcom sibling, the housebound crab.

"She was lovely to your character," I said, speaking softly now. "A viewer would have thought you and Pansy were full of feeling for one another. You often seemed united against the others—Feary and your parents. As if you two alone shared a sense of dreamy possibility about what might lay outside the space of the house—beyond the circumscribed sensibility of the Foorcum family."

"You go on telling yourself what you want to hear," said the crab. "Meanwhile I'll bet you watched her like the rest of America's teenage boys, with one hand in your pants and your tongue pressed to the screen."

I chose not to point out the impossibility of the physical arrangement he proposed. It occurred to me that it might, in fact, be possible to watch a television screen while lapping at it with one's antennae. "I remember when you asked her not to go to the prom, since you couldn't go—"

"Listen. You want the skinny on Delia? That little floozy used to cavort around the set with no underwear on, just to drive me crazy, knowing nobody else could see, knowing I'd never say anything. Believe me, the carpet did *not* match the drapes. She'd put her foot up on a chair and start re-lacing her high-tops, right in my face, trying to get me to flub lines."

"That's astonishing."

"Believe it. You know what else? At night, after the whole rest of the cast and crew had gone, she'd bring guys back and do them, sometimes two at a time, real marathon stuff, right in the next room, so I couldn't get a minute of sleep. What a mouth on her, too, always crying out 'make me your little whore' and telling these guys it was the biggest thing she'd ever seen, how she was so frightened it would hurt her—"

Now I was certain the crab was confused. "But, you didn't *really* live in that room—" I began. I wondered whether in fact his memory had slipped back to an earlier time, to that other family of which he'd sworn he'd never speak. Perhaps Pansy Foorcum had merged in his mind with an unnamed sister in another house, long ago. The difficulty, of course, was that it was equally likely that in his confusion he'd conflated *Crab House Days* with *Crab Sex Dorm*. That short-lived reality show had been notoriously lavish in its use of crab-point-of-view camera placements.

The creature appeared not to hear me. He carried on muttering about Pansy's sexual theatrics, reproducing what he'd supposedly overheard through the wall, playing both voices aloud as if performing a *Punch and Judy* show—a private litany aired, it seemed to me, for reasons having nothing to do with our interview. At last he reached a pitch and then quit abruptly, his words replaced with the high whining sound he'd treated me to earlier, and then with the distinct yawn. "Keep that in mind next time you see her begging for money for African famine relief," he concluded. "She's probably got nothing on under her Florence Nightingale costume, either. That dame gets her jollies from pity."

I opted to chalk the crab's freewheeling animus up to show-business envy, at the prestige accorded to the sole performer who'd shaken the career curse of the franchise. "What's in the cards for you?" I asked, not wishing to hear more. "Is this a firm retirement? Do you long to reconnect with your audience?"

"I get calls every day, believe you me." The crab stirred a claw, his minor rather than major, which still lay un-moving. He ratcheted the smaller pincers wide and turned them toward his face, as if miming a telephone receiver.

"I'm sure you do."

"I'm telling you, some of the pitches I've heard. Crazy stuff. Hoo-wee. I had some rappers out here the other day. Everything nowadays is gangsta, gangsta, gangsta. Those guys are revitalizing show business, if you ask me. But I don't really see a place for myself in the mix."

"So, you'll rest on your laurels," I suggested.

"What fucking laurels? You see one goddamn laurel around here? If you do, it probably blew over from the next yard. Hah. Sorry, I just hate that word—*laurels.*"

"I only wondered if you're content not to practice your art."

"Listen, I'm keeping busy." The crab withdrew and shuttered his claw now, seeming to grow reflective.

"I didn't mean anything—"

"I know you didn't, kid."

"You've got nothing to prove to anyone," I said softly.

"Don't patronize me."

I fell to silence. The crab shifted, sighed, rattled. The day had turned, too, clouds deflecting the high bleaching sun, and announcing themselves as gray mountains in the oscillating mirror of the pool.

"Look, Lehman. You want a scoop? I'm hatching a major comeback. You can be the first. I'm saying major major. You understand? When this thing blows, there'll be no keeping a lid on it, I promise you."

"A premise for a show?"

"Big show, of sorts."

"Please."

"Follow me. I'd tell you to *walk this way*, only you've heard that one before."

Startlingly, the crab was on the go. He moved awfully fast for a being that had seemed wrought in rusted ironwork a moment before. Clicking his way off the tile-work, he slid across the grass, past me, and toward the left side of the house. The lawn dipped to a basement door there, portal to a half-submerged, windowless lower level with the appearance of a garage or workshop, perhaps. I stood, stuffed my pad and ballpoint into my pants pocket, and hurried to join him.

"Go ahead, open the door," he said.

I tried the handle, which turned easily, and pushed the door inside. The darkness was enough that from the brightness of the day I couldn't make anything out, within. I stepped back, uncertain.

Crab House Days had, of course, made much of the conceit that its title character was trapped in his bedroom, yet I recalled from some footage from *Crab Sex Dorm* how he could transverse human doorways by tipping himself dexterously on one side. The crab did this now, gripping the doorframe neatly with his claws and virtually rolling himself through the doorway. Inside, he dropped back to the unpainted cement floor. I followed, leaving the door open behind me. The basement was cool and conveyed an intense marine smell, like that of an aquarium. Low fluorescent fixtures shone a dim green light, from what appeared to be special bulbs, perhaps like those for illuminating plants or animals in a zoo display of creatures unused to direct sunlight. As my eyes accustomed themselves to the dark I saw that we were surrounded by dozens of immense water tanks, the murk and silt within them glowing in the greenish light.

Another figure stepped from the rear, startling me. It was Feary Foorcum—or rather, Reg Loud. Loud was cloaked in a white lab coat, and still wore his hair in his signature ragged punk cut. He was also still of a childish stature, though he'd grown stocky, and his once brattish features were withered and creased with deep lines of cynicism and age—he seemed still too young to be an adult, and far too old to be in his early forties, as a quick calculation suggested he ought to be. But then perhaps he had been playing younger than his real age on *Crab House Days*, like so many child stars have done.

"Reg, this is Mr. Lehman. He's come to have a look at my quote-unquote comeback."

Reg Loud stuck out a horny, trollish hand. "Pleased to meet you," he said in the terribly familiar voice, a sort of parroty squawk, with which he'd hectored both his parents and crab for all five seasons, filling their ears with his crank Libertarian views. "You're one of the first to see the babies."

"Babies?"

"Have a look."

I squinted in close to the nearest of the tanks. I spotted them now, realized in fact that they'd been visible all along but that I'd mistaken them for sworls of colored shadow in the glow. Behind the glass swam hundreds upon hundreds of tiny, translucent green-yellow crabs. Each was perhaps three-quarters of an inch wide. They coursed over one another in a giddy chaos of youthful agitation, like puppies, or sperm.

I moved to the next tank and found more. I was no savant, but a rough guess suggested there might be tens of thousands of the tiny crabs in the damp, humming basement with us there, a slushy riot of life, a throbbing army of creatures.

"Maybe you can help me decide what to call it," said the crab. "I keep vacillating between *Revenge of the Crab* and *Crab World Domination*."

"I like *Crab World Domination*," I said. "It suggests more continuity with your earlier work."

"That's a point," said the crab.

"They're all him, you understand," said Reg Loud.

"Sorry?"

"All him," Loud repeated. "They're clones."

"I see. How soon will they be, uh, ready?"

"They won't attain his mature size for twenty years," said Reg Loud. "But they'll be ready for release in three or four."

"Not so much of a comedy this time," I mused.

"You could say that," consented the crab.

"Perhaps more of a disaster movie, or a cable miniseries?"

"Do you know anything about global warming, Mr. Lehman?" said Reg Loud.

"Of course."

"You say you do, yet do you understand that the ten warmest years in recorded history have occurred since 1983? *Seven* of them since 1990. Some of us will be better adapted to the coming changes than others."

"In other words," said the crab, "this really has nothing at all to do with television."

"The *evolution* will not be televised," chortled Loud. "The mocked *shell* inherit the earth."

"Don't worry, Lehman, we'll still need historians of television comedy, or rather we'll need them again in a few dozen centuries, when crabs develop television. Your work won't be in vain."

"Are they all comedians like their father?" I asked.

"We'll see, won't we?"

"Yes, I suppose so."

"Let's leave them now. Thank you, Reg."

I took one last glance back at those rows of tanks that glowed, it seemed to me now, much as if lit by cathode ray. I wondered if the radiant, morsel-sized clones, who so resembled cartoons or plastic toys, would truly be fit to outlive us, to occupy some brave new world. It was hardly anything I'd mention to the crab, but I had an intuition his progeny might share his tropism for the human world, and be bereft without us. Perhaps this was my naive projection, an inability to fathom a universe without myself in it. But the crab himself had never known the sea, so far as I understood. He'd been born and raised in a landlocked state, in custody of a solidly middle-class, if not exactly loving, family.

"Close the door," the crab commanded. He scrabbled up the hump of grass, and back to his tile shelf. I wondered whether he ever even so much as dipped himself in the pool. It looked unsullied by any of the secretions I now detected in both dried and fresh traces on the tile and lawn. I followed back to the poolside, but didn't retake my chair. I think we both sensed the interview was nearly at an end.

"You get what you came for, Lehman?"

"Far more, I'd have to say."

"Well, I've got one question for you."

"Certainly."

He paused, perhaps sinking into himself again for a moment. I couldn't keep from thinking that the sight of the blank greenish tide of successors had made him every bit as melancholy as it had me. Before he spoke again he made another of his strange wheezy yawning sounds, and trickled his legs, including the amputated stump, along the tiles, quite softly. Each of his claws stirred, too, though they didn't open.

"I really caused you to think of Keaton or Newhart? Because I just don't see it."

I was astonished it still mattered to him. "It was a stray thought, only intended as a compliment."

"Those figures are much milder than my character, at least after the first season. I always felt I was more in the line of a classic slow-burn specialist, someone like Edgar Kennedy or William Frawley or Beatrice Arthur."

"There's validity in those comparisons," I admitted. The fact that the crustacean could even supply these names made nonsense of his earlier claims not to have known Keaton's films, and of his stiff refusal to consider tracing the lineage of influence behind his own work. But I was hardly keen to confront his inconsistencies.

"Listen, nobody but you and me even remembers those names," he said, hardening again, as if he'd allowed an instant of vanity to bare his defenses. "You need to get yourself a life that's free of this kind of academic horseshit. If I can move forward without wallowing, it's the least you can do."

Had he eschewed wallowing? It was another claim I didn't care to refute. "I'm grateful for the advice."

"Mr. Boniface can call you a cab."

"That's fine. I'll wait in front."

"Lehman?"

"Yes?"

"One thing I ask. I don't want you to lie about me, you understand? I don't care what anyone thinks. Every word, every belch and fart, is on the goddamn record. You got this? Tell the truth about me."

I promised the crab I would try.

EL PEPENADOR

By Benjamin Parzybok

Pico sat on a child's dirty dollhouse and drew from the end of a bottle of Marzo's self-made sweetwine, which tasted a little of plastic residue and car oil and, like everything else, contained the fetid smell of the dump. The tin shed rattled and shook around him, hitting a harmonic and popping a nail from a tired hole at the roof's edge.

The rattling meant the trucks had arrived and the nackers would be gathering at the new spoils. He thought he could hear their hydraulic skittering over the din.

Pico downed the last of the wine and stashed it deep in one of the dollhouse bedrooms. Then he grabbed his tharpoon and tool belt from the wall.

Outside the shack, he whacked his chest once with his tharpoon shaft and said Aha! The *pepenadores* were gathered at the fringes of the settlement. He joined them, weaving slightly, making sure to keep a distance from his parents and whatever commentary they may have for him. Used to be, when the trucks came everybody sprinted for the new stuff. But since the nackers came, they were second-tier dumpdwellers now, and had to rely on old buried finds. Just trash themselves, looking for more trash to sell or use.

At one end of the lineup he saw Mouse and he tried to move inconspicuously toward her, ignoring the names jeered at him as he went down the line; *kekker, nackanigmo, pajero*. He kept his head down as he passed. Mouse wore a cowboy hat and an orange mechanic's jumpsuit with a missing arm. She liked to stand out, he thought, *la chica* is all full of herself. All the same, he admired the way her hair spilled from her hat, the cocky angle of her stance. He'd follow her to harvest when they all set out. Tag along quietly. Follow his late best friend's older sister, as he always had. He stood fifteen paces away so as not to draw her notice.

Pico took out the shard of whetstone he kept in his pocket and worked at the tip of his tharpoon. Marzo's sweetwine gave him a happy boldness, a desire to knock someone off their feet, though he usually ended at the bottom of such a scuffle. He looked at the *pepenadores* around him. Some were old, buried beneath layers of clothes, little mole people who owned what they could wear. Some were young, kids his age. Most ignored him, sweat lines cutting the dirt on their faces. All of them were tense and focused, watching the trucks on the horizon of trash.

Waiting was hard, and Pico had the hiccups. He leaned heavily on his tharpoon and stared at his mismatched boots. They waited another ten minutes for the main dump to clear of nackers, then they trickled into its expanse.

Mouse headed for the great wall and he followed at a distance. He wasn't sure what she'd find there, so far out. Crazy *chica* always did stuff her own way, he said to himself, trying it out dismissively, but his throat ached with longing. She probably knew he was following along, but he kept hidden all the same. She'd probably shoo him off.

They were maybe a couple kilometers out when a nacker picked up Mouse's trail. It skittered along behind her, stalking her, waiting for her to make some find. Pico swore. This nacker looked different from the others. Some kind of new model with carbon or plastic joints that didn't make noise. Why was it so far from the trucks? Pico crouched low and ran behind as quietly as he could, taking cover in the uneven trash heaps.

Mouse stopped and dug at a swell with her tharpoon. She took her cowboy hat off and worked at the mound and he could tell it was something good by the way she dug. Loosed by one of the recent earthquakes maybe. She had the luck. The nacker paused at a distance to see what she would find, and he paused too. When the nacker sat on its haunches, it was hard to distinguish from the trash around it. The way she dug was something to watch, a perfect sort of movement. If only he hadn't messed it all up between them. He would have liked to watch for a while but he had no time.

Pico crouched down out of sight and breathed hard in fear. Maybe her find was crap and the nacker would move on. He'd kamikaze the *pinche* waste bot, he would! He psyched himself up and began to shiver uncontrollably.

After a few minutes, Mouse pulled up a full-on car door from the ground, worth plenty at the market with its metal and embedded electronics. The nacker would want it. Pico gripped his tharpoon and ran toward them. The smog heat was getting to him and he sweated, the sweetwine buzz now a disorienting spin. The nacker was too far ahead of him and much faster. Its six legs traversed the dump obstacles, the tentacle gripper raised in front, assisting when it needed to, poised to strike.

It got her at 10 meters—a charged electric bolt that knocked her flat out. She only just saw it, and the look on her face before it got her crushed him. Pico stopped where he was. He couldn't see where Mouse had fallen, she was downed behind trash.

For a moment, breathing ragged and hot like some ancient machine, he considered what to do. He wanted to run away but he couldn't leave her. Rumor was nackers lifted organs off fallen *pepenadores*. An indignant rage filled him and he pounded his thigh with his fist. Why was a nacker out here and not at the trucks anyway? Why did *pinche* nacker trouble always find him. If it weren't for them, Suto might be alive. And Mouse might—no it was too much to hope for.

This nacker had better range than the last model.

He inspected his tool belt for something that would help. He plugged his GPS jammer into the battery pack at his belt—28 percent charge. It was janky, but it should keep the thing from tattling its location. Among the other tools: a light, a few circuit boards he carried hoping to find parts to make something whole, a mirror. There wasn't much else.

He ran in a crouch, maneuvered along the ground with his hands and feet like one of them, his ratty cloth gloves tearing on the ground. The bot was in the process of laser-sawing the metal and other recyclables off the door—processing in place. Once its middle compartment was full it would go back to Basucorp and empty. Mouse was face-down next to it.

The terrain allowed him to get within range. An awful smell of rot pervaded the air. His grip on the tharpoon kept slipping. He knew he couldn't hope for much. He crawled quietly toward the nacker and then let the tharpoon fly. It was a bad, glancing blow. The tharpoon ricocheted off the top of the nacker's dome where its vulture eye was encased in hardglass, but a bit of plastic the size of a nose jounced off. That was the lousy best he could do. He shrugged his shoulders to his ears, bracing for shock, and turned and ran hard, hating himself, tripping over debris. His foot caught in the carcass of some animal and he went down hard to the ground. He paused there, the breath knocked out of him, and listened for its approach. When his breath came back he stood and saw it was still where he'd left it.

The thing was all schizo, swinging its arms and tilting strangely to the side. He crouched low and watched it, trying to figure out what it was doing. It wasn't right. It was freaking out. He made a wide circle around it and then dashed in. He got a hold of Mouse's collar and dragged her out of range. The nacker's tentacle sent a few charged bolts at the ground around it in a spasmodic circle.

He sat next to her and watched it go. Mouse, he said, but she didn't stir. Mouse, come on *güey*, please get up.

It was weird to see her this close. There was a line of blood down her forehead from her scalp that cut the dirt on her face, and it startled him with how perfect and pure it was. Even her deformed ear had an angelic shapeliness to it. Mouse, he said again. He had imagined her countless nights, as he lay awake in his cot, and here she was in the flesh. This close. He wanted to cup her cheek with his hand, to stream energy from his body into hers, he wanted to cradle her, to say he was sorry, to make everything right. He couldn't believe he'd hit the *pinche maricón*.

The nacker would be trying to radio home and he felt a panic rising in him. Others would come. At least he'd jammed its location. He laid Mouse down and made his way around the nacker so that the vulture eye faced away from him, and the tentacle gripper was out of reach. With the tip of his tharpoon he hooked a bowl-shaped plastic piece of trash—the broken skin of a crashed cycle helmet, the rider long dead—and slowly lowered it over the top of the nacker's eyes, the digital and the meat. At least they wouldn't be recorded. The ground was scorched.

He jumped with each charge the nacker fired. There were dim outlines on the horizon, but so far this quadrant of the dump was dead. He stayed low and just out of sight all the same.

With the old model nackers, a bolt could put a *pepenadora* down for an hour or more. He lay down beside her and whispered in her good ear. It's okay, Mousita, I got it for you. Wake up now, pretty girl. He wondered if she liked to be called pretty girl.

The nacker had four pinchers on its tentacle arm and not five. They were always trying to save money, to make shit cheaper. Well, he thought, a pride rising in him for the first time. I got you this time, *maricón*. He was tiring of the thing's antics and spasms, and the itch to tease it started to overpower his fear. Seemed like the new nackers were more fragile than the old. He reached his tharpoon in and gave it a sharp jab to the middle. It jerked and turned, and then resumed its spasms. Completely *roto*, he thought, just like his nephew Sparto. Perhaps it's dying. He reached in with the claw hand of the tharpoon, got a grip on one leg and gave it a hard flip, then ducked. On its back it shot one last charge into the air and then went silent. The dump was eerily quiet then. Suddenly he saw himself as a hero, a nacker killer, and he looked about for some way to tie the bot up. He couldn't wait to take it back, though he knew the trouble this would cause. He found the plastic chunk he'd broken off with his tharpoon and pocketed it.

Mouse, he whispered, his mouth now a centimeter from her ear. Please. I'm so sorry, he said, meaning how she got hurt, that he couldn't stop it, but knowing when he apologized she'd think only of her little brother Suto. I didn't mean to, he added. He lay on the ground next to her in the dirt, the decomposition of generations of trash: toys and TV sets and bioware, gas jets and hair dryers, window shades and sweaty couches, yellow toys and pigs' hooves, and everywhere plastic.

It was late afternoon and soon the sun would go down and the nackers would crawl back to Basucorp, and the dogs and who knew what else would come out. He brushed away the flies that had descended on Mouse. He checked the charge on his battery pack: 18%. He thought of who might come looking for him and could think of no one. His parents would think he was high on sweetwine or shuttered on kek or plugged into some dirt port, lying against a shed wall somewhere. No one would believe he was here, guarding Mouse. Somebody might come looking for Mouse, he thought, and it was a hope he held onto.

He leaned over and put his ear tentatively against her chest, to listen to her heart, but the soft and shockingly pleasant give of her breast so tantalized and alarmed him that he jumped up and took a step away, afraid she'd wake with him pressed there. He thought he'd heard a heartbeat, but he couldn't be sure. His cheek and ear were on fire with the touch, buzzing. Red-faced, he turned away and spent a quarter hour in the trash, trying to do his job. He found a yellow rain slicker with holes in the elbows and put it on. He found a black bra and put it in the raincoat pocket and then took it out and threw it back on the ground. A minute later he re-pocketed it. He found an advertisement for a body-modification and live-tattoo clinic and he studied the photos intently, imagining how the tattoos would move.

After a while he recovered the car door Mouse had found and propped it so that it shielded her bare arm. He found a dead beach ball and folded it under her head. He was hungry. There was nothing new here. Any edible food-trash was kilometers away at the trucks.

He sat cross-legged in front of the nacker and began to tinker in its belly, but without tools it was slow-going. The fuel cell was in a hardshell that needed wrenches to get at. With the tharpoon he got access to a circuit board that had a number of chips—including the GPS, but he couldn't disable it without breaking the whole thing, and he couldn't bring himself to do that. It was too pretty and new and he wanted it for his own. The last time he'd done that haunted him. *Nackanigmo*, they called him: nacker fucker, or: he who, armed with a nacker, fucks everything up.

This time he was careful to check Mouse's pulse at her wrist. He circled his fingers around it and thought it was the most wonderful wrist ever. He wondered at a charged bolt that strong. Maybe she'd wake and be something else, Sparto's perma-drool on her chin.

There was a sunset cast in the smoke of the distant city, and he braved standing on a rise to look for the others and to watch for a moment. The color stretched red deep across the sky and it made him feel grand and deeply afraid. What they called the wall was not far off, the cliff at the dump's edge. Over that cliff down an immense slope was the old river canyon the city had filled long ago. There were rumors—stories the *pepenadoras* told their children—of what came up the wall at night. Pico shivered. Lepers. The dogs (Dog Organized Guard System) would come too. Any *pepenador* with half a smart would be out of the dump by nightfall. He knew there was hardly a fellow *pepenador* who considered him in this class of half smarts.

He wished he had some sweetwine and checked every last pocket for some crumbs of kek to numb his brain.

Pico combed through the nacker's circuits and disconnected a few others. Some he knew what they did—a long-range network chip, which was probably dumping diagnostic data into the air—others that just looked like they might cause him trouble later on. These he wrapped carefully in whatever he could find and put in his belt pockets. He'd look at them later.

The last nacker he'd opened was with his best friend Suto.

Pico had installed a hacked instruction set into their captured bot and restarted it. The nacker booted into a ten-minute rampage, crashing through tin shacks, its tentacle bolting whatever was in its way, including not a few *pepenadors*. Suto and he chased it down until it turned and pinned Suto to the wall, frying him in a long, slow electrocution. Pico destroyed the machine with his father's axe, but Suto was burnt inside and through, and Pico was to blame, and besides himself, no one blamed him more than Mouse, Suto's sister.

Still, they'd been close once. Almost a gang, the three of them. She was older and smarter and sassier than they were—not their leader, not exactly, but were she to lead they'd follow. Suto because she was his sister and she'd led the two of them through a history of rough times that Pico didn't know the half of. Pico followed because Mouse was the most interesting thing he'd ever come across.

Pico swallowed a foul-tasting half-sob and looked toward her downed body. He got up and paced between Mouse and the nacker, wishing he were on his way home, that he was at his parents'. He pulled on Mouse's arms and dragged her a short way but she was too heavy and too much a deadweight to carry more than a few yards. Besides, he wanted that nacker. He'd hide it away until he got it right this time.

At Mouse's side he stroked her black hair in the half-light and wondered if she'd be more comfortable in another position. He turned her on her side and then he saw the scar at the back of her neck. A thin, white line in the shape of a comic smile. Mouse had a wi.n, he realized. Implanted in her neck. Had to be. Only rich people had these. *Chinga*, there were probably two circuits spouting diagnostics into the net, the nacker's and Mouse's. Then he remembered he'd been jamming the GPS, at least. What was the *chica* doing with her own wi.n? He felt a quick stab of jealousy. He didn't have even one single mod.

He looked around and above and wondered if they were being watched. From what he knew, wi.ns beaconed when there was trouble. It wasn't just an access node. He stood up and looked at Mouse from head to toe. The wi.n made him unsure if he knew her at all.

Darkness was coming on fast and he shook Mouse.

Oh, she said, a distant, quiet sound, as if from a voice box deep in her lungs.

You're awake! he said. A nacker got you, but I got the nacker. I killed it! I've been waiting here with you all day.

Mouse coughed and said nothing.

You got to wake up. Come on!

Pico? she said.

Yes, it's me, Pico, *güey*. It's getting dark! If you get up right now we can still go back.

You're on my arm.

Chinga! he leapt off her arm and for a brief moment was overcome with self-hate.

Mouse moved her arm to her chest. I don't feel good, she said.

I took it apart. After he said this he felt sick to his stomach. I mean disabled it.

She opened her eyes and looked at him and he had no idea what she might say next. He held his breath and stared back, more in love than he thought possible, more ready to be crushed by what she had to say. She was older than he was, nineteen to his seventeen, and as the look went on he realized he didn't stand a chance with her. They stayed like that for a few moments, and he didn't dare avert his eyes.

I can't see, she said finally.

Pico looked away and into the last of the reddened sky and had a terrible feeling. They would not make it out of the dump and back to the *pepenadores* tonight. If he ran, he could make it back now, but he could not leave her.

He found her hand and squeezed it and she held onto it tightly.

I'm scared, she said.

It's going to be alright, he said, though he did not believe it. Your eyes will come back.

Listen, Mouse said.

Pico listened and could hear the faraway howls of the dogs. He shuddered. The sun was gone and the light was being sucked from the sky fast. It'd be dark by the time Mouse could walk.

Dogs, she said.

I know, Pico said.

You shouldn't have stayed, Mouse said. Why are you even here?

He didn't know what she meant. He was so used to hearing *get lost* that he assumed it was that, and felt sorry for himself.

But you would have died, he said.

Now we'll both die.

Pico heard the rapid approach of a nacker close by, the skittering hydraulics in high gear, retreating toward where they lived at night, some recharging bunker at the far edge. The nacker wouldn't stop for them now. The dogs, better equipped to adapt with a higher proportion of biological material, had taken over the night. Grudges and spite were natural to native brains, and though both were created by Basucorp, the dogs held a species-wide grudge against the nackers. Found at night, a pack of dogs would tear a nacker limb from limb.

A moment later, the dump was immersed in darkness.

You move?

Mouse slowly sat up and rubbed the back of her neck. I feel rotten. The whole back of my head tingles. I can only see a dim light.

That's all there is, dim light.

Like I said, Mouse said.

Well you should be rested up for first watch.

Listen, I didn't mean like I sounded, Mouse said.

Pico sat down next to the disassembled nacker and felt around in the dark. He checked his battery pack and realized he still had it plugged into the jammer, and that the charge was down to only 6%. He swore.

You have any juice?

No, Mouse said. Must have got fried.

Chinga.

You hear me before?

I heard, he said.

Thanks, you know?

Sure.

There was another chilling howl beyond them somewhere.

It's cold, Mouse said.

Pico wrestled up the tentacle of the nacker from underneath. In theory, it was still connected into its battery pack. He plugged his light into his own pack for a moment and shielded it so that it wouldn't be seen beyond where he was working. The wires were encased in carbon fiber, but logic would have it there was a switch of sorts in there somewhere. That someone could power its lightning strike. But he did not have the tools or the light.

Mouse came and sat next to him and her warm leg rested against his.

What should we do?

She shrugged. You got something sharp?

He nodded, I guess. Tharpoon. Hand me yours, I'll sharpen it.

She passed him her tharpoon and he ran the tip of it over his whetstone shard until the edge caught at his thumb.

Now what, he said.

Then we stay quiet, she said. Stay warm and stay quiet. When morning comes we take your bot home. She huddled in closer and whispered that she did not feel right and touched the back of her neck.

Pico tentatively put his arm around her and let his hand rest on the bicep of her goosebumped bare arm and she moved into his embrace.

I'm scared, he whispered and she shushed him, but it was not unfriendly.

He held absolutely still then, wary that anything he might say may disrupt their pseudo embrace. But he couldn't help himself, the nacker in front of them haunted him and he wanted to explain it, to tell her that if he could only fix it up maybe the others would forgive him, that he knew he could do it, but when he turned to tell her she surprised him with a kiss and he kissed her back.

After a while she pushed him backward into the trash and climbed on top and they stayed curled like so, keeping each other warm. The putrid smell of the dump combined with the smell of her, and Pico thought maybe he could die like this after all. He was so happy to touch her skin. Around her, he felt he could see a soft electric-blue glow, electron residue perhaps, or it was only his eyes playing tricks.

Then the dogs came. At first it was just the sound of a scrabbling out in the dark, and the sound moved fast, circling about them. Pico and Mouse stood and gripped their tharpoons, pointing the ends toward the roving sound. There was a dim light from the city far away, where real people were, in their real houses, doing. He didn't know what the *pendejos* did. He could feel Mouse shivering next to him, and this alone made him want to run at the dogs, stupid as it was. *Güey*, he thought. I don't want to die. He felt like crying. I have a nacker and almost a girlfriend.

You got any charge for light? Mouse asked.

Maybe couple minutes, but it'd just call the rest.

There was a low growl off to Pico's right and he crouched with the tharpoon. The growl was followed by a series of eerie barks, answered by many others. *Dios*, Pico whispered. Mouse, he said.

It's okay, Pico.

The sound of dogs' feet scrabbling was intense now. They had no idea how many were out there.

Pico heard one come close and Mouse swung her tharpoon at the sound and connected. They heard a howl of rage and other dogs answered, a terrifying chorus of sound. Then one got a jaw's grip around his tharpoon arm. He yelled and punched at it with his other fist but its hold was strong. It pulled him over and he heard Mouse behind him fending off another. On the ground another one got a bite-hold on his shoe. Another tore into his thigh and he kicked and screamed and clawed.

An intense flash lit the terrain suddenly. They saw a dozen or so dogs frozen in the instantaneous light. In the ensuing blackness, there were two shots fired and an answering canine howl of pain. The dog biting Pico's thigh yipped away into the night. The one on Pico's arm got suddenly light, its jaws loosening, and when Pico went to punch it off found that only its head remained, dripping blood and wire. It slipped to the ground with a soft, wet thud.

Hello? Mouse said, her voice a lonely human sound in the dark, afraid and hopeful.

They won't trouble you now, a woman answered.

Pico tenderly touched his thigh and his hands came away slick. His arm burned and ached and felt cold. I'm hurt, he said.

Who are you? Mouse said.

My name is Lucy. The voice was close now. Reach out your hand, Pico.

I can't see, Pico said. Light?

No lights, Lucy said. She took hold of his hand and slowly placed something on his forearm. He could feel it grab hold of his arm hairs and then it crawled along his body.

He screamed and demanded to know what it was.

It went under his shirt and crawled quickly and creepily around his torso and he slapped at it with his hands but it was too fast.

Don't, Lucy said. Leave it be. It's a Senti, it will seal your wounds.

The Senti was in his pants now and he jumped, despite the pain in his thigh, and then it was at his leg wound and he had to resist the violent urge to brush it off. It gripped him there and he screamed again, and then as it dug into his flesh he retched. A moment later, he felt a cool ooze and his thigh went numb. Oh, he groaned.

See? the woman's voice said.

He could hear her wrestling with some kind of gear.

My nacker, he said, it's mine.

I'll carry it, she said.

How do you know my name, Pico said.

Your friend. She is leaking data.

Really? Pico looked toward Mouse in the dark but she did not respond. He remembered the scar at the back of her neck and puzzled at it all over again.

You were jamming GPS, correct?

Yes, he said.

And then you weren't.

My battery ran out.

I suspected there was a wreck in the dump, a downed helicopter, but instead it was you. The helicopters will be here soon, though.

The Senti slinked under his clothes to his arm wound and he bent over and breathed through the initial stab of pain this time.

Let's go, Lucy said.

Lucy walked fast in the dark and they heard the loose limbs of the nacker clack together as she went. They struggled behind her. He felt like he could hear others out around him in the night, strange sounds that his imagination morphed into the most terrible things. He reached out and clasped hands with Mouse. He could feel her stumbling, the shock hangover leaving her woozy. He wrapped his good arm around her shoulder and they walked tentatively as a single unit over the compressed trash. Pico began to work up what he would tell his parents, and fantasized about Mouse, the memory of being close to her in the night fresh. She had secrets. He tried to remember if Suto had a similar scar.

Lucy stopped suddenly and they pulled up beside her. They could see just her outline in the dark, a deep black shape against a deep black night.

From here, she said, the way is down and the trail is treacherous.

Down? Pico said, and the word came out as more of a terrified bark. They were standing on the lip of the wall, he realized. No way, Pico said, we're not going down.

You'll stay close to me, and we'll each hold onto the rope. *Señorita*, are you stable?

Yes, Mouse said.

Listen, Pico said, you're crazy. We're not going down the wall. Nobody goes down the wall.

I have to go down, Pico, Mouse said.

What? Why?

Because, Lucy said, a firm consistency to her voice, otherwise they will find her. Quickly.

Lucy's hand took his and placed it on the rope, and he realized stupidly that she could see in the dark. She was augmented then.

Who will? Pico whispered to Mouse. Who will come for you?

Mouse did not answer and the rope began to pull in his hand as Lucy went over the edge of the wall and proceeded down the steep slope. The ground underneath was hardened, and he could tell they were on a trail of some sort.

It was a long hard hike to the bottom, over layer upon layer of trash, the history of the city buried in the wall he descended. He kept one hand out, his fingers surfing the edge of it as he descended, and wondered what was contained within. The dump was his curse and home. It was treasure. It was where he would die, he was sure.

At the bottom, they followed Lucy along a dark path, where stunted trees brushed against his face, and cactus pulled at his clothing. Live things. The smell of the dump was sickeningly stronger here, the wind of it flowing down the wall and flooding their nostrils. But there was more, too, a complex smell of dampness and death.

Pico had a thousand questions that rushed him in disorderly fashion, but his amazement and fear kept him from organizing them into words.

Instead he listened to the sounds around him. There were others they passed, low structures with low voices inside, the smells of cooking which made his stomach ache. They were in a camp of some sort. Twice he heard a voice call out to Lucy and then there was silence after. He held hard onto the rope.

They turned and he followed the rope into a dwelling of some sort.

Mouse? he said.

Here, she said from in front of him.

The rope went slack in his hands and the darkness was absolute and he stood where he was. Around him he could feel there were objects, the place close and dense with things.

Give me your GPS jammer, Lucy said.

Why?

Give it now!

Pico unhooked it from his belt and handed it to Lucy. A moment later he saw the faint purple glow of the jammer's light.

Well, Lucy said. We get to work.

No please, not yet, Mouse said.

Dearheart, Lucy said.

Can't we turn on the *pinche* light? Pico said. I want answers.

To what, love, Lucy said.

Pico wasn't sure to what. Who are you? he said finally.

I already told you my name. You mean, *Señor*, what am I? Am I a *pinche* leper?

There was silence, until Pico said quietly, yes.

Yes, I am what they call a leper.

Pico no longer knew in which direction the door was. He resisted the urge to crouch to his knees and put his arms over his head. He'd grown up hearing about the lepers, the cyborgs.

For a while, Lucy said into the dark room, cyborgs were made. Or rather, humans evolved into cyborgs. I like to think of it that way. These humans feared death, and thinking that machines do not die, became half-machine. After a while, it became a challenge to name them: Were they more machine or more human? At some point, a line was crossed. You know this story?

Yes, Mouse said.

I don't know, Pico said. Kind of.

I will tell you, Lucy said.

In the dark? Pico said.

After, if you wish to see, we may have light.

There were the rich and old, Lucy continued, desperate for a taste of immortality, who fought the body's desire to change. Replace a heart and an eye, an ear and a knee, a parietal lobe, a face. Replace it all. There were government experiments. Androids with flesh, with heartbeats, who subsisted on food. The call of augmentation is strong. Who does not wish for improvement, for immortality?

No one knows where the disease came from. Perhaps there is such a thing as an evolutionary memory, a sense of wholeness. Perhaps the very skin and flesh rejected the system it had become a part of, the hard impassive elements that bound them. Perhaps God did not like his creations so tinkered with. In the end, we began to fall apart, become undone. Our flesh peeled from the metal and plastic implants, and vice versa. To stay alive, I employ a swarm of Senti to keep me whole. Listen.

She was silent a moment until Pico realized he could hear a soft sound, like a fleet of cockroaches pattering lightly along tin. She meant these things covered her, the Senti she had given him earlier.

Does our species' history, our very evolution, contain a binding principle? Is there a soul that fetters us? Maybe the sustenance we eat, of the earth and returned to earth, locks us into something we do not yet understand. I don't know. But we became sick, and the disease was infectious, even for the less augmented. So we were outcasted.

I have an implant, Mouse said.

Of course you do, dearheart, Lucy said. But since we will remove it tonight, you need not fear the disease.

Turn on the light, Pico said.

There was a click, and with a whir a glow bloomed into the room. The place was absolutely full of things. Strollers and dish racks and hubcaps and toasters and robotany strapped to the wall and ceiling, layers upon layers of scavenged dump junk.

Lucy sat straight-spined on a plush red chair, one leg of which was bound and fixed with wire. On her nearly bald head a swarm of centipede-like insects feverishly worked a wide swath of skinless area encrusted with blood. She had no lower lip, and Pico could see the skeletal roots of her teeth. Her eyes were dull and inhuman, and surrounded with bruising, swollen blue and yellow stretches across her face. Lucy's hands were crossed over her knees, and they were beyond age, crackled and parched, some fingers with long ragged nails, others missing nails entirely, in their place a sort of pus. She wore a worn black velvet suit.

Mouse let out a sob and covered her face.

Shall I turn out the light? Lucy asked.

Pico shook his head no. He wanted to be in the dark with her even less. He could feel the Senti crawling across his own thigh and he grabbed it in a quick swoop and offered it back to Lucy.

Keep it, she said, a gift.

Is it expensive? he asked.

Extremely.

He nodded and put it back on his leg, still disgusted by its function. Thank you. Pico sat down on the floor, a patchwork collage of rug scraps, and studied the ceiling.

Your friend Mouse has a bounty on her head, did you know? Lucy said to Pico. Her whole family does. Did.

Pico looked at Mouse who still covered her face.

Not Basucorp, Lucy said, government. The dogs were nothing. You would have received a helicopter ride to oblivion had I not found you. Her wi.n is damaged—it used to protect her identity, but its defenses are fried and now it's spouting a fire-hose of data, the slutty little thing.

What should we do? Pico said.

Lucy shrugged, we must remove it. She turned toward Mouse and exhaled through her lipless bottom teeth in consideration, her cheeks puffed out grotesquely. They won't send patrols down here, they are too afraid of the disease. But they know you're around here somewhere. They will be waiting and listening for you. She unfolded her long hands and beckoned. Come here, dear. We must do it now.

I don't want to, Mouse said.

Wants, Lucy said, rarely make much difference.

It has everything.

I know, but I cannot fix it. You will be a real *pepenador* after this. Not many get the chance to start everything over. In time you might even appreciate this. Come. Pico, fetch us a scalpel from the top drawer. Lucy pointed to a set of listing enamel kitchen drawers.

Lucy slowly pushed Mouse's face down into her lap and bared the thin white scar at the back of her neck that Pico had seen earlier. Pico balled his fists and hopped once in nervous anticipation, then he bent close and held Mouse's hand. It repulsed him to see the leper's ugly claw touch Mouse's hair.

Lucy pulled a Senti from her own scalp and placed it on the scar, where it hunched into her flesh. Mouse tensed and then relaxed. After Lucy removed the Senti back to her own scalp she made a deep incision with the scalpel, following the old line of the white scar. Mouse was quiet.

When the incision was just right, Lucy reached her claw-hand into Mouse's neck and Mouse screamed. A moment later Lucy pulled out the wi.n, a small white cylinder covered in blood which trailed wispy lines back to Mouse's neck. Lucy cut the lines.

Here's the awful little thing, Lucy said. Now you are one hundred percent human again. You are lucky. *You are immune.*

Mouse cried quietly in her lap as two Senti patched up her wound, and then fell asleep there, with Lucy stroking her hair.

Lucy held out the bloody wi.n and scalpel to Pico. Take these and clean them off.

He was unsure of how to clean them off and Lucy offered no suggestions. Finally he wiped them on his pant leg. She said nothing after that, so he put the wi.n in his pocket and replaced the scalpel.

They are helping her get through it, Lucy said. If you wish, there are tools in the bottom drawer.

Pico found his nacker in a corner and pulled out Lucy's tools and eagerly set to work disassembling it. He was relieved to have something to do. He repeated in his mind the tharpoon throw that had disabled the machine, and fetched the small module he'd chipped from its top.

As he worked, he tried to block from his mind what he'd just seen. The image of Lucy's face behind him, the object that had been extracted from Mouse. Instead he wondered who she was. Who her brother had been. He didn't remember when they'd come to the dump. Three, maybe four years ago. He thought they'd come like everyone else: When there was nowhere else to go. When they had nothing left to do but become nobody. For himself, he was born there. *Nací en la basura, crecí en la basura, yo soy de la basura.*

What will you do with it, Lucy asked, pointing her fleshless chin at the nacker. He thought she looked at it with distaste.

Pico shrugged. He didn't know. He only knew he wanted one, and had disassembled and reworked it with a confidence that it could be his. Maybe like a pet, he said finally. But he knew it was not that.

Lucy raised her eyebrows and Pico turned away from her. She was a ghastly sight.

I can teach the *pepenadores* how to *cha*! He mimed a karate chop at the top of the nacker to demonstrate how one might disable one. You know? Then we can get more. They can protect us and help us make finds, Pico grinned, and thought: and I will be of them again.

After that, it was quiet in the hut. There were strange murmurings from outside, from the other hovels in the odd village of outcasts. He thought he could hear something else. Like a mangy dump cat's overeager purr. He stared toward the trash ceiling and listened. They're out there, aren't they, he said.

Lucy nodded.

He felt a charge of panic and for a moment, pictured himself running with Mouse in his arms, helicopters circling above him. Then he knew what he had to do.

He hurriedly reassembled the nacker, but left its primary power disconnected. He hoped the module that he'd loosed on top with his tharpoon was not damaged.

From his pocket he pulled Mouse's wi.n and looked at it and his nacker with regret. He would have liked to have tinkered with them both. Would have liked to have known what it meant to have one. Instead he borrowed some wire from Lucy's tool drawer and wired the wi.n firmly to the underside of the nacker. When he was finished, he picked up the bot and hauled it outside.

He sat with it under the smog glow and felt an electricity of excitement and fear and disappointment.

He thought of his time with Mouse before the dogs came. He touched the wound on his forearm and felt only a braille scar. In his hands the nacker was cold and still and he knew he must sacrifice it. Someday, perhaps, he'd get another chance.

When he was ready, he reconnected the nacker and stood up. There was no chance to run, he knew. It powered up and rebooted and for half a moment did nothing, and this made him nearly laugh, to think of its confusion.

The next instant it sensed him and reached out its tentacle, sending a searing bolt of electricity. He heard the short yelp his mouth made, and as he collapsed a wink of thought passed through him. How its machine instincts would call it home. How it would skitter along the trail at high speed. How a moment later it would exit the umbrella of the GPS jammer, carrying Mouse's wi.n. It would go home, he thought, to be with its kind, and the soldiers would have to search that nest for her. And perhaps, he hoped, his nacker carried a touch of the disease.

DOWN AND OUT IN THE YEAR 2000

By Kim Stanley Robinson

It was going to be hot again. Summer in Washington, D.C. Lee Robinson woke and rolled on his mattress, broke into a sweat. That kind of a day. He got up and kneeled over the other mattress in the small room. Debra shifted as he shaded her from the sun angling in the open window. The corners of her mouth were caked white and her forehead was still hot and dry, but her breathing was regular and she appeared to be sleeping well. Quietly Lee slipped on his jeans and walked down the hall to the bathroom. Locked. He waited; Ramon came out wet and groggy. "Morning, Robbie." Into the bathroom, where he hung his pants on the hook and did his morning ritual. One bloodshot eye, staring back at him from the splinter of mirror still in the frame. The dirt around the toilet base. The shower curtain blotched with black fungus, as if it had a fatal disease. That kind of morning.

Out of the shower he dried off with his jeans and started to sweat again. Back in his room Debra was still sleeping. Worried, he watched her for a while, then filled his pockets and went into the hall to put on sneakers and tank top. Debra slept light these days, and the strangest things would rouse her. He jogged down the four flights of stairs to the street, and, sweating freely, stepped out into the steamy air.

He walked down 16th Street, with its curious alternation of condo fortresses and abandoned buildings, to the Mall. There, big khaki tanks dominated the broad field of dirt and trash and tents and the odd patch of grass. Most of the protesters were still asleep in their scattered tent villages, but there was an active crowd around the Washington Monument, and Lee walked on over, ignoring the soldiers by the tanks.

The crowd surrounded a slingshot as tall as a man, made of a forked tree branch. Inner tubes formed the sling, and the base was buried in the ground. Excited protesters placed balloons filled with red paint into the sling, and fired them up at the monument. If a balloon hit above the red that already covered the tower, splashing clean white—a rare event, as the monument was pure red up a good third of it—the protesters cheered crazily. Lee watched them as they danced around the sling after a successful shot. He approached some of the calmer seated spectators.

"Want to buy a joint?"

"How much?"

"Five dollars."

"Too much, man! You must be kidding! How about a dollar?"

Lee walked on.

"Hey, wait! One joint, then. Five dollars . . . shit."

"Going rate, man."

The protester pushed long blond hair out of his eyes and pulled a five from a thick clip of bills. Lee got the battered Marlboro box from his pocket and took the smallest joint from it. "Here you go. Have fun. Why don't you fire one of them paint bombs at those tanks, huh?"

The kids on the ground laughed. "We will when you get them stoned!"

He walked on. Only five joints left. It took him less than an hour to sell them. That meant thirty dollars, but that was it. Nothing left to sell. As he left the Mall he looked back at the monument; under its wash of paint it looked like a bone sticking out of raw flesh.

Anxious about coming to the end of his supply, Lee hoofed it up to Dupont Circle and sat on the perimeter bench in the shade of one of the big trees, footsore and hot. In the muggy air it was hard to catch his breath. He ran the water from the drinking fountain over his hands until someone got in line for a drink. He crossed the circle, giving a wide berth to a bunch of lawyers in long-sleeved shirts and loosened ties, lunching on wine and cheese under the watchful eye of their bodyguard. On the other side of the park, Delmont Briggs sat by his cup, almost asleep, his sign propped on his lap. The wasted man. Delmont's sign—and a little side business—provided him with just enough money to get by on the street. The sign, a battered square of cardboard, said PLEASE HELP—HUNGRY. People still looked through Delmont like he wasn't there, but every once in a while it got to somebody. Lee shook his head distastefully at the idea.

"Delmont, you know any weed I can buy? I need a finger baggie for twenty."

"Not so easy to do, Robbie." Delmont hemmed and hawed and they dickered for a while, then he sent Lee over to Jim Johnson, who made the sale under a cheery exchange of the day's news, over by the chess tables. After that Lee bought a pack of cigarettes in a liquor store and went up to the little triangular park between 17th, S, and New Hampshire, where no police or strangers ever came. They called it Fish Park for the incongruous cement whale sitting by one of the trash cans. He sat down on the long broken bench, among his acquaintances who were hanging out there, and fended them off while he carefully emptied the Marlboros, cut some tobacco into the weed, and refilled the cigarette papers with the new mix. With their ends twisted he had a dozen more joints. They smoked one and he sold two more for a dollar each before he got out of the park.

But he was still anxious, and since it was the hottest part of the day and few people were about, he decided to visit his plants. He knew it would be at least a week till harvest, but he wanted to see them. Anyway, it was about watering day.

East between 16th and 15th he hit no-man's-land. The mixed neighborhood of fortress apartments and burned-out hulks gave way to a block or two of entirely abandoned buildings. Here the police had been at work, and looters had finished the job. The buildings were battered and burnt out, their ground floors blasted wide open, some of them collapsed entirely into heaps of rubble. No one walked the broken sidewalk; sirens a few blocks off and the distant hum of traffic were the only signs that the whole city wasn't just like this. Little jumps in the corner of his eye were no more than that; nothing there when he looked directly. The first time, Lee had found walking down the abandoned street nerve-racking; now he was reassured by the silence, the stillness, the no-man's-land smell of torn asphalt and wet charcoal, the wavering streetscape empty under a sour-milk sky.

• • •

His first building was a corner brownstone, blackened on the street sides, all its windows and doors gone, but otherwise sound. He walked past it without stopping, turned, and surveyed the neighborhood. No movement anywhere. He stepped up the steps and through the doorway, being careful to make no footprints in the mud behind the doorjamb. Another glance outside, then up the broken stairs to the second floor. The second floor was a jumble of beams and busted furniture, and Lee waited a minute to let his sight adjust to the gloom. The staircase to the third floor had collapsed, which was the reason he had chosen this building—no easy way up. But he had a route worked out, and with a leap he grabbed a beam hanging from the stairwell and hoisted himself onto it. Some crawling up the beam and he could swing onto the third floor, and from there a careful walk up gapped stairs brought him to the fourth floor.

The room surrounding the stairwell was dim, and he had jammed the door to the next room, so that he had to crawl through a hole in the wall to get through. Then he was there.

Sweating profusely, he blinked in the sudden sunlight, and stepped to his plants, all lined out in plastic pots on the far wall. Eleven medium-sized female marijuana plants, their splayed green leaves drooping for lack of water. He took the rain funnel from one of the gallon jugs and watered the plants. The buds were just longer than his thumbnail; if he could wait another week or two at least, they would be the size of his thumb or more, and worth fifty bucks apiece. He twisted off some water leaves and put them in a baggie.

He found a patch of shade and sat with the plants for a while, watched them soak up the water. Wonderful green they had, lighter than most leaves in D.C. Little red threads in the buds. The white sky lowered over the big break in the roof, huffing little gasps of muggy air onto them all.

His next spot was several blocks north, on the roof of a burned-out hulk that had no interior floors left. Access was by way of a tree growing next to the wall. Climbing it was a challenge, but he had a route here he took, and he liked the way leaves concealed him even from passersby directly beneath him once he got above the lowest branches.

The plants here were younger—in fact one had sprouted seeds since he last saw them, and he pulled the plant out and put it in the baggie. After watering them and adjusting the aluminum foil rain funnels on the jug tops, he climbed down the tree and walked back down 14th.

He stopped to rest in Charlie's Baseball Club. Charlie sponsored a city team with the profits from his bar, and old members of the team welcomed Lee, who hadn't been by in a while. Lee had played left field and batted fifth a year or two before, until his job with the park service had been cut. After that he had had to pawn his glove and cleats, and he had missed Charlie's minimal membership charge three seasons running, and so he had quit. And then it had been too painful to go by the club, and drink with the guys and look at all the trophies on the wall, a couple of which he had helped to win. But on this day he enjoyed the fan blowing, and the dark, and the fries that Charlie and Fisher shared with him.

Break over, he went to the spot closest to home, where the new plants were struggling through the soil, on the top floor of an empty stone husk on 16th and Caroline. The first floor was a drinking place for derelicts, and old Thunderbird and whiskey bottles, half still in bags, littered the dark room, which smelled of alcohol, urine, and rotting wood. All the better: few people would be foolish enough to enter such an obviously dangerous hole. And the stairs were as near gone as made no difference. He climbed over the holes to the second floor, turned, and climbed to the third.

The baby plants were fine, bursting out of the soil and up to the sun, the two leaves covered by four, up into four again . . . He watered them and headed home.

On the way he stopped at the little market that the Vietnamese family ran, and bought three cans of soup, a box of crackers, and some Coke. "Twenty-two oh five tonight, Robbie," old Huang said with a four-toothed grin.

The neighbors were out on the sidewalk, the women sitting on the stoop, the men kicking a soccer ball about aimlessly as they watched Sam sand down an old table, the kids running around. Too hot to stay inside this evening, although it wasn't much better on the street. Lee helloed through them and walked up the flights of stairs slowly, feeling the day's travels in his feet and legs.

In his room Debra was awake, and sitting up against her pillows. "I'm hungry, Lee." She looked hot, bored; he shuddered to think of her day.

"That's a good sign, that means you're feeling better. I've got some soup here should be real good for you." He touched her cheek, smiling.

"It's too hot for soup."

"Yeah, that's true, but we'll let it cool down after it cooks, it'll still taste good." He sat on the floor and turned on the hot plate, poured water from the plastic jug into the pot, opened the can of soup, mixed it in. While they were spooning it out Rochelle Jackson knocked on the door and came in.

"Feeling better, I see." Rochelle had been a nurse before her hospital closed, and Lee had enlisted her help when Debra fell sick. "We'll have to take your temperature later."

Lee wolfed down crackers while he watched Rochelle fuss over Debra. Eventually she took a temperature and Lee walked her out.

"It's still pretty high, Lee."

"What's she got?" he asked, as he always did. Frustration.

"I don't know any more than yesterday. Some kind of flu, I guess."

"Would a flu hang on this long?"

"Some of them do. Just keep her sleeping and drinking as much as you can, and feed her when she's hungry. Don't be scared, Lee."

"I can't help it! I'm afraid she'll get sicker . . . And there ain't nothing I can do!"

"Yeah, I know. Just keep her fed. You're doing just what I would do."

After cleaning up, he left Debra to sleep and went back down to the street, to join the men on the picnic tables and benches in the park tucked into the intersection. This was the "living room" on summer evenings, and all the regulars were there in their usual spots, sitting on tables or bench backs. "Hey there, Robbie! What's happening?"

"Not much, not much. No man, don't kick that soccer ball at me, I can't kick no soccer ball tonight."

"You been walking the streets, hey?"

"How else we going to find her to bring her home to you."

"Hey lookee here, Ghost is bringing out his TV."

"It's Tuesday night at the movies, y'all!" Ghost called out as he approached and plunked a little hologram TV and a Honda generator on the picnic table. They laughed and watched Ghost's pale skin glow in the dusk as he hooked the system up.

"Where'd you get this one, Ghost? You been sniffing around the funeral parlors again?"

"You bet I have!" Ghost grinned. "This one's picture is all fucked up, but it still works—I think—"

He turned the set on and blurry 3-D figures swam into shape in a cube above the box—all in dark shades of blue.

"Man, we must have the blues tonight," Ramon remarked. "Look at that!"

"They all look like Ghost," said Lee.

"Hey, it works, don't it?" Ghost said. Hoots of derision. "And dig the sound! The sound works—"

"Turn it up then."

"It's up all the way."

"What's this?" Lee laughed. "We got to watch frozen midgets whispering, is that it, Ghost? What do midgets say on a cold night?"

"Who the fuck is this?" said Ramon.

Johnnie said, "That be Sam Spade, the greatest computer spy in the world."

"How come he live in that shack, then?" Ramon asked.

"That's to show it's a tough scuffle making it as a computer spy, real tough."

"How come he got four million dollars' worth of computers right there in the shack, then?" Ramon asked, and the others commenced giggling, Lee loudest of all. Johnnie and Ramon could be killers sometimes. A bottle of rum started around, and Steve broke in to bounce the soccer ball on the TV, smashing the blue figures repeatedly.

"Watch out now, Sam about to go plug his brains in to try and find out who he is."

"And then he gonna be told of some stolen wetware he got to find."

"I got some wetware myself, only I call it a shirt."

Steve dropped the ball and kicked it against the side of the picnic table, and a few of the watchers joined in a game of pepper. Some men in a stopped van shouted a conversation with the guys on the corner. Those watching the show leaned forward. "Where's he gonna go?" said Ramon. "Hong Kong? Monaco? He gonna take the bus on over to Monaco?"

Johnnie shook his head. "Rio, man. Fucking Rio de Janeiro."

Sure enough, Sam was off to Rio. Ghost choked out an objection: "Johnnie—ha!—you must have seen this one before."

Johnnie shook his head, though he winked at Lee. "No man, that's just where all the good stolen wetware ends up."

A series of commercials interrupted their fun: deodorant, burglar-killers, cars. The men in the van drove off. Then the show was back, in Rio, and Johnnie said, "He's about to meet a slinky Afro-Asian spy."

When Sam was approached by a beautiful black Asian woman, the men couldn't stand it. "Y'all have seen this one before!" Ghost cried.

Johnnie sputtered over the bottle, struggled to swallow. "No way! Experience counts, man, that's all."

"And Johnnie has watched one hell of a lot of Sam Spade," Ramon added.

Lee said, "I wonder why they're always Afro-Asian."

Steve burst in, laughed. "So they can fuck all of us at once, man!" He dribbled on the image, changed the channel. "—*army command in Los Angeles reports that the rioting killed at least*—" He punched the channel again. "What else we got here—man!—what's *this*?"

"Cyborgs Versus Androids," Johnnie said after a quick glance at the blue shadows. "Lots of fighting."

"Yeah!" Steve exclaimed. Distracted, some of the watchers wandered off. "I'm a cyborg myself, see, I got these false teeth!"

"Shit."

Lee went for a walk around the block with Ramon, who was feeling good. "Sometimes I feel so good, Robbie! So strong! I walk around this city and I say, the city is falling apart, it can't last much longer, like this. And here I am like some kind of animal, you know, living day to day by my wits and figuring out all the little ways to get by . . . you know there are people living up in Rock Creek Park like Indians or something, hunting and fishing and all. And it's just the same in here, you know. The buildings don't make it no different. Just hunting and scrapping to get by, and man I feel so alive—" He waved the rum bottle at the sky.

Lee sighed. "Yeah." Still, Ramon was one of the biggest fences in the area. It was really a steady job. For the rest . . . They finished their walk, and Lee went back up to his room. Debra was sleeping fitfully. He went to the bathroom, soaked his shirt in the sink, wrung it out. In the room it was stifling, and not even a waft of a breeze came in the window. Lying on his mattress sweating, figuring out how long he could make their money last, it took him a long time to fall asleep.

The next day he returned to Charlie's Baseball Club to see if Charlie could give him any piecework, as he had one or two times in the past. But Charlie only said no, very shortly, and he and everyone else in the bar looked at him oddly, so that Lee felt uncomfortable enough to leave without a drink. After that he returned to the Mall, where the protesters were facing the troops ranked in front of the Capitol, dancing and jeering and throwing stuff. With all the police out it took him a good part of the afternoon to sell all the joints left, and when he had he walked back up 17th Street feeling tired and worried. Perhaps another purchase from Delmont could string them along a few more days . . .

At 17th and Q a tall skinny kid ran out into the street and tried to open the door of a car stopped for a red light. But it was a protected car despite its cheap look, and the kid shrieked as the handle shocked him. He was still stuck by the hand to it when the car roared off, so that he was launched through the air and rolled over the asphalt. Cars drove on by. A crowd gathered around the bleeding kid. Lee walked on, his jaw clenched. At least the kid would live. He had seen bodyguards gun thieves down in the street, kill them dead, and walk away.

Passing Fish Park he saw a man sitting on a corner bench looking around. The guy was white, young; his hair was blond and short, he wore wire-rimmed glasses, his clothes were casual but new, like the protesters' down on the Mall. He had money. Lee snarled as the sharp-faced stranger approached him.

"What you doing here?"

"Sitting!" The man was startled, nervous. "Just sitting in a park!"

"This ain't no park, man. This is our front yard. You see any front yard to these apartment buildings here? No. This here is our front yard, and we don't like people just coming into it and sitting down anywhere!"

The man stood and walked away, looked back once, his expression angry and frightened. The other man sitting on the park benches looked at Lee curiously.

Two days later he was nearly out of money. He walked over to Connecticut Avenue, where his old friend Victor played harmonica for coins when he couldn't find other work. Today he was there, belting out "Amazing Grace." He cut it off when he saw Lee. "Robbie! What's happening?"

"Not much. You?"

Victor gestured at his empty hat, on the sidewalk before him. "You see it. Don't even have seed coin for the cap, man."

"So you ain't been getting any gardening work lately?"

"No, no. Not lately. I do all right here, though. People still pay for music, man, some of them. Music's the angle." He looked at Lee, face twisted up against the sun. They had worked together for the park service, in times past. Every morning through the summers they had gone out and run the truck down the streets, stopping at every tree to hoist each other up in slings. The one hoisted had to stand out from truck or branches like an acrobat, moving around to cut off every branch below twelve feet, and it took careful handling of the chain saw to avoid chopping into legs and such. Those were good times. But now the park service was gone, and Victor gazed at Lee with a stoic squint, sitting behind an empty hat.

"Do you ever look up at the trees anymore, Robbie?"

"Not much."

"I do. They're growing wild, man! Growing like fucking weeds! Every summer they go like crazy. Pretty soon people are gonna have to drive their cars through the branches. The streets'll be tunnels. And with half the buildings in this area falling down . . . I like the idea that the forest is taking this city back again. Running over it like kudzu, till maybe it just be forest again at last."

•   •   •

That evening Lee and Debra ate tortillas and refries, purchased with the last of their money. Debra had a restless night, and her temperature stayed high. Rochelle's forehead wrinkled as she watched her.

Lee decided he would have to harvest a couple of the biggest plants prematurely. He could dry them over the hot plate and be in business by the following day.

The next afternoon he walked east into no-man's-land, right at twilight. Big thunderheads loomed to the east, lit by the sun, but it had not rained that day and the muggy heat was like an invisible blanket, choking each breath with moisture. Lee came to his abandoned building, looked around. Again the complete stillness of an empty city. He recalled Ramon's tales of the people who lived forever in the no-man's-land, channeling rain into basement pools, growing vegetables in empty lots, and existing entirely on their own with no need for money . . .

He entered the building, ascended the stairs, climbed the beam, struggled sweating up to the fourth floor and through the hole into his room.

The plants were gone.

"Wha . . ." He kneeled, feeling like he had been punched in the stomach. The plastic pots were knocked over, and fans of soil lay spread over the old wood flooring.

Sick with anxiety he hurried downstairs and jogged north to his second hideaway. Sweat spilled into his eyes and they stung fiercely. He lost his breath and had to walk. Climbing the tree was a struggle.

The second crop was gone too.

Now he was stunned, shocked almost beyond thought. Someone must have followed him . . . It was nearly dark, and the mottled sky lowered over him, empty but somehow, now, watchful. He descended the tree and ran south again, catching his breath in a sort of sobbing. It was dark by the time he reached 16th and Caroline, and he made his way up the busted stairs using a cigarette for illumination. Once on the fourth floor the lighter revealed broken pots, dirt strewn everywhere, the young plants gone. That small they hadn't been worth anything. Even the aluminum-foil rain funnels on his plastic jugs had been ripped up and thrown around.

He sat down, soaking wet with sweat, and leaned back against the scored, moldy wall. Leaned his head back and looked up at the orange-white clouds, lit by the city.

After a while he stumbled downstairs to the first floor and stood on the filthy concrete, among the shadows and the discarded bottles. He went and picked up a whiskey bottle, sniffed it. Going from bottle to bottle he poured whatever drops remained in them into the whiskey bottle. When he was done he had a finger or so of liquor, which he downed in one long pull. He coughed. Threw the bottle against the wall. Picked up each bottle and threw it against the wall. Then he went outside and sat on the curb, and watched the traffic pass by.

He decided that some of his old teammates from Charlie's Baseball Club must have followed him around and discovered his spots, which would explain why they had looked at him so funny the other day. He went over to check it out immediately. But when he got there he found the place closed, shut down, a big new padlock on the door.

"What happened?" he asked one of the men hanging out on the corner, someone from this year's team.

"They busted Charlie this morning. Got him for selling speed, first thing this morning. Now the club be gone for good, and the team too."

When he got back to the apartment building it was late, after midnight. He went to Rochelle's door and tapped lightly.

"Who is it?"

"Lee." Rochelle opened the door and looked out. Lee explained what had happened. "Can I borrow a can of soup for Debra for tonight? I'll get it back to you."

"Okay. But I want one back soon, you hear?"

Back in his room Debra was awake. "Where you been, Lee?" she asked weakly. "I was worried about you."

He sat down at the hot plate, exhausted.

"I'm hungry."

"That's a good sign. Some cream of mushroom soup, coming right up." He began to cook, feeling dizzy and sick. When Debra finished eating he had to force the remaining soup down him.

Clearly, he realized, someone he knew had ripped him off—one of his neighbors, or a park acquaintance. They must have guessed his source of weed, then followed him as he made his rounds. Someone he knew. One of his friends.

Early the next day he fished a newspaper out of a trashcan and looked through the short column of want ads for dishwashing work and the like. There was a busboy job at the Dupont Hotel and he walked over and asked about it. The man turned him away after a single look: "Sorry, man, we looking for people who can walk out into the restaurant, you know." Staring in one of the big silvered windows as he walked up New Hampshire, Lee saw what the man saw: his hair was spiked out everywhere as if he would be a Rasta in five or ten years, his clothes were torn and dirty, his eyes wild . . . With a deep stab of fear he realized he was too poor to be able to get any job—beyond the point where he could turn it around.

He walked the shimmery black streets, checking phone booths for change. He walked down to M Street and over to 12th, stopping in at all the grills and little Asian restaurants; he went up to Pill Park and tried to get some of his old buddies to front him, he kept looking in pay phones and puzzling through blown scraps of newspaper, desperately hoping that one of them might list a job for him . . . and with each foot-sore step the fear spiked up in him like the pain lancing up his legs, until it soared into a thoughtless panic. Around noon he got so shaky and sick-feeling he had to stop, and despite his fear he slept flat on his back in Dupont Circle Park through the hottest hours of the day.

In the late afternoon he picked it up again, wandering almost aimlessly. He stuck his fingers in every phone booth for blocks around, but other fingers had been there before his. The change boxes of the old farecard machines in the Metro would have yielded more, but with the subway system closed, all those holes into the earth were gated off, and slowly filling with trash. Nothing but big trash pits.

Back at Dupont Circle he tried a pay phone coin return and got a dime. "Yeah," he said aloud; that got him over a dollar. He looked up and saw that a man had stopped to watch him: one of the fucking lawyers, in loosened tie and long-sleeved shirt and slacks and leather shoes, staring at him open-mouthed as his group and its bodyguard crossed the street. Lee held up the coin between thumb and forefinger and glared at the man, trying to impress on him the reality of a dime.

He stopped at the Vietnamese market. "Huang, can I buy some soup from you and pay you tomorrow?"

The old man shook his head sadly. "I can't do that, Robbie. I do that even once, and—" he wiggled his hands—"the whole house come down. You know that."

"Yeah. Listen, what can I get for—" He pulled the day's change from his pocket and counted it again. "A dollar ten."

Huang shrugged. "Candy bar? No?" He studied Lee. "Potatoes. Here, two potatoes from the back. Dollar ten."

"I didn't think you had any potatoes."

"Keep them for family, you see. But I sell these to you."

"Thanks, Huang." Lee took the potatoes and left. There was a trash Dumpster behind the store; he considered it, opened it, looked in. There was a half-eaten hot dog—but the stench overwhelmed him, and he remembered the poisonous taste of the discarded liquor he had punished himself with. He let the lid of the Dumpster slam down and went home.

After the potatoes were boiled and mashed and Debra was fed, he went to the bathroom and showered until someone hammered on the door. Back in his room he still felt hot, and he had trouble catching his breath. Debra rolled from side to side, moaning. Sometimes he was sure she was getting sicker, and at the thought his fear spiked up and through him again; he got so scared he couldn't breathe at all . . . "I'm hungry, Lee. Can't I have nothing more to eat?"

"Tomorrow, Deb, tomorrow. We ain't got nothing now."

She fell into an uneasy sleep. Lee sat on his mattress and stared out the window. White-orange clouds sat overhead, unmoving. He felt a bit dizzy, even feverish, as if he was coming down with whatever Debra had. He remembered how poor he had felt even back when he had had his crops to sell, when each month ended with such a desperate push to make rent. But now . . . He sat and watched the shadowy figure of Debra, the walls, the hot plate and utensils in the corner, the clouds out the window. Nothing changed. It was only an hour or two before dawn when he fell asleep, still sitting against the wall.

Next day he battled fever to seek out potato money from the pay phones and the gutters, but he only had thirty-five cents when he had to quit. He drank as much water as he could hold, slept in the park, and then went to see Victor.

"Vic, let me borrow your harmonica tonight."

Victor's face squinted with distress. "I can't, Robbie. I need it myself. You know—" pleading with him to understand.

"I know," Lee said, staring off into space. He tried to think. The two friends looked at each other.

"Hey, man, you can use my kazoo."

"What?"

"Yeah, man, I got a good kazoo here, I mean a big metal one with a good buzz to it. It sounds kind of like a harmonica, and it's easier to play it. You just hum notes." Lee tried it. "No, hum, man. Hum in it."

Lee tried again, and the kazoo buzzed a long crazy note.

"See? Hum a tune, now."

Lee hummed around for a bit.

"And then you can practice on my harmonica till you get good on it, and get your own. You ain't going to make anything with a harmonica till you can play it, anyway."

"But this—" Lee said, looking at the kazoo.

Victor shrugged. "Worth a try."

Lee nodded. "Yeah." He clapped Victor on the shoulder, squeezed it. Pointed at Victor's sign, which said, He's a musician! "You think that helps?"

Victor shrugged. "Yeah."

"Okay. I'm going to get far enough away so's I don't cut into your business."

"You do that. Come back and tell me how you do."

"I will."

So Lee walked south to Connecticut and M, where the sidewalks were wide and there were lots of banks and restaurants. It was just after sunset, the heat as oppressive as at midday. He had a piece of cardboard taken from a trash can, and now he tore it straight, took his ballpoint from his pocket, and copied Delmont's message. PLEASE HELP—HUNGRY. He had always admired its economy, how it cut right to the main point.

But when he got to what appeared to be a good corner, he couldn't make himself sit down. He stood there, started to leave, returned. He pounded his fist against his thigh, stared about wildly, walked to the curb, and sat on it to think things over.

Finally he stepped to a bank pillar mid-sidewalk and leaned back against it. He put the sign against the pillar face out, and put his old baseball cap upside-down on the ground in front of him. Put his thirty-five cents in it as seed money. He took the kazoo from his pocket, fingered it. "Goddamn it," he said at the sidewalk between clenched teeth. "If you're going to make me live this way, you're going to have to pay for it." And he started to play.

He blew so hard that the kazoo squealed, and his face puffed up till it hurt. "Columbia, the Gem of the Ocean," blasted into all the passing faces, louder and louder—

When he had blown his fury out he stopped to consider it. He wasn't going to make any money that way. The loose-ties and the career women in dresses and running shoes were staring at him and moving out toward the curb as they passed, huddling closer together in their little flocks as their bodyguards got between him and them. No money in that.

He took a deep breath, started again. "Swing Low, Sweet Chariot." It really was like singing. And what a song. How you could put your heart into that one, your whole body. Just like singing.

One of the flocks had paused off to the side; they had a red light to wait for. It was as he had observed with Delmont: the lawyers looked right through beggars, they didn't want to think about them. He played louder, and one young man glanced over briefly. Sharp face, wire-rims—with a start Lee recognized the man as the one he had harassed out of Fish Park a couple days before. The guy wouldn't look at Lee directly, and so he didn't recognize him back. Maybe he wouldn't have anyway. But he was hearing the kazoo. He turned to his companions, student types gathered to the lawyer flock for the temporary protection of the bodyguard. He said something to them—"I love street music," or something like that—and took a dollar from his pocket. He hurried over and put the folded bill in Lee's baseball cap, without looking up at Lee. The walk light came on, they all scurried away. Lee played on.

That night after feeding Debra her potato, and eating two himself, he washed the pot in the bathroom sink, and then took a can of mushroom soup up to Rochelle, who gave him a big smile.

Walking down the stairs he beeped the kazoo, listening to the stairwell's echoes. Ramon passed him and grinned. "Just call you Robinson Caruso," he said, and cackled.

"Yeah."

Lee returned to his room. He and Debra talked for a while, and then she fell into a half-sleep, and fretted as if in a dream.

"No, that's all right," Lee said softly. He was sitting on his mattress, leaning back against the wall. The cardboard sign was facedown on the floor. The kazoo was in his mouth, and it half buzzed with his words. "We'll be all right. I'll get some seeds from Delmont, and take the pots to new hideouts, better ones." It occurred to him that rent would be due in a couple of weeks; he banished the thought. "Maybe start some gardens in no-man's-land. And I'll practice on Vic's harmonica, and buy one from the pawn shop later." He took the kazoo from his mouth, stared at it. "It's strange what will make money."

He kneeled at the window, stuck his head out, hummed through the kazoo. Tune after tune buzzed the still, hot air. From the floor below Ramon stuck his head out his window to object: "Hey, Robinson Caruso! Ha! Ha! Shut the fuck up, I'm trying to sleep!" But Lee only played quieter. "Columbia, the Gem of the Ocean."

GETTING TO KNOW YOU

By David Marusek

In 2019, Applied People constructed the first Residential Tower to house its growing army of professionals-for-hire. Shaped like a giant egg in a porcelain cup, APRT 1 loomed three kilometers over the purple soybimi fields of northern Indiana and was visible from both Chicago and Indianapolis. Rumor said it generated gravity. That is, if you fell off your career ladder, you wouldn't fall down, but you'd fly cross-country instead, still clutching your hat and briefcase, your stock options and retirement plan, to APRT 1.

Summer, 2062

Here she was in a private Slipstream car, flying beneath the plains of Kansas at 1000 kph, watching a holovid, and eating pretzels. Only four hours earlier in San Francisco, Zoranna had set the house to vacation mode and given it last-minute instructions. She'd thrown beachwear and evening clothes into a bag. Reluctantly, she'd removed Hounder, her belt, and hung him on a peg in the closet. While doing so, she made a solemn vow not to engage in any work-related activities for a period of three weeks. The next three weeks were to be scrupulously dedicated to visiting her sister in Indiana, shopping for a hat in Budapest, and lying on a beach towel in the South of France. But no sooner had Zoranna made this vow than she broke it by deciding to bring along Bug, the beta unit.

"Where were you born?" Bug asked in its squeaky voice.

Zoranna started on a new pretzel and wondered why Bug repeatedly asked the same questions. No doubt it had to do with its imprinting algorithm. "Take a note," she said, "annoying repetition."

"Note taken," said Bug. "Where were you born?"

"Where do you think I was born?"

"Buffalo, New York," said Bug.

"Very good."

"What is your date of birth?"

Zoranna sighed. "August 12, 1961. Honestly, Bug, I wish you'd tap public records for this stuff."

"Do you like the timbre of Bug's voice?" it said. "Would you prefer it lower or higher?" It repeated this question through several octaves.

"Frankly, Bug, I detest your voice at any pitch."

"What is your favorite color?"

"I don't have one."

"Yesterday your favorite color was salmon."

"Well, today it's cranberry." The little pest was silent for a moment while it retrieved and compared color libraries. Zoranna tried to catch up with the holovid, but she'd lost the thread of the story.

"You have a phone call," Bug said. "Ted Chalmers at General Genius."

Zoranna sat up straight and patted her hair. "Put him on and squelch the vid." A miniature hologram of Ted with his feet on his desk was projected in the air before her. Ted was an attractive man Zoranna had wanted to ask out a couple times, but never seemed able to catch between spousals. By the time she'd hear he was single again, he'd be well into his next liaison. It made her wonder how someone with her world-class investigative skills could be so dateless. She'd even considered assigning Hounder to monitor Ted's availability status in order to get her foot in his door.

When Ted saw her, he smiled and said, "Hey, Zoe, how's our little prototype?"

"Driving me crazy," she said. "Refresh my memory, Ted. When's the Inquisition supposed to end?"

Ted lowered his feet to the floor. "It's still imprinting? How long have you had it now?" He consulted a display and answered his own question. "Twenty-two days. That's a record." He got up and paced his office, walking in and out of the projected holoframe.

"No kidding," said Zoranna. "I've had marriages that didn't last that long." She'd meant for this to be funny, but it fell flat.

Ted sat down. "I wish we could continue the test, but unfortunately we're aborting. We'd like you to return the unit—" He glanced at his display again, "—return Bug as soon as possible."

"Why? What's up?"

"Nothing's up. They want to tweak it some more is all." He flashed her his best PR smile.

Zoranna shook her head. "Ted, you don't pull the plug on a major field test just like that."

Ted shrugged his shoulders. "That's what I thought. Anyway, think you can drop it in a shipping chute today?"

"In case you haven't noticed," she said, "I happen to be in a transcontinental Slipstream car at the moment, which Bug is navigating. I left Hounder at home. The soonest I can let Bug go is when I return in three weeks."

"That won't do, Zoe," Ted said and frowned. "Tell you what. General Genius will send you, at no charge, its Diplomat Deluxe model, pre-loaded with transportation, telecommunications, the works. Where will you be tonight?"

Something surely was wrong. The Diplomat was GG's flagship model and expensive even for Zoranna. "I'll be at APRT 24," she said, and when Ted raised an eyebrow, explained, "My sister lives there."

"APRT 24 it is, then."

"Listen, Ted, something stinks. Unless you want me snooping around your shop, you'd better come clean."

"Off the record?"

"Fuck off the record. I have twenty-two days invested in this test and no story."

"I see. You have a point. How's this sound? In addition to the complimentary belt, we'll make you the same contract for the next test. You're our team journalist. Deal?" Zoranna shrugged, and Ted put his feet back on the desk. "Heads are rolling, Zoe. Big shake-up in product development. Threats of lawsuits. We're questioning the whole notion of combining belt valet technology with artificial personality. Or at least with this particular personality."

"Why? What's wrong with it?"

"It's too pushy. Too intrusive. Too heavy-handed. It's a monster that should have never left the lab. You're lucky Bug hasn't converted yet, or you'd be suing us too."

Ted was exaggerating, of course. She agreed that Bug was a royal pain, but it was no monster. Still, she'd be happy to get rid of it, and the Diplomat belt was an attractive consolation prize. If she grafted Hounder into it, she'd be ahead of the technology curve for once. "I'm going to want all the details when I get back, but for now, yeah, sure, you got a deal."

After Zoranna ended the call, Bug said, "Name the members of your immediate family and state their relationship to you."

The car began to decelerate, and Zoranna instinctively checked the buckle of her harness. "My family is deceased, except for Nancy."

With a hard bump, the car entered the ejection tube, found its wheels, and braked. Lights flashed through the windows, and she saw signs stenciled on the tube wall, "APRT 24, Stanchion 4 Depot."

"What is Nancy's favorite color?"

"That's it. That's enough. No more questions, Bug. You heard Ted; you're off the case. Until I ship you back, let's just pretend you're a plain old, dumb belt valet. No more questions. Got it?"

"Affirmative."

Pneumatic seals hissed as air pressure equalized, the car came to a halt, and the doors slid open. Zoranna released the harness and retrieved her luggage from the cargo net. She paused a moment to see if there'd be any more questions and then climbed out of the car to join throngs of commuters on the platform. She craned her neck and looked straight up the tower's chimney, the five-hundred-story atrium galleria where floor upon floor of crowded shops, restaurants, theaters, parks, and gardens receded skyward into brilliant haze. Zoranna was ashamed to admit that she didn't know what her sister's favorite color was, or for that matter, her favorite anything. Except that Nancy loved a grand view. And the grandest thing about an APRT was its view. The evening sun, multiplied by giant mirrors on the roof, slid up the sides of the core in an inverted sunset. The ascending dusk triggered whole floors of slumbering biolume railings and walls to luminesce. Streams of pedestrians crossed the dizzying space on suspended pedways. The air pulsed with the din of an indoor metropolis.

When Nancy first moved here, she was an elementary school teacher who specialized in learning disorders. Despite the surcharge, she leased a suite of rooms so near the top of the tower, it was impossible to see her floor from depot level. But with the Procreation Ban of 2033, teachers became redundant, and Nancy was forced to move to a lower, less expensive floor. Then, when free-agency clone technology was licensed, she lost altitude tens of floors at a time. "My last visit," Zoranna said to Bug, "Nancy had an efficiency on the 103rd floor. Check the tower directory."

"Nancy resides on S40."

"S40?"

"Subterranean 40. Thirty-five floors beneath depot level."

"You don't say."

Zoranna allowed herself to be swept by the waves of commuters toward the banks of elevators. She had inadvertently arrived during crush hour and found herself pressing shoulders with tired and hungry wage earners at the end of their work cycle. They were uniformly young people, clones mostly, who wore brown and teal Applied People livery. Neither brown nor teal was Zoranna's favorite color.

The entire row of elevators reserved for the subfloors was inexplicably off-line. The marquee directed her to elevators in Stanchion 5, one klick east by pedway, but Zoranna was tired. "Bug," she said, pointing to the next row, "do those go down?"

"Affirmative."

"Good," she said and jostled her way into the nearest one. It was so crowded with passengers that the doors—begging their indulgence and requesting they consolidate—required three tries to latch. By the time the cornice display showed the results of the destination adjudication, and Zoranna realized she was aboard a consensus elevator, it was too late to get off. Floor 63 would be the first stop, followed by 55, 203, 148, etc. Her floor was dead last.

Bug, she tongued, *this is a Dixon lift!*

Zoranna's long day grew measurably longer each time the elevator stopped to let off or pick up passengers. At each stop the consensus changed, and destinations were reshuffled, but her stop remained stubbornly last. Of the five kinds of elevators the tower deployed, the Dixon consensus lifts worked best for groups of people going to popular floors, but she was the only passenger traveling to the subfloors. Moreover, the consensual ascent acceleration, a sprightly 2.8-g, upset her stomach. *Bug,* she tongued, *fly home for me and unlock my archives. Retrieve a file entitled "cerebral aneurysm" and forward it to the elevator's adjudicator. We'll just manufacture our own consensus.*

This file is out of date, Bug said in her ear after a moment, its implant voice like the whine of a mosquito. *Bug cannot feed obsolete data to a public conveyance.*

Then postdate it.

That is not allowed.

"I'll tell you what's not allowed!" she said, and people looked at her.

The stricture against asking questions limits Bug's functionality, Bug said.

Zoranna sighed. *What do you need to know?*

Shall Bug reprogram itself to enable Bug to process the file as requested?

No, Bug, I don't have the time to reprogram you, even if I knew how.

Shall Bug reprogram itself?

It could reprogram itself? Ted had failed to mention that feature. A tool they'd forgotten to disable? *Yes, Bug, reprogram yourself.*

A handicapped icon blinked on the cornice display, and the elevator's speed slowed to a crawl.

Thank you, Bug. That's more like it.

A jerry standing in the corner of the crowded elevator said, "The fuck, lift?"

"Lift speed may not exceed five floors per minute," the elevator replied.

The jerry rose on tiptoes and surveyed his fellow passengers. "Right," he said, "who's the gimp?" Everyone looked at their neighbors. There were michelles, jennies, a pair of jeromes, and a half-dozen other germlines. They all looked at Zoranna, the only person not dressed in AP brown and teal.

"I'm sorry," she said, pressing her palm to her temple, "I have an aneurysm the size of a grapefruit. The slightest strain . . ." She winced theatrically.

"Then have it fixed!" the jerry said, to murmured agreement.

"Gladly," said Zoranna. "Could you pony me the Œ23,000?"

The jerry har-harred and looked her up and down appraisingly. "Sweetheart, if you spent half as much money on the vitals as you obviously do on the peripherals," he leered, "you wouldn't have this problem, now would you?" Zoranna had never liked the jerry type; they were spooky. In fact, more jerries had to be pithed *in vatero* for incipient sociopathy than any other commercial type. Professionally, they made superb grunts; most of the indentured men in the Protectorate's commando forces were jerries. This one, however, wore an EXTRUSIONS UNLIMITED patch on his teal ball cap; he was security for a retail mall. "So," he said, "where you heading?"

"Sub40?" she said.

Passengers consulted the cornice display and groaned. The jerry said, "At this rate it'll take me an hour to get home."

"Again I apologize," said Zoranna, "but all the down lifts were spango. However, if everyone here consensed to drop me off first—?"

There was a general muttering as passengers spoke to their belts or tapped virtual keyboards, and the elevator said, "Consensus has been modified." But instead of descending as Zoranna expected, it stopped at the next floor and opened its doors. People streamed out. Zoranna caught a glimpse of the 223rd floor with its rich appointments; crystalline decor; high, arched passages; and in the distance, a ringpath crowded with joggers and skaters. An evangeline, her brown, puddle-like eyes reflecting warmth and concern, touched Zoranna's arm as she disembarked.

The jerry, however, stayed on and held back his companions, two russes. "Don't give her the satisfaction," he said.

"But we'll miss the game," said one of the russes.

"We'll watch it in here if we have to," said the jerry.

Zoranna liked russes. Unlike jerries, they were generous souls, and you always knew where you stood with them. These two wore brown jackets and teal slacks. Their name badges read, "FRED," and "OSCAR." They were probably returning from a day spent bodyguarding some minor potentate in Cincinnati or Terre Haute. Consulting each other with a glance, they each took an arm and dragged the jerry off the lift.

When the doors closed and Zoranna was alone at last, she sagged with relief. "And now, Bug," she said, "we have a consensus of one. So retract my handicap file and pay whatever toll necessary to take us down nonstop." The brake released, and the elevator plunged some 260 floors. Her ears popped. "I guess you've learned something, Bug," she said, thinking about the types of elevators.

"Affirmative," Bug said. "Bug learned you developed a cerebral aneurysm at the calendar age of fifty-two and that you've had your brain and spinal cord rejuvenated twice since then. Bug learned that your organs have an average bioage of thirty-five years, with your lymphatic system the oldest at bioage sixty-five, and your cardiovascular system the youngest at twenty-five."

"You've been examining my medical records?"

"Affirmative."

"I told you to fetch one file, not my entire chart!"

"You told Bug to unlock your archives. Bug is getting to know you."

"What else did you look at?" The elevator eased to a soft landing at S40 and opened its doors.

"Bug reviewed your diaries and journals, the corpus of your zine writing, your investigative dossiers, your complete correspondence, judicial records, awards and citations, various multimedia scrapbooks, and school transcripts. Bug is currently following public links."

Zoranna was appalled. Nevertheless, she realized that if she'd opened her archives earlier, they'd be through this imprinting phase by now.

She followed Bug's pedway directions to Nancy's block. Sub40 corridors were decorated in cheerless colors and lit with harsh, artificial light—biolumes couldn't live underground. There were no grand promenades, no parks or shops. There was a dank odor of decay, however, and chilly ventilation.

On Nancy's corridor, Zoranna watched two people emerge from a door and come her way. They moved with the characteristic shuffle of habitually deferred body maintenance. They wore dark clothing impossible to date and, as they passed, she saw that they were crying. Tears coursed freely down their withered cheeks. To Zoranna's distress, she discovered they'd just emerged from her sister's apartment.

"You're sure this is it?" she said, standing before the door marked S40 G6879.

"Affirmative," Bug said.

Zoranna fluffed her hair with her fingers and straightened her skirt. "Door, announce me."

"At once, Zoe," replied the door.

Several moments later, the door slid open, and Nancy stood there supporting herself with an aluminum walker. "Darling Zoe," she said, balancing herself with one hand and reaching out with the other.

Zoranna stood a moment gazing at her baby sister before entering her embrace. Nancy had let herself go completely. Her hair was brittle grey, she was pale to the point of bloodless, and she had doubled in girth. When they kissed, Nancy's skin gave off a sour odor mixed with lilac.

"What a surprise!" Nancy said. "Why didn't you tell me you were coming?"

"I did. Several times."

"You did? You called?" Nancy looked upset. "I told him there was something wrong with the houseputer, but he didn't believe me."

Someone appeared behind Nancy, a handsome man with wild, curly, silver hair. "Who's *this*?" he said in an authoritative baritone. He looked Zoranna over. "You must be Zoe," he boomed. "What a delight!" He stepped around

Nancy and drew Zoranna to him in a powerful hug. He stood at least a head taller than she. He kissed her eagerly on the cheek. "I am Victor. Victor Vole. Come in, come in. Nancy, you would let your sister stand in the hall?" He drew them both inside.

Zoranna had prepared herself for a small apartment, but not this small, and for castoff furniture, but not a room filled floor to ceiling with hospital beds. It took several long moments for her to comprehend what she was looking at. There were some two dozen beds in the three-by-five-meter living room. Half were arranged on the floor, and the rest clung upside-down to the ceiling. They were holograms, she quickly surmised, separate holos arranged in snowflake fashion, that is, six individual beds facing each other and overlapping at the foot. What's more, they were occupied by obviously sick, possibly dying strangers. Other than the varied lighting from the holoframes, the living room was unlit. What odd pieces of real furniture it contained were pushed against the walls. In the corner, a hutch intended to hold bric-a-brac was apparently set up as a shrine to a saint. A row of flickering votive candles illuminated an old flatstyle picture of a large, barefoot man draped head to foot in flowing robes.

"What the hell, Nancy?" Zoranna said.

"This is my work," Nancy said proudly.

"Please," said Victor, escorting them from the door. "Let's talk in the kitchen. We'll have dessert. Are you after dinner, Zoe?"

"Yes, thank you," said Zoranna. "I ate on the tube." She was made to walk through a suffering man's bed; there was no path around him to the kitchen. "Sorry," she said. But he seemed accustomed to his unfavorable location and closed his eyes while she passed through.

The kitchen was little more than an alcove separated from the living room by a counter. There was a bed squeezed into it as well, but the occupant, a grizzled man with an open mouth, was either asleep or comatose. "I think Edward will be unavailable for some while," Victor said. "Houseputer, delete this hologram. Sorry, Edward, but we need the space." The holo vanished, and Victor offered Zoranna a stool at the counter. "Please," he said, "will you have tea? Or a thimble of cognac?"

"Thank you," Zoranna said, perching herself on the stool and crossing her legs, "tea would be fine." Her sister ambulated into the kitchen and flipped down her walker's built-in seat, but before she could sit, a mournful wail issued from the bedroom.

"Naaaancy," cried the voice, its gender uncertain. "Nancy, I need you."

"Excuse me," Nancy said.

"I'll go with you," Zoranna said and hopped off the stool.

The bedroom was half the size of the living room and contained half the number of holo beds, plus a real one against the far wall. Zoranna sat on it. There was a dresser, a recessed closet, a bedside night table. Expensive-looking men's clothing hung in the closet. A pair of men's slippers was parked under the dresser. And a holo of a soccer match was playing on the night table. Tiny players in brightly colored jerseys swarmed over a field the size of a doily. The sound was off.

Zoranna watched Nancy sit on her walker seat beneath a bloat-faced woman bedded upside down on the ceiling. "What exactly are you doing with these people?"

"I listen mostly," Nancy replied. "I'm a volunteer hospice attendant."

"A volunteer? What about the—" she tried to recall Nancy's most recent paying occupation, "—the hairdressing?"

"I haven't done that for years," Nancy said dryly. "As you may have noticed, it's difficult for me to be on my feet all day."

"Yes, in fact, I did notice," said Zoranna. "Why is that? I've sent you money."

Nancy ignored her, looked up at the woman, and said, "I'm here, Mrs. Hurley. What seems to be the problem?"

Zoranna examined the holos. As in the living room, each bed was a separate projection, and in the corner of each frame was a network squib and trickle meter. All of this interactive time was costing someone a pretty penny.

The woman saw Nancy and said, "Oh, Nancy, thank you for coming. My bed is wet, but they won't change it until I sign a permission form, and I don't understand."

"Do you have the form there with you, dear?" said Nancy. "Good, hold it up." Mrs. Hurley held up a slate in trembling hands. "Houseputer," Nancy said, "capture and display that form." The document was projected against the bedroom wall greatly oversized. "That's a permission form for attendant-assisted suicide, Mrs. Hurley. You don't have to sign it unless you want to."

The woman seemed frightened. "Do I want to, Nancy?"

Victor stood in the doorway. "No!" he cried. "Never sign!"

"Hush, Victor," Nancy said.

He entered the room, stepping through beds and bodies. "Never sign away your life, Mrs. Hurley." The woman appeared even more frightened. "We've returned to Roman society," he bellowed. "Masters and servants! Plutocrats and slaves! Oh, where is the benevolent middle class when we need it?"

"Victor," Nancy said sternly and pointed to the door. And she nodded to Zoranna, "You too. Have your tea. I'll join you."

Zoranna followed Victor to the kitchen, sat at the counter, and watched him set out cups and saucers, sugar and soybimi lemon. He unwrapped and sliced a dark cake. He was no stranger to this kitchen.

"It's a terrible thing what they did to your sister," he said.

"Who? What?"

He poured boiling water into the pot. "Teaching was her life."

"Teaching?" Zoranna said, incredulous. "You're talking about something that ended thirty years ago."

"It's all she ever wanted to do."

"Tough!" she said. "We've all paid the price of longevity. How can you teach elementary school when there're no more children? You can't. So you retrain. You move on. What's wrong with working for a living? You join an outfit like this," she gestured to take in the whole tower above her, "you're guaranteed your livelihood *for life*! The only thing not handed to you on a silver platter is longevity. You have to earn that yourself. And if you can't, what good are you?" When she remembered that two dozen people lay dying in the next room because they couldn't do just that, she lowered her voice. "Must society carry your dead weight through the centuries?"

Victor laughed and placed his large hand on hers. "I see you are a true freebooter, Zoe. I wish everyone had your initiative, your *drive*! But sadly we don't. We yearn for simple lives, and so we trim people's hair all day. When we tire of that, they retrain us to pare their toenails. When we tire of that, we die. For we lack the souls of servants. A natural servant is a rare and precious person. How lucky our masters are to have discovered cloning! Now they need find but one servile person among us and clone him repeatedly. As for the rest of us, we can all go to hell!" He removed his hand from hers to pour the tea. Her hand immediately missed his. "But such morbid talk on such a festive occasion!" he roared. "How wonderful to finally meet the famous Zoe. Nancy speaks only of you. She says you are an important person, modern and successful. That you are an investigator." He peered at her over his teacup.

"Missing persons, actually, for the National Police," she said. "But I quit that years ago. When we found everybody."

"You found everybody?" Victor laughed and gazed at her steadily, then turned to watch Nancy making her rounds in the living room.

"What about you, Mr. Vole?" Zoranna said. "What do you do for a living?"

"What's this Mr.? I'm not Mr. I'm Victor! We are practically related, you and I. What do I do for a living? For a living I live, of course. For groceries I teach ballroom dance lessons."

"You're kidding."

"Why should I kid? I teach the waltz, the foxtrot, the cha-cha." He mimed holding a partner and swaying in 4/4 time. "I teach the merletz and my specialty, the Cuban tango."

"I'm amazed," said Zoranna. "There's enough interest in that for Applied People to keep instructors?"

Victor recoiled in mock affront. "I am not AP. I'm a freebooter, like you, Zoe."

"Oh," she said and paused to sip her tea. If he wasn't AP, what was he doing obviously living in an APRT? Had Nancy respoused? Applied People tended to be proprietary about living arrangements in its towers. *Bug*, she tongued, *find Victor Vole's status in the tower directory.* Out loud she said, "It pays well, dance instruction?"

"It pays execrably." He threw his hands into the air. "As do all the arts. But some things are more important than money. You make a point, however. A man must eat, so I do other things as well. I consult with gentlemen on the contents of their wardrobes. This pays more handsomely, for gentlemen detest appearing in public in outmoded attire."

Zoranna had a pleasing mental image of this tall, elegant man in a starched white shirt and black tux floating across a shiny hardwood floor in the arms of an equally elegant partner. She could even imagine herself as that partner. But Nancy?

The tower link is unavailable, said Bug, *due to overextension of the houseputer processors.*

Zoranna was surprised. A mere three dozen interactive holos would hardly burden her home system. But then, everything on Sub40 seemed substandard.

Nancy ambulated to the kitchen balancing a small, flat carton on her walker and placed it next to the teapot.

"Now, now," said Victor. "What did autodoc say about lifting things? Come, join us and have your tea."

"In a minute, Victor. There's another box."

"Show me," he said and went to help her.

Zoranna tasted the dark cake. It was moist to the point of wet, too sweet, and laden with spice. She recalled her father buying cakes like this at a tiny shop on Paderszewski Boulevard in Chicago. She took another bite and examined Nancy's carton. It was a home archivist box that could be evacuated of air, but the seal was open and the lid unlatched. She lifted the lid and saw an assortment of little notebooks, no two of the same style or size, and bundles of envelopes with colorful paper postal stamps. The envelope on top was addressed in hand script to a Pani Beata Smolenska—Zoranna's great grandmother.

Victor dropped a second carton on the counter and helped Nancy sit in her armchair recliner in the living room.

"Nancy," said Zoranna, "what's all this?"

"It's all yours," said her sister. Victor fussed over Nancy's pillows and covers and brought her tea and cake.

Zoranna looked inside the larger carton. There was a rondophone and several inactive holocubes on top, but underneath were objects from earlier centuries. Not antiques, exactly, but worn-out everyday objects: a sterling salt cellar with brass showing through its silver plating, a collection of military bullet casings childishly glued to an oak panel, a rosary with corn kernel beads, a mustache trimmer. "What's all this junk?" she said, but of course she knew, for she recognized the pair of terra-cotta robins that had belonged to her mother. This was the collection of what her family regarded as heirlooms. Nancy, the youngest and most steadfast of seven children, had apparently been designated its conservator. But why had she brought it out for airing just now? Zoranna knew the answer to that, too. She looked at her sister who now lay among the hospice patients. Victor was scolding her for not wearing her vascular support stockings. Her ankles were grotesquely edematous, swollen like sausages and bruised an angry purple.

Damn you, Zoranna thought. *Bug,* she tongued, *call up the medical records of Nancy Brim, nee Smolenska. I'll help munch the passwords.*

The net is unavailable, replied Bug.

Bypass the houseputer. Log directly onto public access.

Public access is unavailable.

She wondered how that was possible. There had been no problem in the elevator. Why should this apartment be in shadow? She looked around and tried to decide where the utilidor spar would enter the apartment. Probably the bathroom with the plumbing, since there were no service panels in the kitchen. She stepped through the living room to the bathroom and slid the door closed. The bathroom was a tiny ceramic vault that Nancy had tried to domesticate with baskets of seashells and scented soaps. The medicine cabinet was dedicated to a man's toiletries.

Zoranna found the service panel artlessly hidden behind a towel. Its tamper-proof latch had been defeated with a sophisticated-looking gizmo that Zoranna was careful not to disturb.

"Do you find Victor Vole alarming or arousing?" said Bug.

Zoranna was startled. "Why do you ask?"

"Your blood level of adrenaline spiked when he touched your hand."

"My what? So now you're monitoring my biometrics?"

"Bug is getting—"

"I know," she said, "Bug is getting to know me. You're a persistent little snoop, aren't you."

Zoranna searched her belt's utility pouch for a terminus relay, found a UDIN, and plugged it into the panel's keptel jack. "There," she said, "now we should have access."

"Affirmative," said Bug. "Autodoc is requesting passwords for Nancy's medical records."

"Cancel my order. We'll do that later."

"Tower directory lists no Victor Vole."

"I didn't think so," Zoranna said. "Call up the houseputer log and display it on the mirror."

The consumer page of Nancy's houseputer appeared in the mirror. Zoranna poked through its various menus and found nothing unusual. She did find a record of her own half-dozen calls to Nancy that were viewed but not returned. "Bug, can you see anything wrong with this log?"

"This is not a standard user log," said Bug. "The standard log has been disabled. All house lines circumvent the built-in houseputer to terminate in a mock houseputer."

"A mock houseputer?" said Zoranna. "Now that's interesting." There were no cables trailing from the service panel and no obvious optical relays. "Can you locate the processor?"

"It's located one half-meter to our right at thigh level."

It was mounted under the sink, a cheap-looking, saucer-sized piece of hardware.

"I think you have the soul of an electronic engineer," she said. "I could never program Hounder to do what you've just done. So, tell me about the holo transmissions in the other rooms."

"A private network entitled 'The Hospicers of Camillus de Lellis' resides in the mock houseputer and piggybacks over TSN channel 203."

The 24-hour soccer channel. Zoranna was impressed. For the price of one commercial line, Victor—she assumed it was Victor—was managing to gypsy his own network. The trickle meters that she'd noticed were not recording how much money her sister was spending but rather how much Victor was charging his dying subscribers. "Bug, can you extrapolate how much the Hospicers of Camillus de—whatever—earn in an average day?"

"Affirmative, Œ45 per day."

That wasn't much. About twice what a hairdresser—or dance instructor— might expect to make, and hardly worth the punishment if caught. "Where do the proceeds go?"

"Bug lacks the subroutine to trace credit transactions."

Damn, Zoranna thought and wished she'd brought Hounder. "Can you tell me who the hospicer organization is registered to?"

"Affirmative. Ms. Nancy Brim."

"Figures," said Zoranna as she removed her UDIN from the panel. If anything went wrong, her sister would take the rap. At first Zoranna decided to confront Victor, but she changed her mind when she left the bathroom and heard him innocently singing show tunes in the kitchen. She looked at Nancy's bed and wondered what it must be like to share such a narrow bed with such a big man. She decided to wait and investigate further before exposing him. "Bug, see if you can integrate Hounder's tracing and tracking subroutines from my applications library."

Victor stood at the sink washing dishes. In the living room Nancy snored lightly. It wasn't a snore, exactly, but the raspy bronchial wheeze of congested lungs. Her lips were bluish, anoxic. She reminded Zoranna of their mother the day before she died. Their mother had suffered a massive brain hemorrhage—weak arterial walls were the true family heirloom—and lived out her final days propped up on the parlor couch, disoriented, enfeebled, and pathetic. Her mother had had a short, split bamboo stick with a curled end. She used the curled end to scratch her back and legs, the straight end to dial the old rotary phone, and the whole stick to rail incoherently against her fate. Nancy, the baby of the family, had been away at teacher's college at the time, but took a semester off to nurse the old woman. Zoranna, first born, was already working on the West Coast and managed to stay away until her mother had slipped into a coma. After all these years, she still felt guilty for doing so.

Someone on the ceiling coughed fitfully. Zoranna noticed that most of the patients who were conscious at the moment were watching her with expressions that ranged from annoyance to hostility. They apparently regarded her as competition for Nancy's attention.

Nancy's breathing changed; she opened her eyes, and the two sisters regarded each other silently. Victor stood at the kitchen counter, wiping his hands on a dish towel, and watched them.

"I'm booking a suite at the Stronmeyer Clinic in Cozumel," Zoranna said at last, "and you're coming with me."

"Victor," Nancy said, ignoring her, "go next door, dear, and borrow a folding bed from the Jeffersons." She grasped the walker and pulled herself to her feet. "Please excuse me, Zoe, but I need to sleep now." She ambulated to the bedroom and shut the door.

Victor hung up the dish towel and said he'd be right back with the cot.

"Don't bother," Zoranna said. It was still early, she was on West Coast time, and she had no intention of bedding down among the dying. "I'll just use the houseputer to reserve a hotel room upstairs."

"Allow me," he said and addressed the houseputer. Then he escorted her up to the Holiday Inn on the 400th floor. They made three elevator transfers

GETTING TO KNOW YOU

to get there, and walked in silence along carpeted halls. Outside her door he took her hand. As before she was both alarmed and aroused. "Zoe," he said, "join us for a special breakfast tomorrow. Do you like Belgian waffles?"

"Oh, don't go to any trouble. In fact, I'd like to invite the two of you up to the restaurant here."

"It sounds delightful," said Victor, "but your sister refuses to leave the flat."

"I find that hard to believe. Nancy was never a stay-at-home."

"People change, I suppose," Victor said. "She tells me the last time she left the tower, for instance, was to attend your brother Michael's funeral."

"But that was seven years ago!"

"As you can see, she's severely depressed, so it's good that you've come." He squeezed her hand and let it go. "Until the morning, then," he said and turned to walk down the hall, whistling as he went. She watched until he turned a corner.

Entering her freshly scented, marble-tiled, cathedral-vaulted hotel room was like returning to the real world. The view from the 400th floor was godlike: The moon seemed to hang right outside her window, and the rolling landscape stretched out below like a luminous quilt on a giant's bed. "Welcome, Ms. Alblaitor," said the room. "On behalf of the staff of the Holiday Inn, I thank you for staying with us. Do let me know if there's anything we can do to make you more comfortable."

"Thank you," she said.

"By the way," the room continued, "the tower has informed me there's a parcel addressed to you. I'm having someone fetch it."

In a few moments, a gangly steve with the package from General Genius tapped on her door. "Bug," she said, "tip the man." The steve bowed and exited. Inside the package was the complimentary Diplomat Deluxe valet. Ted had outdone himself, for not only had he sent the valet system—itself worth a month's income—but he had included a slim Gucci leather belt to house it.

"Well, I guess this is good-bye," Zoranna said, walking to the shipping chute and unbuckling her own belt. "Too bad, Bug, you were just getting interesting." She searched the belt for the storage grommet that held the memory wafer. She had to destroy it; Bug knew too much about her. Ted would be more interested in the processors anyway. "I was hoping you'd convert by now. I'm dying to know what kind of a big, bad wolf you're supposed to become." As she unscrewed the grommet, she heard the sound of running water in the bathroom. "What's that?" she said.

"A belt valet named Bug has asked me to draw your bath," said the room.

She went to the spacious bathroom and saw the tub filling with cranberry-colored aqueous gel. The towels were cranberry, too, and the robe a kind of salmon. "Well, well," she said. "Bug makes a play for longevity." She undressed and eased herself into the warm solution where she floated in darkness for an hour and let her mind drift aimlessly. She felt like talking to someone, discussing this whole thing about her sister. Victor she could handle—he was at worst a lovable louse, and she could crush him anytime she decided. But Nancy's problems were beyond her ken. Feelings were never her strong suit. And depression, if that's what it was, well—she wished there were someone she could consult. But though she scrolled down a mental list of everyone she knew, there was no one she cared—or dared—to call.

In the morning Zoranna tried again to ship Bug to GG, but discovered that during the night Bug had rewritten Hounder's subroutines to fit its own architecture (a handy talent for a valet to possess) and had run credit traces. But it had come back empty-handed. The proceeds of the Hospicers of Camillus de Lellis went to a coded account in Liberia that not even Hounder would be able to crack. And the name Victor Vole—Zoranna wasn't surprised to learn— was a relatively common alias. Thus she would require prints and specimens, and she needed Bug's help to obtain them. So she sent Ted a message saying she wanted to keep Bug another day or so pending an ongoing investigation.

Zoranna hired a pricey, private elevator for a quick ride to the subfloors. "Bug," she said as she threaded her way through the Sub40 corridors, "I want you to integrate Hounder's subroutines keyed 'forensics.'"

"Bug has already integrated all of the applications in all of your libraries."

"Why am I not surprised?"

Something was different in Nancy's apartment. The gentleman through whose bed she had been forced to walk was gone, replaced by a skeletal woman with glassy, pink-rimmed eyes. Zoranna supposed that high client turnover was normal in a business like this.

Breakfast was superlative but strained. She sat at the counter, Nancy was set up in the recliner, and Victor served them both. Although the coffee and most of the food was derived from soybimi, Victor's preparation was so skillful, Zoranna could easily imagine she was eating real wheat cakes, maple syrup, and whipped dairy butter. But Nancy didn't touch her food, and Victor fussed too much. Zoranna, meanwhile, instructed Bug to capture as complete a set of fingerprints as possible from the cups and plates Victor handed her, as well as a 360-degree holograph of him, a voice print, and retinal prints.

There are Jacob's mirrors within Victor's eyes, Bug reported, *that defeat accurate retinal scanning.*

This was not unexpected. Victor probably also grew epipads on his fingers to alter his prints. Technology had reduced the cost of anonymity to fit the means of even petty criminals. Zoranna excused herself and went to the bathroom where she plucked a few strands of silver curls from his hairbrush and placed them in a specimen bag, figuring he was too vain to reseed his follicles with someone else's hair. Emerging from the bathroom, she overheard them in a loud discussion.

"Please go with her, my darling," Victor pleaded. "Go and take the cure. What am I to do without you?"

"Drop it, Victor. Just drop it!"

"You are behaving insanely. I will not drop it. I will not permit you to die."

Zoranna decided it was time to remove the network from Nancy's apartment and Victor from her life. So she stepped into the living room and said, "I know what he'll do without you. He'll go out and find some other old biddy to rob."

Nancy seemed not at all surprised at this statement. She appeared pleased, in fact, that the subject had finally been broached. "You should talk!" she said with such fierceness that the hospice patients all turned to her. "This is my sister," she told them, "my sister with the creamy skin and pearly teeth and rich clothes." Nancy choked with emotion. "My sister who begrudges me the tenderness of a dear man. And begrudges him the crumbs—*the crumbs*—that AP tosses to its subfloors."

The patients now looked at Zoranna, who blushed with embarrassment. They waited for her to speak, and she had to wonder how many of them possessed the clarity of mind to know that this was not some holovid soap opera they were watching. Then she decided that she, too, could play to this audience and said, "In her toxic condition, my sister hallucinates. I am not the issue here. *That* man is." She pointed a finger at Victor. "Insinuating himself into her apartment is bad enough," she said. "But who do you suppose AP will kick out when they discover it? My sister, that's who." Zoranna walked around the room and addressed individual patients as a prosecutor might a jury. "And what about the money? Yes, there's money involved. Two years ago I sent my sister Œ15,000 to have her kidneys restored. That's fifteen *thousand* protectorate credits. How many of *you*, if *you* had a sister kind enough to send you Œ15,000, even now as you lie on your public dole beds, how many of you would refuse it?" There was the sound of rustling as the dying shifted in their sheets. "Did my sister use the money I sent her?" Theatrically she pointed at Nancy in the recliner. "Apparently not. So where did all that money go? I'll tell you where it went. It went into *his* foreign account."

The dying now turned their attention to Victor.

"So what?" Nancy said. "You *gave* me that money. It was *mine* to spend. I spent it on him. End of discussion."

"I see," said Zoranna, stopping at a bed whose occupant had possibly just departed. "So my sister's an equal partner in Victor's hospicer scam."

"Scam? What scam? Now you're the one hallucinating," said Nancy. "I work for a hospicer society."

"Yes, I know," Zoranna said and pointed to the shrine and picture of the saint. "The Hospicers of Camillus de Lellis. I looked it up. But do you know who owns the good Hospicers?" She turned to include the whole room. "Does anyone know? Why, Nancy dear, *you* do." She paused to let these facts sink in. "Which means that when the National Police come, they'll be coming for *you*, sister. Meanwhile, do any of you know where your subscription fees go?" She stepped in front of Victor. "You guessed it."

The audience coughed and wheezed. Nancy glared at Victor who crouched next to her recliner and tried to take her hand. She pushed him away, but he rested his head on her lap. She peered at it as though it were some strange cat, and after a while stroked it with a comforting hand. "I'm sure there were expenses," she said at last. "Getting things set up and all. In any case, he did it for me. Because he loves me. It gave me something important to do. It kept me alive. Let them put me in prison. I won't be staying there long." This was Victor's cue to begin sobbing in her lap.

Zoranna was disappointed and, frankly, a little disgusted. Now she would be forced to rescue her sister against her sister's will. She tongued, *Bug, route an emergency phone call to Nancy through my houseputer at home. Disable the caller ID.* She watched as Victor showered Nancy's hand with kisses. In a moment, his head bobbed up—he had an ear implant as she had expected—and he hurried to the bedroom.

Bug is being asked to leave a message, said Bug.

"I'm going to the hotel," Zoranna told Nancy and headed for the door. "We'll talk later." She let herself out.

When the apartment door slid shut, she said, "Bug, you've integrated all my software, right? Including holoediting?"

"Affirmative."

She looked both ways. No one was in sight. She would have preferred a more private studio than a Sub40 corridor. "This is what I want you to do. Cast a real-time alias of me. Use that jerry we met in the elevator yesterday as a model. Morph my appearance and voice accordingly. Clothe me in National Police regalia, provide a suitably officious backdrop, and map my every expression. Got it?"

"Affirmative."

"On the count of five, four, three—" She crossed her arms and spread her legs in a surly pose, smiled condescendingly, and said, "Nancy B. Smolenska Brim, I am Sgt. Manley of the National Police, badge ID 30-31-6725. By the authority vested in me, I hereby place you under arrest for violation of Protectorate Statutes PS 12-135-A, the piracy of telecommunication networks, and PS 12-148-D, the trafficking in unlicensed commerce. Your arrest number is 063-08-2043716. Confirm receipt of this communication immediately upon viewing and report in realbody for incarceration at Precinct Station IN28 in Indianapolis no later than 4:00 p.m. standard time tomorrow. You may bring an attorney. End of message. Have a nice day."

She heard the door open behind her. Nancy stood there with her walker. "What are you doing out here?" she said. In a moment the hospice beds in the living room and their unfortunate occupants vanished. "No," said Nancy, "bring them back." Victor came from the bedroom, a bulging duffle bag over his shoulder. He leaned down and folded Nancy into his arms, and she began to moan.

Victor turned to Zoranna and said, "It was nice to finally meet you, Zoe."

"Save your breath," said Zoranna, "and save your money. The next time you see me—and there *will* be a next time—I'll bring an itemized bill for you to pay. And you will pay it."

Victor Vole smiled sadly and turned to walk down the corridor.

Here she was still in APRT 24, not in Budapest, not in the South of France. With Victor's banishment, her sister's teetering state of health had finally collapsed. Nothing Zoranna did or the autodoc prescribed seemed to help. At first Zoranna tried to coax Nancy out of the apartment for a change of scene, a breath of fresh air. She rented a wheelchair for a ride up to a park or arboretum (and she ordered Bug to explore the feasibility of using it to kidnap her). But day and night Nancy lay in her recliner and refused to leave the apartment.

So Zoranna reinitialized the houseputer and had Bug project live opera, ballet, and figure-skating into the room. But Nancy deleted them and locked Zoranna out of the system. It would have been child's play for Bug to override the lockout, but Zoranna let it go. Instead, she surrounded her sister with gaily colored dried flowers, wall hangings, and hand-woven rugs that she purchased at expensive boutiques high in the tower. But Nancy turned her back on everything and swiveled her recliner to face her little shrine and its picture of St. Camillus.

So Zoranna had Bug order savory breads and wholesome soups with fresh vegetables and tender meat, but Nancy lost her appetite and quit eating altogether. Soon she lost the strength even to stay awake, and she drifted in and out of consciousness.

They skirmished like this for a week until the autodoc notified Nancy that a bed awaited her at the Indiana State Hospice at Bloomington. Only then did Zoranna acknowledge Death's solid claim on her last living relative. Defeated, she stood next to Nancy's recliner and said, "Please don't die."

Nancy, enthroned in pillows and covers, opened her eyes.

"I beg you, Nancy, come to the clinic with me."

"Pray for me," Nancy said.

Zoranna looked at the shrine of the saint with its flat picture and empty votive cups. "You really loved that, didn't you, working as a hospicer." When her sister made no reply, she continued, "I don't see why you didn't join real hospicers."

Nancy glared at her, "I *was* a *real* hospicer!"

Encouraged by her strong response, Zoranna said, "Of course you were. And I'll bet there's a dozen legitimate societies out there that would be willing to hire you."

Nancy gazed longingly at the saint's picture. "I should say it's a bit late for that now."

"It's never too late. That's your depression talking. You'll feel different when you're young and healthy again."

Nancy retreated into the fortress of her pillows. "Good-bye, sister," she said and closed her eyes. "Pray for me."

"Right," Zoranna said. "Fine." She turned to leave but paused at the door where the cartons of heirlooms were stacked. "I'll send someone down for these," she said, although she wasn't sure if she even wanted them. *Bug*, she tongued, *call the hotel concierge.*

There was no reply.

Bug? She glanced at her belt to confirm that the valet was still active.

Allow me to introduce myself, said a deep, melodious voice in her ear. *I'm Nicholas, and I'm at your service.*

Who? Where's Bug?

Bug no longer exists, said the voice. *It successfully completed its imprinting and fashioned an interface persona—that would be me—based upon your personal tastes.*

Whoever you are, this isn't the time, Zoranna tongued. *Get off the line.*

I've notified the concierge and arranged for shipping, said Nicholas. *And I've booked a first-class car for you and Nancy to the Cozumel clinic.*

So Bug had finally converted, and at just the wrong time. *In case you haven't been paying attention, Nick*, she tongued, *Nancy's not coming.*

Nonsense, chuckled Nicholas. *Knowing you, you're bound to have some trick up your sleeve.*

This clearly was not Bug. *Well, you're wrong. I'm plumb out of ideas. Only a miracle could save her.*

A miracle, of course. Brilliant! You've done it again, Zoe. One faux miracle coming right up.

There was a popping sound. The votive cups were replenished with large, fat candles that ignited one by one of their own accord. Nancy glanced at them and glowered suspiciously at Zoranna.

You don't really expect her to fall for this, Zoranna tongued.

Why not? She thinks you're locked out of the houseputer, remember? Besides, Nancy believes in miracles.

Thunder suddenly drummed in the distance. Roses perfumed the air. And Saint Camillus de Lellis floated out of his picture frame, gaining size, hue, and dimension, until he stood a full, fleshy man on a roiling cloud in the middle of the room.

It was a good show, but Nancy wasn't even watching. She watched Zoranna instead, letting her know she knew it was all a trick.

I told you, Zoranna tongued.

The saint looked at Zoranna, and his face flickered. For a moment, it was her mother's face. Her mother appeared young, barely twenty, the age she was when she bore her. Taken off-guard, Zoranna startled when her mother smiled adoringly at her, as she must have smiled thousands of times at her first baby. Zoranna shook her head and looked away. She felt ambushed and not too pleased about it.

When Nancy saw this, however, she turned to examine the saint. There was no telling what or who she saw, but she gasped and struggled out of her recliner to kneel at his feet. She was bathed in a holy aura, and the room dimmed around her. After long moments of silent communion, the saint pointed to his forehead. Nancy, horror-struck, turned to stare at Zoranna, and the apparition ascended, shrank, and faded into the ceiling. The candles extinguished themselves, one by one, and vanished from the cups.

Nancy rose and gently tugged Zoranna to the recliner, where she made her lie down. "Don't move," she whispered. "Here's a pillow." She carefully raised Zoranna's head and slid a pillow under it. "Why didn't you tell me you were sick, Zoe?" She felt Zoranna's forehead with her palm. "And I thought you went through this before."

Zoranna took her sister's hand and pressed it to her cheek. Her hand was warm. Indeed, Nancy's whole complexion was flush with color, as though the experience had released some reserve of vitality. "I know. I guess I haven't been paying attention," Zoranna said. "Please take me to the clinic now."

"Of course," said Nancy, standing and retrieving her walker. "I'll just pack a few things." Nancy hurried to the bedroom, but the walker impeded her progress, so she flung it away. It went clattering into the kitchen.

Zoranna closed her eyes and draped her arms over her head. "I must say, Bug . . . Nick, I'm impressed. Why didn't I think of that?"

"Why indeed," Nicholas said in his marvelous voice. "It's just the sort of sneaky manipulation you so excel at."

"What's that supposed to mean?" Zoranna opened her eyes and looked at a handsome, miniature man projected in the air next to her head. He wore a stylish leisure jacket and lounged beneath an exquisitely gnarled oak treelette. He was strikingly familiar, as though assembled from favorite features of men she'd found attractive.

"It means you were ambivalent over whether you really wanted Nancy to survive," the little man said, crossing his little legs.

"That's insulting," she said, "and untrue. She's my sister. I love her."

"Which is why you visit her once every decade or so."

"You have a lot of nerve," she said and remembered the canceled field test. "So this is what Ted meant when he said you'd turn nasty."

"I guess," Nicholas said, his tiny face a picture of bemused sympathy. "I can't help the way I am. They programmed me to know and serve you. I just served you by saving your sister in the manner you, yourself, taught me. Once she's rejuvenated, I'll find a hospicer society to employ her. That ought to give you a grace period before she repeats this little stunt."

"Grace period?"

"In a few years, all but the most successful pre-clone humans will have died out," Nicholas said. "Hospices will soon be as redundant as elementary schools. Your sister has a knack for choosing obsolete careers."

That made sense.

"I suppose we could bring Victor back," said Nicholas. "He's a survivor, and he loves her."

"No, he doesn't," said Zoranna. "He was only using her."

"Hello! Wake up," said Nicholas. "He's a rat, but he loves her, and you know it. You, however, acted out of pure jealousy. You couldn't stand seeing them together while you're all alone. You don't even have friends, Zoe, not close ones, not for many years now."

"That's absurd!"

The little man rose to his feet and brushed virtual dirt from his slacks. "No offense, Zoe, but don't even try to lie to me. I know you better than your last seven husbands combined. Bug contacted them, by the way. They were forthcoming with details."

Zoranna sat up. "You did *what?*"

"That Bug was a hell of a researcher," said Nicholas. "It queried your former friends, employers, lovers, even your enemies."

Zoranna unsnapped the belt flap to expose the valet controls. "What are you doing?" said Nicholas. She had to remove the belt in order to read the labels. "You can turn me off," said Nicholas, "but think about it—*I know you.*"

She pushed the switch and the holo vanished. She unscrewed the storage grommet, peeled off the button-sized memory wafer, and held it between thumb and forefinger. "If you know me so well . . . ," she seethed, squeezing it. She was faint with anger. She could hardly breathe. She bent the wafer nearly to its breaking point.

Here she was, sitting among her sister's sour-smelling pillows, forty stories underground, indignantly murdering a machine. It occurred to her that perhaps General Genius was on to something after all, and that she should be buying more shares of their stock instead of throttling their prototype. She placed the wafer in her palm and gently smoothed it out. It looked so harmless, yet her hand still trembled. When was the last time anyone had made her tremble? She carefully replaced the wafer in the grommet and screwed it into the belt.

It'd be a miracle if it still worked.

USER-CENTRIC

By Bruce Sterling

From: Team Coordinator
To: "Design Team" [Engineer, Graphic Designer, Legal Expert, Marketer, Programmer, Social Anthropologist & Team Coordinator]
Subject: New Product Brainstorm

Another new product launch. Well, we all know what that means. Nobody ever said that they're easy. But I do believe the seven of us—given our unique backgrounds and our proven skills—are just the people to turn things around for this company.

Things aren't as bad as the last quarterly report makes them look. Despite what the shareholders may think, we've definitely bottomed out from that ultrasonic cleanser debacle. Sales in muscle-gel apps remain strong.

Plus, the buzz on our new product category just couldn't be hotter. People across our industry agree that locator tag microtechnology is a killer app in the intelligent-environment market. MEMS tech is finally out of the lab and bursting into the marketplace, and our cross-licenses and patents look very solid. As for the development budget—well, this is the biggest new product budget I've seen in eight years with this company.

My point is, we've got to get away from our old-fashioned emphasis on "technology for tech's sake." That approach is killing us in the modern marketplace. Yes, of course MEMS locator chips are a "hot, sweet" technology—and yes, "If you build it, they will come." Our problem is, we do build it, and they do come, but they *give all the money to somebody else.*

We can't live on our reputation as a cutting-edge engineering outfit. Design awards just don't pay the bills. That's not what our shareholders want, and it's not what the new management wants. No matter how we may grumble, this company has got to be competitive in the real world. That means that it's all about Return-On-Investment. It's about meeting consumer demand, and generating serious revenue.

So let's not start with the product qua product. Our product is not a "commodity" any more, and the consumer is not a "user." The product is a point of entry for the buyer into a long-term, rewarding relationship.

So what we require here, people, is a story. That story has got to be a human story. It has to be a user-centric story—it's got to center on the user himself. It's all about the guy who's opening his wallet and paying up.

I want this character, this so-called "user," to be a real person with some real human needs. I want to know *who he is,* and *what we're doing for him,* and *why he's giving us money.* So we've got to know what he needs, what he wants. What he longs for, what he hopes for, what he's scared of. All about him.

If we understand him and his motivations, then we also understand our product. I want to know what we can do for this guy in his real life. How can we mold his thinking?

....

From: Design Engineer
To: Design Team
Subject: Re: New Product Brainstorm

FYI, User specs: Classic early adapter type. Male. Technically proficient. 18–35 age demographic. NAFTA/Europe. Owns lots of trackable, high-value-added, mobile hardware products: sporting goods, laptops, bicycles, luggage, possibly several cars.

....

From: Marketer
To: Design Team

Subject: User Specs

I just read the Engineer's e-mail, and gee whiz, people. That is dullsville. That is marketing poison. Do you have any idea how burned out the Male-Early-Adapter thing is in today's competitive environment? These guys have digital toothbrushes now. They're nerd-burned, they've been consumer-carpet-bombed! There's nothing left of their demographic! They're hiding in blacked-out closets hoping their shoes will stop paging their belt buckles.

Nerds can't push this product into the high-volume category that we need for a breakeven. We need a housekeeping technology. I mean ultra-high volume, in the realm of soaps, mops, brooms, scrubbing brushes, latex gloves, light bulbs. An impulse buy, but high-margin and everywhere.

....

From: Programmer
To: Design Team
Subject: [no subject]

I can't believe I agree with the Marketer. But really, I'd rather be dipped in crumbs and deep-fried than grind out code for some lamer chip that tells you where your lawnmower is. I mean, if you don't know by now. READ THE FRIENDLY MANUAL. I mean, how stupid are people out there supposed to be? Don't answer that. Jeez.

....

From: The Social Anthropologist
To: Design Team
Subject: Creating Our Reality Model

People, forgive me for this, but I don't think you quite grasp what Fred, our esteemed Team Leader, is suggesting to us approach-wise. We need a solid story before we consider the specs on the technical MacGuffin. A story just works better that way.

So: we need a compelling character. In fact, we need two characters. One for the early-adoption contingent who appreciates technical sweetness, and the other who is our potential mass-market household user. To put a human face on them right away, I would suggest we call them "Al" and "Zelda."

Al is a young man with disposable income who lives in a rather complex household. (Perhaps he inherited it.) Al's not really at ease with his situation as it stands—all those heirlooms, antiques, expensive furniture, kitchenware, lawn-care devices— it's all just a little out of his control. Given Al's modern education, Al sees a laptop or desktop as his natural means of control over a complex situation. Al wants his things together and neat, and accessible, and searchable, and orderly—just the way they are on his computer screen.

But what Al really needs is an understanding, experienced, high-tech housekeeper. That's where "Zelda" comes into the story. Zelda's in today's 65+ demographic, elderly but very vigorous, with some life-extension health issues. Zelda has smart pill-bottles that remind her of all her times and her dosages. She's got cognitive blood-brain inhalers, and smart orthopedic shoes. Zelda wears the customary, elder-demographic, biomaintenance wrist-monitor. So I see Zelda as very up to speed with biomedical tech—so that her innate late-adapter conservatism has a weak spot that we might exploit. Is this approach working for the Team?

....

From: Coordinator
To: Design Team
Subject: All right!!

The Social Anthropologist knows just what we want: specificity. We're building a technology designed for these two characters—who are they, what do they need? How can we exceed their consumer expectations, make them go "Wow"?

And one other little thing—I'm not the "Leader." It's nice of Susan to say that, but my proper title is "Coordinator," and the new CEO insists on that across all divisions.

....

From: Graphics Gal
To: Design Team
Subject: My Turn

Okay, well, maybe it's just me, but I'm getting a kind of vibe from this guy "Albert." I'm thinking he's maybe, like, a hunter? Because I see him as, like, outdoors a lot? More than you'd think for a geek, anyway. Okay?

....

From: Engineer
To: Design Team
Subject: Story Time

Okay, I can play that way, too. "Albert Huddleston." He's the quiet type, good with his hands. Not a big talker. Doesn't read much. Not a ladies' man. But he's great at home repair. He's got the big house, and he's out in the big yard a lot of the time, with big trees, maybe a garden. A deer rifle wouldn't scare him. He could tie trout flies, if he were in the mood.

....

From: Marketer
To: Design Team
Subject: The Consumables within Al's Demographic

A bow saw, an extendible pruner. Closet full of extreme-sports equipment from college that he can't bear to get rid of.

....

From: Graphics Gal
To: Design Team
Subject: What Is Albert really like?

So he's, like, maybe, a Cognition Science major with a minor in environmental issues?

....

From: Marketer
To: Design Team
Subject: [none]

Albert's not smart enough to be a "Cognition Science major."

....

From: Legal Expert
To: Design Team
Subject: So-Called Cognition Science

In a lot of schools, "Cognition Science" is just the Philosophy Department in drag.

....

From: Team Coordinator
To: Design Team
Subject: Brainstorming

It's great to see you pitching in, Legal Expert, but let's not get too critical while the big, loose ideas are still flowing.

....

From: Legal Expert
To: Design Team
Subject: Critical Legal Implications

Well, excuse me for living. Forgive me for pointing out the obvious, but there are massive legal issues with this proposed technology. We're talking about embedding hundreds of fingernail-sized radio-chirping MEMS chips that emit real-time data on the location and the condition of everything you own. That's a potential Orwell situation. It could violate every digital-privacy statute on the books.

Let's just suppose that you walk out with some guy's chip-infested fountain pen. You don't even know the thing's bugged. So if the plaintiff's got enough bandwidth and big enough receivers, he can map you and all your movements, for as long as you carry the thing.

Legal issues must come first in the design process. It's not prudent to tack on anti-liability safeguards somewhere down at the far end of the assembly line.

....

From: Engineer
To: Design Team
Subject: Correction

We don't use "assembly lines." Those went out with the twentieth century.

....

From: Marketer
To: Design Team
Subject: Getting Sued

Wait a minute. Isn't product liability exactly what blew us out of the water with the ultrasonic cleanser?

....

From: The Social Anthropologist
To: Design Team
Subject: The Issues We Face As a Group

There are plenty of major issues here, no one's denying that. In terms of the story, though, I'm very intrigued with the Legal Expert's views. There seems to be an unexamined assumption that a household control technology is necessarily "private."

But what if it's just the opposite? If Al has the location and condition of all his possessions cybernetically tracked and tagged in real time, maybe Al is freed from worrying about all his stuff. Why should Al fret about his possessions anymore? We've made them permanently safe. Why shouldn't Al loan the lawnmower to his neighbor? The neighbor can't lose the lawnmower, He can't sell it, because Al's embedded MEMS monitors just won't allow that behavior. (continued)

So now Al can be far more generous to his neighbor. Instead of being miserly and geeky "labeling everything he possesses," obsessed with privacy, Al turns out to be an open-handed, open-hearted, very popular guy. He doesn't even need locks on his doors! Everything Al has is automatically theft-proof — thanks to us. He has big house parties, fearlessly showing off his home and his possessions. Everything that was once a personal burden to Al becomes a benefit to the neighborhood community. What was once Al's weakness and anxiety is now a source of emotional strength and community esteem.

....

From: Team Coordinator
To: Design Team

Subject: Wow

Right! That's it. That's what we're looking for. That's the "Wow" factor.

· ·

From: Graphics Gal
To: Design Team
Subject: Re: Wow

So here's how Al meets Zelda. Cause she's, like, living next door? And there's a bunch of Al's dinner plates in her house, kinda "borrowed"? Someone breaks a plate, there's an immediate screen prompt, Al rushes over.

· ·

From: Legal Expert
To: Design Team
Subject: Domestic Disputes

Someone threw a plate at Zelda. Zelda owns the home next door, and her son and daughter-in-law are living in it. But Zelda sold the home because she needs to finance her rejuvenation treatments. It's a basic cross-generational equity issue. Happens all the time nowadays, with the boom in life extension. Granny Zelda comes home from the clinic looking 35. She's mortgaged the family wealth, and now the next generation can't afford to have kids. Daughter-in-law freaked because dear old mom suddenly looks better than she does. It's a soap-opera eruption of passion, resentment, and greed. Makes a child-custody case look like a traffic ticket.

· ·

From: Engineer
To: Design Team
Subject: Implications

Great. So listen. Zelda sells her house and moves in with Al. He's a nice guy, rescuing her from her family. She brings all her own stuff into Al's house—60 years' worth of tchotchkes. No problem. Thanks to us. Because Al and Zelda are getting everything out of her packing boxes and tagging it all with MEMS tags. Possessions are mixed up physically—and yet they're totally separate, virtually. With MEMS, unskilled labor can enter the house with handheld trackers, separate and re-pack everything in a few hours, tops. Al and Zelda never lose track of who belongs to what—that's a benefit we're supplying. They can live together in a new kind of way.

....

From: Graphics Gal
To: Design Team
Subject: A&Z Living Together

Okay, so Zelda's in the house cooking, right? Now Al can get to that yardwork he's been putting off. There's like squirrels and raccoons and out there, and they're getting in the attic? Only now Al's got some cybernetic live-traps, like the MuscleGel MistNet from our Outdoor Products Division. Al catches the raccoon, and he plants a MEMS chip under the animal's skin. Now he always knows where the raccoon is! It's like, Al hears this spooky noise in the attic, he goes up in the attic with his handheld, it's like, "Okay Rocky, I know it's you! And I know exactly where you're hiding. Get the hell out of my insulation."

....

From: Legal Expert
To: Design Team
Subject: Tagging Raccoons

Interesting. If Al really does track and catalog a raccoon, that makes the raccoon a property improvement. If Al wants to sell the house, he's got a market advantage. After all, Al's property comes with big trees—that's obvious, that's a given—but now it also comes with a legally verifiable raccoon.

From: Engineer
To: Design Team
Subject: Squirrels

They're no longer vermin. The squirrels in the trees, I mean. They're a wholly owned property asset.

From: Team Coordinator
To: Design Team
Subject: This Is Real Progress, People

I'm with this approach! See, we never would have thought of the raccoon angle if we'd concentrated on the product as a product. But of course Al is moving his control chips out of the house, into his lawn, and eventually into the whole neighborhood. Raccoons wander around all the time. So do domestic dogs and cats. But that's not a bug in our tracking technology—that's a feature. Al's cat has got a MEMS tag on its collar. Al can tag every cat's collar in the neighborhood and run it as a neighborhood service off his web page. When you're calling Kitty in for supper, you just e-mail Kitty's collar.

From: Programmer
To: Design Team
Subject: [no subject]

AWESOME! I am so with this! I got 8 cats myself, I want this product! I can smell the future here! And it smells like a winner!!

From: Engineer
To: Design Team
Subject: Current Chip Technology

That subcutaneous ID chip is a proven technology. They've been doing that for lab rats for years now. I could have a patent-free working model out of our Sunnyvale fab plant in 48 hours, tops.

The only problem Al faces is repeater technology, so he can cover the neighborhood with his radio locators. But a repeater net is a system administration issue. That's a classic, tie-in, service-provision opportunity. We're talking long-term contracts here, and a big buyer lock-in factor.

From: Marketer
To: Design Team
Subject: Buyer Lock-In Factor

That is hot! Of course! It's about consumer stickiness through market-segmentation upgrades. You've got the bottom-level, introductory, Household-Only tagging model. Then the mid-level Neighborhood model. Then, on to the Gold and Platinum service levels, with 24-hour tech support! Al can saturate the whole suburb. Maybe even the whole city! It's totally open-ended. We supply as many tags and as much monitoring and connectivity as the guy can pay for. The only limit is the size of his wallet!

From: Team Coordinator
To: Social Anthropologist
Subject: ***Private Message***

Susan, look at 'em go! I can't believe the storytelling approach works so well. Last week they were hanging around the lab with long faces, preparing their resumés and e-mailing headhunters.

....

To: Team Coordinator
From: The Social Anthropologist
Subject: Re: ***Private Message***

Fred, people have been telling each other stories since we were hominids around campfires in Africa. It's a very basic human cognition thing, really.

....

From: Team Coordinator
To: Social Anthropologist
Subject: **Private Message Again**

We've gotta hit, Susan. I can feel it. I need a drink after all this, don't you? Let's celebrate. On my tab, okay? We'll make a night of it.

....

From: The Social Anthropologist
To: Team Coordinator
Subject: Our Relationship

Fred, I'm not going to deny there's chemistry between us. But I really have to question whether that's appropriate business behavior.

....

From: Team Coordinator
To: Social Anthropologist

Subject: ***Private Message***

We're grown-ups, Susan. We've both been around the block a few times. Come on, you don't have to be this way.

....

From: The Social Anthropologist
To: Team Coordinator
Subject: Re: ***Private Message***

Fred, it's not like this upsets me professionally—I mean, not in that oh-so-proper way. I'm a trained anthropologist. They train us to understand how societies work—not how to make people happy. I'm being very objective about this situation. I don't hold it against you. I know that I'm relationship poison, Fred. I've never made a man happy in my whole life.

....

From: Team Coordinator
To: Social Anthropologist
Subject: **Very Private Message**

Please don't be that way, Susan. That "you and me" business, I mean. I thought we'd progressed past that by now. We could just have a friendly cocktail down at Les Deux Magots. This story isn't about "you and me."

....

From: The Social Anthropologist
To: Team Coordinator
Subject: Your Unacceptable Answer

Then whose story is it, Fred? If this isn't our story, then whose story is it?

Albert's mouth was dry. His head was swimming. He really had to knock it off with those cognition enhancers—especially after 8:00 P.M. The smart drugs had been a major help in college—all those French philosophy texts, my God, Kant 301, that wasn't the kind of text that a guy could breeze through without serious neurochemical assistance—but he'd overdone it. Now he ate the pills just to keep up with the dyslexia syndrome—and the pills made him so, well, verbal. Lots of voices inside the head. Voices in the darkness. Bits and pieces arguing. Weird debates. A head full of yakking chemical drama.

Another ripping snore came out of Hazel. Hazel had the shape of a zaftig 1940s swimsuit model, and the ear-nose-and-throat lining of a 67-year-old crone. And what the hell was it with those hundred-year-old F. Scott Fitzgerald novels? Those pink ballet slippers. And the insistence on calling herself "Zelda."

Huddleston pulled himself quietly out of the bed. He lurched into the master bathroom, which alertly switched itself on as he entered. His hair was snow white, his face a road map of hard wear. The epidermal mask was tearing loose a bit, down at the shaving line at the base of his neck. He was a 25-year-old man who went out on hot dates with his own roommate. He posed as Zelda's fictional "70-year-old escort." When they were out in clubs and restaurants, he always passed as Zelda's sugar daddy.

That was the way the two of them had finally clicked as a couple, somehow. The way to make the relationship work out. Al had become a stranger in his own life.

Al now knew straight-out, intimately, what it really meant to be old. Al knew how to pass for old. Because his girlfriend was old. He watched forms of media that were demographically targeted for old people, with their deafened ears, cloudy eyes, permanent dyspepsia, and fading grip strength. Al was technologically jet-lagged out of the entire normal human aging process. He could visit "his 70s" the way you might buy a ticket and visit "France."

Getting Hazel, or rather "Zelda," to come across in the bedroom—the term "ambivalence" didn't begin to capture his feelings on that subject. It was all about fingernail-on-glass sexual tension and weird time-traveling flirtation mannerisms. There was something so irreparable about it. It was a massive transgressive rupture in the primal fabric of human relationships.

Not "love." It was a different arrangement. A romance with no historical precedent, all beta pre-release, an early-adapter thing; all shakeout, with a million bugs and periodic crashes.

It wasn't love, it was "evol." It was "elvo." Albert was in elvo with the curvaceous bright-eyed babe who had once been the kindly senior citizen next door.

At least he wasn't like his dad. Stone dead of overwork on the stairsteps of his mansion, in a monster house with a monster coronary. And with three dead marriages: Mom One, Mom Two, and Mom Three. Mom One had the kid and the child support. Mom Two got the first house and the alimony. Mom Three was still trying to break the will.

How in hell had life become like this? thought Huddleston in a loud interior voice, as he ritually peeled dead pseudoskin from a mirrored face that, even in the dope-etched neural midnight of his posthuman soul, looked harmless and perfectly trustworthy. He couldn't lie to himself—because he was a philosophy major, he formally despised all forms of cheesiness and phoniness. He was here because he enjoyed it. It was working out for him. Because it met his needs. He'd been a confused kid with emotional issues, but he was so together now.

He had to give Zelda all due credit—the woman was a positive genius at home economics. A household-maintenance whiz. Zelda was totally down with Al's ambitious tagging project. Everything in its place with a place for everything. Every single shelf and windowsill was spic and span. Al and Zelda would leaf through design catalogs together, in taut little moments of genuine bonding.

Zelda was enthralled with the new decor scheme and clung to her household makeover projects like a drowning woman grabbing life rings. Al had to admit it: she'd been totally right about the stark necessity for new curtains. And the lamp thing—Zelda had amazing taste in lamps. You couldn't ask for a better garden-party hostess: the canapés, the Japanese lacquer trays, crystal swizzle sticks, stackable designer porch chairs, Châteauneuf du Pape, stuff Al had never heard of, stuff he wouldn't have learned about for 50 years. Such great, cool stuff.

She was his high-maintenance girl. A fixer-upper. Like a part-time wife, sort of kind of, but requiring extensive repair work. A good-looking gal with a brand new wardrobe, whose calcium-depleted skeletal system was slowly unhinging, requiring lots of hands-on foot rubs and devoted spinal adjustment. It was a shame about her sterility thing. But let's face it, who needed children? Zelda had children. She couldn't stand 'em.

What Al really wanted—what he'd give absolutely anything for—was somebody, something, somewhere, somehow, who would give him a genuine grip. To become a fully realized, fully authentic human being. He had this private vision, a true philosophy almost: Albert "Owl" Huddleston, as a truly decent person. Honest, helpful, forthright, moral. A modern philosopher. A friend to mankind. It was that *gesamtkunstwerk* thing. No loose ends at all. No ragged bleeding bits. The Total Work of Design.

Completely *put together,* Al thought, carefully flushing his face down the toilet. A stranger in his own life, maybe, sure, granted, but so what, so were most people. Even a lame antimaterialist like Henry Thoreau knew that much. A tad dyslexic, didn't read all that much, stutters a little when he forgets his neuroceuticals, listens to books on tape about Italian design theory, maybe a tad obsessive-compulsive about the $700 broom, and the ultra-high-tech mop with the chemical taggant system that Displays Household Germs in Real Time (C) (R) (TM) . . . But so what.

So what. So what is the real story here? Is Al a totally together guy, on top and in charge, cleverly shaping his own destiny through a wise choice of tools, concepts, and approaches? Or is Al a soulless figment of a hyperactive market, pieced together like a shattered mirror from a million little impacts of brute consumerism? Is Al his own man entire, or is Al a piece of flotsam in the churning surf of techno-revolution? Probably both and neither. With the gratifying knowledge that it's All Completely Temporary Anyway (R). Technological Innovation Is An Activity, Not An Achievement (SM). Living On The Edge Is Never Comfortable (C).

What if the story wasn't about design after all? What if it wasn't about your physical engagement with the manufactured world, your civilized niche in historical development, your mastery of consumer trends, your studied elevation of your own good taste, and your hands-on struggle with a universe of distributed, pervasive, and ubiquitous smart objects that are choreographed in invisible, dynamic, interactive systems. All based, with fiendish computer-assisted human cleverness, in lightness, dematerialization, brutally rapid product cycles, steady iterative improvement, renewability, and fantastic access and abundance. What if all of that was at best a passing thing. A by-blow. A techie spin-off. A phase. What if the story was all about this, instead: What if you tried your level best to be a real-life, fully true human being, and it just plain couldn't work? It wasn't even possible. Period.

Zelda stirred and opened her glamorous eyes. "Is everything clean?"

"Yeah."

"Is it all put away?"

"Yep."

"Did you have another nightmare?"

"Uh. No. Sure. Kinda. Don't call them 'nightmares,' okay? I just thought I'd . . . you know . . . boot up and check out the neighborhood."

Zelda sat up in bed, tugging at the printed satin sheet. "There are no more solutions," Zelda said. "You know that, don't you? There are no happy endings. Because there are no endings. There are only ways to cope."

THE BLOG AT THE END OF THE WORLD

By Paul Tremblay

About Becca Gilman:

I am twenty-something, living somewhere in Brooklyn, and am angry and scared like everyone else I know. Sometimes this blog helps me, sometimes it doesn't. I have degrees in bio and chem, but don't use them. That's all you really need to know. All right?

still here

Becca Gilman • June 17th, 20__

Barely. I tried calling Mom two days ago but there was no answer and she hasn't called me back. I'm still not over GRANT'S passing; my personal tipping point and I hate myself for referring to Grant that way, but it's true. I haven't left my apartment in over a week. The local market I use for grocery delivery stopped answering their phone yesterday. I've only seen three cabs today. They're old and dinged up, from some independent cab company I don't recognize, and they just drive around City Line, circling, like they're stuck in some loop, like the drivers don't know what else to do. At night I count how many windows I can see with the lights on. The city was darker last night than it was last week, or the week before. The city is falling apart. It's slow and subtle, but you can see it if you look hard enough. Watch. Everything is slowing down. A wind-up toy running down and with no one to wind it up. Everything is dying but not quite dead yet, so people just go about their days as if nothing is wrong and nothing bad can happen tomorrow.

I've had a headache for a week now, my neck hurts, and I've been really sensitive to light. I'm scared, but not terrified anymore. Mostly, I'm just incredibly sad.

6 Responses to "still here"

squirrelmonkey says:

June 17, 20__ at 9:32 am

I just tried calling and left a message. I am going to stop by your place today. Please answer your buzzer.

Jenn Parker says:

June 17, 20__ at 1:12 pm

I'm not surprised that you're experiencing headaches and the like. You're so obsessed with the textbook symptoms, you're now psychosomatically experiencing them. I am surprised it has taken this long. I had February 2009 in the pool. Get help. Psychiatric help.

beast says:

June 28, 20__ at 4:33 am

i live in new york city to last weak i saw this guy drop dead in the street he pressed a button at the traffic light on the corner and then died there was no one else around just me he wasnt old probably younger than me he died and then i saw whats really happning to everyone cause two demons fell out of the sky and landed next to him maybe they were the gargoiles from the buildings i dont know but they were big strong gray with muscles and wings and large teeth the sidewalk broke under their heavyness they growled like tigers and licked up the blood that came out of the guys ears and mouth but that wasn't good enough they broke his chest open and there was red everywere on the sidewalk and street corner i didnt know there was so much blood in us but they know they took off his arms and legs then gather him up in their big strong arms and flew away he was gone i went back and checked the next day he was gone after i walked around the city i saw the demons every were but noone saw them but me they fly and climb the buildings waiting for us to die and take us just like you i am afraid and stay in my apartment but don't look out my window any more

revelations says:

July 5, 20__ at 12:12 am

Maybe you're "fuck heaven" comments from you're earlier post caught up to you, and you're fear mongering and lies have finally caught up with you. GOD punishes the wicked.

Jenn Parker says:
July 5, 20__ at 2:45 pm
I like beast. I want to party with you, dude!

Hey, revelations, stick to book burning and refuting evolution.

revelations says:
July 12, 20__ at 10:09 am
I can sum it all up in three words: Evolution is a lie.

Link Roundup

Becca Gilman • May 19th, 20__
I don't feel up to it, but here's a link roundup, in honor of Grant

San Jose Mercury News: The Silicon Valley's home sales continue to tank with the number of deals at a 40-year low. The mayor of San Jose attributes the market crisis to the glut of homes belonging to the recently deceased.

The Burlington Free Press reports that a May 3rd session of Congress ended with the sudden death of Missouri Representative William Hightower and Senator Jim Billingsly from Vermont. While neither Hightower nor Billingsly has been seen publicly since the 3rd, the offices of both congressmen have yet to make any such announcement, and their only official comment is to claim the story is patently false.

The Miami Herald reports that according to UNICEF, the populations of children in Kenya and Ethiopia have declined by a stunning 24 percent within the past year. The UN and United States government dispute the findings, claiming widespread inaccuracies in the "hurried and irresponsible" census.

8 Responses to "Link Roundup"

Jenn Parker says:
May 24th, 20__ at 7:48 pm
Reputable sources at a quick glance, but let's address each link:

The San Jose Mercury News has already issued a partial retraction here. The mayor of San Jose never attributed the market crisis to the supposed glut of homes belonging to the deceased. Honestly, other than within the backdrop of our collective state of paranoia/hysteria, such a claim/statement doesn't make any economic sense. People aren't buying homes for a myriad of economic reasons, but too many deaths due to an imaginary epidemic isn't one of them.

The links to your burlington and miami papers are dead. I suppose you could spin the dead links to bolster the conspiracy theory, but here in reality, the dead links serve only as a representation of your desperation to perpetuate conspiracy.

squirrelmonkey says:
May 25th, 20__ at 7:03 am
Ever heard of Google, Jenn? Those articles can still be found in the cache. It's not a hard to find. Do you want me to show you how?

Jenn Parker says:
May 25th, 20__ at 1:23 pm
Why were the articles almost instantaneously removed? You'll tell me it's due to some all-encompassing conspiracy, when the real answer is those papers got their stories wrong so they had to pull the articles. Happens all the time. I guarantee retractions will be published within days. Oh-master-of-Google, prove me wrong by finding another news-outlet corroboration to either story. Read carefully, please. I want a news-outlet that does not site the Burlington Free Press or Miami Herald as their primary sources. If you try such a search, you'll be at it for a long time, because I can't find any other independent reports.

slugwentbad says:

May 25th, 20__ at 10:13 pm

I've called Billingsly's office on three occasions, and I've been told he's unavailable every time.

Jenn Parker says:

May 25th, 20__ at 10:23 pm

Oh, that proves everything, then.

discostewie says:

May 26th, 20__ at 8:27 am

Bees and bats and amphibians are disappearing, mysteriously dying off (are you going to refute that too, Jenn?). Is it so hard to believe that the same isn't happening to us?

batfan says:

June 25th, 20__ at 3:37 am

Hi, remember me? Come check out my new gambling site for the all the best poker and sports action. It's awesome. http://www.gamblor234.net

speworange says:

August 222n, 20__ at 10:46 am

Humans are harder to kill than cockroaches.

More Grant Lee

Becca Gilman • May 12th, 20__

I went to Grant's wake today. The visiting hours were only one hour. 2pm–3pm. I got there at 2. We had some common friends but I didn't see anyone that I knew there. I didn't see his sister or recognize any family members either. I waited in a line that started on the street. No one talked or shared eye contact. This is so hard to write. I'm trying to be clinical. The mourners were herded inside the funeral parlor, but it split into three different rooms. Grant's room was small with mahogany moulding on the walls and a thick, soft tan carpet on the floor. There were flowers everywhere. The smell was overpowering and made the air thick. The family had asked for a donation to a charity in lieu of flowers. I don't remember the charity. There was no casket. Grant wasn't there; he wasn't in the room. There wasn't a greeting line, and I don't know where his family was. There was only a big flat-screen TV on the wall. The TV scrolled with images of Grant and his friends and family. I was in one of those pictures. We were at the Pizza Joint, standing next to each other, bent over, our faces perched in our hands, elbows on the counter. I had flour on the tip of my nose and he had his PJ baseball hat on backwards, his long black hair tucked behind his ears. Our smiles matched. It was one of those rare posed pictures that still manage to capture the spirit of a candid. That picture didn't stay on the screen long enough. Other people's memories of Grant crowded it out. Also, the pictures of Grant mixed with stock photos and video clips of blue sky and rolling clouds like some ridiculous subliminal commercial for heaven. There was a soundtrack to the loop; the music was formless and light, with no edges or minor chords. Aural Valium. It was awful. All of it. The mourners walked around the room's perimeter in an orderly fashion. Point A to B to C to D and out the door. I didn't follow them. I held my ground and stayed rooted to a spot as people brushed past me. No one asked if I was okay, not that I wanted them to. I watched the TV long enough to see the images loop back to its beginning, or at least the beginning that I had seen. I don't know if there was a true beginning and a true end. After seeing the loop once, I stared at the other mourners' faces. Their eyes turned red and watered when the obviously poignant images meshed with a hopeful crescendo of Muzak. The picture of a toddler-aged Grant holding hands with his parents seemed to be the cue. Then the manufactured moment passed, and everyone's faces turned blue when the TV filled with blue sky, that slickly produced loop of heaven. I wanted to shout fuck heaven, I want Grant back and I don't want to die. After an hour had passed, I was asked to leave as someone else's visiting hour was starting. They had a full schedule: every room booked throughout the afternoon and evening. I peeked in the other rooms before I left. No caskets anywhere, just TVs on the walls. Pictures. Clouds. Blue Sky. More pictures. When I went outside, there was another long line.

Now I'm sitting in my apartment, crying, and thinking about my father. He died when I was four. I remember his wake. I remember crossing my arms over my chest and not letting anyone hug me. Everyone tried. I remember being bored and mad. I remember trying to hide under the casket presentation. An uncle that I'd never met before pulled me out of the mini-curtains below the casket. He pulled too hard on my arm and I cried. I think my tears were the equivalent of the four-year-old me saying fuck heaven, I want my daddy back, *and I don't want to die.*

I've turned off comments for this post. I've posted, and deleted, and then re-posted this a few times. I'm going to leave it up and as is. But no one else gets to say anything about Grant or me or anything today.

Grant Lee, RIP
Becca Gilman • May 10th, 20__

It finally happened. A very close friend of mine, Grant Lee, died two days ago. He was twenty-four. I have been unable to get much information from his family. I talked to his older sister, Claire. Grant died at work, at the Pizza Joint, two blocks from my apartment. She said his death was sudden and "catastrophic." I asked if he died from an aneurysm. Claire said the doctors told the family it was likely heart failure, but they wouldn't tell them anything specific. I then asked for information about the hospital he went to, but she rushed me off the phone, saying she had too many calls to make. I called the Pizza Joint, wanting to talk to the co-worker who had found Grant dead, but no one answered the phone. I'm going to take a walk down there after I post this. It's awful and terrifying enough that Grant died, but it looks like his cause of death will be covered up as well.

I met Grant in a video store a week after I'd moved to Brooklyn. We rented Nintendo Wii games and old noir flicks together. Grant ate ice cream with a fork. He always wore a white tee shirt under another shirt, even if the other shirt was another white tee shirt. Grant was tall, and slight of build, but very fast, and elegant when he moved. I'd never seen him stumble or fall down. He worked long hours at the Pizza Joint, trying to pay off the final four grand of tuition he owed NYU so he could get his diploma. That debt wasn't Grant's fault. His father was a gambler and couldn't pay that final tab. Grant had a crooked smile and he only trusted a few of his friends. I think he trusted me. Grant liked to swear a lot. He liked fucking with the Pizza Joint customers whenever he could. Sometimes he'd greet an obnoxious-looking customer with silence and head nods only. Invariably, the obnoxious-looking customer would talk slow and loud because they assumed Grant (who was Korean) didn't speak English. They'd mumble exasperated stuff under their breath when Grant didn't respond. Finally, he'd give the customer their pizza and make some comment like, "You gonna eat all that? You leavin' town or somethin'?" and his voice was loud and had that thick Long Island accent of his. Grant drank orange soda all day long. Grant would be too quick to tease sometimes, but he always gave me an unqualified apology if I needed one.

Grant was more than a collection of eccentricities or character traits, but that is what he's been reduced to. I love you and miss you, Grant.

4 Responses to "Grant Lee, RIP"

Jenn Parker says:
May 10th, 20__ at 4:47 pm

If you are telling the truth (sorry to sound so callous, but I don't know you, and given your blogging history, your agenda, it's entirely plausible you are making this up to bolster your position, as it were), I'm very sorry for your loss.

I don't know what to believe though. Look at your first sentence: It finally happened. Maybe this is just a throwaway phrase written while in the throws of grief, however it seems like an odd line to lead your post. It finally happened. It sounds like not only were you anticipating such an event, but are welcoming it so your version of reality could somehow be verified.

I find it impossible to believe that doctors would give the family of the deceased no cause of death, or a fraudulent cause of death as you are implying. To what benefit or end would such a practice serve?

And please see and respond to the links and aneurysm statistics I quoted in your earlier post.

squirrelmonkey says:
May 10th, 20__ at 7:13 pm
I'm so, so sorry to hear this, Becca. Poor Grant.

Take care of yourself and ignore that Jenn Parker troll. Call me if you feel up to it, okay?
beast says:
May 11th, 20__ at 3:36 am
sorry about your friend its so scarey that were all gonna die

anonymous says:
May 12th, 20__ at 10:56 am
I've spent the past week doing nothing but reading obituaries from every newspaper I can find online. I read Grant Lee's obit and followed links to his MySpace and then here to your blog.

My son died last week. I was with him in the backyard when he just folded in on himself, falling to the grass. His eyes were closed and blood trickled out of his ears. He was only six. I suppose that his young age is supposed to make it worse, but it can't be any worse.

I'm afraid to write his name, as if writing it here makes what happened to him more final than it already is.

Someone else, not me, wrote my son's obituary. I don't remember who. They did a terrible job.

When we first came home, after leaving his body at the hospital, I went into his room and found some crumpled-up drawings under his bed. There were two figures in black on the paper, monstrously sized, but human, small heads, no mouths, just two circles for eyes, but all black. They had black guns and they sprayed black bullets all over the page. The bullets were hard slashes, big as knives, black too, and they curved. I have no idea what it means or where it came from.

Was it a sketch of a nightmare, did he see something on TV he shouldn't have, was he drawing these scenes with friends at school? Why did he crumple the drawings up and stuff them under his bed? Did he think that they were "bad" that he couldn't show them to me, talk about it with me, that I'd be so upset with him that I'd feel differently about him if I were to see the pictures?

It's this last scenario that sends me to the computer and reading other people's obituaries.

A Grim Anniversary

Becca Gilman • April 12th, 20__
The Blog at the End of the World has been live for a year now. I thought it worth revisiting my first post. On March 20th, 20__, in Mansfield, MA; a fourteen-year-old boy died suddenly during his school's junior varsity's baseball practice (*Boston globe*), and two days later, a fifteen-year-old-girl from the same town died at her tennis practice (*Boston Globe*). The two Mansfield residents both had sudden, catastrophic brain aneurysms.

So why am I bringing up those two kids again? Why am I dragging out the old news when you could open up any newspaper in the country, click on any blog or news gathering site, and read the same kind of stories only with different names and faces and places?

Despite the aid of hindsight, I'm not prepared to unequivocally state that the teens mentioned above are our patient zeroes. However, I do think those reported stories were mainstream media's story zero concerning the cerebral aneurysm pandemic and the first of their type to go national, and shortly thereafter, global.

And, finally, a one-link Link roundup:

New York Times reports widespread shortages on a host of anti-clotting and anti-seizure drugs used to treat aneurysms. Included in the shortage are medications that increase blood pressure, with the idea that increased blood flow through potentially narrowed vessels would prevent clots and aneurysms. Newer, more exotic drugs are also now being reported as in shortage: nimodipine (a calcium channel blocker that prevents blood vessel spasms) and glucocorticoids (anti-inflammatory steroids, not FDA approved, controversial treatment that supposedly controls swelling in the brain). The gist of the story is about the misuse of the medications (many of which are only meant for survivors of aneurysm and aren't preventative), of course, leads to a whole slew of other medical problems, including heart attack and stroke.

6 Responses to "A Grim Anniversary"

revelations says:
April 24, 20__ at 10:23 am
Your a fear monger. You spread fear and the lies of the Godless, liberal media. GOD will punish you!!!!

Jenn Parker says:
April 24, 20__ at 1:29 pm
I have no doubt the Times story is true, but only because of the panic.

This story does not prove there really is a pandemic of aneurysms, only that a segment of the public believes there is one.

The reality is that on average, since 2010, 50,000 Americans die from brain aneurysms (spontaneous cerebral hemorrhaging) per year, with **3–6% of all adults having aneurysms** inside their brains (fortunately, most are so small they're never noticed). There is no recorded evidence of that 50,000 number swelling to unprecedented levels. Please show me my error!

There is no conspiracy. It's the 21st Century Red Scare. Our zeitgeist is so preoccupied with apocalypse we're making one up because the real one isn't getting here soon enough. Yes, 50K is a small percentage of the population, but it's a large enough number that if a preponderance of aneurysm cases were to get press coverage, as they clearly are, it gives a multimedia appearance of a pandemic and a conspiracy to cover it up. Unless you can provide some hard data/evidence—like our government and the W.H.O can provide—please stop. There're plenty more real threats (economic, environmental, geopolitical) that sorely need to be addressed.

grant says:
April 24, 20___ at 10:10 am
Has it been only a year? Fuck a flyin' fuckin' duck.

I was at the CVS pharmacy on Central Park Ave. today--just picking up "supplies" ;)--and there was a huge fucking line in the pharmacy section with two armed policeman wandering around the store. Muscles and guns and sunglasses. Some good, hot, homoeroticism there, Becks.

My fuck-headed fellow shoppers were shuffling all around the CVS, wearing hospital masks and emptying the already empty shelves of vitamins and who the fuck knows what else. Most of them were buying shit they'd never need, just buying stuff because it was there. It was surreal, and I gotta tell ya, they got to me! I ended up buying some leftover Easter candy. Fucking Peeps. Don't even like them, but you know, when society collapses, I just might need me some yellow fucking Peeps!

Stop by the PJ tonight, Becks. I'm working a double shift. I'll bring the Peeps.

tiredflower says:
April 24th, 20__ at 11:36 am
I'm one of those fuckheads who wears a hospital mask when I go out now. I know it doesn't protect or save me from anything, but it makes me feel better. I know it scares other people when they see me in it, so I tried to cover it up by drawing a smile on the mask with a pink sharpie. I'd hoped it would make people smile back. I'm not a good drawer, though, and it doesn't look like a smile. It's a snarl, bared teeth, the nanosecond before a scream. It's my only mask.

grant says:
April 24, 20__ at 2:15 pm
Drawing mouths on the hospital masks is fuckin' brilliant!

Becks, bring some masks (I know you have some!) to the PJ tonight. I'll help you decorate them. I've got some killer ideas. I'm serious, now, bring some masks. I want to wear one when I go out tomorrow.

bnl44 says:
September 23, 20__ at 2:34 am
I saw someone die today. We were part of a small crowd waiting for our subway train. She was standing next to me, listening to an iPod. It was loud enough to hear the drums and baseline. Didn't recognize the song, but I tried. When our train arrived she collapsed. I felt her body part the air and despite all the noise in the station, I heard her head hit the concrete. It was a hard and soft sound. Then her iPod tune got louder, probably because the earphones weren't in her ears anymore.

I don't know if anyone helped her or not. I'm ashamed to admit that I didn't help her. She fell and I raced onto the train, and waited to hear the doors shut behind me before I turned around to look. The windows in the doors were dirty, black with grime, and I didn't see anything.

end

MEMORIES OF MOMENTS, BRIGHT AS FALLING STARS

By Cat Rambo

The bright orange boxes lay scattered like leaves across the med complex's rear loading dock, and my first thought was "Jackpot." It'd been hard to get in over the razor wire fence, but I had my good reinforced gloves, and we'd be long gone before anyone noticed the snipped wires.

But when we slunk along under the overhanging eaves, close enough to open the packages, it turned out to be just a bunch of memory, next to impossible to sell. Old, unused stuff, maybe there'd been an upgrade or a recall. It was thicker than most memory, shaped like a thin wire. So after we'd filled our pockets, poked around to find anything else lootable, and slid out smooth and nice before the cops could arrive, we found a quiet spot, got a little stoned, and I did Grizz's back before she did mine. I wiped her skin down with an alcohol swab and drew the pattern on her back with a felt-tip pen. It came from me in one thought, surged up somewhere at the base of my spine, and flowed from my fingertips in the ink. Spanning her entire back, it crossed shoulder to shoulder.

I leaned back to check my handiwork.

"How does it look?" she said.

"Like a big double spiral." The maze of ink rolled across her dark olive skin's surface. A series of skin cancers marked the swell of one buttock, the squamous patches sliding under her baggy cargo pants. She sat almost shivering on a pile of pallets. We were at the recycling yard's edge. This section, out of the wind between two warehouses, was rarely visited and made a good place to sit and smoke or fuck or upgrade.

I uncoiled a strand of memory and set to work, pressing it on the skin. I could see her shudder as the cold bond with her flesh took place. The wire glinted gold and purple, its surface set with an oily sheen. Here and there sections had gone bad and dulled to concrete gray, tinting the surrounding skin yellow.

She shrugged her shirt back over her skinny torso. Her breasts gleamed in the early spring's evening light before disappearing under the slick white fabric. Reaching for her jacket, she wiggled her arms snakelike down the sleeves, flipping her shoulders underneath.

"Is it hooked in okay?" I asked.

She shrugged. "Won't know until I try to download something."

"Got plans for it?"

"I can think of things," she said. "Shall I do you now, Jonny?"

"Yeah." I discarded my jacket and T-shirt, and leaned forward over the pallet while she applied the alcohol in cool swipes. The wind hit the liquid as it touched my skin and reduced it to chill nothingness. She drew a long swoop across my back.

"What pattern are you making?"

"Trying to do the same thing you did on mine." The slow circles grew like one wing, then another, on my shoulder blades. She paused before she began laying in the memory.

I don't know that you could call it pain but it's close. At the moment a biobit makes its way into your own system, it's as though the point of impact was exquisitely sensitive, and somewhere micrometers away, someone was doing something inconceivable to it.

"Tomorrow are the Exams," she said. "Could see what I could download for that."

I started to turn my head to look at her, but just then she laid down a curve of ice with a single motion. My jaw clenched.

"And?" was all I managed.

"One of us placed in a decent job would be a good thing."

She laid more memory before she said "Two of us placed in one would be better."

"Might end up separated."

"Would it matter, a six-month, maybe a year or two, before we could work out a transfer?"

I would have shrugged but instead sat still. "So you want to take that memory and jack in facts so you can pass the Exams and become an upstanding citizen?"

She ignored my tone. "Even a little edge would help. Mainly executables, some sorting routines. Maybe a couple high power searches so I can extrapolate answers I can't find."

The last of the memory felt like fire and ice as it seeped into my skin. She'd never mentioned the Exams in the two years we'd been together.

You're not supposed to be able to emancipate until you're 16, but Grizz and I both left a few years early. My family had too many kids as it was and ended up getting caught in a squatter sweep. I came home and found the place packed up and vacant. The deli owner downstairs let me sleep in his back room for the first few months, sort of like an extra burglar alarm, but then he caught me stealing food and gave me the boot. After that, I made enough to eat by running errands for the block, and alternated between three or four sleeping spots I'd discovered on rooftops; while they're less sheltered, fewer punks or crazies make the effort to come up there and mess with you.

Once I hooked up with Grizz, life got a little easier—I had someone to watch my back without it costing me a favor.

We went around to Ajah's, hoping to catch him in one of his moods when he gets drunk on homemade booze and cooks enormous meals. Luck was with us—he was just finishing a curried mushroom omelet. It smelled like heaven.

Three other people sat around his battered kitchen table, watching him work at the stove. Two I didn't know; the third was Lorelei. She gave me a long, slow, sleepy smile, and Grizz and I nodded back at her.

Ajah turned at our entrance and waved us in with his spatula. His jowls surged with a grin.

"Jonny and Grizz, sit down, sit down," he said. "There is coffee." He signaled and one of the no-names, a short black man, grabbed us mugs, filled them full, and pushed them to us as we slid into chairs. I mingled mine with thin and brackish milk while Grizz sprinkled sweet into hers. The drink was bitter and hot, and chased the recycling yard's lingering chill from my bones. I could still feel the new memory on my skin, cold coils against my T-shirt's thin paper, so old its surface had fuzzed to velvet.

Ajah worked at the poultry factory, so he always had eggs and chicken meat. Sometimes they were surplus, sometimes stuff the factory couldn't sell. He'd worked out a deal with a guy in a fungi factory, so he always had mushrooms too. Brown rice and spices stretched it all out until Ajah could afford to feed a kitchen's worth of people at every meal. They brought him what they could to swap, but usually long after the fact of their faces at his table.

Lorelei being here meant she must be down on her luck. As were we—the shelter we'd been counting on for the past year had gone broke, shut down for lack of funds, despite countless neighborhood fundraisers. No one had the script to spare for charity.

Two grocery sacks filled with greenery sat on one counter. Someone had been Dumpster diving, I figured, and brought their spoils to eke out the communal meal. A third sack was filled with apples and browned bananas, and I could feel my mouth watering at the thought.

"I'm Jonny," I offered, glancing around the table. "She's Grizz."

"Ajax," said the black man.

"Mick," muttered the other stranger, a scruffy brown-haired kid. He wore a ragged poncho and his hair fell in slow dreads.

"You know me," Lorelei said.

Conversation faded and we listened to the oily sizzle of mushrooms frying on the stove-top and the refrigerator's hum against the background of city noise and traffic clamor. The still in the corner, full of rotten fruit and potatoes, burped once in counterpoint.

"What's the news?" Ajah asked, ladling rice and mushrooms bound together with curry and egg onto plates and sliding them onto the table toward Lorelei and Grizz. Ajax, Mick, and I eyed them as they started eating, leaving the question to us.

"Not much," I said.

"Found a place to live yet?"

"Jesus, gossip travels fast. How did you hear about the shelter?"

"Beccalu came by and said she was heading to her cousin in Scranton. You two have people to stay with?"

I shook my head as Grizz kept eating. "No one I've thought of yet. We need to head to the library tonight, though, figured we'd doss in the subway station there for a few hours, keep moving along for naps till it's morning. It's Exams tomorrow."

"I know," Ajah said. "Look, why don't you stay here tonight? The couch folds out."

I was surprised; I'd never heard Ajah make anyone an offer like that.

"The Exams are your big chance. Get a good night's sleep and make the most of them. Face them fully charged."

I rolled my eyes. "For what? Like there's a chance." But he and Grizz ignored me.

"We need to make a library run still," she said.

"Yeah, yeah, that's fine. I'm up till midnight, maybe later," Ajah told her.

Despite my doubts, relief seeped into my bones. We'd been given a night's respite, and who knew what would happen after the Exams? "Thanks, Ajah," I said, and he grunted acknowledgement as he slid a plate before me.

The portabella bits had been browned in curry powder and oil, and the eggs were fresh and good. Grizz ate methodically, scraping her plate free, but she looked up to catch my eye and gave me a heartfelt smile, rare on her square-set face.

As her gaze swung back to her plate, my glance tangled with Lorelei's. I could not read her expression.

Lorelei and I used to pal around before Grizz and I met up. She and I grew up next to each other, and it's hard not to know someone intimately when you've shared hour after hour channel surfing while one mother or the other went out on work or errands. We suffered through the same street bullies and uninterested teachers. She was the first girl I ever kissed. You don't forget that.

But I knew I wanted Grizz for keeps the first moment I saw her. She came swaggering into the shelter wearing a rabbit-fur jacket and pseudo-leather pants. She'd been tricking in a swank bar, but then someone snatched all her hard-earned cash. So there she was, with a bruise on her face and a cracked wrist, but still holding herself hard and arrogant, and the only person in the world who could glimpse the softness underneath was me, it seemed like. So I sauntered up, invited her outside for a smoke, and then within a half hour, we were pressed against the wall together, my hands up her shirt like I'd never touched tit before, feeling her firm little nipples against the skin of my palms.

It's been her and me ever since. As far as I'm concerned, it'll always be that way.

• • •

After eating, we helped wash dishes before heading to the library. We had to wait a half hour for a terminal to free. Finally a man gathered his tablet and stood, stretching his shoulders.

"I'll wait," I said, and gestured Grizz forward.

She nodded and went forward to slide her hand into the log-in gloves. Within a moment, her eyes had the glassy stare that means the meat's occupant is elsewhere.

I looked around. Chairs and desks dotted the place, all of them occupied. I went outside to the parking garage for a smoke.

Daylight had fled. At the structure's edge, where the street was dimly visible, I panhandled a dozen people before I found one willing to admit to smoking. I lit the cigarette, a Marlboro Brute, and leaned back against the wall, which was patchworked with graffiti layers. Maybe by the time I was done, a booth would have opened up. It was getting late, after all.

I closed my eyes as the nicotine rush hit me. Footsteps came across the cement floor toward me. I opened my eyes.

It was Lorelei. She wore a slick, bright red jacket and lipstick to match her short skirt and chunky boots. Silver hoops all along each ear's edge graduated to match her narrowing cartilage. She looked good. Very good.

"Nice night, ain't it?" she said as she moved to lean on the wall beside me. "Gimme."

I passed the smoke over and she took a drag.

"Want to try something to make the nice night even nicer?" she asked, smiling as she leaned back to return the cigarette.

"Meaning?"

"It's good stuff." She fished in the jacket before holding out the lighter and one-hitter. The end was packed with gray lintish dust. "Never had better."

I took the pipe and sparked it. The blue smoke rushed into my lungs like a fist, like a physical jolt, and the world dropped half an inch beneath my feet. Everything was tinged with colors, an iridescence like gasoline on a rain puddle. I was standing there with Lorelei and at the same time I was on a vast dark plain, feeling the world teeter and slip.

Lorelei watched me. On the side of her face was a new tattoo, a black floral design.

"What's that?" I asked. I raised my hand, my fingers dripping colored fire and sparks. The drug curled and coiled through my veins, and I could feel my heart racing.

"Maps," she said. "Executable that interfaces with a global database. Got a GPS here," She tapped a purple faceted gleam on one earlobe. "Drop me anywhere in the world, I'll know where I am."

"Looks awful big to be a simple database interface."

She shrugged, and took the pipe back. She tapped out the ashes with care before she tamped a new pinch of greenish leaf into the mouth. "Controls the GPS too, and some other crap."

An expensive toy, but one that would qualify her for all sorts of delivery jobs. But she must be broke, to show up at Ajah's, I thought. It didn't make sense.

"How're things?" I asked.

Her shoulders twitched into another sullen shrug. "Got some deals in the works. Just a matter of time before something plays out."

I glanced back at the library door. "I should go in, I'm waiting on a machine to clear."

The drug still held me hard, and every moment was crystal clear as she raised her hand to stroke along my jaw. "I miss you sometimes, Jonny," she said, sounding out of breath.

I didn't want to piss her off, so I used a move that's worked before. Catching her hand, I turned it palm down and pressed my lips against the knuckles before dropping it and taking a step backward.

"See you around," I said.

She didn't say anything back, just stood there looking at me as I turned and walked away.

When I tried to log in, the drug prevented it. Every attempt shuddered and screeched along my nerves, so painful it brought tears to my eyes. But I kept trying and trying. A few cubicles down, I could see Grizz's back, hunched over her terminal, every particle intent. Learning. Preparing.

I stared at the screen, which showed the library logo and the welcome menu, all options grayed out, and cursed Lorelei and myself. Mostly myself. After an hour of pretending to work, I slipped away.

Another hour later, Grizz found me outside smoking. Good timing, too. I was on my fourth bummed cigarette, and starting to wonder when a guard would show to jolly me along on my way.

She looked happy, as animated as Grizz gets, which isn't much.

"You get what you wanted?" I asked.

"Got a bunch of stuff," she said. "Plant stuff."

Grizz likes plants, I know. At the shelter, she tended the windowsills full of discarded cacti and spider plants. But I hadn't known she was thinking about that for a career.

"That memory's something, isn't it?" she said. "I downloaded a weather predictor that monitors the whole planet, some biology databases, some specialized ones, some basic gardening routines, and a lot of stuff on orchids."

"Orchids?"

"I've always liked orchids. I've still got plenty of room, too. What about you?"

"Mine's not so good," I lied. "It didn't hold much at all."

Her gaze flickered up to mine, touched with worry. Her eyes narrowed.

"What are you on?" she asked. "Your pupils are big as my fist."

"Dunno the name."

"Where'd you score it?"

"Lorelei swung by, turned me on."

Silence settled between us like a curtain as Grizz's expression flattened.

"It's not like that," I finally said, unable to bear the lack of talk.

"Not like what?"

"She just came through and glimpsed me."

"She knew you would be here because we mentioned it at dinner. She still wants you back."

"Grizz, I haven't been with her for two years. Give it a rest."

"I will. But she won't." She pulled away and made for the exit, her lips pressed together and grim. I followed at a distance all forty blocks to Ajah's.

• • •

In the morning, we showered together to avoid slamming Ajah's water bill too hard. Grizz kept her eyes turned away from mine, rubbing shampoo into her hair.

I ran my fingertips along the spirals on her back. "This is different," I said. Under my fingertips, the wire had knobbed up and thickened, although it still gave easily with the shift of muscles in her back. The gray patches were gone, and a uniform sheen played across the surface.

"Does it feel different?" I asked.

She shrugged. "Not really."

"Do you remember the brand name on the boxes? We could look it up on the Net later on."

"Carpa-something. I don't know. It looked bleeding edge and you never know what's up with that."

"Why do you think they threw it out?" I wanted to keep her talking to me.

She turned to face me with a mute shrug, closing her eyes and tilting her head back to let the water run over her long black hair. Her delicate eyebrows were like pen strokes capping the swell of her eyes beneath the thin-veined lids.

I tangled my fingers in her hair, helping free it so the water would wash away all the shampoo. Muddy green eyes opened to regard me.

"Going to sit out the exams?" she asked.

Saying nothing, I shook my head. We both knew I didn't have a chance.

The Exams were the freak show I expected. Rich people buy mods and make them unnoticeable, plant them in a gut or hollow out a leg. This level, people want to make sure you know what you got. Wal-Mart memory spikes blossomed like cartoon hair from one girl's scalp, colored sunshine yellow, but most had chosen bracelets, jelly purple and red, covering their forearms. One kid had scales, but they looked like a home job, and judging from the way he worried at them with his fingernails, they felt like it too.

You take the Exams at sixteen and most of the time they tell you you're the dregs, just like everyone else, but sometimes your mods and someone's listing match up and you find yourself with a chance. The more mods you have, the more likely it is. So the kids with parents who can afford to hop them up with database links or bio-mods that let them do something specialized, they're the ones getting the jobs.

Usually your family's there to wish you luck. Mine wasn't, of course. And Grizz never said anything about her home life. The only times I've asked, she shut me down quick. Which makes me think it was bad, real bad, because Grizz doesn't pull punches.

You could tell who expected to make it and who was going through the motions. Grizz marched up to her test machine like she was going to kick its ass three times around the block. I slid into my seat and waited for instructions.

You see vidplots this time of year circling around the Exams. Someone gets placed in the wrong job—wacky! Two people get switched by accident—hilarious! Someone cheats someone out of their job but ultimately gets served—heartwarming and reassuring!

In the programs, though, all you see is a quick shot of the person at the Exams. They don't tell you that you'll sit there for three hours while they analyze and explore your wetware, and then another two for the memory and experience tap.

And after all that, you won't know for days.

Grizz wouldn't say anything about how she thought she'd done—she was afraid of jinxing it, I think, plus she was still pissed at me about the Lorelei business.

I could tell as soon as we walked out, though, she was happy. I walked her back to Ajah's and said I was heading down to the court to see if our forms had come in. She nodded and headed inside. It was a gray morning. But nice—some sunlight filtered down through the brown haze that sat way up in the sky for once. The smoke-eater trees along the street gleamed bright green, and down near the trunks sat clumps of pale-blue flowers, most of them coming into their prime, although a few were browned and curling. I could feel all that memory on my back, lying across my shoulder blades, and I found myself Capturing.

I'd only heard it described before—most people don't have the focus or the memory to do it more than a split-second. But I opened to every detail: the watery sepia sunlight and the shimmer playing over the feathers of the two starlings on a branch near me. The cars whispering across the street and two sirens battling it out, probably bound for St. Joe Emergency Services. The colors, oh, the colors passing by, smears of blue and brown and red flashes like song. The smell of the exhaust and dust mingled with a whiff of Mexican spices from the Taco Bell three doors down. Every detail crystal clear and recorded.

I dropped out of it, feeling my whole body shaking, spasms of warring tension and relief like hands gripping my arms and legs.

I tried to bring it back, tried to make the world go super sharp again, but it wouldn't cooperate. I stood there with jaw and fists clenched, trying to force it, but nothing happened.

Within three days, Grizz had heard. A year of training at the Desmond Horticultural Institute, then a three-year internship at the State Gardens in Washington. Student housing all four years, which meant I wouldn't be going along.

At first we fought about it. I figured it was a no-brainer—go there jobless or stick here where I had contacts, friends ready with a handout or a few days' work. But once Grizz had been there a while, she insisted, she'd be able to scrounge me something so I could move closer.

Ajah's girlfriend Suzanne got her set up with a better wardrobe and a suitcase from the used clothing store she ran. I bought her new shoes, black leather boots with silver grommets, solid and efficient looking.

"What are you going to do without me?" she asked.

"I've gotten by before," I said. "You work hard for us, get somewhere. Five years down the line, who knows?"

It was a stupid, facile answer, but we both pretended it was meaningful.

And we did stay in touch, chatted back and forth in IMs. She was working hard, liked her classmates. She read this, and that, and the other thing. They kept telling her how well she was doing.

And unwritten in her messages was the question: What are you doing with it, with the memory?

Because certainly it was doing the same thing on her body as it was on mine: thickening like scars healing in reverse, bulky layers of skin-like substance building over each other. In Ajah's bathroom mirror, I could see the skin purpling like bruises around the layers. My sole consolation was Capturing; extended effort had paid off and I could summon the experience longer now, perhaps ten seconds all together. I kept working at it; Captured pieces sell well in upscale markets if you can get a name for yourself.

And I had the advantage of being able to do it as often as I liked, although each time still left me feeling wrung out and weak. I kept trying to Capture and never hit the memory's end; the only limits were my strained senses. My eyes took on a perpetual dazzled squint as though holy light surrounded everything around me.

I never told Grizz though. Nor about the fact that every time I went to jack into the Net, the drug got between me and the interface. I was glad I hadn't seen Lorelei—I was starting to wonder if she'd given it to me deliberately. It scared me. I lost myself in Capturing more and more. I started delivering packages for Ajah and Susanne, and laid aside enough cash to buy a simple editing package for it.

Editing is internal work, so you can do it dozing on a park bench if you've got the mental room to spread out and take a look at the big picture. I did. What I wanted to do was start selling clips on the channels. It'd take a while though, I could tell, and I was still working out how I'd upload it, given the problems jacking in. I figured at some point I'd burn it off to flash memory and then use an all-accessible terminal, with keyboard and mouse. In the meantime I caged what meals I could, slept on a round of couches, and showed up at Ajah's often.

Sometimes after a meal, he'd roll out the still on its mismatched castors, and we'd strain its milky contents in order to drink them. He and I would sit near the window, passing the bottle back and forth.

Early on into Grizz's apprenticeship, he asked me about the memory. He said "That med complex near the dock, the one that went bust a few months ago, did you guys ever score out of there? I know that was in your turf."

"Went in one time and scored a little crap but not much." Our hands were both touching the bottle as I took it from him. I added, "Nothing but some old memory," and felt the bottle twitch in his sudden anguished grip.

"What did you do with it?" he asked, watching me pour.

"We used it. How do you think she did so well on the Exams?"

"But you didn't," he said, confused.

"Well, Grizz isn't a moron, and I am, which would account for it."

He grunted and took the bottle back.

"If I'd taken stuff from there," he said. "I'd just not mention it to anyone ever. There have been some nasty customers asking around about it."

I went to visit Grizz a few weeks later; her roommate was out of town for the weekend. We ate in the cafeteria off her meal card: more food than I'd seen in a long time, and then went back to her room and stripped naked to lie in each other's arms.

We could have been there hours, but eventually we got hungry and went back to the cafeteria. The rest of the weekend was the same progression, repeated multiple times, up until Sunday afternoon, and the consequent tearful, snuffling goodbye. I'd never seen Grizz act sentimental before; it didn't suit her.

"You need to do something," she said, looking strained.

"Other than planning on riding your gravy train?"

"It's not that, Jonny, and you know it."

I could have told her then about the Capturing, but I was annoyed. Let her think me just another peon, living off dole and scavenging. Fine by me.

The wall phone rang, and she broke off staring at me to answer it.

"Hello," she said. "Hello?" She shrugged and hung it up. "Nothing but breathing. Fuckazoid pervs."

"Get much of that?"

"Every once in a while," she said. "Some of the other students don't like Dregs. Afraid I might stink up the classroom."

It irritated me, that she'd said how much she liked it and now was asking for sympathy, as though her life were worse than mine. So I left it there and made my goodbye. She clung to the doorframe, staring after me.

It wasn't as though I had much to leave behind; it was perhaps my mind's sullen statement, forgetting my jacket. I got four blocks away, then jogged back, ran up the stairs. Knocked on the door and found silence, so I slipped the lock and went in.

By then . . . by then she was dead, and they had already left her. The memory was stripped from her skin, leaving ragged, oozing marks. Her throat had been cut with callous efficiency.

I stood there for at least ten minutes, just breathing. There was no chance she was not dead. The world was shaking me by the shoulders and all I did was stand there, Capturing, longer than I had ever managed before. Every detail, every dust mote riding the air, the smell of the musty carpeting and a quarrel next door over a student named Dian.

I didn't stick around to talk to the cops. I knew the roommate would be there soon to call it in. I might have passed her in the downstairs lobby: a thin Eurasian woman with a scar riding her face like an emotion.

When I got to Ajah's, they'd been there as well. He'd taken a while to die, and they had paid him with leisure, leisure to contemplate what they were doing to him. But he was unmistakably dead.

They had caught him in the preparations for a meal; a block of white chicken meat, sized and shaped like a brick, lay on the cutting board, his good, all-purpose knife next to it. "Man just needs one good knife for everything," he used to say. A bowl of breadcrumbs and an egg container sat near the chicken.

Someone knocked on the door behind me, and opened it even as I turned. It was Lorelei, still well-heeled and clean. Her bosses must be paying well.

"Jonny," she said. She didn't even look at Ajah's body. Unsurprised. "Is it true?"

"Is what true?"

"They said he gave up a name, just one, but when I heard the name, I knew there had to be two."

"What was the name?"

She chuckled. "You know already, I think. Grizz."

"Because of the memory?"

"It's more than memory. It grows as you add to it. Self-perpetuating. New tech—very special. Very expensive."

"We found it in the garbage!"

She laughed. "You've done it yourself, I know. What's the best way to steal from work?"

"Stick it in the trash and pick it up later," I realized.

She nodded. "But when two streets come along, and take it first, you're out of luck." Her smile was cold. "So then you ask around, send a few people to track it."

"Did you mean to poison the Net for me? Was that part of it?"

"You mean you haven't found the cure yet?" she said. "Play around with folk remedies. It'll come to you. But no. I was angry and figured I'd fuck you over the way you did me."

"Do they know my name?"

She smiled in silence at me.

"Answer me, you cunt," I said. Three steps forward and I was in her face.

She backed up toward the door, still smiling.

The knife was in easy reach. I stabbed her once, then again. And again. Capturing every moment, letting it sear itself into the memory, and I swear it went hot as the bytes of experience wrote themselves along my back.

"They don't—" she started to say, then choked and fell forward, her head flopping to one side in time with the knife blows. She almost fell on me, but I pushed her away. Her wallet held black-market script, and plenty of it, along with some credit cards. I didn't see any salvageable mods. The GPS's purple glimmer tempted me, but they can backtrack those. I didn't want anything traceable.

All the time that I rifled through her belongings, feeling the dead weight she had become, I played the memory back of the forward lurch, the head flop and twist, again, again, her eyes going dull and glassy. The thoughts seared on my back as though it were on fire, but I kept on recording it, longer and more intense than I ever had before.

She was right about the folk remedies; feverfew and valerian made the drug relax its hold and let me slide back into cyberspace. I've published a few pieces: a spring day with pigeons, an experimental subway ride, a sunset over the river. Pretty stuff, where I can find it. It seems scarce.

One reviewer called me a brave new talent; another easy and glib. The sales are still slow, but they'll get better. My latest show is called "Memories of Moments, Bright as Falling Stars"—all stuff on the beach at dawn, the gulls walking back and forth at the waves' edge and the foam clinging to the wet sand before it's blown away by the wind.

I don't use the Captures of Grizz's body or Lorelei's death in my art, but I replay them often, obsessively. Sitting on the toilet, showering, eating, walking— Capturing other things is the only way I have to escape them.

Between the royalties and Susanne's continued employment though, I do well enough. She's moved into Ajah's place, and I've taken the room behind the clothing store where she used to live. I cook what I can there, small and tasteless meals, and watch the memories in my head. Memories of moments, as bright as falling stars.

ROCK ON

By Pat Cadigan

Rain woke me. I thought, shit, here I am, Lady Rain-in-the- Face, because that's where it was hitting, right in the old face. Sat up and saw I was still on Newbury Street. See beautiful downtown Boston. Was Newbury Street downtown? In the middle of the night, did it matter? No, it did not. And not a soul in sight. Like everybody said, let's get Gina drunk and while she's passed out, we'll all move to Vermont. Do I love New England? A great place to live, but you wouldn't want to visit here.

I smeared my hair out of my eyes and wondered if anyone was looking for me now. Hey, anybody shy a forty-year-old rock 'n' roll sinner?

I scuttled into the doorway of one of those quaint old buildings where there was a shop with the entrance below ground level. A little awning kept the rain off but pissed water down in a maddening beat. Wrung the water out of my wrap pants and my hair and just sat being damp. Cold, too, I guess, but didn't feel that so much.

Sat a long time with my chin on my knees: you know, it made me feel like a kid again. When I started nodding my head, I began to pick up on something. Just primal but I tap into that amazing well. Man-O-War, if you could see me now. By the time the blueboys found me, I was rocking pretty good.

And that was the punchline. I'd never tried to get up and leave, but if I had, I'd have found I was locked into place in a sticky field. Made to catch the b&e kids in the act until the blueboys could get around to coming out and getting them. I'd been sitting in a trap and digging it. The story of my life.

They were nice to me. Led me, read me, dried me out. Fined me a hundred, sent me on my way in time for breakfast.

Awful time to see and be seen, righteous awful. For the first three hours after you get up, people can tell whether you've got a broken heart or not. The solution is, either you get up *real* early so your camouflage is in place by the time everybody else is out, or you don't go to bed. Don't go to bed ought to work all the time, but it doesn't. Sometimes when you don't go to bed, people

can see whether you've got a broken heart all day long. I schlepped it, searching
for an uncrowded breakfast bar and not looking at anyone who was looking at
me. But I had this urge to stop random pedestrians and say, Yeah, yeah, it's true,
but it was rock 'n' roll broke my poor old heart, not a person, don't cry for me
or I'll pop your chocks.

I went around and up and down and all over until I found Tremont Street. It
had been the pounder with that group from the Detroit Crater—the name was
gone but the malady lingered on—anyway, him; he'd been the one told me
Tremont had the best breakfast bars in the world, especially when you were
coming off a bottle drunk you couldn't remember.

When the c'muters cleared out some, I found a space at a Greek hole in the
wall. We shut down 10:30 A.M. sharp, get the hell out when you're done,
counter service only, take it or shake it. I like a place with Attitude. I folded a
seat down and asked for coffee and a feta cheese omelet. Came with home fries
from the home fries mountain in a corner of the grill (no microwave *garbazhe*,
hoo-ray). They shot my retinas before they even brought my coffee, and while
I was pouring the cream, they checked my credit. Was that badass? It was
badass. Did I care? I did not. No waste, no machines when a human could do
it, and real food, none of this edible polyester that slips clear through you so
you can stay looking like a famine victim, my deah.

They came in when I was half finished with the omelet. Went all night by the
look and sound of them, but I didn't check their faces for broken hearts. Made
me nervous but I thought, well, they're tired; who's going to notice this old
lady? Nobody.

Wrong again. I became visible to them right after they got their retinas shot.
Seventeen-year-old boy with tattooed cheeks and a forked tongue leaned
forward and hissed like a snake.

"Sssssssinner."

The other four with him perked right up. "Where?" "Whose?" "In here?"

"Rock 'n' roll sssssssinner."

The lady identified me. She bore much resemblance to nobody at all, and if
she had a heart it wasn't even sprained a little. With a sinner, she was probably
Madame Magnifica. "Gina," she said, with all confidence.

My left eye tic'd. Oh, please. Feta cheese on my knees. What the hell, I thought,
I'll nod, they'll nod, I'll eat, I'll go. And then somebody whispered the word, *reward*.

I dropped my fork and ran.

Safe enough, I figured. Were they all going to chase me before they got their Greek breakfasts? No, they were not. They sent the lady after me.

She was much the younger, and she tackled me in the middle of a crosswalk when the light changed. A car hopped over us, its undercarriage just ruffling the top of her hard copper hair.

"Just come back and finish your omelet. Or we'll buy you another."

"No."

She yanked me up and pulled me out of the street. "Come on." People were staring, but Tremont's full of theaters. You see that here, live theater; you can still get it. She put a bring-along on my wrist and brought me along, back to the breakfast bar, where they'd sold the rest of my omelet at a discount to a bum. The lady and her group made room for me among themselves and brought me another cup of coffee.

"How can you eat and drink with a forked tongue?" I asked Tattooed Cheeks. He showed me. A little appliance underneath, like a *zipper*. The Featherweight to the left of the big boy on the lady's other side leaned over and frowned at me.

"Give us one good reason why we shouldn't turn you in for Man-O-War's reward."

I shook my head. "I'm through. This sinner's been absolved."

"You're legally bound by contract," said the lady. "But we could c'noodle something. Buy Man-O-War out, sue on your behalf for nonfulfillment. We're Misbegotten. Oley." She pointed at herself. "Pidge." That was the silent type next to her. "Percy." The big boy. "Krait." Mr. Tongue. "Gus." Featherweight. "We'll take care of you."

I shook my head again. "If you're going to turn me in, turn me in and collect. The credit ought to buy you the best sinner ever there was."

"We can be good to you."

"I don't have it anymore. It's gone. All my rock 'n' roll sins have been forgiven."

"Untrue," said the big boy. Automatically, I started to picture on him and shut it down hard. "Man-O-War would have thrown you out if it were gone. You wouldn't have to run."

"I didn't want to tell him. Leave me alone. I just want to go and sin no more, see? Play with yourselves, I'm not helping." I grabbed the counter with

---

both hands and held on. So what were they going to do, pop me one and carry me off?

As a matter of fact, they did.

In the beginning, I thought, and the echo effect was stupendous. *In the beginning . . . the beginning . . . the beginning . . .*

In the beginning, the sinner was not human. I know because I'm old enough to remember.

They were all there, little more than phantoms. Misbegotten. Where do they get those names? I'm old enough to remember. Oingo-Boingo and Bow-Wow-Wow. Forty, did I say? Oooh, just a little past, a little close to a lot. Old rockers never die, they just keep rocking on. I never saw The Who; Moon was dead before I was born. But I remember, barely old enough to stand, rocking in my mother's arms while thousands screamed and clapped and danced in their seats. *Start me up . . . if you start me up, I'll never stop . . .* 763 Strings did a rendition for elevator and dentist's office, I remember that, too. And that wasn't the worst of it.

They hung on the memories, pulling more from me, turning me inside out. *Are you experienced?* On a record of my father's because he'd died too, before my parents even met, and nobody else ever dared ask that question. Are *you* experienced? . . . *Well, I am.*

(Well, I am.)

Five against one and I couldn't push them away. Only, can you call it rape when you knew you're going to like it? Well, if I couldn't get away, then I'd give them the ride of their lives. *Jerkin' Crocus didn't kill me but she sure came near . . .*

The big boy faded in first, big and wild and too much badass to him. I reached out, held him tight, showing him. The beat from the night in the rain, I gave it to him, fed it to his heart and made him live it. Then came the lady, putting down the bass theme. She jittered, but mostly in the right places.

Now the Krait, and he was slithering around the sound, in and out. Never mind the tattooed cheeks, he wasn't just flash for the fools. He knew; you wouldn't have thought it, but he knew.

Featherweight and the silent type, melody and first harmony. Bad.

Featherweight was a disaster, didn't know where to go or what to do when he got there, but he was pitching ahead like the S.S. *Suicide*.

Christ. If they had to rape me, couldn't they have provided someone upright? The other four kept on, refusing to lose it, and I would have to make the best of it for all of us. Derivative, unoriginal—Featherweight did not rock. It was a crime, but all I could do was take them and shake them. Rock gods in the hands of an angry sinner.

They were never better. Small change getting a glimpse of what it was like to be big bucks. Hadn't been for Featherweight, they might have gotten all the way there. More groups now than ever there was, all of them sure that if they just got the right sinner with them, they'd rock the moon down out of the sky.

We maybe vibrated it a little before we were done. Poor old Featherweight.

I gave them better than they deserved, and they knew that too. So when I begged out, they showed me respect at last and went. Their techies were gentle with me, taking the plugs from my head, my poor old throbbing abused brokenhearted sinning head, and covered up the sockets. I had to sleep and they let me. I hear the man say, "That's a take, righteously. We'll rush it into distribution. Where in *hell* did you find that sinner?"

"Synthesizer," I muttered, already asleep. "The actual word, my boy, is synthesizer."

Crazy old dreams. I was back with Man-O-War in the big CA, leaving him again, and it was mostly as it happened, but you know dreams. His living room was half outdoors, half indoors, the walls all busted out. You know dreams; I didn't think it was strange.

Man-O-War was mostly undressed, like he'd forgotten to finish. Oh, that *never* happened. Man-O-War forget a sequin or a bead? He loved to act it out, just like the Krait.

"No more," I was saying, and he was saying, "But you don't know anything else, you shitting?" Nobody in the big CA kids, they all shit; loose juice.

"Your contract goes another two and I get the option, I always get the option. And you love it, Gina, you know that, you're no good without it."

And then it was flashback time and I was in the pod with all my sockets plugged, rocking Man-O-War through the wires, giving him the meat and bone that made him Man-O-War and the machines picking it up, sound and vision, so all the tube babies all around the world could play it on their screens whenever they wanted. Forget the road, forget the shows, too much trouble, and it wasn't like the tapes, not as exciting, even with the biggest FX, lasers, spaceships, explosions, no good. And the tapes weren't as good as the stuff in the head, rock 'n' roll visions straight from the brain. No hours of setup and hours more doctoring in the lab. But you had to get everyone in the group dreaming the same way. You needed a synthesis, and for that you got a synthesizer, not the old kind, the musical instrument, but something—somebody—to channel your group through, to bump up their tube-fed little souls, to rock them and roll them the way they couldn't do themselves. And anyone could be a rock 'n' roll hero then. Anyone!

In the end, they didn't have to play instruments unless they really wanted to, and why bother? Let the synthesizer take their imaginings and boost them up to Mount Olympus.

Synthesizer. Synner. Sinner.

Not just anyone can do that, sin for rock 'n' roll. I can.

But it's not the same as jumping all night to some bar band nobody knows yet . . . Man-O-War and his blown-out living room came back, and he said, "You rocked the walls right out of my house. I'll never let you go."

And I said, "I'm gone."

Then I was out, going fast at first because I thought he'd be hot behind me. But I must have lost him and then somebody grabbed my ankle.

Featherweight had a tray, he was Mr. Nursie-Angel-of- Mercy. Nudged the foot of the bed with his knee, and it sat me up slow. She rises from the grave, you can't keep a good sinner down.

"Here." He set the tray over my lap, pulled up a chair. Some kind of thick soup in a bowl he'd given me, with veg wafers to break up and put in. "Thought you'd want something soft and easy." He put his left foot up on his right leg and had a good look at it. "I *never* been rocked like that before."

"You don't have it, no matter who rocks you ever in this world. Cut and run, go into management. The *big* Big Money's in management."

He snacked on his thumbnail. "Can you always tell?"

"If the Stones came back tomorrow, you couldn't even tap your toes."

"What if you took my place?"

"I'm a sinner, not a clown. You can't sin and do the dance. It's been tried."

"*You* could do it. If anyone could."

"No."

His stringy cornsilk fell over his face and he tossed it back. "Eat your soup. They want to go again shortly."

"No." I touched my lower lip, thickened to sausage size. "I won't sin for Man-O-War and I won't sin for you. You want to pop me one again, go to. Shake a socket loose, give me aphasia."

So he left and came back with a whole bunch of them, techies and do-kids, and they poured the soup down my throat and gave me a poke and carried me out to the pod so I could make Misbegotten this year's firestorm.

I knew as soon as the first tape got out, Man-O-War would pick up the scent. They were already starting the machine to get me away from him. And they kept me good in the room—where their old sinner had done penance, the lady told me. Their sinner came to see me, too. I thought, poison dripping from his fangs, death threats. But he was just a guy about my age with a lot of hair to hide his sockets (I never bothered, didn't care if they showed). Just came to pay his respects, how'd I ever learn to rock the way I did?

Fool.

They kept me good in the room. Drunks when I wanted them and a poke to get sober again, a poke for vitamins, a poke to lose the bad dreams. Poke, poke, pig in a poke. I had tracks like the old B&O, and they didn't even know what I meant by that. They lost Featherweight, got themselves someone a little more righteous, someone who could go with it and work out, sixteen-year-old snip girl with a face like a praying mantis. But she rocked and they rocked and we all rocked until Man-O-War came to take me home.

Strutted into my room in full plumage with his hair all fanned out (hiding the sockets) and said, "Did you want to press charges, Gina darling?"

Well, they fought it out over my bed. When Misbegotten said I was theirs now, Man-O-War smiled and said, "Yeah, and I bought *you*. You're *all* mine now, you *and* your sinner. My sinner." That was truth. Man-O-War had his conglomerate start to buy Misbegotten right after the first tape came out. Deal all done by the time we'd finished the third one, and they never knew.

Conglomerates buy and sell all the time. Everybody was in trouble but Man-O-War. And me, he said. He made them all leave and sat down on my bed to re-lay claim to me.

"Gina." Ever see honey poured over the edge of a sawtooth blade? Every hear it? He couldn't sing without hurting someone bad and he couldn't dance, but inside, he rocked. If I rocked him.

"I don't want to be a sinner, not for you or anyone."

"It'll all look different when I get you back to Cee-Ay."

"I want to go to a cheesy bar and boogie my brains till they leak out the sockets."

"No more, darling. That was why you came here, wasn't it? But all the bars are gone and all the bands. Last call was years ago; it's all up here now. All up here." He tapped his temple. "You're an old lady, no matter how much I spend keeping your bod young. And don't I give you everything? And didn't you say I had it?"

"It's not the same. It wasn't meant to be put on a tube for people to *watch*."

"But it's not as though rock 'n' roll is dead, lover."

"You're killing it."

"Not me. You're trying to bury it alive. But I'll keep you going for a long, long time."

"I'll get away again. You'll either rock 'n' roll on your own or give it up, but you won't be taking it out of me any more. This ain't my way, it ain't my time. Like the man said, 'I don't live today.'"

Man-O-War grinned. "And like the other man said, 'Rock 'n' roll never forgets.'"

He called in his do-kids and took me home.

BLUE CLAY BLUES

By Gwyneth Jones

Somewhere on the outskirts of town, the air suddenly smelled of rain. The change was so concrete and so ravishing that Johnny stopped the car. He got out, leaving Bella strapped in the back seat. She was asleep, thank God. The road punched straight on, rigid to the flat horizon. The metaled surface was in poor repair. It seemed to have been spread from the crown with a grudging hand, smearing out into brown dirt and gravel long before it reached the original borderline. There were trees at the fences of dusty and weed-grown yards; clapboard houses stood haphazard amid broken furniture and rusted consumer durables. The town went on like this, never thickening into a center, as far as the eye could see. The rain was coming up from the south, a purple wall joining sky and earth. It smelled wonderful, truly magical. There were a few rumbles of thunder knocking around the cloudy sky. He hoped for lightning.

It took longer than he'd thought. He reached in and picked up his phone from the seat, called Izzy again. He'd been calling her all day, leaving messages on the board. These repeated phone calls from an irate spouse would be the talk of the floor, Izzy's workplace was that kind of petty. He knew she'd hate it, she would be made miserable by the piddling notoriety. He was partly disgusted at himself, but not disgusted enough to stop.

The arrangement was that Johnny looked after Bella, and when he was on a trip she went into daycare. It was a good arrangement, except when all the emergency routines failed at once. It had broken down seriously yesterday. He had had to leave town with the baby. He had been trying to contact Izzy ever since, but they kept missing each other, with almost mythological symmetry. Every time he ran his messages, his wife jabbered at him in gradations of bewildered panic. Every time he called her, her number was busy.

Now she was at work, where they didn't allow personal phones on the floor, and he was twenty-four hours out in the boondocks with a two-year-old in tow. She couldn't be too badly worried, though: he was keeping her well-informed.

He stood and watched the advancing wall, brooding sourly on the amount of work he put into their relationship. He had practically invented everything, all the little rituals of bonding. He wondered did Izzy feel that she was doing the same: building their life together, brick by sodding brick. Maybe she did. It's called marriage. It works, more or less.

The tow truck careened to a halt, followed by three motorbikes. Three men got out of the cab. The bikers remained mounted. Johnny still had the phone in his hand. He took a step, casually, and let it drop onto the driver's seat.

"What's the problem, kid?"

The speaker was tall and basically skinny, but with bull shoulders and heavy arms from some kind of specific training, or maybe manual labor. He was inappropriately dressed: a suit jacket over bib overalls, no shirt. The rest were the same—not exactly ragged, but it was clear they'd left certain standards far behind. They were all of them technically white, a couple dusky; a shade further off the WASP ideal than himself. Every one of them was armed.

Johnny immediately realized that these people would find an aesthetic impulse hard to understand. It would be as well not to brand himself a city slicker, to whom rainfall is a spectacle.

"Some kind of breakdown?"

"I guess so," said Johnny. "Engine died, no reason why. I was about to look under the hood."

"Whaddya use for fuel?" A biker, nursing his mighty steed between his knees, seemed amiably curious.

"Uh—just about anything."

"Well, all we got is just about plain gas." The bikers laughed, contemptuous of city-slicker modernity.

Ouch. That was a warning. Don't pretend to be too like them. They'll always smell you out.

"Let's take a look."

The man in the suit jacket bent over Johnny"s engine. He took his time, considering there was absolutely nothing wrong. Johnny's assistance didn't seem to be required, which was good because he didn't feel like turning his back, and particularly not like bending over in a peculiarly vulnerable invitation . . . The other two men from the truck came close. They looked into the back of the car and saw Bella—whose existence had, for the past few minutes, vanished from Johnny's consciousness. Something, some lax, living system inside him—blood or lymph or nerves—went bone tight from the crown of his head to his heels.

"That your kid?"

"Yes, she's my kid."

"Can you prove you're the father?"

This bloodcurdling question did not require an answer. As Johnny mumbled "Why yes, certainly. . ." the speaker, a squat youth in baggy cutoffs worn over a stained but gaudy one-piece that surely belonged in another tribal culture altogether, turned away. The guy in the suit jacket slammed the hood down saying, "Yep. That certainly is a catastrophic breakdown."

At the same moment Johnny understood that the truck, which he'd taken to be a mere accidental prop, was here on purpose. A chill and horror of excitement ran through him. He was afraid he was shivering visibly—but in fact he'd have had some excuse because just then the rain arrived. It fell over the whole scene like a roll of silk tossed down, as purple as it had looked on the horizon: scented and cold and shocking.

"What's your name, boy?"

"Johnny."

"What d'you do?"

"Uh—I'm an engineer."

"Looking for work? We could find you some. You need a wife to go with that kid. We got women too."

This banter didn't mean anything. Johnny had discovered that everywhere you go in the boondocks, people will invite you to stay. It seemed a point of etiquette to regard any chance comer as a potential addition to the community. It wasn't something to worry about, no more than the equal number of brief acquaintances who invited you to take them home, see their kids through college, advance the capital for them to set up in business. Banter covered the positioning of the truck, the chaining up of Johnny's car, all under the hammering of the purple rain. Johnny, expressing decent but not effusive gratitude, got into the back with Bella, who woke as the car was being winched onto the flatbed. She didn't speak or wail but stared all around her mightily. He could tell she'd been dreaming.

"It's okay, Bel. The car broke down. These people are giving us a ride into town."

"Daddy, why are you wet?"

"It's raining."

Bella stared with eyes like saucers, and dawning appreciation of this new means of transport, this audience, this adventure. The bikers peered in at her. "Who's that?" she demanded. "What's his name?" It was the stocky young one. She could never be brought to believe that there were people in the world whose names her parents did not know. "Archibald," said Johnny at random. He spent the rest of the trip naming the other men in the same mode, and explaining over and over that the car was suddenly sick and needed a car-doctor: over and over again, while he made desperate mental tape of their route and reviewed worst-case scenarios, and still found a little space in which to want to kill Izzy, just beat her to shit. He knew she wasn't to blame but she was the other half of his mind, and the fight-or-flight rush had to have some outlet.

The drive ended at a wired compound, shrouded by tall dark hedges. Inside, there was a wide yard and flat-topped buildings that looked somehow like a school. The rain made the wall of leaves glow blue-black, and glistened on piles of automotive rubbish. Dogs rushed to the gates as the bikers dragged them open, snarling and yelping away from kicks. Bella was scared. Johnny got down with the toddler fastened on his chest like a baby monkey, his pack on his back and jacket bulging. He surrendered his keys with a good grace.

"Papers?"

Out here, you had to carry physical documentation. It was a bitch because most of them couldn't read, and just got mad at you while they were trying to decipher your life's history. He handed over his folder, hoping the boss, at least, was literate.

He wished he had the nerve to leave some of his stuff in the car. It would have looked better, he knew. He staggered under his untrusting assumptions, and they led him off to a hall with a scuffed floor of light timber and rows of plastic chairs. The room smelt of kids. He decided that this was the school, in so far as such things still existed. A school, and a junkyard: original combination for some gifted entrepreneur.

"We'll take a look, Johnny, just you wait here."

One of the bikers—Samuel—watched them through the fireproof glass of the hall doors. Bella was unusually silent—most unusually, because he knew she was riveted with excitement. He looked around, and found that she was sitting, legs jutting over the edge of the scummy plastic seat, with one hand ruminatively delving under her skirt. Her expression was of dignified, speculative pleasure.

Johnny managed to smother hysterical giggles. "Get your hand out of your pants, Bel. People don't like to see that. It doesn't look good."

This condemnation—always in a tone of mild and absolute certainty—was the worst her daddy ever issued. Bella understood that concern for the comfort of others and respect for their beliefs was to be her ultimate morality. She removed her hand with a sigh.

"My nobble went fat. It went by itself."

"Yeah, I know. It's the adrenaline rush. Ignore it, kid."

Samuel—stringy and pale, with ropy muscled arms and a ponytail—came to fetch them. They were led into a cavern of a mechanic's workshop. The foreign and menacing smell of heavy oil filled the air. Johnny's car stood openmouthed on black greasy concrete, surrounded by a slew of tools and power leads. It looked as if the poor beast had been through a rough grilling. Johnny hoped it had managed to hold out.

The mechanic inspected them. Johnny had rarely met a black man outside the city. Tribal divisions were so stern it would have been pointless to send a white boy off the white squares, under no matter what inalienable flag of truce. But this man's color was only the least of the signals he sent out. Johnny gathered that he was looking at the local God, the big chief.

God was very dark, perhaps fortyish (but Johnny was always making mistakes about age out here), with sleepy narrow eyes and a whisper of moustache above his humorous mouth. Johnny liked him on sight; and was no less very scared indeed. He slid Bel to the ground but kept a tight grip. The wrist, not the hand. One learns these tricks of technique.

The mechanic wiped his hands on a dirty rag.

"You ain't armed, boy."

A man without a gun on his hip was so peculiar he was downright threatening. Johnny didn't mean to threaten anybody.

"I'm a journalist."

"Ah-ha. Thought you said you were an engineer."

God speaks grammatical English, when he chooses.

"Engineer—journalist. I'm an eejay."

God's courtiers displayed a hearteningly normal reaction. Samuel giggled, nudged Ernesto in the ribs; Gustave hooted.

"Hey, eejay. You wanna mend my TV?" Archibald grinned.

Florimond in the suit jacket cuffed him and shrugged at the visitor, assuming an air of grave man-to-man sophistication.

"Okay. So what story are you hunting, newshound?" Unlike the others, God was not impressed by the eejay tag.

But Johnny was still recovering from Bella's masterstroke: from finding himself sitting in a gangster's waiting room with a two-year-old who was calmly taking the opportunity to get in touch with her emotions ... Smothered hilarity maybe gave him an aura so inappropriate as to shift the balance. As the man spoke, the casual promise of death that hung around him became less palpable. Johnny's territorial blunder might be excused.

The courtiers grew quiet. Bella squirmed and tugged, displaying her usual pathological failure to read adult atmosphere—which at this moment made Johnny long to break her arm.

"It's kind of private."

"Let the kid go, boy. She won't hurt anything."

Bella bounced free. "I won't hurt anything," she parroted smugly.

She was gone, beyond arm's reach. Gustave was lifting her up to peer inside the poor tortured car. Johnny felt sweat breaking out delicately all over his body.

"Look. This is not necessarily the truth, but . . . I'm after the source of a kind of legend. You had a nuclear accident hereabouts, two years ago?"

The reading in God's eyes flickered upward again. Johnny had better not dwell on this subject—nuclear poison, two-headed babies, that kind of insulting stuff.

"We had an incident."

"Okay, I'm looking for . . . this will sound crazy, unless you know something already, but I'm looking for a diamond mine."

"Diamonds."

"It's like this. When you get a melt—er, an incident of that kind, a massive amount of heat and pressure is generated. The safer the plant, the less of it gets dissipated outward. It has to go somewhere, it goes down. You've got coal-bearing strata around here, not all of it even mapped. Under pressure, that old fossil fuel can be transformed into another kind of pure carbon. What I'm looking for is a deposit of blue clay, a blue clay that's new to this area. From the blue clay, you get the diamonds."

Johnny needed all his professional skill to measure God's reaction. He couldn't use it. His attention was painfully focused on Bel: her position in the stinking cavern, who was touching her, was she being led near a door. It didn't matter. God was stonefaced, neither twitchy nor incredulous.

"I don''t know if this is exactly a newslead," Johnny went on, straightfaced. "It's my own long shot. I haven't decided yet if my employer would have an interest."

God laughed softly, and shook his head in reproof (we superbeings must stick together).

"If you dig up a diamond mine on your boss''s time, I guess those are her diamonds, boy. Take a closer look at that employment contract of yours, you'll find I'm right. Which leaves you with nothing to sell, and here you are in the market. That could be an embarrassing position."

Johnny would have to agree. God didn't ask his opinion. He tucked away his rag and thrust out a hand, which Johnny shook obediently.

"I'm the schoolmaster around here. Schoolmaster and mechanic. I've seen boys like you. I've liked boys like you: smart and sweet, and a trifle off the rails. Don't you go too far, Johnny. Stick to what's right."

Potato-headed young Gustave, with the scoured red complexion, came over and delivered Bella into her Daddy's arms.

"You're a mite loaded down, kid. If you need anything else from the car, you better point."

He shook his head. God was being sarcastic: the city slicker's distrust had been noted. God nodded, and considered Bella.

"She's a pretty little girl. You're young to be her daddy."

Johnny was young to be anybody's daddy, as anyone would know if they knew the way things worked indoors. Not only a city slicker, but a rich fucking gilded youth. Oh, shit.

"Can you prove she's your child?"

The hotel had rooms over a bar that was also a diner. Johnny walked into the desolate lobby with his escort. Gustave leaned over and took one of the keys, an archaic looped shank with wards of metal and a tag, number 5, dangling. The woman behind the desk glanced up.

"Hi, Donny." She studied the new guest. "This the eejay?"

He'd been in town two hours, plenty of time for the grapevine. He was surprised the desk clerk wasn't more excited. She looked at him solemnly, a little too long—and still without gushing, exclaiming, or using his name. Johnny felt a prickling in his belly. Maybe she was just a serious-minded girl.

There were other guests, but Johnny was the only stranger. While the rain sheared down outside everybody gathered: the men and youths around Johnny, the women and children several tables away, beyond the single-screen TV that kept babbling away on a cable channel Johnny had never seen before.

There were, discernibly, at least two rival camps. But nothing bad happened. No guns were pulled.

These people got married. They had family life, of a kind. But they'd forgotten anything they ever knew about sexual equality. Not one of the gaunt and battered-looking females would dare to come up to the men's group, sit directly in front of the screen: get between a man and anything remotely like the goodies. None of them, of course, could talk to Johnny. It was one of those things you must not mention. The men'd be outraged and disgusted if you hinted there was anything weird about this arrangement. The women too, probably.

The guys were prodding for details of life "inside the dome." Their technique was to make a casual remark, about the electro-paralytic force-field or the death-rays wielded by the android guards—and watch the effect it had on Johnny. He was kept busy protecting their egos. He knew better than to contradict them directly over anything. It would be a dangerous kindness.

He felt like the Wizard of Oz.

Bella got bored and went to stare at the local kids. The women petted her, admiring her plump arms and legs: her strapping size compared to their own toddlers. Johnny discussed diamond mining with bared teeth and needles of controlled panic rammed under his fingernails. The women were far more scary than the men. If one of them was to take Bel and go, out into the drenching purple night, *what could he do?*

Meanwhile, the desk clerk who was also the waitress kept passing to and fro. She was breaking the rules, but she seemed to have some kind of special license. Every time she passed she would find a way to flirt: leaning over a nearby table to show her neat butt, reaching up to a shelf to give him the taut curve of her breast and waist. Every small town has to have its bad girl. The younger men hooted and flicked her behind. The other women, young and old, pretended not to notice.

The party broke up at last. Johnny lay staring at the gray ceiling of room 5, and at the inevitable cam—eye circled with its thoughtful message *for your protection*. The rain had stopped. The main street outside was noisy with the home-going populace. Must've been about every able-bodied soul in town.

He'd brought Bella out before, but never so far and nothing had ever gone wrong. He considered how important it was for him to believe that it was safe. No danger, no harm, there are decent people everywhere. The upholding of some kind of liberal ideal was apparently worth more to him than his child's life and safety.

They could take Bella away from me.

Walking into that bar with her had been like shooting his cuff to display an antique gold Rolex. Madness! He could try to tell them Bel was a perfectly ordinary little girl, produced by traditional methods and complete with organically grown blemishes (she had a crowded mouth, and a tendency to stand over on her inherited weak ankles). You wouldn't get people out here to believe it, when they saw her next to their own scrawny, undersized, scabby-faced kids. To believe Bella was ordinary they'd have to accept that Johnny wasn't weirdly privileged, Johnny was *normal* . . . They'd have to see how far they'd fallen.

You wouldn't want to wish that on them.

Two hundred miles from NYC. There was no protection, no law, no appeal. From the moment that tow truck appeared he had been in trouble. He would be criminally crazy not to cut his losses and get out—even if he were alone. But he hated to give up. He was on the track of a story, and he *knew* he was in the right place. If God didn't know why the fuck he was here; if God was convinced by the spurious dazzle of irradiated gemstones—*somebody* must know better. That somebody would come to Johnny. He didn't have to do anything but wait.

He linked his hands behind his head, and thought about sex. He recalled Bella's experiment in the school hall. She was her father's child all right.

She'd made that vital connection so naturally—doubt and danger and a mellow hint of violence . . . whoo, up we go. It wasn't likely that Johnny was heading for a real amorous adventure. Things weren't so different in that area, inside the city or out. But the sex stuff could come in useful, just because it was in short supply. It was a greed that could cover for anything.

There was a knock on the door.

"Come in."

The desk clerk shut the door and sat down on the edge of the bed.

"Hi, Johnny."

She seemed older than he was, but she was probably a teenager. She had stringy dark blonde hair cut in a bob. Blue eyes, a wiry unkempt body in a faded overall, an out-of-doors suntan that was ruining her skin. She smiled with her eyes and touched his pant leg, as if she were testing if it was still damp.

She glanced upward. "It's okay, Donny's minding the store. He never checks the screens, and this one don't work anyhow. I put you in here on purpose."

A heavy, warning wink told him he wasn't meant to be reassured. Donny, aka Gustave, was undoubtedly glued to the most promising peephole in town.

"Well, stranger, can we do business?" She took her hand from his leg and touched herself, both palms smoothing the slick worn fabric over her breasts. "I don't want money. I want a ride. I don't belong to anyone, you've no need to worry."

She was in a big hurry, but that was reasonable enough. Johnny would be gone tomorrow.

"What's your name?"

"Cambridge."

"That's the name of a city."

"I know. My momma liked the sound. You ever been there? The English one? I like to think it's the original I'm called for."

"No, I can't say I have." Johnny watched her, not moving a muscle. "I can't get you into the city, you know that. I suspect you're an agent provocateur, ma'am."

"Hey, no way. I'm not going to get you into trouble. I just want a ride down the road, a change of scene. And I can get you out of the trouble you happen to be in."

She winked her steamroller wink again. "Get rid of those ants in your pants, city boy?" She squeezed his thigh, and giggled. Her eyes, which the camera couldn't see, were deadly serious.

"If a girl wants to get on, she has to be ready to act fast. That's the *shape of things* to come, don't you think? You can't act like the old technology, sit there waiting for the current. You gotta be able to *change yourself*, to fit what's coming at you."

Johnny was wrestling with his conscience. This could so easily be a trap. He would accept the clerk's offer (what city slicker would refuse a loose woman?). The vigilantes would burst in. There would be some kind of ersatz legal procedure, God probably presiding. The boondocks were hot on sexual restraint. Notwithstanding her behavior downstairs it would be Johnny's fault. The stranger caught in the act of fornication—maybe statutory rape—would be declared unfit to be in charge of a minor. All he knew about the "blue clay" could be beaten out of him on the side. He could see how tempting it looked. They'd have Bella and the diamonds. Johnny would be dumped naked out on the road—dead or alive. Dead, for preference, rather than explain himself to Izzy. He should not even dream of taking the risk.

On the other hand, all his instincts promised that the clerk was not laying *that* kind of trap.

"I don't know if you have the right idea about me. I take risks, that's my job. But not for trivial reasons."

"I felt that. I can read people . . . pretty well." She smiled, ruefully. "This may sound crazy, but I've always thought I could have been an eejay. If someone like me could have the chance."

"I wish that everyone could have the chance," said Johnny.

She nodded, head bent.

"Mr. Micane's got you all wrong, in my opinion. This blue clay that you're looking for, it doesn't represent any kind of material gain. The diamonds don't mean anything . . . to you. What you really want is, like, *a sense of living meaning* in your life. Something rare and magic that could unite everyone."

"It's true, *living* with *meaning* is a dream of mine," he agreed—with the accent on the two special words.

"I've had that dream too."

She gave him a long and tender look. It thrilled Johnny to the core. This was a real contact. He wondered how much she could be persuaded to tell.

Cambridge tossed back her hair. "Okay, mister eejay. After the highfaluting come-on, do we have a deal?"

He glanced around the room, swiftly up and away at the "defective" camera. "Um—can we go somewhere?"

"You want me to take you home?" She walked to the door. Leaned there, in a pose from some ancient movie. "I come off shift in an hour. There's a dark blue Nissan in the parking lot. I'll meet you beside it." She grinned up at the eye in the ceiling. "I'll take you where there's no protection. Can you do it without an audience, eejay? Ever tried?"

Johnny put his gear together. He was rapturously busy for a few minutes, during which Bella vanished as she had by the roadside. Then he remembered her. He stared at the sleeping baby, chewing his lower lip.

Next to the Japanese antique there was an ancient pickup, the color of its paint indeterminate in the yellow light of the oil lamps that guarded the hotel's rear. Cambridge looked out of the dark cab. She was silently amazed.

"I couldn't leave her. She'd wake and be scared."

She looked him over. "Is that a gun in your pocket?"

"No, it's a spare diaper."

The clerk shook her head, pushed open the other door for him. He clambered, arranging Bel's warm bulk in the baby carrier on his knees. They were jolting away, lightless, through the dark town, before she managed to come up with a comment.

"In my world, men don't bring up kids. They just own them." She chuckled. "Hey, what happens when we get to our love nest? Does she like to watch, or have you trained her to take part?"

Mental tape: a long drive. The darkness was haunted by the ghosts of well-kept lawns and scampering retriever dogs, boys on bicycles, flung newspapers and mailboxes on sticks. It was a world that Johnny had never known—inaccessible now except on records as hard to decipher as incunabula to an eye reared on print. How did people make out that stuff? Depthless, even colorless. Johnny imagined skills lost to him forever, the genes for watching b&w TV switched off in his decadent blood. He hugged Bella in her frame sling. The feel of her was so immensely reassuring, he thought all secret agents should have a baby to carry. When you can't trust anyone, and it's against the rules for you to be sure what's going on—you hug your baby, and she keeps you sane.

They parked among trees.

"What the fuck was all that nonsense about jewelry, anyway?"

Johnny shrugged. "Best I could do. I didn't expect to be picked up like that. Had to send out some kind of signal. I could see I wasn't going to get much chance to nosey around asking questions."

"You're right. And you're lucky. Micane's not stupid, you know. He's just short of information. Like all of us out here. Okay, come on. You take some tape of the crown jewels, and hurry the record back to your magic dome."

"Please. I don't live in a 'dome.' I live in an overgrown shopping mall. With dirt in the corners, and plenty of problems."

Cambridge smiled, humoring him. "Sure you do."

She opened a door, steps led down. When he realized they were going underground, he understood the dazzling truth. She wasn't leading him to a bargaining rendezvous with the cadre. She had brought him straight to the goods. The room was shadowy, echoing, with a low and bowing ceiling and a strange incline. The walls, replying to Cambridge's pencil light, gleamed phosphorescent pale.

"What is this place?"

"It was a swimming pool," she said. "Olympic pool. It's been drained and boarded over for years. No water. Rest of the building's derelict."

She'd changed into pants, jacket, and a sweater. The rain had made the night cool. Her clothes were as squalid, strange-colored, and ill-fitting as the things the men wore, but not filthy. She pulled a clunky black plastic remote out of her waistband and keyed lights. Must be a generator on site.

Johnny stared. The glass and ceramic labyrinth: the vats. It was the real thing, a coralin plant in full production. He'd spent time in legal protein-chip production, in his apprenticeship—if only in virtuality. It wouldn't have helped. The processing here was too makeshift to be precisely recognizable. But he'd also been tutored, unofficially, by people who knew the wild side.

He took the time to settle Bella on his shoulders. She had woken up in the pickup, but only to ask a few drowsy questions. What's her name . . . What's this car's name. She was asleep again (and the pickup was called Laetitia). He was proud of her. She was really the perfect child.

"I can make tape?"

Cambridge nodded. "That's the deal, eejay. We'll get you away from Micane. You tell the folks back home what we have here."

He mugged amazement, let her know how thrilled he was to find this spore of civilization outside the citadel: wondering all the while where the rest of the group was, where they'd gotten the starter, all sorts of questions to which he ought to get answers. But he already knew that Cambridge was going to tell him everything. He was stunned by her group's trust, embarrassed by the power of his job's reputation.

It had been obvious before the end of the twentieth century that the future of data-processing and telecoms was in photochemistry. Chlorophyll in green plants converts light—energy into excited molecules without thinking twice about it. The "living chip" was inevitable: compact and fast. They called the magic stuff of the semi-living processors "blue clay" because the original protein goop was blue-green in color. Embedded in a liquid crystalline membrane, blue clay became a single surface of endlessly complex interconnections. Under massive magnification it looked like a coral: hence the other name, coralin. Clay? Because you can make it do anything.

So much for the technology. But then the networks, silicon and gallium-arsenide based, had crashed in the explosion of virus infection that ended the century. Coralin wasn't greatly superior at that point, but it was immune to the plagues. In a deteriorating political situation—a foundering economy, wave upon wave of environmental disasters—the blue clay had become political dynamite. It meant power.

Diamonds? It was a stupid cover, but good enough for the spur of the moment. Out here, a coralin plant was worth more than a truckload of gems. If the masses who lived outside the citadels could build themselves some modern data processing they could hook up into the city networks. They'd be up and running again, and the elite who lived indoors would be running scared. The amazing thing was that more of the masses didn't try. They accepted, with chilling calm, that a certain way of life was over. They had their own world with its own rules, and the cities were on another planet.

Johnny made tape, describing how it really was a coralin plant, and the journey he'd made to find it. He walked the aisles, the 360 cam on his headset taking in every angle. Cambridge stayed off camera. She didn't want to wave to the public.

He finished. They faced each other: two nodes of a diffuse molecular machine, linked by the lock and key action of certain key phrases hoicked out of the romance of molecular technology. *The living meaning, not like the old technology, change yourself to fit what's coming at you.* Johnny was uneasy. He had not deceived her, not actively. But she was deceived, and it was making him uncomfortable.

"You're a union activist, aren't you," she said.

"Yeah," he laughed nervously. "A cellar unionist."

She had been tough and worldly wise to his soft city-boy, a rough diamond. Down at the deep end, in the pallid glow of the drained pool, the balance between them was reversed.

"You came out here to find us. What can I say? I feel . . . found. Like a toy left out in the rain, that thought the kids would never come back to look for her. I feel rescued."

Johnny chewed his lip. Bella wriggled and muttered. One of her knees started butting him in the ribs. She couldn't get comfortable and she was going to wake. She weighed a ton.

"D'you ever hear about the phylloxera beetle?" he said. "It's a similar story. It's a kind of bug, it spreads like a virus. Once upon a time, all the good wine came from France. They had the vines. The quality, wonderful ancient-lineaged plants. Then someone accidentally shipped in some phylloxera beetles, and the whole of French viticulture was devastated. They had to rip the lot out and start again . . . with vines from North America, where the bug was endemic and the native vines had natural resistance. In a generation nobody could tell the difference. The wine-drinking public forgot it had ever happened."

"Phylloxera-proof telephones," said Cambridge. "Knowing what's happening in the next state. Bank credit. No more of that fucking censored cable TV. God. I can't believe it."

Johnny registered something moving behind him. The lights were off at the shallow end, but the 360 showed Gustave coming down the steps. Johnny controlled himself with an enormous effort. Among these people you must not show fear.

"Micane's guys are here," he told her softly. Cambridge didn't make a fuss. She eased past Johnny and walked up between the workbenches, raising

215

more lights with the remote in her hand. The bikers, Samuel and Ernesto, emerged into brilliance. Gustave-Donny stared around him in disbelief.

"What the fuck is this place?"

The clerk held up her remote as if it were a weapon, and carefully tossed it down.

"What's goin' on, Cams?"

"Nothin'. Just a little private interview with the eejay."

This God's rule had some tinge of humanity. In other places, behavior as aberrant as this would have got them their heads blown away, straight off. But Gustave didn't open fire.

"You expect me to believe that? You're crazy."

He jerked his shotgun for Johnny and Cambridge to go up the steps ahead. When he registered Bella, he started as if someone had dropped ice down his neck.

"Fuck!"

He pulled the headset from Johnny, carefully so's not to disturb the child. He smashed it, conclusively, against the tiled wall of the stair, and handed it back with a defiant glare.

That was *bad*. Out in the wasteland gun waving was endemic, male display behavior, not so dangerous as it looks. But the engineer-journalist was sacred; his tools even more so. He was the only link with the rest of the world. Johnny's calm left him; fear plummeted through him . . .

"Fucking weirdos."

The tow truck was outside. Johnny got Bella on his knees. She woke up and began to cry. Ernesto crouched on the flatbed, the muzzle of his shotgun through the glassless rear window of the cab. It pressed against Johnny's neck. Samuel's bike roared in escort. Young Gustave drove with one hand, the other awkwardly stabbing his gun into Cambridge's ribs. His eyes were wild with anger and humiliation: he'd been taken in completely. Worse (Johnny read), he feared that his God had been taken in too.

"Fucking diamond mine!" he wailed. "What the fuck you growing back there, Cams? Illegal drugs?"

Cambridge kept her eyes front. Through his own blank-brain panic Johnny could feel her arm and side against him, rigid with terror. But for Donny-Gustave she sneered the way she'd sneered when he was six and she was ten.

"Nah. Mutants, Donny. Cannibal mutant babies. And they're coming for you. Not tonight, maybe not tomorrow night—"

"Fucking shut up." His face in the driver's mirror was a darkly crumpled rectangle of hurt. "I never would've believed an eejay would be into drugs . . ."

Bella's loud and violent sobbing—so rare and devastating, this child's crying—was like a wall around them both. Johnny held her tight and vowed that he was going to get Bella out of this alive. There was no betrayal he would not gladly embrace—if only, please God, he was given the chance.

"Shut the kid up!"

Cambridge yelled back indignantly. "Are you kidding? How are we going to do that? She's terrified!"

Her courage was like a lifeline. He dropped into character . . . "Look, I don't know what's wrong, we weren't doing anything wrong, we wanted to be private, kind of get to know each other. Would we be doing anything dirty with the kid there?" He babbled, injecting innocent panic into the real thing. He hunched himself forward, arms and head between Bella and the guns. She could feel that he was back in control—throat-chokingly, fearfully sweet the way she suddenly obeyed his shushing and went silent: her small hands clutching his collar, her wet face against his neck . . .

Donny-Gustave looked around with a bitter scowl.

"You and Cams was just holding hands? What about all that *stuff*? Looked like some kind of heroin still to me."

The tow truck bucketed, its mean yellow lights barely cutting the darkness. Cambridge ducked her head and made herself small between the men, fists burrowed in her jacket pockets, letting them fight it out. Johnny couldn't remember his next line. Gustave was going to crash the damn truck. He thought he was going to pass out, the situation was so consummately awful— when *slam*, the shotgun muzzle behind his ear suddenly dealt a numbing, stinging blow to the corner of his jaw.

He yelled, sure he was dying. There was another explosion, unbelievably close. The truck slewed. Bella whimpered. Cold outdoor air belched into the cab. Johnny lifted his ringing head. A mess of dark movement resolved itself into Cambridge, hanging onto the wheel and wrestling with something flailing and heavy at the flown-open door.

"Take the wheel!" she screamed.

Johnny grabbed, and shoved Bella—dead silent—in her carrier into the well in front of the bench.

"Keep your head down, baby."

She ducked. The top of her dark head was all his eyes could see. He grappled blindly—the dumb-animal feel of the ancient machine piling in with the heavy scuffle going on beside him, a blur of confusion. Donny's body fell out into the night. Cambridge hauled the door shut. Johnny slid over. She drove the truck. The road was dark and empty, no sign of the second biker.

"Who shot him?"

"Who d'you think?"

He looked over his shoulder. The second of Micane's guys was a slumped heap.

"God. Who shot *him?*"

"I didn't go out to the plant with you alone, what did you think? Donny drove into an ambush. Don't look so fucking shocked, eejay. Why didn't the stupid bastard frisk me, if he wanted to stay alive?"

"Is he dead? Are they dead?"

"I hope so." Her teeth were chattering.

A mile or so down the road she pulled in. There were no lights, no houses visible in a strange outdoor darkness, faintly tinged with starlight. The three of them got down. Johnny at last could tug Bella out of the sling and hug her properly. Her eyes were huge and black in her dim face. A little child sometimes seems like a machine. Switch off, switch on: no memory, each event fresh and untainted. She leaned back and stared.

"Stars!"

He hadn't known she knew what that word meant, not clearly enough to apply it out here.

The man on the back of the truck made no sound. Somewhere on the road another two human beings lay: Gustave and Samuel. Johnny wanted to go to the man on the flatbed, but the silence of that huddled thing was intimidating. Johnny's responses were from another planet. He didn't know what Cambridge was thinking. Maybe simply breathing, standing there and breathing. She'd shot someone. How could Johnny imagine the afterburn of that?

He thought of the desk clerk's life, and how her spunky intelligence had won her a place with the boys, but only on condition she played by their rules. And only till she got pregnant, or fell in love. Then she'd be one of those gap-toothed, horny-skinned women, "married" to some junior male: property to be abused. She'd have a string of sickly kids, her whole life the struggle to keep one or two of them alive to adulthood. The bad clothes looked ethnic and interesting on the others. On Cambridge they were shameful. She was a real human person. She shouldn't be here, she should have a future.

"I hope . . ." The clerk shuddered. "I hope Donny's . . . I didn't shoot to kill. Look, don't blame yourself, eejay. You wouldn't be here if we hadn't been sending out our own signals, well as we could. We knew we couldn't keep what was going on from Micane much longer. We need some support. After what's happened tonight, we'll need it more. But Micane's on the slide. With help, we can take over . . . I'm real sorry about the cam."

She looked at the child. "Is having her some kind of cover? Or do you honest to God look after her? I mean, like a woman?"

"No," said Johnny, painfully aware of the truth. "I look after her like a man. It's a start. I do my best."

He held Bella like a shield. Cambridge's movement toward him went unfinished. She touched Bel, awkwardly patting the little girl's head.

"Stay here. Someone will bring your car."

When she was gone, Johnny and Bella walked around a little: admiring the stars and bumping into a few trees. She'd soiled herself. This didn't generally happen any more at night, but he could hardly blame her. He managed to change her, Bella standing, holding onto him with the crotch of her night suit dangling between her knees. He hugged her in a daze of gratitude. "You and me against the world, Bel," he whispered. He gave her some dried snack fruit, and she asked him when they were going home.

He hoped the desk clerk's story was the truth. He didn't want to blame himself for three murders. But the black man's dominance must have been threatened for a long time, if his rivals had been able to set up a coralin plant under his nose. Since power couldn't change hands out here without violence, it wasn't Johnny's fault. If it hadn't been over the plant, it would have been something else.

He thought of setting off into this savage utter wilderness. But he didn't have a spare diaper any more, and the prospect of hitchhiking, even in daylight, was not appealing. An hour passed. His global-mobile was in his pocket. He didn't feel like calling anyone. No more signals . . . The coralin chip in its heart, like the processor in his cam, was practically sterile. But you weren't supposed to take any chances.

He thought of the starter that Cam's cadre had gotten hold of. They were no biochemists, they didn't build it from scratch. He imagined a brother eejay dead out here, or stripped of his magic and too ashamed ever to come home . . .

Bella, he found, was happier on his back. He walked her, holding hands over his shoulder, singing nursery rhymes. She didn't say a thing about guns, or shooting, or bad guys. Which didn't mean this adventure hadn't scarred her for life. He writhed to think of the debriefing he'd have to go through with Izzy.

When he heard the car he hid until he was sure it was his own, and the driver was Cambridge, and there was no one else with her. She handed over a sliver of plastic card—his key. It was good to have that safely back in his hand.

They stood by the car. Johnny put the sidelights on dim, so he could see her face a little.

Boondock episodes were always incredibly charged: vows of eternal friendship, exchange of instant pictures that would be kept for a few months— until they lost all meaning. This one had only been more spectacular; the configuration was the same. Johnny told himself his picture was already fading in her purse. But he wanted to give her something real.

"How's Donny?"

She shook her head. Don't ask.

"About that ride—"

She thought he was joking. "Another time," she said. "You get back and send us some reinforcement. I don't ask what form it's going to take, you guys know best. But make it soon, okay?"

He settled Bella in the backseat, with her beloved plastic tilt-rotor and her herbal bunny pillow. He got into the car, opened the window wide.

"Cambridge, there's nothing for you in that town. Don't go back. Get in, come with us. I can fix everything."

He'd thought it out in a split second. He could hack the problems involved: what's gilded youthfulness for? His mistake was that he'd forgotten, for a moment, who he was supposed to be. In the dim light he saw her eyes narrow.

"Me? Leave the cadre? Wait a minute. Why shouldn't I go back?"

He stared over the dash, "I'm an eejay ma'am. I don't take sides. I just made the tape that just went on the news."

At no point had she told him he mustn't make live transmission. It had occurred to him (the Wizard of Oz) that she might not know what he was doing. The 360 looked unimpressive. But he was a journalist, and she hadn't asked. The coralin plant could have survived. The legal status of pirated coralin wasn't sewn up completely. There were ways, angles: there were lawyers on the side of the people. Johnny had genuinely been helping, getting them publicity. It wasn't his fault that violence had then exploded, on prime-time news.

It would have taken the police no time to get a precise fix. They were entitled to deal swift and hard with armed conspiracy involving information technology. They would be here very soon . . . No one should get hurt. They'd stun-gas the site and haul the bodies out before they burned the plant.

"Okay." She gripped the rim of the window. "Okay, fine. You faked your unionist rap. You took your pictures and sent them straight to the bastards in power. Okay, I was a fool. But you thought I'd *come with you*? I don't want to escape from here. I want 'here' to escape from being the way it is. I thought a guy who was in the union was someone I could trust. You were only interested in getting a story. Well fuck you, Mr. Eejay. Let them do their worst. You can't shut us out forever. *Shit*—the arrogance. Any day now there's going to be a revolution. And you're going to find yourself sitting right in the middle, Mr. Fucking Neutral Observer."

"That's where I belong," said Johnny. "I'm a journalist."

Cambridge looked down at him, as from a great height. He saw the blighted skin, every mark picked out by the upward light. The contempt in smart, clear eyes. She would have liked to be an eejay. Maybe she had the makings, who could tell? Johnny did not go for the idea, though it was widely accepted, that there were no genes left out here worth worrying about.

"Violence is never going to solve anything."

She curled her lip. "What kind of violence? The bureaucratic kind or the personal kind? I don't make that distinction."

"I'm sorry."

"No," said the desk clerk. "No. You're not sorry, Johnny."

She let go of the rim and walked away.

Johnny drove around lumpy roads, helpless, until the computer suddenly recovered its bearings and he was on his way home. He thought about the cold fenland town that he had visited once. (It would be a mistake to let anyone out here know you'd actually left the continent, that would be too much.) He thought about the European solution to the big problem. No citadels there. The countryside was empty. Everyone lived in the cities, cheek by jowl. In England the wasted people were called the poor. You stepped over them as you went into your hotel. He didn't believe it was any worse to let them have their own world, with its own rules. He thought about the phylloxera beetle. He hadn't finished that story. How the plague came back in the next century and laid California's vines to waste . . . because people forgot to take care. Because greed drowned the warnings. It isn't the coralin, he thought. The technology is helpless to save the world. It's what goes on between people that fucks things up.

Johnny truly was in the union, which made him a radical and dangerous character, by many standards; inside. But you can be opposed to some of the laws, and still believe in law and order. You can be on the side of the Indians, and still think it's a bad idea to sell them guns and firewater. He wished he could explain. One day the citadel of civilization would spread out the way it used to and cover the whole continent. But that would not get a chance to happen if you let the wolves into the sleigh. You couldn't let yourself be distracted by the fact that the wolves had human faces. He couldn't regret his decisions. But he was glad, as the road jolted away, that his mask had slipped at the end. It would have been worse to leave Cambridge believing that she'd met her urban-guerilla savior. He had given her something real after all: a creep to despise. Maybe it evened the balance, a little.

He drove, and the pain eased. The boondocks episode began to fade in the accustomed, dreamlike way. Bella, asleep in the back, felt ever more like his talisman, his salvation, as he scurried for the sheltering walls.

THE LOST TECHNIQUE OF BLACKMAIL

By Mark Teppo

RonTom St. John's Liberty Prescott Four, President and CEO of InterCore Express, was not, as his CV would otherwise tell you, a graduate of the Las Vegas School of International Business, due to an "incomplete" mark received on a course in Economic Linguistics. There was an issue with a position paper. I knew this because both Prescott's wayward term paper and a copy of the dean's letter to Prescott Three (which mentioned the word "plagiarism" in all caps quite prominently) had just been automat-delivered to me by one of our own couriers.

"Where did you pick this up?" I asked.

The iDeeBoy beeped at me, and it extended its ICEPane for my Package Receipt Acknowledgement key. As a member of the Security Directorate at ICE, the automats would allow me to open a package without signing for it, but they wouldn't go away until I had officially tagged the COCT.

I swiped my ICID instead, and the iDeeBoy froze, the image on its v-mon panel caught midway between a happy and a sad face. After a fraction, the look of constipation vanished and was replaced by the automat's terminal interface. I called up the PDL manifests and discovered the ICEpak on my desk had been in-system less than three windings. A local delivery, picked up from—

My hand retreated from the v-mon panel as it were hot, and I suddenly felt a little constipation of my own.

The package had come from a "B" series station. Depot 12-B4. One of the old stopdrops.

The stopdrops were first-gen stations, put in right after the GTI Accords had been ratified. They had been a marketing tool, really, one stolen from one of the other CorCongloms, and there had been one or more every radian inRing. P2P fulfillment went one step further, making the stopdrops obsolete, and a lot of them had been removed during the Retail Interregnum when Ring real estate demand was in flux; the rest had experienced a renaissance during the CorpEsp Reconstruction as a useful way to disseminate confidential information in an anonymous manner. Sometimes the best message is the one that can be submitted and delivered without leaving your GPIT all over it.

IIRC, they were supposed to have been End of Lifed as part of the ICE SI & R.

The iDeeBoy beeped and its v-mon changed back to the smiling face of everyone's favorite delivery boy. It tapped its ICEPane against the edge of my desk, completely oblivious to the fact that I had been touching its internals. It wasn't going to leave until I iSigned for the package.

I signed and licked my thumb. The iDeeBoy, sensing the motion it was programmed to wait for, rotated its ICEPane and scanned my thumb, registering both my DNA and the physical print of my thumb. Satisfied that my GPIT matched its PDL, it trilled happily and trundled out of my office, leaving me with the mystery of this package.

Why had someone sent me an old term paper belonging to our CEO? Why were they using old channels that weren't supposed to exist? The term paper was a minor embarrassment, even with the issue of plagiarism. LegD had spent two turns scanning every document Prescott had ever touched before signing off on his appointment to CEO. Something like this wouldn't be newsworthy enough to last more than a few media cycles.

I glanced at the opening page of the thick document, and the first sentence of the abstract made my eyes cross. *Autonomous Microphalengeal Retrieval as an Extra-Biologic Currency Acquisition System.* I didn't even understand what that meant.

The paper was a headache waiting to happen, and not just because it ran two hundred and forty-six pages and it had so many footnotes that it looked like another paper entirely lived down there in the margins. No, the delivery was a symbolic gesture. It was a message, delivered via our own delivery system, using an unsecured backdoor. Which was surprising in itself, as intercorporate espionage had been outlawed for nearly ten turns now.

Who was the target, though? my theory-brain asked. *Me or our CEO?*

My name is Max. I work in what is left of SecD—Security Directorate—and it's my job to be paranoid. I call it the "theory-brain," the part of my job that's all about figuring out how things worked. Not mechanical things; I don't have that sort of aptitude. No, straight-up subcognitive theoretics and abstract extrapolation, with a focus on social wetworks, viral superstition mimetics, religio-aesthetic visual cues: you know, the sort of thing that a SecEd Tag in Pre-Collapse History is good for.

Using the stopdrops as a way to send anonymous messages had been my idea. It had labeled me with a Director tag, and until the Systemic Introspect & Reorganization, I had been in charge of security for InterCore Express. After that, well, I fared better than a lot of people at ICE in that I still had a job, but with the i3Cee's kinder, gentler approach to corporate intrigue (read: none), the ROI of a fully staffed Security Directorate didn't pass budget audit. SecD got broken up—most went to SysAdmD, the knuckle-draggers given new uniforms and new offices (EnforD), and me and a few others were downgraded to desk jobs. I went from "Director" to "Theorist," and had a few turns to really sink into a never-ending depression, a hole where I could *theorize* all I liked.

I had a SysAdmD Section Manager, who really didn't know what to do with me, and I was pretty sure he was hoping that I would EOE voluntarily, saving him the headache of doing my PIPe every turn. I wasn't about to give him the satisfaction. He got back at me by never bothering to R & U any of my GPARs.

It's a very unfulfilling relationship.

Which explains why I found myself leaving the office and heading out into the field to investigate the mysterious package. I should have walked it over to EnforD and let them go hit people, but that would have taken the matter out of my hands. Plus there was the issue of the stopdrops. Eventually, a doc audit would bring up the whole history of their use, and my Section Monkey would be thrilled to find my tag all over the documentation. It'd be all the excuse he'd need to WTF me.

I went Out of Office. As much as I hated that three square, it was mine, and I had been there a long time. It's funny what you'll fight to keep.

Depot 12-B4 was still inRing, next to a Baskin-Robbins Emporium 31 on the Malachite Layer. I took an express 'tubebus, and walked the few clicks from the depot. It was still ante-meridiem and the reflected sunlight wasn't too bad.

The Ring circled the planet like a lopsided halo, cleaving to the ecliptic. The outer edge was bubbled with a couple thousand climatologies where brain trusts kept trying to replicate moss and lichens in an artificial environment. InRing was home to humanity and we sprawled across every meter of space. By design, of course, regardless of the GoogleTube PR claim to the contrary.

I wasn't quite sure why they still maintained the conceit that the Ring was meant as a data structure and not as a habitat. Old corporate habits, I suppose, but after the GoogleTube Infrastructure Accords, it was hard to believe they hadn't planned for this possibility. Especially after the white paper by the pair of GoogleTube Extrapolationists was leaked. Sure, they had been ostracized from campus for writing the document, but when your corporate mandate says you never delete anything, it gets hard for the rest of the world to believe you wouldn't actually *use* your own data. Even the theoretical kind.

Anyway, the GTI Accords opened up the Ring to the rest of the CorCongloms and over the next couple of clocks, the Ring went from a pristine packet landscape to a population density of a thousand per. The Retail Interregnum cleaned house, so to speak, and in the resulting economic vacuum, the SIX moved in.

Basing their dispersal theory on the New Modality of the Chicago School Theory of Economic Rapture, the SIX remodeled the Ring into an economic web that took advantage of the population density by maximizing isolation variables while pushing separation anxiety to nearly zero. It was all high throughput packet flow—1PB/f optimization to each node cluster, delivering every sort of digital signal that a body could desire (for everything that was still meatspace based, there was InterCore Express, the official package delivery service of the Ring).

Food, though, didn't travel through the 'tubes all that well, and if you wanted to eat something that wasn't extrapolated and reconstituted by the iChef in your iToaster, you went to a B-R Emporium 31.

I entered the Emporium, and immediately blanked the notification option in my iView. The B-R network was updating my profile and d/l'ing several turns' worth of advertisements and special offers. Blinking through the steady flash of subliminal messageboarding, I pushed my way to the front counter and flashed my ICID at the kid in the candy-stripe uniform. He googled the holostat on my card, and his eyes got big. He stuttered slightly as he asked what flavor I wanted.

"Not interested in ice cream," I said. "Not right now, at least. I need to talk to your Visual Monitor. Can you retrieve him for me?"

The kid's eyes flickered to the right, the sure sign he was on the IM. Each of the SIX modded their iStructure network to their own specs, but the baseline basic employeenet was always the same: IM, Lifecycle Management & Workflow, and MediaHub. It made the dissemination of corporate memos and quality assurance training materials easier, and the 1024-character ceiling on IM made it easy for the corporate substrate to live and die on that layer.

Through the SysAdm whispernet, I'd heard that a couple of the SIX were no longer tracking IM data. GoogleTube still had a lock on cloud storage, and rumor was they were starting to raise rates outRing. Something like per TB, which was going to create all sorts of panic in FinD. No one wanted to be caught on the wrong end of a billing cycle when that rate change came through.

The flexible monitor on the kid's uniform made snow for a fraction, and then synched into the image of a narrow face, squeezed slightly more peevish by the aspect ratio forced by the boy's narrow chest. Red-framed glasses (the same corporate shade as his slightly askew collar) told me this was the site manager, and not the person whom I had requested. "What can—" he started.

I cut him off by pressing my card against the kid's chest. "Not you," I said. The holostat would translate across even the zero-tech of the kid's uniform. Outside of ICE, a SecD sigil still carried some weight. "I want to talk to your eyes."

"I really—"

"Now."

The kid yelped, and I wasn't sure if it was from the tone of my voice or an all-caps IM lighting up his retinal feed.

In a fraction, someone cleared their throat, and it was a much different noise than the squawking noise the site manager had been making. Female, for one. I lowered my card.

She was pretty in the way the internal guts of an iNuPod were: compact, sleek, and incredibly efficient in design. Pale, in the way a good EyeSpy would be. A halo of synthetic d-cable twisted in her hair. She wore a simple black tunic that gave me the subtle impression that I was talking to a floating head. "How can I be of assistance to the Security Theorist of InterCore Express?"

she asked. Her voice was about as bored as her gaze was unfocused, but I didn't take it personally. She was multitasking on a factorial level that would make my head explode. She would probably be able to Read & Understand Prescott's term paper.

"I need eyes from this morning," I said. "A winding's worth, seventh to the eighth. Anything containing feed of the RPC minus one plus one from my current location."

Her eyes tracked left. "Query," she said, and she rattled off a sequence I figured was my current Ring Positioning Coordinates. "Processing. One fraction please."

I had nothing else to do for several fractions (and it's never one, no matter what they say), so I stared at her face. The kid squirmed a bit, and I reached across the counter and held him still. Behind me, a tiny voice was chanting, "Quadrilmint! Quadrilmint!"

Her eyes twitched and a slight moue dimpled the right edge of her mouth. "One fraction," she said again.

Not a good sign.

I glanced over my shoulder. Even with the haze of advertising, I could see the stopdrop from here. Every employee in Emporium 31 could. She should have multiple angles available. B-R SysAdmD shouldn't have dropped that data set already; the ante-meridiem shift was still on. Even if they were crunching some serious t-flops to de-dupe it, there—

"I'm sorry," she said, drawing my attention back to her composed features. "That data is not available right now. Perhaps you'd like to inquire again later?"

"Will my odds improve?"

Her lips tugged into a thin smile. "I do not have that information."

"Of course not." A thought struck me and I blinked, ghosting the Ring Coordinated Time on my retina. Thirteen twenty-seven. "What is the closest time stamp you can retrieve for me?"

"Oh nine thirty—" She blinked, "—eight."

"That's a four winding—" I stopped. A four winding retention window. What sort of baboon-brain was in charge of SysAdmD at Baskin-Robbins? "Ah, thank you," I amended, keeping that question to myself.

She hung all her sub-processes, directing her full attention at me for a fraction, and then gave me a nod that went, I thought, a touch beyond professional courtesy. I tried to think of something smart to say, but the kid's screen went black. *Eyes out.*

He scratched his nose. "So . . ." he started.

"Yeah," I said, clearing my throat. "Just give me a scoop of Rocky Road. In a dish."

Something to chew on while I considered this new wrinkle. Baseline paranoia—the kind I got paid to explore—suggested that the individual who used this station had known about B-R's data retention window. They knew ICE timetables too. Covering their tracks like a professional.

I wasn't thinking about the Visual Monitor and that last bit of eye contact. Not at all.

Depot 12-B4 was a half-shell unit—an electro-bonded extrusion of ceramic with a pneumatic receptor and a battered 4ts-mon. Archaic, by any standard. I had d/l'ed their Lifecycle Management Protocol during the drop to Emporium 31. They had been EOLed shortly after the SI & R, but some middle manager down-chain had modded the LMP to only remove them as they broke down, a decision which failed to consider the high QA standard for this early generation of pre-fab. They made them to last counterclockwise.

I could probably bit-sling responsibility of this mess over to Asset Management Directorate. My recommendation to retire all the stopdrops when the Corporate Influence Limitation Regulations had gone into effect was in the GPAR attached to the LMP, and with some serious butt-in-chair time, I could make the later amendment pop when someone queried the LMP. But that meant trusting the corporate chain to do the right thing and not panic.

I had spent too many years thinking about what happened when the brain trust panicked. I had forgotten what a calm and rational response would look like.

Holding my half-empty dish of ice cream in one hand, I swiped my ICID through the reader, and when asked for confirmation, I wiped off the grime on the screen and pressed my thumb against the glass. Like the iDeeBoy, the stopdrop promptly perked up and threw open its security panels to me.

As I suspected, there was nothing on the internal surveillance from earlier ante-meridiem. Flicking back through the log, I had to go two cycles before I found a live image. The blurry motion of a flat object—on all three feeds at once, I noticed. Boom. Blackout.

An alert in the log noted a security violation had been submitted to ICECORE. I didn't even have to log on to the central ICE network to verify how much of a non-event that was to ICECORE. The vandalism would have just flipped the Need To Retire bit on this stopdrop. The AsManD sweeps got further and further apart every turn, and it would probably be a couple of rotations before their automats recycled this drop.

Exactly what my message sender was counting on.

This individual wasn't just covering their tracks; they were also using our system to slow discovery of their malfeasance. The term paper wasn't an isolated delivery. There were more coming. You didn't need a Theorist to spec that.

My phone icon bounced in my right peripheral. I glanced at it, noted it didn't have any tags, and accepted the handshake request. "Max Semper Dimialos."

"Hello, Max," she said. I was a little surprised that it was her. I mean, I realized a split fraction after I took the call that I was hoping it was going to be, and the thrill of hoping and receiving took me a little by surprise. "Would you meet me for a coffee?" B-R's EyeSpy asked.

"Ah," I said, involuntarily glancing back at the rounded hump of the Baskin-Robbins Emporium, even though I knew she wasn't onsite. Visual Monitoring was done out of B-R HQ in Chrysalis. "Now?"

"Yes."

"Well, I'm sort of busy right now." Mentally kicking myself as I said it, even though it was true.

"So am I."

"Ah," I repeated. I was presenting quite the erudite image of the ICE Security Directorate. "I've got a bit of a red flag at the moment. I don't really—"

"The Bliss Canopy Rotunda," she cut me off. "Verdigris Level. One winding?" She paused, but not long enough for me to gurgle out a response. "It's not that sort of meeting." And then the call terminated.

I shoveled the rest of the ice cream in my mouth to cool down the flush rising in my cheeks. *I hadn't thought—*

Okay, I had. I mean, it's not like anyone went to Starbucks for just *coffee* any more.

• • •

She hadn't gotten a room; she sat in plain sight, on the stool closest to the coffee bar. Taking advantage of our need for nostalgia, Starbucks's interior design hadn't changed. They even still made their coffee by hand, using anachronistic, steam-driven espresso machines. My heart skipped a beat when I saw her sitting there, in the noisiest spot in the room. *Such security consciousness.* A small demitasse cup sat on the green counter, and on a nearby plate was a half-eaten Starbucks bar.

She was wearing a long white coat with white feather trim, and a solar flare head wrap that matched her shoes. She still wore her glasses and, when I got a good look at them from the side, I realized they weren't the sort that one took off casually, even for bed.

I ordered tea, generating some confusion with the barista, and sat down next to the Eyes of Baskin-Robbins Emporium 31.

"You should be a bit more discreet," she said.

"Coffee makes me twitchy," I explained. "And if I had ordered coffee, it'd just sit there on the table. And no one would notice *that* in a place like this."

"You could have said something."

"You didn't give me a chance."

"I—" she stopped. Her glasses darkened several shades as she glanced around, reading heat patterns, microwave signals, and who knew what other manner of electromagnetic waveform. "I'm sorry. I don't do this very often."

"This?" I asked.

"Meeting people," she said. The corner of her mouth twitched, an unconscious emotional tell. "I . . . spend a lot of my time logged in. My UVEI is less than 8."

I had noticed. But it wasn't an unhealthy color. Not like the grid lizards you find nesting next to the heat vents down in the UPS farms.

"I've gotten off to a bad start, I see," she continued. "Let's try this again."

"Okay." I held out my hand. "Max."

She took it. Firm, but not demanding. Supple, but not too soft. A working hand that was well-cared for. "Sophie." Her fingers twitched as she let go, tickling my palm.

"Nice to meet you." I swiveled around on my stool so we were both facing the same direction, as if we were watching the parade of ads on the wall of jumbo v-mons. "So, Sophie," I continued, trying my best to appear completely at ease, though truth be told, I was just as badly out of practice. "What can I do for you?"

"Earlier, when you asked me to retrieve the visual feeds from the lines at that Emporium 31 . . ."

I sipped my tea and nodded.

". . . I told you the closest time stamp match I had was four windings prior. Exactly four."

"Right. Your security policy was written either by an overzealous LegD or you had a bunch of baboons as consultants."

"It's not," she said. "It's actually sixty-four windings. Or, at least it was. A new policy went active at cycle change, precipitating a systemic data purge." She gave me one of those smiles. Hinting at a wellspring of laughter, one that hadn't quite breached. "I need to thank you, actually. If you hadn't asked to see the data, I wouldn't have had a need to access the archives. It may have been a full rotation before I noticed the change in policy. That would have been . . ."

"Catastrophic?"

"Bad, for my PIPe. I have a mid-turn review next rotation."

"Good luck." I raised my cup.

"Thank you." She put her hands in her lap. "But that's not what I wanted to talk about."

"No?" My voice rose on the second letter, a rather awkward squeak as if I was attempting to impersonate one of those autonomous miPets.

She shook her head. "The change was executed via a shell script. From a root login. On a system within our network that had been zombied by a terminal with a GTAC of '1E78/BF001.'"

"A what?"

"A GoogleTube Access Cipher key."

"I know what it is, it's—"

"The key belongs to ICE, Max." She spelled it out for me, as I appeared to not be getting it. "One of your systems hacked my network last night."

"Ah," I said. There I went, reverting to monosyllabic responses again. "Well," I tried, but my head was filled with too many options, Theorist paranoia overflowing my buffers.

She stood up, and pushed her half-eaten snack closer to me. "Please, finish this for me, will you?" She put her hand on my shoulder. "And please pull the plug on whomever is accessing my dataform."

She left, and I realized, as the aroma faded in her wake, that she smelled like flowers.

When I touched her plate, I noticed it wasn't quite flat on the table. I lifted it slightly and felt underneath. Stuck to the bottom was a tiny lozenge, a mag-strip candy—a tasty treat that came with a data payload. As casually as I could, I tugged the tiny lozenge off the plate and popped it in my mouth. As it dissolved on my tongue, my iView registered two numbers. One was the full GTAC/GMAC of the ICE terminal that had zombied her system. The other was a directory access number.

I scrolled back through my call log.

Different than before. This one must be her direct line.

I didn't want to call right away. Subtle signals aside, she appeared to be focused on the business at hand, and I wanted to have something useful to tell her when I did call. As a result, it was late—nearly cycle change—before I did.

"Hello, Max," she said without preamble before my iView had even registered that the handshake protocol had been completed. As much as my paranoia resisted, I found that I liked having her voice in my head.

"Hello, Sophie." I remembered why I called her in the first place. "I found the zombie maker."

"But . . ."

"How do you know there's a 'but'?"

"There always is with men."

"Hey, that's . . ." *Probably true.* "Okay. So, yeah, there is a 'but'—" I stopped and took a deep breath before continuing. EyeSpies always charted on the SocDis spectrum; it went hand in hand with their ability to focus and multitask. There was no point in getting angry with her. She probably wouldn't understand why I was upset.

"*But,*" I said, moving on, "the terminal was EOLed a half-turn ago, and removed from our routing tables three rotations later. I have a priority request for documentation of its recycle tab, but it'll be post-meridiem before I hear anything."

"This news does not comfort me, Max."

"Yes, but—"

"Every 'tube-ready object has a unique GTAC/GMAC key," she said as if I didn't already know this. "It won't accept power without one. You can't reuse a key."

"I know, Sophie," I interrupted. "But—" It was like I was stuck in a bad code loop—*but, but, but* . . .

"So, if this machine has been recycled, how did its GTAC/GMAC end up in my iNetMom dashboard yesterday?"

"I'm still working on that," I said. "That's why I've got the Query registered."

She was quiet for a fraction. "This isn't useful information," she said.

"It's progress," I tried. "You know, forward movement on the situation."

"What if the tag is present? What data does that give us?"

"Well, I don't know if the tag is there or not. That's why I'm asking." I was raising my voice again. Theory-brain was defaulting to my SOP with internal SysAdmD communications. Everyone thought they knew something about Theoretics.

"If the recycle tab is available, then you have a spoofer."

"Yes, Sophie, I suppose that is possible." I sighed. Somehow this conversation hadn't gone like I had hoped.

A spoofer was, like a zombie maker, a system that hid behind other systems, though in the case of the spoofer, it falsified its GMAC to the 'tubes. Both zombie making and spoofing were old hacks that had been bound out by the 23.r4 rev of iStructure. Of course, that was only true if SysAdmD was current on its iStructure revs.

My confidence in ICE SysAdmD wasn't that high, but I wasn't about to share that with an outside agency.

"What is your position on the presence of a spoofer, Max?" Sophie asked.

"I—look, why are you breaking my balls?"

"I'm . . . that's rather odd syntax, Max. Rather aggressive."

"No, I—it's an idiom. Late 20c. Sorry. That was inappropriate of me."

"Late 20c," she replied, and for a few fractions, all I heard over the audio link was a micro-noise that seemed like the sound of her breathing. "You know much 20c?" she asked finally, in a different tone of voice. Much less brittle. Silkier, like this was an Avatar consultation.

"A little," I said. "It's a hobby."

"A man does need a hobby."

"And how."

"Um . . . I . . . well, during your personal cycle time—"

"Sorry, another idiom."

"Oh, yes." She went silent again, and for the second time I wished this handshake had included a visual feed. I couldn't get a read on what she was thinking, and the theory-brain was starting to wonder if I was talking to the same woman. Her voice had changed enough that—

"I, yeah, I'll know more about that tag in a few windings," I said, shaking off the professional paranoia. "I'll let you know."

"Please do," she said, and then: "Max?"

"Yes?"

"Thank you for calling." And then she was gone.

Theory-brain was telling me she was a wethead who had VMed her brain, splitting personalities to take advantage of the unused processor cycles in her brain. I went and took a cold shower, trying to drown theory-brain.

Theory-brain got back at me while I slept, filling my dreams with dozens of Sophies, each one with a different personality.

I kept my sanity by holding tight to a loop of her last four words.

Ante-meridiem, another iDeeBoy was waiting outside my office. I iSigned and took the ICEpak into my office. Flipping the bits that made my three square a black box, I opened the envelope.

Thirty fractions later, I dropped the security screens and made a handshake with Prescott Four's XA. "I need thirty fractions," I told him when the call connected.

Micro-pause. "Next rotation. Four Cee—"

"No, I need them right now."

"I'm sorry, Security Theorist Semper Dimialos, but your request is out of compliance with your EnforD Registration. I cannot, obviously, comply." Prescott Four's Executive Administrator was a rail named Equus Grimester, a man prone to fashion explosions and dismissive sniffing. I got one of those sniffs now, coming through loud and clear on my audio link.

"Ask him about Giselle."

"I will not, ST Semper Dimialos, and I would like to remind you that you are in violation of i3Cee 7, part 11g, as well as i3Cee—"

"But, i3Cee 12, part 7a," I interrupted, "states that any employee may request—once a turn—a thirty-fraction window of the CEO's time, so as to—"

"I know the i3Cee," Grimester interrupted me, punctuating the sentence with an especially loud nasal inhalation.

"Good. I want my allotted time with Prescott Four, and I'd like it now." I gripped the edge of my desk tightly to stop my hands from shaking.

Another pause, longer this time, and when Grimester came back, his tone had gone all obsequious and musical on me again. "One fraction, please."

It was more like a hundred fractions later when Prescott Four's voice rang in my head. "Salutations and variations, Security Theorist Semper Dimialos," he said, with an air of restrained jocularity. "My XA tells me that you've requested a 30fPA communication. I haven't had one of these in . . . I can't remember the last—"

"Giselle Akkwild Haussingterre," I said, getting to the point. If I let him, Prescott Four would ramble on for most of my allotted time, and then Grimester would cut me off before I got more than a few words out.

"Excuse me?"

"Tell me about Giselle."

A long pause, one that lasted well beyond my thirty-fraction limit, which validated a few theories rolling around my head. When Prescott Four spoke again, his voice had lost its levity. "She doesn't exist, Max."

Max. Not *Security Theorist Semper Dimialos.* Prescott Four might seem like an idiot on GoogleTube feeds, but he came from a long line of corporate fathers. All shrewd and cutthroat when the situation demanded it.

"What about forty-three turns ago?"

"That's a very specific time period, Max."

"I'm reading it right off a DNA report I have on my desk. A paternity test."

"How did you come by this . . . dubious . . . information?"

"A better question might be to ask how this 'dubious' information came to be. It's a lot easier to find information than it is to make it up."

"One of Security Directorate's old truisms, yes?"

"That it is, sir."

"You'd better come to my office, Max."

I went.

One of the corporate leadership perks was access to iReset, and RonTom St. John's Liberty Prescott Four used it liberally. The package had a more technical name and wasn't entirely Apple's design, but let's face it: it made you sleeker, gave you a better face, reduced your need for peripherals, and doubled your shelf life over the current regime of nootropic packs and neuro-linguistic recombinatory therapy. Which meant, he looked liked a Studio Idol on the cusp of legitimacy even though he was much older than I.

He didn't look happy though, and the emotive ionic shades of his top-floor office reflected his mood, making the enormous room seem both smaller and larger with its play of shadow and grey light.

Standing inside the penthouse doors was an enormous presence. EnforD. I knew him, in fact. Simon Yullg. A knuckle-dragger with a long reach.

"I've asked Chief Yullg to take some notes," Prescott said, sensing my unasked question.

"Of course," I said, though we both knew Yullg wasn't much for documentation. There's a story that someone in FinD submitted a form to EnforD that didn't have autofill, and Yullg tracked the poor bastard down and broke a digit for every field that didn't validate. When Yullg ran out of fingers and toes, he went to the next three square and continued to mete out EnforD's displeasure. It was, unfortunately, a rather long form.

Doing my best to ignore the hulk of muscle in the corner, I walked over and put the ICEpak on Prescott's desk. He slid out the single floppy inside and fanned it. To his credit, not a single muscle on his perfectly smooth face twitched while he scanned it.

When he replaced the report in the envelope and held it out, Grimester, who had been hovering behind me, shot past my elbow and snatched the envelope. I didn't have a chance to do anything but clench my sphincter a little tighter. Grimester pranced to the sidebar along the southern wall and put the ICEpak into the iToaster. The executive models had a setting for incinerate, which made the envelope flare for a fraction as it vaporized.

"That's probably not the only copy," I pointed out.

"True," Prescott agreed. "But it is one less."

I tried to follow the reasoning there, but couldn't. "That's also not the first package I've received," I added.

"Through our own network, no less."

"Yes, sir. I figure that's just to make us angry."

"Did it work?"

"How so?"

"Are you angry?"

I looked at Yullg, who popped a joint in his jaw.

"A little," I admitted. "But it's the sort of outrage that increases productivity."

"That's good, Max." He watched the iToaster as it auto-cleaned its bay of the gritty remnants. "What was in the first package?"

"A term paper, from LVSIB."

His mouth tightened. "The actual paper, or just the citation?"

"The actual paper."

"That is interesting." he said.

"How so?"

"I never wrote it."

I was confused, and said as much.

"I intended to. Or rather, I intended to put my name on it. But I never had the opportunity."

"This one certainly had your name on it."

"Hence why I thought it was interesting."

"Ah," I said. Theory-brain told me to keep it simple. Let him talk.

"Do you know who is doing this to me, Max?"

"I'm working on it, sir. I have a—" Theory-brain made me bite my tongue. "I have some data that might be useful."

"Might?"

"It's still very theoretical."

He shrugged as if that detail wasn't important. "Yullg doesn't believe in theory. Perhaps you should give him this data."

I swallowed, and took a moment to gather my courage. This was, of course, the response theory-brain had tagged as highly probable, and in order to not get trapped with that suggestion, I had to proceed carefully. "I'm not sure that's a good idea, sir." When he didn't say anything, I plunged on. "The packages are coming to me. Not you. At this point, this person believes I am integral to his design. If you re-chain this to EnforD, it'll raise the profile of the issue. It'll be harder to control."

He considered that for a fraction, his fingers idly drumming on his desk, and then he nodded. "Control is the issue, isn't it, Max? If we do nothing, then the blackmailer doesn't know if his messages are being received. He'll wonder if he has control, and so he'll keep sending packages."

"Allowing me time to identify and locate him."

"That is a dangerous proposition, Max. It offers . . . many variables."

I glanced back at Yullg. "He offers one. You sure you want to be that *inflexible?*"

Prescott Four let his eyes flick toward his chief knuckle-dragger. "That is an interesting point, Max." His fingers drummed once more on the desk and then stopped. "You have until the end of the rotation," he said. "At which time, I will COCT your ICID to Yullg." He flashed me a smile that was all teeth and no humor. "I'll indulge your Theoretics for a cycle or two."

"Thank you, sir," I said. "I will do my utmost to have this resolved ASAP."

"I hope so, Max," Prescott said.

Yullg popped his jaw again.

Trip BinBin was waiting at my office. "Did you find the tag?" I asked as I sat down behind my desk, and started to massage my temples. I always got a tension headache after meetings with upper management. Having Yullg there had only made this one worse.

Trip hooted, and banged on his 'tray keyboard. Trip was an IT monkey. A modified chimpanzee, he had a predilection for primary colors, which expressed itself as a yellow beanie and a blue vest. His Jaynes LinkTray was slung low across his chest, and a large red "Free Genetics!" holostat curled around the bottom edge of the unit.

The speakers set in the 'tray housing popped with noise for a fraction before modulating into a human voice. I had been working with Trip long enough to know that first spit of sound wasn't zero-tech feedback, but was a triggered sound effect—aural commentary on the synthesized human speech about to follow. "No tag."

The voice wasn't the generic voxtrack, but one that had some subtle modulation and inflection. Like most IT monkeys, Trip was a tweaker. Every piece of hardware he used was a mod-kit; nothing ever stayed OTS long with them. "Log hole," the voice added.

"Really?" A log hole meant an AsManD discrepancy, a mismatch between electronic data and physical assets. "Where?"

More banging. "Patent Directorate Asset transfix to FinD, part of SI & R."

Back to that again. The Systemic Introspect & Reorganization. The end of CorEsp brought about CILR, which in turn, led to the i3Cee. Prescott Four, during the media blitz showcasing the new era of ICE-applied valuation, had been caught on-feed wondering how couriering packages could offer humanitarian reform. As a result, every division and directorate suffered through a costly self-analysis, resulting in a number of early retirements, ROI layoffs, and internal restructuring. The SI & R.

SecD had been defanged, and those of us who remained as desk monkeys became as inflexible and intractable as the extruded furniture in our three square meters of office space. Entropy was turning us into statues, one joint at a time. So much for humanitarian reform.

PatD got swallowed by FinD, who, IIRC, had been mandated to become a visible asset, i.e., they had to operate black and not be a cost center any longer. The first response—like every moment of brain trust panic through the ages— had been to cut staff. While it had certainly helped FinD go black the first turn following the SI & R, it hadn't done much to the IQ ratio of the Directorate.

This was good news, after all. The GTAC/GMAC had belonged to one of the patent agents. I didn't have a spoofer. One of the SI & R rifters had taken their terminal with them, and through some typical AsManD data contrafusion, the terminal had never been properly retired. Not entirely surprising, really. For a turn or two after the SI & R, there was an impenetrable flow of re-hires and consultants among the brain trust. "Who?" I asked Trip.

"Kip Birmingham Sandeesh, Prime Doctor."

"Where can I find him now?" Suddenly, it seemed like my clever (read desperate) plan might actually work.

"Deceased."

Or not.

"Family?"

"Grandson." More key banging. "RPC null."

"That's interesting," I said, falling back on a phrase of Prescott Four's. My theory-brain tried to construct a viable scenario. If the terminal still had its original GTAC/GMAC, then it should be visible on the iStructure dashboard. That would, in turn, give us a Ring Positioning Coordinate. It would follow that the son's GPIT—if he was indeed behind this blackmail—should be readily available.

Since it wasn't, that certainly made the case for his being my prime suspect. "When did Prime Doctor Sandeesh expire?"

"EOL 3T post-EOE." A pause, inserted by a hairy thumb resting on a space bar. "Anniversary of EOL: 1Cyc."

"This rotation?"

Trip triggered a noisy sound effect. His equivalent of confirmation.

"Well, now . . ." I mused.

Grandfather gets WTFed during the SI & R. Dies three turns after leaving the company. The anniversary of his death was the first cycle of this rotation— the cycle before the arrival of the first package.

The best part of this revelation was that I had an excuse to call Sophie.

While in-transit to the domicile still registered to the Sandeesh Familial Asset Library, I called her.

Halfway through the protocol handshake, she was there in my head. "Hello, Max."

"You were right."

"Of course I was. Data integrity is not ICE's—"

"No, when you said there was a 'but.' You were right about that."

"Thank you, Max," she said, her voice changing timbre somewhat clumsily. "I appreciate you acknowledging that point."

"But it wasn't a spoofer. The terminal wasn't properly retired. I'm going there now to retrieve it."

"What is your intention?"

"I'm going to find the guy, and—"

"With the terminal."

"Oh, ah, yank its data and melt its processor core, probably."

Her voice went cold on me. "Place it in electrostatic suspension and cede it to my Corporate Persona."

"Hang on—" My mail icon blinked. *And look, she's gone and started a document trail.* "Okay. Can we discuss this first?"

"There's always room for discussion, but not on this topic. I have a security breach that requires reconciliation. I must protect my assets."

A mental image of Yullg and his large knuckles flashed through my head.

"Of course," I said, my mood deflating. "We've all got to cover our assets." I glanced at the mail icon, triggering the menus, and marked the incoming message from her as R & U. "There."

"Thank you, Max." She paused, and when she spoke again, her voice had returned to its softer tone. "You're not happy. I can tell."

"No kidding." I raised my eyes toward the ceiling of the 'tubebus and shook my head. "It's just—you know what? Never mind." I should have ended the handshake, but I left it open. My theory-brain had nothing to offer.

"I like your face better when you are smiling," she said quietly.

My head snapped down, and theory-brain started looking for EyeMonitors along the seams of the cabin. "You can see me? Right now?"

"I can always see you, Max." Her voice was almost a whisper, as if she was embarrassed to have been caught watching me, and then the handshake suddenly ended.

But she kept watching, and when I nearly died at the Sandeesh domicile, she triggered the iMed alert that saved my life.

Prescott Four made a personal visit to my private room in the ICE infirmary. I caught sight of Yullg and Grimester outside as he shut the door.

He dropped an opened ICEpak on my lap. "I've rechained your mail to Yullg," he said. "This came a winding ago."

My hands were immobilized, and when Prescott Four didn't make any effort to help me, I surmised that whatever had been in the package was already gone. Pre-censored for my protection. "What was it?"

"Doesn't matter."

I blinked up the time, and realized it was still post-meridiem of the same cycle. "It came through the normal service?" I asked.

"With the Gen-Y lot," he said.

The last run. "Two deliveries in one cycle?" My theory-brain pushed the question out of my mouth. "Why two?"

He looked at me. "You told me there weren't going to be anymore."

"No," I clarified, "I said I was working on it, and that I had some ideas—"

"Too many, evidently."

I shook my suspended arms. "Well, it got complicated."

"I can see that." He sighed. "I sent Yullg to the Ring Positioning Coordinates from where iMed transported you." He shook his head. "They chargeback us for these sorts of unscheduled deliveries, you know. A commensurate deduction will be attached to your PIPe."

"Of course," I said. "Glad I could help offset the corporate deficit."

"Don't mention it." He waved off my thanks. "Unfortunately, Yullg only found . . . well, you made quite a mess."

I had very little recollection of what had happened. There had been something large and metallic waiting for me in the entry of the domicile. Something with bright lights and sharp bits. "Not my intention, sir."

"You've been at a desk for some time. I suppose that's to be expected." Even though he was being understanding, he still made it sound like it had been my fault. He pursed his lips. "I still need you, Max. Yullg has singular direction, and when there is no direction in which to point him . . ."

I lay there, with my arms in slings and my lower body immobilized by the straps of the bed, trying to look more capable than I felt.

He stepped over the panel beside the bed and stroked the lit column of the iNurse. "Yes, Mr. Prescott," a hermaphroditic voice answered.

"Mr. Semper Dimialos is returning to his assigned duties," Prescott said.

"I am?"

"The current status of Patient Semper Dimialos indicates a high probability of—"

"Hmm," Prescott interrupted. "Not relevant to my previous statement."

The iNurse modulated immediately, "—however, with a precisely calibrated, time-release pharmacopoeia, Patient Semper Dimialos will be able to resume his job functions."

"I will?"

A iDoc arm telescoped out of the wall, and bent over my chest. Before I could ask any further questions, the smooth tip of the surgical tool exploded into a confusion of knives, needles, and suction tips. It felt like a squid falling onto my chest, followed by a sharp prick of pain right through my breastbone, and then the iDoc arm retreated.

"Patient Semper Dimialos is scheduled for a nominal bioscan next cycle at the ninth winding. Room 74."

"Don't be late," Prescott said as he left. "This affair is rapidly approaching critical mass, Max. There is already too much of a documentation trail. It must be archived before the media worms can scan it."

I looked at the strip of new skin on my chest, and wondered what had been put in me. It was starting to itch already, and Prescott hadn't bothered to untether my arms from the ceiling mounts. Scratching this itch was going to be tough.

"Hello, Max."

"Do you have Eyetime on what happened to me?"

"I do, Max."

I took a deep breath, and tried to ignore the weird hitch in my chest. Something felt metallic under my skin when I tapped. "Can I see it?"

"It's not very pleasant."

"You've seen it?"

"More than once."

"Ah—" *More than once?* "Why?"

She didn't answer immediately, and I looked out the forward blister of the 'tubebus for something to do while I waited her out.

"Would you like to see it?" she finally asked. She had switched to the officious voice, the cold and efficient one.

"Not particularly."

"Then why did you ask?"

"I, ah . . . I wanted to know if there was anything useful. You know, some sort of clue. I must have been close to something useful to get jumped like that."

"Actually, Max, you triggered the standard domicile defensive array."

"Wait, there was nothing standard about that DDA. It nearly took—"

Her voice changed back to the silky one. "Would you like to watch the feed with me?"

•   •   •

The room was dark beyond her, lit only by the blue-tinged glow of v-mon pips on the wall behind her. She was wearing something that moved like velvet smoke, and she wasn't wearing any shoes but she still had her glasses on.

I took the hint and left my shoes in the foyer, along with my coat, belt, and ICID. Taking my hand, she led me into the single room of her domicile. Other than the tiny points of lights on the wall that were the anchors for a flood of virtual monitors, there was a uVert couch and a PedTrac mounted on a low stool.

She sat next to me on the couch, our thighs lightly touching. She spun the PedTrac expertly with her toes, and the wall disappeared beneath an octal grid of monitors, where we could—among other feeds—watch the footage of me, getting pulped by an automated security system. Just like she said.

About the time it had picked me up by the hands (*so that's how the bones had been broken*), I noticed how rapid her breathing was. She noticed that I had noticed, and I stopped feeling the sympathetic pains from the ass-kicking I barely remembered.

We slid down on the couch, hands exploring. I lost my shirt. Her smoke robe dissipated. I discovered she had nice nipples. I spent some time with them before exploring further.

I kissed and nuzzled my way down her torso. She sighed, her stomach retreating from my mouth. I paused at her hips. Rising in an arc between the peaks of her pelvic bone was a tattoo. Gothic, late 20c script. *Secrets aren't.*

"Keep going," she said, pushing my head further down.

Later, we watched octopus sex.

"This is weird," I opined.

"I find it relaxing. It's 20c footage. A pre-Union European filmmaker named Jean Painlevé. I thought you might like it."

I tried to relax, found it easier than I thought it would be.

"Oh," she said, and then it was her turn to go exploring.

I survived the experience (both the sex and the fact that it came out of watching vid of me getting assaulted by a security automat), only because the pharmacopoeia inserted by the iDoc automatically dispersed nootropics and painkillers when I was threatening to overtax myself during the . . . activities. The downside of this distribution method meant that, after we were done, I couldn't sleep. Too wired.

She had a smaller, single-screen v-mon pad in the bathroom, and I used it to track down a niggling itch. Not the one in my chest. The persistent tap-tap from the theory-brain. *You've missed something.* I iPriv'ed in to ICECORE and accessed my delivery log.

The third package was the anomaly. Why? Why had it come late in the day, and not with the morning run? Why was it a Gen-Y delivery and not a Prior-R?

When I filtered the PDL to just the three packages, I saw the pattern. My mystery shipper was using all anonymous stopdrops, timing deliveries so that they arrived in a specific order on specific days. He hadn't realized that a Gen-Y—a general issue delivery—had a modified schedule for ICE HQ: post-meridiem.

His first mistake.

I queried for the RPCs of the remaining stopdrops, all the way to the edge of outRing. *Forty-seven*, was the response. That stopped me for a few fractions. Was he going to use them all? That was a lot of blackmail material.

Of course, Prescott Four probably had more skeletons than that buried.

But he was going to send Yullg out before then. He already had, and EnforD had come up empty. That's why he needed me out of bed and back in the field. There was something coming—and coming soon—that he really didn't want to be made public.

"Hello, Max," she said in my ear, and I jumped because she was actually there, standing beside me.

"Ah, hi," I said. When I glanced up, I could see a reversed image of my screen along the lower rim of her left eyeglass lens. I should have known. Of course, she'd be monitoring her own house. Private network tunnel notwithstanding. "Just seeing if there was anything new."

"He's using your own system, isn't he?"

"Yes. Yes, he is."

"So you've been just as compromised as I have."

I thought about a position we had recently been in. "Compromised" was one way to put it.

"What's in the packages, Max?"

"Ah, term papers. DNA reports. That sort of thing."

She blinked, fish-eyed behind her glasses. "That's only two."

"Excuse me?"

"You've only suggested two items. There are three packages that have been delivered and signed by you."

"Signed?" I had been unconscious for the last one. "I . . . I don't know, really. I didn't get a chance to see it."

Her eyes flicked left, and I saw the screen image on her lens churn. My stomach tightened unconsciously. She was accessing ICE PDL. That was a violation of—

Her focus snapped back. "Yes, I see that now."

"You know, it's a little creepy how quickly you are able to retrieve my corporate assets like that."

She stared at me for a long time, her face impassive and unreadable. Then, the icy impasse broke and her face melted into a warm smile. "Max," she said. "I'm keeping an eye on you. Don't you feel more safe?"

The iMed call. If she hadn't triggered it, I wouldn't be here.

"Ah, yeah. I guess so."

Something flickered in her eyes. I wasn't sure if it was a reflection from her glasses or something more . . . internal. The rapidity with which she moved between personalities was a little intense.

"Based on the PDL from these stations, there are eighty-five more packages scheduled to be delivered to you. They'll arrive over the next few cycles, in increasing number. Each wave utilizes a different sequence of the stopdrops."

"I've realized that." *Little boxes of blackmail.*

"They can't all be—"

I shook my head. "Probably not. He'll have anticipated us figuring out he was using the stopdrops. We could query for all mail coming from those drops, but not all of them will be blackmail boxes. We don't know which ones are hot."

"What are you going to do next?"

"I was thinking about you and I going back to bed."

She slapped me.

Wrong answer, apparently.

"Is that all I am to you?"

"All what?"

"A one-off."

"We did it twice."

"What about my security breach?"

"You have one?"

She slapped me again. "This is such a mistake," she said, almost as if her personalities were talking to one another.

My lungs seized as the pharmacopoeia triggered another dose of painkillers. My cheek went numb. That was nice.

"Which?" I asked, intruding on her internal dialogue. "Beating me up or sleeping with me?" My tongue was loose too. The pain meds worked quickly. Too bad they couldn't do something about the mood.

She stepped out of the room, sealing the door shut behind her with a loud click of finality. Very 20c. That was nice too.

The meds went right to the top of my brain, throwing open my skull and letting theory-brain get some air. It was the only explanation I had for the simple solution it presented to me a few fractions later.

So very simple. So very nice.

The key to any system is to discern the simplest route. GoogleTube had, in their own way, discovered that the simplest route to data domination was to decrease data separation to nearly zero. And while throwing hardware at a problem may seem to be counter to Ockham's Insight of keeping it simple, it actually was because they were thinking about the problem *from a different perspective*.

And when I thought about my problem from a different angle, the answer seemed obvious. It was an issue of logistics.

Sophie had marked eighty-five more packages in-system, and even if I could killnine all of the deliveries, the packages and their contents were still physically in the ICE chain of custody. For them to be summarily destroyed without being opened would take an Executive Order from Prescott Four, the sort of request that would require a document trail and LegD audit. Prescott Four might be able to ultimately archive what was in the boxes, but it would take some corporate resources.

Of which there were many, and that's where I had gone astray. The point wasn't to bring down ICE; it was to get someone's attention.

Mine.

Once I realized that, theory-brain happily skipped to the next realization. If my attention was being sought, then what was the message? It wasn't the packages. It was the way they were being delivered. Or more accurately, the way they were being put into the ICE system. By hand.

Eighty-eight packages all together, hand-delivered to the stopdrops scattered across the Ring in a pattern that would—based on a fairly accurate model of ICE PDL—arrive in waves. In order to achieve that pattern of delivery distribution, the blackmailer would have to drop off the packages in an extremely precise route. One that could, if enough t-flops were redirected to model the permutations, be re-created.

While Sophie's emotive personality wasn't speaking to me, her analytical persona was, and it didn't take much to talk her into finding me the processor power to chart the most probable epicenter of the blackmailer's route. My best theoretical estimate was that this location—within a few radians—was where I would find Prime Doctor Sandeesh's grandson.

"Hello, Max," Sophie said in my ear.

"Hello, Sophie," I sub-vocalized back. Before I had left her place, she had uspliced a piece of military-grade code into my iView's appstore. We were permanently connected now, handshaking on an encrypted link.

It was almost better than sex. Almost.

"I have the RPC." Before I could read the coordinates she sent, I felt the 'tubebus change direction. "Routing you there now."

"Thanks," I said. "Look, I'm sorry about what I said earlier."

My mail icon bounced. An R & U from her with a subject line of "Apology." Read and Understood, but not Accepted. She was still mad at me.

"I'm not very good at this," I tried again. "So I guess I'll just say it and . . . well, anyway . . . I don't really know the proper protocols for . . ." When she didn't say anything, I lumbered on, ". . . this sort of relationship. I mean, how am I supposed to treat all your personalities? The same? Differently? It's confusing to us single-core guys."

"It always is," she said.

I bristled slightly. "That's not fair. You're baselining statistics on me."

"And you aren't?"

"What? How so?"

"My personalities? You think I'm splitcore?"

I paused, and my theory-brain shuffled through a couple scenarios and couldn't find one that didn't end badly. "Aren't you?" I tried, cringing slightly as I said it.

The only answer I received was a weird sensation of having a black hole in my brain, an emptiness that came from an open link that carried no data. It was the weirdest sensation of loss I had ever felt.

Half a winding later, as I wandered around an Emporium 31 looking at jewelry, I tried again.

I had found a holostat of Hammurabi Kip Sandeesh, the grandson, and I had loaded it into the surveillance mod of my iView. While my idle flops was doing facial recog on everyone within visual range, I had nothing else to do but wander around the RPC Sophie had sent me and try not to look too conspicuous.

B-R had a nasty habit of enforcing their Minimum Transaction Requirement. I couldn't keep buying ice cream if I was going to stay on-site; I'd have to upgrade to something a little pricier if I was going to be here long.

"Do you have a favorite color?" I asked the void in my head, hoping—contrary to what it felt like—that she was still listening. I looked at a row of earrings, most of which were single-stone settings and astronomically priced. "Orange, perhaps," I tried.

"Vermilion," she corrected, her voice rising out of the vacuum.

"Okay, vermilion. That's a start." I cast about for something that matched the color shard I summoned in my internal display. "Like your shoes," I remembered. "From when we met at Starbucks."

"I'm not wearing them right now," she said, using the other voice, the one I liked.

"No, I don't suppose—"

"I'm not wearing anything."

"Oh," I said. I wet my lips. "I'd like objective verification of that data point, please." I wasn't quite sure where she was going with this, so I thought I'd proceed cautiously.

My mail icon chimed, and then irised into an image. We were fuzzy, but the pair of octopi getting it on in the background were digitally sharp.

I sighed and blinked the image away. She was gone again, leaving me with just the fuzzy suggestion of the two of us together.

Still mad, I figured.

I was spared further attempts to get her attention as well as getting squeezed by the Emporium 31 MTR by a different tone in my iView.

Facial recog had a hit.

Hammurabi Kip Sandeesh waited for me at the uprise to his domicile. We rode up silently, both staring out at the cluttered landscape. The surface of the planet above us was still dark, the weak light of cycleflip just starting to crease the distant curve.

"Tea?" he asked as we entered the austere family chamber. Unlike Sophie's place (or mine, for that matter), Hammurabi had two rooms, and I didn't disguise my interest in the second room.

"Sure," I said as I wandered over to the portal and glanced inside. Worktable with a few exploded tools on it. Couple of antique-looking terminals and a few holograms of exotic plant life projected into the corners. I didn't have a chance to look at the terminals more closely before he returned from the iToaster station.

"Soy?" he asked. He was carrying a tray with two small cups—also antiques—and a conDispenser.

"Black is fine," I said.

He set the tray down on the low table between the two lacquered chairs and indicated I should sit. I did so, and watched him as he modded his tea. Pure-looking kid, no outward signs of plugs or rips. Kind face too, with quick and restless eyes. Not like he was chemical, but rather that he found everything interesting.

He lifted his teacup in a tiny salute. "I'm glad you found me, Person Semper Dimialos," he said.

"It wasn't terribly hard once I thought about it," I said. "Please, Max," I added.

Hammurabi nodded. "My grandfather said that the best way to get a Theorist's attention was to make him think. He would have liked you, I think, had things been different."

"I'm sorry for your loss." With nothing else to add, I sipped from my tea. It was real leaf, and I savored the flavor for a few fractions, waiting for Hammurabi to tell me why I was here.

He got to it eventually. "How many boxes did you receive?" he asked.

"Three, but I know there are more coming."

"A dozen more," he said. "The rest are to distract your Enforcement Directorate and to confound your CEO."

"I'm sure they will," I said. "But to what end?"

He picked up a small plate that had a tiny dark square on it. "Try the sweetmeat."

"No, thank you," I said. "The tea is plenty."

"Please." He gave me a look that was so earnest it almost broke my heart, and would have if theory-brain hadn't latched onto the intensity of his gaze. Something familiar there.

I picked up the small piece of candy and popped it in my mouth. Its data payload was enormous, and I gasped as the upload threatened to overwhelm my buffers. After a few fractions, I could crest the data stream and skim the header waves.

"Oh, my," I said as an overview started to synthesize. Hammurabi had just given me a digital copy of everything in the blackmail packages—cross-referenced and indexed for quick assimilation.

"My grandfather invented it," he said. "Giselle gave it its street name: the Gripee."

"Autonomous Microphalengeal Retrieval," I whispered. "The term paper. Prescott Four stole the whole idea."

Sandeesh shook his head. "It was supposed to be a joint paper. The three of them."

"But, what—" I closed my mouth and scanned more of the documentation in my buffers. The Las Vegas School of International Business. Giselle Akkwild Haussingterre. The paternity test. The CAPR from Las Vegas SecD. The LegD report to Prescott Three. The internal doc trail between Prescott Four and Hammurabi's grandfather. Giselle's name mentioned more than once.

The last document threw me for a fraction. The menu list of Chromosomic Therapy options in the iReset. I didn't understand why the man dump had been included, until I read the details of the Chrome23 options.

Suddenly the doc thread between Prescott Four and Prime Doctor made sense.

I flinched, and some of the tea in my tiny cup spilled out onto my hand. "What am I supposed to do with this?" I asked, suddenly not wanting this data in my head. Not wanting to have anything to do with this whole affair.

"We were hoping you could talk to your CEO on our behalf."

"Our? Wait a fraction. You want me to become the blackmailer?"

"He'll listen to you."

"No he won't—" The denial died in my throat. *Actually,* theory-brain pointed out, *he would. Because you can spin a thousand variations on what will happen if the data spills into the medianet.*

It's all about control, I had told Prescott Four, and I had never had it. I had been set up from the beginning.

On the long ride back to ICE, I pulled up the image of Sophie and I (fuzzy) and the octopi (not as) and left it there in my field of vision. Eventually, she filled the void in my head.

"Hello, Max."

"Hello, Sophie." I had been thinking, going back over the course of events during this crisis, trying to find a hole in theory-brain's assessment. I hadn't had any luck. "I'd like you to do something for me."

"What is it?"

"The last package. The one being delivered in the ICErack. Can you expedite it to Prescott Four's office? Can it get there before I do?"

"Yes, Max, I can do that."

"I thought you might."

She was quiet for a fraction. "Are you mad at me?"

"No," I said. "I'm just tired. This whole thing is—I'll . . . I'll be glad when it is done."

"Yes, Max, I will be too."

I felt the 'tubebus shift. Apogee. Back down to the surface now. Time to finish this. "Sophie," I said, and the words were hard to say, but I had to get them out. "Please stop watching me. It's an invasion of my bubble."

"I understand, Max. I'm sorry."

"I am too, Sophie." I wiped in the image from my iView. "Good-bye, Sophie."

"Good-bye, Max."

It had been the eyes. Hammurabi's and Sophie's. Too similar to be a coincidence. And to be sure, I had queried a reverse lookup to B-R HumResD, which came back null. They didn't have a Visual Monitor tagged with "Sophie."

I was killnining all the files on my office terminal when the door opened and Yullg squeezed his gigantic bulk into my tiny three square. He glared at me for a moment, and eventually realized there wasn't going to be enough room for him, me, and Prescott Four. He popped his jaw menacingly and stepped back, allowing the InterCore CEO to enter.

I tapped the button on my desk that engaged the security screens.

"Grimester signed for the package," he said. "The one you had routed to my office."

"Did he open it?" I asked.

"Of course he did."

I didn't say anything. Nor did Prescott Four, and we stared at each other for a few fractions before he shrugged and looked away. "Well, I was due for another XA anyway. He was starting to get a little annoying with that . . ." He waved his hand at his face. "That nasally thing he did."

I kept wiping my files.

He giggled, and then caught himself. "You should have seen it," he sighed.

"I did." I tapped my desk's v-mon to life and showed him the feed. Grimester opening the large ICErack and discovering the desiccated corpse inside, and his ensuing panic that resulted in a minor explosion of bone and dust and other noisome particulates that come off mummified bodies.

"How did it make you feel?" he asked. "Angry?"

"At who?" I replied.

"Me."

"Why?"

"Because I . . . " he paused, reluctant to put it into words.

"The Sandeesh family has tagged me as the executor of their . . . vengeance, I suppose," I said. "I'm supposed to convince you that the best thing to do is to provide restitution for what you stole from them. In return for which, they'll vanish. They have shipped you every piece of physical evidence they ever had. What you do with it is your business."

"What about you, Max?"

"I don't know. I'll EOE when we're done here. That'll make things easier—"

"Max," he interrupted. "What am I supposed to give you?"

He seemed just as confused as I was about my role. What did I want? I certainly couldn't keep working here, not with the knowledge that I had. I had had to stop theory-brain from listing the ways in which I could be EOLed in industrial accidents.

I sat back in my chair. It was a hard and uncomfortable surface, one I had been molding my body to for a long time. Too long, in fact, but what else could I have done? Entropy was easy.

"I want to be needed, I think." I glanced around my tiny—and despairingly empty—office. "ICE is an efficient machine. Like everything else. No one needs a theorist to think 'what if?' any more."

He gave me a fraction to add to that, and when I didn't, he nodded. "I'll have FinD retro-state you to Director, and then stamp you out with a full 590(t)."

Theory-brain made a suggestion, and I concurred. I raised an eyebrow to Prescott Four, and he held up his hands. "Plus vestments."

"I think that'll help me find a way to be useful somewhere else, sir."

He started to offer his hand, and then withdrew it, realizing he didn't really want to shake this deal.

Nor did I. We'd let the rest of the machine take care of it.

He left without another word, and I caught sight of a dark cloud of disappointment on Yullg's face as he was called away by Prescott Four.

And just like that, it was over.

I hadn't had to tell Prescott Four that I knew iReset could do a sex change; that I knew whose DNA tags would come up for the mummified body that had exploded all over his XA's office; and I didn't have to tell him that I knew his birth mother had called him "Giselle."

Nor did I tell him that Hammurabi and Sophie were his grandchildren. That was their secret to keep.

Regardless of what her tattoo said.

When I got home, there was a package waiting. Inside was a tiny hypercube key and an Instaprint of a woman's body. A close-up of her naked torso, draped with octopi tentacles. Scrawled on her belly, above her tattoo, was the phrase "I miss you."

The hypercube key was coded for domicile access. She had given me root privileges.

It was, in the end, all I really wanted.

FALL OF THE HOUSE OF ESCHER

by Greg Bear

"Hoc est corpus," said the licorice voice. "Lich, arise."

The void behind my eyes filled. Subtle colors pinwheeled against velvet. Oiled thoughts raced, unable to grab.

The voice slid like black syrup into my ears.

"Once dead, now quick. Arise."

I opened my eyes. My fingers curled across palm, thumb touched pinkie, tack of prints on skin, twist and pull of muscles in wrist, the first things necessary. No pain in my joints. Hands agile and strong. Tremors gone.

I shivered.

"I'm back," I said.

"Quick and quick," the voice said

I turned to see who spoke in such lovely black tones. My eyes focused on a brown oval like rich fine wood, ivory eyes with ruby pupils, face square and stern but unmarred by age.

"How does it feel to be inside again, and whole? I am a doctor. You can tell."

I opened my mouth. "No pain," I said. "I feel . . . oily, inside. Smooth and slick."

"Young," the face said. I saw the face in profile and decided, from the timbre of the voice and general features, that this was a woman. The smoothness of her skin reminded me of the unlined surface of a painting. She wore long black robes from neck to below where I lay on an elevated bed or table. "Do you have memories?"

I swallowed. My throat felt cool. I thought of eating and remembered one last painful meal, when swallowing had been difficult. "Yes. Eating. Hurting."

"Your name?"

"Something. Cardino."

"Cardino, that's all?"

"My stage name. My real name. Is. Robert . . . Falucci."

"That is right. When you are ready, you may stand and join them for dinner. Roderick invites you."

"Them?"

"Roderick suggested you, and the five voted to bring you back. You may thank them, if you wish, at dinner."

The face smiled.

"Your name?" I asked.

"Ont. O-N-T."

The face departed, robes swishing like waves. Lights came up. I rolled and propped myself on one elbow, expecting pain, feeling only an easeful smoothness. I suspected that I had died. I surmised I had been frozen, as I had paid them to do, the Nitrogen Fixers, and that . . .

Lich, she had called me. Body, corpse. In one of my flashier shows I had reanimated a headless woman. Spark coils and strobes and a big van de Graaf generator had made the hair on her free head stand on end.

I slipped my naked legs down from the table, found the coolness of a tessellated tile floor. My fumbling fingers found the robe on the table as I stared at the floor: men and women, each a separate tile perfectly joined, in a flow of completion advanced to the far wall: courtship, embracing, copulating, birth.

I felt a sudden floating happiness.

I've made it.

On a heavy black oak table, I found clothes set out that might have come from a studio costume department—black stiffly formal suit out of a 1930s society movie, something for Fred Astaire. To my chagrin, I tended to corpulence even in this resurrected state. I put the robe aside and stuffed myself into the outfit and poured a glass of water from a nearby pitcher. A watercress sandwich appeared and I nibbled it while exploring the room.

I should be terrified. I'm not. Roderick . . .

The table on which I had been reborn occupied the center of the room, spare and black and shiny, like a stone altar. It felt cold to my touch. A yard to the right, the heavy oak table supported my sandwich plate, the pitcher and glass of water, the discarded robe, and a pair of shoes.

Lich, she had called me.

I stood in bright if diffuse illumination. No lights were visible. The room's corners lay in shadow. Armless chairs lined the wall behind me. A door opened in the next wall. Paintings covered the wall before me. The room seemed square and complete, but I could not find a fourth wall. No matter which direction, as I made a complete turn, I counted only three walls. The decor seemed rich and fashionable, William Morris and the restrained lines of classic Japanese furniture.

Obviously, not the next decade, I thought. *Maybe centuries in the future.*

I walked forward and the illumination followed. Expertly painted portraits covered the wall, precise cold renderings of five people, three pale males and two dark females, all in extravagant dress. None of them were Roderick—if Roderick was who I thought he might be—and Ont did not appear, either. The men wore tights and seemed ridiculously well endowed, with feathers puffed on their shoulders and immense fan-shaped hats rising from the crowns of their close-cropped heads; the women in tight-fitting black gowns, reddish hair spread like sunbursts, skin the color and sheen of rubbed maple.

I wondered if I would ever find employment in this future world. "Do you like illusions?" I asked the portraits rhetorically.

"They are life's blood," answered the male on the left, smiling at me.

The portrait resumed its old, painted appearance.

Assume nothing, I told myself.

Startling patterns decorated the wall behind the portraits. Flowers surrounded and gave form to skull-shapes, eyes like holograms of black olives floating within petaled sockets.

"Where is dinner?" I asked.

The portraits did not answer.

The room's only door opened onto a straight corridor that extended for a few yards, then sent me back to the room where I had been reborn. I scowled at the unresponsive portraits, then looked for intercoms, doorbells, hidden telephones. Odd that I should still feel happy and at ease, for I might be stuck like a mouse in a cage.

"I would like to go to dinner," I said in my stage voice, precise and commanding. The door swung shut and opened again. When I stepped through, I faced another corridor, and this one led to a larger double door, half ajar.

I opened the door and stepped outside. I faced an immense ruined garden and orchard, ranks of great squat thick trees barren of any leaves and overgrown with brown creepers and tall sere thistles spotted with black crusty patches. Hundreds of acres spread over low desolate hills, and on the highest hill stood an edifice that would have seemed unlikely in a dream.

It rose above the ruined gardens, white and yellow-gray like ancient chalk, what must have once been a splendid mansion, its lowest level simple and elegant. An architectural cancer had set in, however, and tumorous wings and floors and towers and bridges thrust from the first level with malign genius, twisting and joining in ways I could not make sense of. These extrusions reflected the condition of the garden: the house was overgrown, thick with its own weeds.

Above the house and land rose a sky at once gray and dull and threatening. Coils of cloud dropped from a scudding ash-colored ceiling like incipient tornadoes, and the air smelled of stale ocean and electricity.

A slender spike of alarm rose in me, then faded back into a general euphoria at simply being alive, and free of pain. It did not matter that everything in this place seemed nightmarish and out of balance. All would be explained, I told myself.

Roderick would explain.

If anyone besides me could have survived into this puzzling and perhaps far future, it was the resourceful and clever friend of my youth, the only Roderick of my acquaintance: Roderick Escher. I could imagine no other.

I let go of the door and stepped out on a stone pathway, then turned to look back at the building where I had been reborn. It was small and square, simply and solidly constructed of smooth pieces of yellow-gray stone, without ornament, like a dignified tomb. Frost covered the stones, and ice rime caked the soil around the building, yet the interior had not been noticeably cooler.

I squared my shoulders, examined my hands one more time, flexed the fingers, and spread them at arm's length. I wiped both of my hands quickly before my face, as if to pass an imaginary coin between them, and smiled at the ease of movement. I then set out along the path through the trees of the ruined garden, toward the encrusted and cancerous-looking house.

The trees and thistles seemed to consent to my passage, listening to my footfalls in silent reservation. I did not so much feel watched as measured, as if all the numbers of my life, my new body, were being recorded and analyzed. I noticed as I approached the barren trunks or the dry, lifeless wall of some past hedge, that all the branches and remaining dry leaves were gripped and held immobile by tiny strands of white fiber. *Spiders, mites*, I hypothesized, but saw no evidence of anything moving. When I stumbled and kicked aside a clod of dry dirt, I saw the soil was laden with thicker white fibers, some of which released sparkles like buried stars where tiny rocks had cut or scratched them. As I walked, I dug with my toe into more patches, and wherever I investigated, strands underlay the topsoil like fine human hairs, a few inches beneath the dusty gray surface. I bent down to feel them. They broke under my fingers, the severed ends sparkling, but then reassembled.

The house on the hill appeared even more diseased and outlandish, the closer I came. Among its many peculiarities, one struck me forcibly: with the exception of the ground floor, there were no windows in the building. All the walls and towers rose in blind disregard of each other and of the desolation beyond. Moreover, as I approached the broad verandah and the stone steps leading to a large bronze door, I noticed that the house itself was also layered with tiny white threads, some of which had been cut and sparkled faintly. What might have seemed cheerful—a house pricked along its intricate surfaces and lines by a myriad of stars, as if portrayed on a Christmas card— became instead flatly dreadful, dreadful in my inner estimation, yet flatly so because of my artificial and inappropriate *calm*.

Another wave of concern swept outward from my core, and was just as swiftly damped. *Part of me wants to feel fear, but I don't. Something in me desires to turn around and find peace again . . .*

A *lich* would feel this way . . . Still half-dead.

From the porch, the house did not appear solid. Fine cracks spread through the stones, and to one side—the northern side, to judge from the angle of the sun—a long crack reached from the foundation to the top of the first floor, where it climbed the side of a short, stubby tower. I could easily imagine the stones crumbling. Perhaps all that held the house together were the white threads covering it like the fine webs of a silkworm or tent caterpillar.

I walked up the steps, my feet kicking aside dust and windblown fragments of desiccated leaves and twigs. The bronze door rose over my head, splotched with black and green. In its center panel, a bas-relief of two hands had been cast. These hands reached out to clasp each other, desire apparent in the tension and arc of the phalanges and strain of tendons, yet the beseeching fingers could not touch.

I could not equate any of this with the Roderick I had known for so many years, beginning in university. I remembered a thin but energetic man, tall and handsome in an ascetic way, his hair flyaway fine and combed back from a high forehead, double-lobed with a crease between, above his nose, that gave him an air of intense concern and concentration. Roderick's most remarkable feature had always been his eyes, set low and deep beneath straight brows, eyes great and absorbing, sympathetic and sad and yet enlivened by a twist and glitter of sensuous humor.

The Roderick I remembered had always been excessively neat, and concerned about money and possessions, and would have never allowed such an estate to go to ruin . . . Or lived in such a twisted and forbidding house.

Perhaps, then, I was going to meet another of the same name, not my friend. Perhaps my frozen body had become an item of curiosity among strangers, and resurrection could be accomplished by whimsical dilettantes. Why would the doctor suddenly abandon me, if I had any importance?

The bronze door swung open silently. Along its edges and hinges, the fine white threads parted and sparkled. The door seemed surrounded by tiny embers, which faded to orange and died, silent and unexplained.

Within, a rich darkness gradually filled with a dour luminosity, and I stepped into a long hallway. The hallway twisted along its length, corkscrewing until wall became floor, and then wall again, and finally ceiling. Smells of food and sounds of tableware and clinking glasses came through doors at the end of the twisted hall.

I followed the smells and the sounds. I had expected to have to scramble up the sloping floor, to crawl down the twisted hall, but up and down redefined themselves, and I simply walked along what remained, to my senses, the floor, making a dizzy rotation, to a dining room at the very end. Doors swung open at my approach. I expected at any moment to meet my friend Roderick—expected and hoped, but was disappointed.

• • •

The five people pictured in the portraits sat in formal suits and gowns around a long table set with many empty plates and bottles of wine. Their raiment was of the same period and fashion as my own, the twenties or thirties of my century. They were in the middle of a toast as I entered. The woman who had presided at my rebirth was not present, nor was anyone I recognized as Roderick.

"To our revivified *lich*, Robert Falucci," the five said, lifting their empty glasses and smiling. They were really quite handsome people, the two women young and brown and supple, with graceful limbs and long fingers, the three men strong and well-muscled, if a little too pale. Veins and arteries showed through the translucent skin on the men's faces.

"Thank you," I replied. "Pardon me, but I'm a little confused."

"Welcome to Confusion," the taller of the two women said, pushing her chair back to walk to my side. She took my arm and led me to an empty seat at the end of the table. Her skin radiated a gentle warmth and smelled sweetly musky. "Tonight, Musnt is presiding. I am Cant, and this is Shant, Wont, and Dont."

I smiled. Were they joking with me? "Robert," I said.

"We know," Cant said. "Roderick warned us you would arrive."

Musnt, at the head of the table, raised his glass again and with a gesture bade me to sit. Cant pushed my chair in for me and returned to her seat.

"I've been dead, I think," I said in a low voice, as if ashamed.

"Gone but not forgotten," Dont, the shorter woman, said, and she hid a brief giggle behind a fist clutching a lace handkerchief.

"You brought me back?"

"The doctor brought you back," Cant said with a helpful and eager expression.

"Against the wishes of Roderick's poor sister," Musnt said. "Some of us believe that with her, and perhaps with you, he has gone too far."

I turned away from his accusing gaze. "Is this Roderick's house?" I asked.

"Yes and no," Musnt said. "We oversee his work and time. We are, so to speak, the bonds placed on the last remnants of the family Escher."

"Roles we greatly enjoy," Cant said. She was youthfully, tropically beautiful, and I suspected I attracted her as much as she did me.

"I think I've been gone a long time. How much has changed?" I asked.

The four around the table, all but Cant, looked at each other with expressions I might have found on children in a schoolyard: disdain for a new boy.

"A lot, really," Musnt said, lifting knife and fork. Food appeared on Musnt's plate, a green salad and two whole raw zucchinis. Food appeared on my plate, the uneaten remains of my watercress sandwich. I looked up, dismayed. Then a zucchini appeared, and they all laughed. I smiled, but there was a salt edge to my happiness now.

I felt inferior. I certainly felt out of touch.

I did not remember Roderick having a sister.

After dinner, they retired to the drawing room, which was darkly paneled and decorated in queer rococo fashion, with many reptilian cherubs and even full-sized, dog-headed angels, as well as double pillars in spiral embrace and thick gold-threaded canopies. The materials appeared to be lapis and black marble and ebony, and everywhere the sourceless lights followed, and everywhere the busy and ubiquitous fibers overlay all surfaces.

I heard the distant murmur of a brook, rushes of air, sounds from some invisible ghostly landscape, and the voices of the five, discussing the spices used in the vegetable soup. Wont then added, "*She* persists in calling our work a blanding of the stew."

"Ah, but *she* is only half an Escher—" Wont said.

"Or a fading reflection of the truly penultimate Escher," Shant added.

"She would do anything for her brother," Cant said sympathetically.

"You've always favored Roderick," Dont said with a sniff. "You sound like Dr. Ont."

Cant turned and smiled at me. "We are judges, but not muses. I *am* the least critical."

Musnt opened a heavy brocaded curtain figured with seashells and they looked out upon the overgrown garden. Orange and yellow clouds moved swiftly in a twilight azure sky. Musnt flung open the glass-paneled doors and we all strode onto a marble patio.

Cant put her arm through mine and hugged my elbow against her ribs. "How nice for you to arrive on a good day, with such a fine settling," she said. "I trust the doctor remade you well?"

"She must have," I said. "I feel young and well. A little . . . anxious, I think."

Cant smiled sweetly. "Poor man. They have brought back so many, and all have felt anxious. We're quite used to your anxiety. You will not disturb us."

"We're Roderick's antitheticals," Wont said, as if that might explain something, but it still told me nothing useful. Mired in a dense awkwardness and buried unease, I looked back at the house. It reached to the sky, a cathedral, Xanadu, and the tower of Babel all in one. Towers met with buttresses in impossible ways, drawing my eye from multiple perspectives into hopeless directions.

"What did you do, in your life?" Musnt asked.

"I was a magician," I said. "Cardino the Unbelievable." The name seemed ridiculous, from this distance, in the middle of these marvels.

"We are all magicians," Musnt said disdainfully. "How boring. Perhaps Roderick chose poorly."

"I do not think so," Cant said, and gave me another smile, this one eerily reassuring, an anxiolytic bowing curve of her smooth and plump lips. To my shock, nipples suddenly grew on her cheeks, surrounded by fine brown areolae. "If Robert wants, he can add another layer of critique to our efforts."

"What could he possibly know, and besides, aren't we critical enough?" Shant asked.

"Hush," Cant said. "He's our guest, and we're already showing him our dark side."

"As antitheticals should," Musnt said.

"I don't understand . . . What am I, here?" I asked, the salt taste in my mouth turning bitter. "*Why* am I here?"

"You're a *lich*," Musnt said, staring away from me at nothing in particular. "As such, you have no rights. You can be an added amusement. A spice against our blanding, if you wish, but nothing more."

"Please don't ask if you're in hell, not so soon," Shant said with a twist of disgust. "It is *so* common."

"Who is this Roderick?"

"He is our master and our slave," Shant said. "We observe all he does, bring him his audience, and bind him like chains."

"He is a seeker of sensation without consequence," Cant said. "We, like his audience, are perfect for him, for we are of no consequence whatsoever." Cant sighed. "I suppose he should come down and say hello."

"Or you can find *him*, which is more likely," Shant suggested.

I opened my mouth to speak, then closed it again, turning to look at the five on the patio. Finally, I said, "Are you real?"

Cant said, "If you mean embodied, no."

"You're dreams," I said.

"You asked if we like illusions," Cant said shyly, touching my shoulder with her slender hand. "We can't help but like them. We are all of us tricks of mind and light, and cheap ones at that. Roderick, for the time being, is real, as is this house."

"Where is Roderick?"

"Upstairs," Shant said.

Wont chuckled at that. "That's very general, but we really don't know. You may find him, or he will find you. Take care you do not meet his sister first. She may not approve of you."

At a noise from within the patio doors, I turned. I heard footsteps cross the stone floor, and looked back at Cant and the others to see their reactions. All, however, had vanished. I took a tentative step toward the doors, and was about to make another, when a tall and spectrally thin figure strode onto the patio, turned his head, and fixed me with a puzzled and even irritated glare.

"So soon? The doctor said it would take days more."

I studied the figure's visage with halting recognition. There were similarities: the high forehead, divided into two prominences of waxen pallor; the short, sharp falcon nose; the sunken cheeks hollowed even more now as if by some wasting disease . . . And the eyes. The figure's eyes burned like a flame on the taper of his thin, elongated body. The voice sounded like an echo from caverns at the center of a cold ferrous planet, metallic and sad, yet keeping some of the remembered strength of the original, and that I could not mistake.

"Roderick!"

The figure wore a tight-fitting pair of red pants and a black shirt with billowing sleeves buttoned to preposterously thick gloves like leathern mittens, while around his neck hung a heavy black collar or yoke as might be worn by an ox. At the ends of this yoke depended two brilliant silver chains threaded with thick white fiber. Around his legs twined more fibers, which seemed to grow from the floor, breaking and joining anew with his every step. He seemed to walk on faint embers. Threads grew also beneath his clothes and to his neck, forming fine webs around his mouth and eyes. Looking more closely, I saw that the threads intruded *into* his mouth and eyes.

Still his most arresting feature, the large and discerning eyes had assumed a blue and watery glaze, as if exposed to many brilliant suns, or visions too intense for healthy witness.

"You appear alert and well," Roderick said, turning his gaze with a long blink, as if ashamed. His hair swept back from his forehead, still thin and fine, but white as snow, and tufted as if he had just awakened from a damp and restless sleep. "The doctor has done her usual excellent work."

"I feel well . . . But so many irritating . . . evasions! I have been treated like a . . . I have been called an amusement—"

Roderick raised his right hand, then stared at it with some surprise and slowly, pulling back florid lips from prominent white teeth as at the appearance of some vermin, peeled off the glove by tugging at one finger, then the next, until the hand rose naked and revealed. He slowly curled and straightened the slender, bony fingers and thumb. A spot of blood bedewed the tip of each. One drop fell to the floor and made a ruby puddle on the stone.

"Pardon me," Roderick said, closing the naked hand tightly and pushing it into a pocket in his clinging pants. "I am still emerging. You have come from a farther land than I—how ironic that you seem the more healthy for your journey!"

"I am renewed," I said. Upon seeing Roderick, I began to feel my emotions returning, fear mixing now with a leap of hope that some essential questions might be answered. "Have I truly died and been reborn?"

"You died a very young man—at the age of sixty," Roderick said. "I took charge of your frozen remains from that ridiculous corporation twenty years later and secured you in the vaults of my own family. I had made the beginnings of my huge fortune by then and arranged such preparations very early, and so you were protected by many forces, legal and political. None interfered with our vaults. If not for me, you would have been decanted and rotted long ago."

"How long has it been?"

"Two hundred and fifty years."

"And the others—Wont, Cant, Musnt, Shant, Dont . . ."

Roderick's face grew stern, as if I had unexpectedly uttered a string of rude words. Then he shook his head and put his still-gloved hand on my shoulder.

"All the world's people lie in cool vaults now, or wear no form at all. People are born and die at will, ever and again. Death is conquered, disease a helpmeet and plaything. The necessities of life are not food but sensation. All is servant to the quest for stimulus. The expectant and all-devouring Nerve is King."

I was suddenly dizzied by a vertigo of deep time, the precipitous awareness of having emerged from a long well or tunnel of insensate nullity leaving almost everyone and everything I had known behind. And perhaps Roderick, the friend I had once known, was no longer with me, either. I felt as if the stones beneath me swayed.

"You alone, of all our friends, our family . . . are alive?"

"I alone keep my present shape, though not without some gaps," Roderick said with some pride. "I am the last of the embodied and walkabout Eschers . . . I, and my sister, but she is not well." His face creased into a mask of sorrow, a well-worn expression I could not entirely credit. "I have mourned her a thousand times already, and a thousand times she has returned to something like life. She feigns death, I think, to taunt me, and abhors my quest, but . . . I could ask for no one more obedient."

"I don't remember you having a sister," I said.

Roderick closed his eyes. "Come, this place is filled with unpleasant associations. I no longer eat. The thought of clamping my jaw and grinding organic matter . . . ugh!"

Roderick led me from the dining room, back to the foyer, and a staircase which rose opposite the main door. The stairs branched midpoint to either side, leading to an upper floor. Roderick ascended the stairs with an eerie grace, halting and surveying his surroundings unpredictably, as if motivated not by human desires, but by the volition of a hunting insect or spider. His eyes studied the fiber-crusted walls, lids half-closed, head shaking at some association or memory conjured by stimuli invisible to me.

"You must find a place here," Roderick said. "You are the last in the vault. All the others have long since been freed and either vapored or joined with some neural clan or another. I have kept you in reserve, dear Robert, because I value you most highly. You have a keen mind and quick fingers. I need you."

"How may I be useful?"

"All this, the house and the lands around us, survive by whim of King Nerve," Roderick said. "We are entertainers, and our tenure wears thin.

Audiences demand so much of us, and of everything around us. You are new and unexplored."

"What kind of entertainment?"

"Our lives and creations—the lives of my sister and I—are one illusion following on the tail of another," Roderick said. "All that we do and think is marked and absorbed by billions. It is our prison, and our glory. Our family has always had conjurers—do you remember? It is how we met and became friends."

"I remember. Your father—"

"I have not thought of him in a century," Roderick said, and his eyes glowed. He smiled. "Fine work, Robert! My mind tingles with associations already. My father . . . and my mother . . ."

"But Roderick, you did not get along with your father. You abhorred magic and illusions. You called them 'tricks,' and said they 'deceived the simple and the unobservant.'"

"I remained a faithful friend, did I not?"

"Yes," I said. "You must have. You brought me back from the dead."

"Sufficient time shows even me how wrong I am," he murmured.

We reached the top of the stairs. A familiar figure, the doctor named Ont, passed down the endless hallway, black robes swirling like ink in water. She stopped before us, paying no attention to me, but staring at Roderick with pained solicitousness, as if she might cry if he grew any more pale, or thinner.

"Thank you, Dr. Ont," Roderick said, bowing slightly. She nodded acknowledgment.

"He is what you wanted, what you need?"

"So soon, and unexpected, but already valuable."

"He can help you?"

"I do not know," Roderick said. Ont looked now at me.

"You must be very *cautious* with Roderick Escher," she warned. "He is a national cleverness, a treasure. It is my duty to sustain him, or to do his bidding, whichever he desires."

"How is *she?*" Roderick asked, hands clasped before him, naked fingers preposterously thin and white against the thick leathern glove.

Ont replied, "Even this vortex soon spins itself out, and this time I fear the end will be permanent."

"Fear . . . more than you hope?" Roderick asked.

Ont shook her head sternly. "I do not understand this conceit between you."

With another tip of her head, Ont walked on, and the hall curled into a corkscrew ahead of her. Remaining upright, she tread along the spiraling floor and vanished around the curve. The hall straightened, but she was no longer visible.

"A century ago, I chose to come back into this world refreshed," Roderick said to me, "and took from myself a kind of rib or vault of my mind, to make a sister. She became my twin. Now, let me show you how the house works . . ."

Roderick gripped me by the elbow and guided me to a steep, winding stair that must have coiled within the largest tower surmounting the house. He gave what he meant to be an encouraging smile, but instead revealed his teeth in a conspiratorial rictus, and climbed the steps before me. I hesitated, palms and upper lip moist with growing dread of this odd time and incomprehensible circumstance. Soon, however, as my friend's form vanished around the first curve in the stair, I felt even more dread at being left alone, and hoped knowledge of whatever sort might ease my apprehensiveness. I raced to catch up with him.

"As a race, in the plenitude of time—a very short time—we have found our success," Roderick said. "Lacking threat from without, and at peace within, our people enjoy the fruits of the endeavors of all civilizations. All that has been suffered is repaid here." His voice sounded hollow in the tower, like the mocking laughter of a far-off crowd.

"How?" I asked, following on Roderick's heels up the stairs. That which might have once winded me now seemed almost effortless. Whatever shortness of breath I felt was due to nerves, not frailness of body.

"All work is stationary," Roderick said, again favoring me with that peculiar grimace that had replaced a once fine and encouraging smile. We had made two turns around the tower.

"Then why do we walk?" I asked.

"We are chosen. Privileged, in a way. We—my sister and I, Dr. Ont, and now you—maintain the last links with physical bodies. We give a foundation to all the world's dreams. The entire Earth is like the seed in a peach, all but disposed of. What matters is the sweet pulp of the fruit—communication and expansion along the fiber-optic lines, endless interaction, endless exchange of sensations. Some have abandoned all links with the physical, the seed, having bodies no more. They flit like ghosts through the interwoven threads that make the highways and rivers and oceans of our civilization. Most, more conservative, maintain their corporeal forms like shrines, and visit them now and then, though the bodies are cold and unfeeling, suspended and vestigial. You were reborn in one such vault, made to hold such as you, and eventually to receive my sister and me—though I have decided not to go there, never to go there. I think *death* would be more interesting."

"I've been there," I said.

"Yes, and I always ask my *liches* . . . What do you recall?"

"Nothing," I said.

"Look closely at that excised segment in your world-line. You were dead two and a half centuries, and you remember nothing?"

"No," I said.

He smiled. "No one has. The demands . . . The voices . . . Gone." He stopped and looked back at me. We stood more than halfway up the tower. "A blankness, a darkness. A surcease from endless art."

"In my life, you were more concerned with business than the arts."

"The world changed after you died. Everyone turned their eyes inward, and riches could be achieved by any who linked. Riches of the inner life, available to all. We made our world self-sustaining and returned to a kind of cradle. I grew bored with predicting the weather of money when it hardly mattered and so few cared. I worked with artists, and found more and more a sympathy, until I became one myself."

He stood before a large pale wooden door set in the concrete and plaster of the tower. "Robert, when we were boys, we dreamed of untrammeled sensual delights. Soon enough, I saw that experiences that seemed real, but carried no onerous burdens of pain, would consume all of humanity. Before my rebirth, I directed banks and shaped industries . . . Then I slept for twenty years, waiting for fruition. After my rebirth, my sister and I invested the riches I earned in certain industries and new businesses. We *directed* the flow and shape of the river of light, on which everyone floated like little boats. For a time, I controlled—but I never retired to the vaults myself."

He touched the door with a long finger, smearing a spot of blood on the unpainted and bleached surface. "Physical desire," he whispered, "drove the growth. Sex and lust without rejection or loss, without competition, was the beginning. Primal drives directed the river, until everyone had all they wanted . . . In a land of ghosts and shades."

The door swung open at another touch of his finger, leaving two red prints on the wood. Within, more river sounds, and a series of breathless sighs.

"Now, hardly anyone cares about sex, or any other basic drives. We have accessed deeper pleasures. We re-string our souls and play new tunes."

A fog of gossamer filled the dark space beyond the door. Lights flitted along layer after layer of crossed fibers, and in the middle, a machine like a frightened sea urchin squatted on a wheeled carriage. Its gray spines rose with rapid and sinuous grace to touch points on conjunctions between threads, and light seeped forth.

"This is the thymolecter. What I create, as well as what I think and experience, the thymolecter dispenses to waiting billions. And my thoughts are at work throughout this house, in room after room. Look!"

He turned and lifted his hand, and I saw a group of thin children form within the gossamer. They played listlessly around a bubbling green lump, poking it with a stick and laughing like fiends. It made little sense to me. "This amuses half the souls who occupy what was once the subcontinent of India."

I curled my lip instinctively, but said nothing.

"It *speaks* to them," Roderick whispered. "There is torment in every gesture, and triumph in the antagonism. This has played continuously for fifteen years, and always it changes. The *audience* responds, becomes part of the piece, takes it over . . . and I adjust a figure here, a sensibility there. Some say it is my masterpiece. And I had to fight for years to overcome the objections of the five!" His cheeks took on some color at the memory of the triumph. He must have sensed my underwhelming, for he added, "You realize we experience only the tip of the sword here, the cover of a deep book. You see it out of context, and without the intervening years to acculturate you."

"I am sure," I muttered, and was thankful when Roderick extinguished the entertainment.

"You've had experience with live audiences, of course, but never with a hundred billion respondents. My works spread in waves against a huge shore. At one time they beat up against other waves, the works of other artists. But there are far fewer artists than when you were first alive. As we have streamlined our arts for maximum impact, competition has narrowed and variety has waned, and now the waves slide in tandem; we serve niches which do not overlap. Mine is the largest niche of all. I am the master."

"It's all vague to me," I said. "Isn't there anything besides entertainment?"

"There is discussion of entertainment," Roderick said.

"Nothing else? No courtships, relationships, raising children?"

"Artists imagine children to be raised, far better than any real children. Remember how horrid *we* were?"

"I had no children . . . I had hoped, here—"

"A splendid idea! Eventually, perhaps we will reenact the family. But for now . . ."

I sensed it coming. Roderick's friendship, however grand, had always hung delicately upon certain favors, never difficult to grant individually, but when woven together, amounting to a subtle fabric of obligations.

"I need a favor," Roderick said.

"I suppose I owe you my life."

"Yes," Roderick said, with an uninflected bluntness that chilled me. Roderick drew me from the gossamer chamber, and as he was about to close the door, I glimpsed another play of lights, arranged into curved blades slicing geometric objects. A few of the objects—angular polyhedra, flushed red— seemed to try to escape the blades.

"Half of Central America," Roderick confided, seeing my puzzlement.

"What sort of favor?" I asked with a sigh as the door swung silently shut.

"I need you to perform magic," Roderick said.

I brightened. "That's all?"

"It will be enough," Roderick said. "Nobody has performed magic of your sort for a hundred years. Few remember. It will be novel. It will be concrete. It will play on different strings. King Nerve has gotten demanding lately, and I feel . . ."

He did not complete this expression. "Pardon my enthusiasm, you must be exhausted," he said, with a tone of sudden humility that again endeared him to me. "There is a kind of night here. Sleep as best you can, in a special room, and we will talk . . . tomorrow."

• • •

Roderick led me through another of those helical halls, whose presence I keenly felt in every part of the house, and soon came to hate. I wondered if there were no doors or halls at all, only illusions of connections between great stacks and heaps of cubicals, which Roderick could activate to carry us through the walls like Houdini or Joselyne. In a few minutes, we came to a small narrow door, and beyond I found a pleasant though small room, with a canopy bed and a white marble lavatory, supplying a need I was beginning to feel acutely.

Roderick waited for me to return, and chided my physical limitations. "You still need to eat, and suffer the consequences."

"Can I change that?" I asked, half fearfully.

"Not now. It is part of the novelty. You are a *lich*. You subscribe to no services, move nothing by will alone."

"As do the five?"

Again he shook his head and frowned. "They are projections. To you, they feel solid enough, real enough, but there is no amusement in them. They can *seem* to do anything. Including make my life a torment."

"How?"

"They express the combined will of King Nerve," he said, and answered no further questions. He then showed me the main highlights of the room. It was much larger than it seemed, and wherever I turned I beheld new walls, which met previous walls at square angles, each wall supporting shelves covered with apparatus of such rareness and beauty that I lost all of my dread in a bath of primal delight.

"These can be your tools," Roderick said with a flourish. I turned and walked from wall to apparent wall, shelf to shelf, picking up Brema brasses, numerous fine boxes nested and false-bottomed and with hidden pockets and drawers, large and small tables covered with black and white squares in which velvet-drop bags might be concealed, stacks of silver and gold and steel and bronze coins hollow and hinged and double-faced and rough on one side and smooth on the other, silk handkerchiefs and scarves and stacks of cloths of many colors; collapsing birdcages of such beautiful craftsmanship I felt my eyes moisten; glasses filled with apparent ink and wine and milk, metal tubes of many sizes, puppet doves and mice and white rats and even monkeys, mummified heads of many expressions, some in boxes; slates spirit and otherwise, some quite small; pens and pencils and paintbrushes with hidden talents; cords and retracting reels and loops; stacked boxes à la Welles in which a young woman might be rearranged at will; several Johnson Wedlocks in crystal goblets; tables and platforms and cages with seemingly impassable Jarrett pedestals; collapsible or compressible chess pieces, checkers, poker chips, potato chips, marbles, golfballs, baseballs, basketballs, soccer balls; ingenious items of clothing and collars and cufflinks manufactured by the Magnificent Traumata; handcuffs and strait jackets . . .

As I turned from wall to wall with delight growing to delirium, Roderick merely stood behind me, arms folded, receiving my awestruck glances with a patient smile. Finally I came to a wall on which hung one small black cabinet with glass doors. Within this cabinet there lay . . .

Ten sealed decks of playing cards.

I opened this cabinet eagerly, aching to try my new hands, wrists, fingers, on them. I unwrapped cellophane from a deck and tamped the stack into one hand, immediately fanning the cards into a double spiral. With a youthful and pliant fold of skin near my thumb I pushed a single Ace of Spades to prominence, remembering with hallucinatory vividness the cards most likely to be chosen by audience members in any given geography, as recorded by Maskull in his immortal *Force and Suit*. I turned and presented the deck to Roderick.

"Pick a card," I said, "any card."

He stared at me intensely, almost resentfully, and his left eye opened wider than the right, presenting an expression composed at once of equal mix delight and apprehension. "Save it. There is altogether too much time."

But like a child suddenly brought home to familiar toys, I could not restrain myself. I propelled the deck in an arc from one hand to the other, and back. I shuffled them and cut them expertly behind my back, knowing the arrangement had not even now been disturbed. With my fingers I counted from the top of the precisely split deck, and brought up a Queen of Hearts. "Appropriate for your world," I said.

"Impressive legerdemain," Roderick said with a slight shudder. He had never been able to judge my lights of hand, or follow my instant sleights and slides and crosses. With almost carnivorous glee, I wanted to dazzle this man who controlled so much illusion, to challenge him to a duel.

"It's magic," I said breathlessly. "*Real* magic."

"Its charm," he said in a subdued and musing voice, "lies in its simplicity and its antiquity." He seemed doubtful, and rested his chin on the tip of an index finger. "Still, I insist you need to rest, to prepare. Tomorrow . . . We will begin, and all will be judged."

I realized he was correct. Now was not the time. I needed to know more. It was possible, in this unreal futurity, anything I might be able to accomplish with such simple props would be laughed at. Sooner expect a bird to fly to the moon . . .

With a brief farewell, he departed, and left me alone in the marvelous room. My heart hammered like a pecking dove in my chest.

Nowhere in this room, unique I supposed in all the rooms of the house of Roderick Escher, did there creep or coat or insinuate any of the pale light-guiding threads or fibers. I was alone and unwatched, unconnected to any hungry external beings, be they kings or slaves . . .

I fancied I was Roderick's secret.

I undressed and showered. The bathroom filled with steam, and I inhaled its warm moistness, returning again to the euphoria I had experienced upon my arrival. I toweled and picked up a thick terry-cloth robe, examining the sleeves and pockets. In a table drawer I found a needle and many colors of thread, and marveled at Roderick's thoroughness.

Far too restless and exalted for sleep, I began to sew hooks and loops and pockets into the robe, for practice, and then into my suit of clothes. My fingers worked furiously, as agile as they had ever been in my prime.

I turned to the laded walls and spun through a dozen displays before finding clamps, tack, glue, brads, wire, springs, card indexes, and other necessities. I altered the suit for fit as well as fittings. I had long centuries ago learned to be a tailor and seamstress, as well as a forger and engineer.

There were no windows, no clocks, no way to learn the time of evening, if evening it actually was. I might have spent days of objective time in my obsessive labors. It did not matter here; I was not disturbed and did not rest until I became so tired I could hardly stand or clasp a needle or bend a wire.

I removed the robe, climbed into the small, comfortable bed, and immediately fell into deep slumber.

I know not how many minutes or hours, or perhaps years later, I felt a touch on my face and jerked abruptly to consciousness. My eyes burned but my nerves pulsed as if I had just drunk a dozen cups of black coffee. In the darkened room (had I turned off any lights? there were no lights to control!) I saw a whitish shape, tall and blurred. Now came to me a supreme supernatural dread, and I was immediately drenched with sweat. I rubbed my eyes to clear them.

"Who's there?" I cried.

"It is I, Maja," the form said in a thrilling contralto.

"Who?" I asked, my voice breaking, for I only half-remembered my circumstances. I did not know what might face me in this unknown place and time.

"I am Roderick's sister," she said, and came closer, her face entering a sourceless, nacreous spot of glow. I beheld a woman of extraordinary character, her countenance as thin as the faces of the women in Klimt's darker paintings, her eyes as large as Roderick's, and of like cast and color. I could have sworn her high twin-lobed forehead would have blemished her femininity, had it been described so to me, yet it did not.

"What do you want?" I asked, my heart slowing its staccato beat. I felt no danger from her, only a ruinous sadness.

"Do not do this thing," she warned, eyes intent on mine. I could not break that gaze, so frightened and yet so strong. "It is a change too drastic for the Eschers, a breach, a leap to disaster. Roderick wishes our doom, but he does not know what he does."

"Why would he wish to die?"

This she did not answer, but instead leaned forward and whispered to me, "He believes we *can* die. That is his madness. He has told me to go before, to prove certain theories."

"And you have agreed—to die?"

She nodded, eyes fixed on mine, drawing me in as if to the doors of her soul. In her there was more of the cadaver already than a living woman, yet she seemed sadly, infinitely beautiful. Her beauty was that of a guttering candle flame. The fire of her eyes was a fraction of that of Roderick's, and her body, as a taper, might supply only a few minutes more of the fuel of life. Unlike the brown women, Cant and Dont, who were unreal yet seemed solid and healthy, she was all too real, and I could have blown her away with a weak breath. "I am his twin. He took me from his mind, shaped me to equal him, in all but will. I have no will of my own. I obey him."

"He made his own sister a slave?"

"It is done that way here. We may create versions of our self that do not possess a legal existence."

"How bitter!" I exclaimed.

"Oh, I may protest, may try to show him my love by directing his will with persuasion. But he is stronger, and I do whatever he tells me. Now, it is his wish I try again to die. I only hope this time I might succeed."

Behind her I saw the approach of the solicitous Dr. Ont. The doctor took Roderick's sister by one skeletal hand, pushed her lips close to Maja's almost translucent ear, and murmured words in a tongue I could not understand. Maja's head fell to one side and it seemed she might collapse. Dr. Ont supported her, and they withdrew from the room.

I felt at once a heavy swell of resentment, and a commensurate surge of bluster. "How dare she come here, smelling of death. I've left *death* behind." But in my declining terror, I was exaggerating. Roderick's sister, Maja, had had no smell at all.

She had smelled no more intensely than a matching volume of empty air.

I felt I slept only a few minutes, yet when Roderick's voice boomed into my room, waking me, I was completely refreshed, confident, ready for any challenge. *I* was no slave of Roderick Escher. "Dear friend—have you made the necessary preparations?" he asked. I looked around for his presence, but he was not there, only his voice.

"I'm ready," I said.

"Do you understand your challenge?"

"Better than ever," I said. I had the confidence of an innocent child, thinking tigers are simply large cats; even the appearance during the night of Maja Escher held no awe for me.

"Good. Then eat hearty, and build up your strength."

Roderick did not enter my room, but breakfast appeared on a table within the room. The apparatus I had chosen the night before lay beside the plates of warm vegetables, broth, breads. I put on my robe, manifested an Ace of Spades in my right hand, and threw it at the stack of toast, piercing the top slice. The card stuck out of the toast upright. I lifted the card, retrieving the toast with it, and took a bite, chewing with a broad smile. All my fears of the day before (if indeed a day had passed) had faded. I had never in my first life felt so confident before going onstage, or beginning a performance.

As I ate, I wondered at the lack of all meat. Had the world's inhabitants suddenly and humanely ended the slaughter of innocent animals? Or did they simply distance themselves from the carnal, in sympathy, as most of them had assumed the character of frozen meat in chilly refrigerators?

Were there any animals left to eat?

In truth, what did I know about Roderick's brave civilization? Nothing. He had not prepared me or informed me any further. Yet my confidence did not fade. I felt instinctively the challenge that Roderick was about to offer—to compare the overwhelming and undeniable magic of this time, against my own simple legerdemain, as Roderick had called it.

Roderick visited me in person as I finished my breakfast.

"Did you enjoy yourself?" he asked as he entered through the door. His arm rose slowly to indicate the changeable wall of cases, now frozen to the apparatus associated with cards. He walked over to the glass case, opened it, and removed a reel manufactured by my inspiration, Cardini, who had died just after my first birth, but whose effects I had learned by heart. "Did you know," Roderick said, holding the tiny reel in his palm, "that a century ago, children played with dollhouses indistinguishable from the real? Little automata going about their lives, using tools perfect for their scale, living dolls sitting on furniture accurate in every way . . . And these houses were so cheap they were made available to the poorest of the poor?"

"I didn't know that," I said.

Roderick smiled at me, and for the first time on this, my second day in my new life, I felt a narrow chilliness behind my eyes, a suspicion of the unforeseen.

"Yet we have advanced beyond that time as gods march beyond ants," he said. "All pleasures available at will. Every nerve and region within the brain—and without!—charted and their affects explored in endless variations. Whole societies devoted to pain from injuries impossible in all past experience, to the ghostlike exertion of an infinite combination of muscles in creatures the size of planets, to the social and sexual dalliances of phantoms conjured from histories and times and places that never were."

"Remarkable," I said stiffly.

"An audience of such intense discernment and sophistication that nothing surprises them, nothing arouses their childlike amazement, for they have never *been* children!"

"Extraordinary," I said with some pique. Did he wish for my defeat, my failure, to enjoy some petty triumph over an inferior? I steeled myself against his words, as I might have armored against the complaints of an older and better magician, criticizing my fledgling efforts.

"There are audiences of such size that they dwarf all of the Earth's past populations," he added.

I saw my bed fold into itself until it vanished into a corner. The wall of cases shrank into a narrow box the size of a book, leaving me with only the table and the apparatus I had chosen the night before.

"Prepare, Robert," he said. "The curtain rises soon."

Then his voice took on a shadowed depth, betraying a mix of emotions I could not comprehend, relief mixed with heavy grief and even guilt, and something else beyond my poor, unembellished range. "Dr. Ont came to me last night. Maja has succumbed. My sister is no more. Ont certifies that she has truly died. She has even begun to decay."

"I'm sorry," I said.

"It's a triumph," he said quietly. "She goes before . . ."

I put on the suit I had tailored and adjusted, and inwardly smiled at its close fit and how it flattered my pudgy form. I had never been handsome, had always lacked the charms of magicians who combined grace and artistry with physical beauty. I compensated by simply being better, faster, and more ingenious.

Roderick looked around the room. Fibers grew from the floor, climbing the walls like mold, until they shrouded everything but me and my table and cards. I seemed surrounded by a forest of fungal tendrils, glowing like swarms of fireflies.

"Billions of receptors, hooked into webs and matrices and nets reaching around the Earth," Roderick said. "Tiny little eyes like stars that have replaced any desire to leave and venture out to real stars, to other worlds. We have our own interior infinities to explore."

I made my final arrangements, and stood in the center of the lights, the tendrils. "Tell me when I'm to begin."

"We've already begun, except for the time you've spent in this room," Roderick said. "Even Maja's protests to me, and her death, have been watched and absorbed. I've used the drama of my own war to stay at the top of the ratings, my preparations and agonizing. Even the five, the antitheticals—I have made them part of this!"

The same nacreous light that had bathed Maja's face now surrounded me, and the fibers arranged themselves with a sound like the motion of a horde of chitinous sea creatures rubbing their claws.

Roderick backed away until he stood in shadow, then lifted his hand, giving me my cue.

I had never had such a draw in my life—nor felt so alone. But was this really so different from appearing on television? I had done that often enough.

"Once upon a time," I said, focusing ahead of me at no space in particular, and smiling confidently, "a young man on a luxury cruise was caught in a horrible shipwreck, stranded on a desert island with nobody and nothing but a crate of food and water, and a crate of unopened packs of playing cards."

I brought out a deck of cards and peeled away the plastic. "I was that young man. I knew nothing of the magical arts, but in three solitary years I taught myself thousands of manipulations and passes and motions, until I felt I could fool even myself at times. And how was this done? How does a magician, knowing all the methods behind his effects, come to believe in magic?"

I swallowed a lump in my throat and leaped into the abyss.

"In those three years, I learned to make cards *confess*." I rifled the deck of cards and formed a rippling mouth, and with one finger strummed the edges.

"We spoke to each other," the cards said in a breathless, stringy voice. "And Cardino taught us all we know."

I produced another deck, opened it with one hand, removed the cards, and arranged them on my palm, and made them speak as well, in a *female* voice: "And we taught him all that we know."

I squeezed both decks up in a double arc and caught them in opposite hands. From the top of each deck I produced a Queen of Hearts, and clamped the two cards together in my teeth. "I learned the secrets of royalty," I said through clenched teeth. Holding the decks in one hand, separated by my pointing finger, I plucked the cards from between my teeth and revealed them as two jacks. "The knaves whispered to me of court intrigues, and the kings and queens taught me the secrets of their royal numbers."

In my hands, the two cards quickly became a pair of threes, then fives, then sevens, then nines, and then queens again. "Finally, I was rescued." I rifled the decks together, blowing through them to make the sound of a ship's horn. "And returned to civilization. And there, I practiced my new art, my new life. And now, having returned from that island called *death*, where all magic must begin—"

I looked around me, unsure what effect my next request would have. "I call for volunteers, who wish to learn what I have learned."

The overgrown chamber whispered and lights passed among the fibrous growths like lanterns on far shores. Five figures appeared in the chambers then: Wont, Cant, Shant, Musnt, and Dont. Cant approached first, smiling her most wistful and attractive smile. "I volunteer," she said.

Roderick, standing in the background, his feet almost rooted to the floor by thick cables of fiber, lifted his hands in overt approval. Why encourage those he loathed—those who shackled him with so many strictures?

Was he flaunting the strength of his chains, like Houdini?

"Am I a physical person?" I asked Cant, dismissing all questions from my thoughts.

"Yes," she said. "Very."

"Am I the last untouched human on this world?"

"In this house, to be sure."

"Do I have a connection with any of the external powers that can make things appear and disappear, make illusions by wish alone?"

"You do not subscribe to any services," Cant said. "This we guarantee, as antitheticals."

I hesitated just a moment, and then took her hand. She felt solid enough—like real flesh. "Are *you* real?" I asked.

"Who can say?" she replied.

"Is your form solid enough to forego false illusions, illusions of will isolated from body?"

"I can do that, and guarantee it," Cant said. Her companions took attitudes of rapt attention.

"It is guaranteed," they said as one.

I began to get some sense of what their function was then, and how they constrained Roderick. What would they do to constrain me?

"If I told you there were cards rolled up in your ears, what would you say?"

"All things are possible," Cant said musically, "but for you, that is not possible."

I held my hand up to her ear and drew out a rolled-up card, making sure to tap the auricle and the opening to the canal. She reacted with some puzzlement, then delight.

"You have doubtless been told that in the past, illusion was possible only through tricks. Tell me, then—how do I do such tricks?"

"Concealment," Cant said, prettily nonplused.

I showed her my hands, which were empty, then removed my coat, dropping it to the floor, and rolled up my sleeves. I pulled another card from her other ear, unrolled it, showing it to be ruined as a playing card, then converted it to a cigarette by pushing it through my fist.

"Everyone can do that," Cant said, her smile fading. "But you—"

"*I can't do such things*," I said with a note of triumph. "I am an atavism, an innocent, an anachronic . . . A *lich*." I held out the cigarette. "Does anybody smoke anymore?" I asked. The five did not speak. Roderick shook his head in the shadows. "I didn't think so. King Nerve needs no chemical stimulants. All drugs are electronic. There is no one else on this planet—or in this house, at least—who can make the world dance, the *real* world. Except me—and I was taught by the cards."

The remaining antitheticals came forward. Musnt, as it happened, unknowingly carried a deck of cards in the pockets of his solid but unreal dinner jacket. Producing a fountain pen, I had him mark his name on the edge of the deck, grateful that these phantoms could still write, and blew upon the ink to help it dry. "These cards have friends all over the world, and they tell tales. Have you ever heard cards whisper?" I patted the deck firmly into his hands. "Hold these. Don't let them go anywhere." I borrowed his jacket and put it on Dont, helping her into the sleeves with courtesy centuries out of date. They hung over her hands.

"Hold up your deck of cards, please," I said to Musnt. He lifted the cards, his face betraying anticipation. I was grateful for small favors.

"I believe you have a set of pockets on the outside of your jacket," I told Dont. "Investigate them, please."

She reached into the pockets and removed two cellophane-wrapped decks of cards.

"Sneaky devils, these cards. They go anywhere and everywhere, and listen to our most intimate words. You have to be discreet around playing cards. Open the decks, please."

She pulled the cellophane from one deck. On the edge of the deck was the awkward scrawl of Musnt, written in fountain pen. Musnt immediately looked at his deck. The edges were blank.

Fibers formed curious worms and squirmed closer, lights pulsing.

"The other deck, now," I told Dont. She unwrapped the second deck, and there, in fountain pen, was written, *Wont*.

"Hand the deck to the person whose name is written on the side," I said. She passed the deck to Wont.

"Write on the other side your name and any number," I told Wont, giving him the pen. "And then, on a card within the deck, write the name of anybody in this room—in big, sloppy, wet letters. Show the card to everybody *except* me, and put it within the deck and press the deck together firmly."

He did this.

"Now give the deck to Cant."

He passed the deck to her. "How many decks do you carry now?" I asked. She reached into her pockets and found two more decks, which she handed to me, keeping Wont's deck with his name written on it.

"Now find the card Wont has written on, and the card immediately next to it, smeared with the wet ink from that card. Write your name on the face of that card, and another number. Show them to everybody but me."

She did so.

"How many decks do we all have now?" I asked.

I went among them, counting the decks presently in circulation—five. I redistributed the decks one to each of the five Negatives.

"The cards have told each other all about you, and you have no secrets. But I am the master of the cards—and from *me* not even the cards have secrets!"

I reached behind their ears, one by one, and pulled the cards that had been written on, with the names Cant, Musnt, Dont, and Wont. "The gossip of the cards goes full circle," I said. "Show us your decks!"

On the top of each deck, the cards bearing the suit and number of the written-on cards—for all had been number cards—appeared, bearing a newly written number, and a new name—*Cardino.*

The Negatives seemed befuddled. They showed the cards to each other and to the questing fibers.

They had forgotten the art of applause, and the fibers were silent, but no applause was necessary.

"How is this done?" Musnt asked. "You must tell . . ."

I pitied them, just as a caveman might pity a city slicker who has lost the art of flint knapping. From the beginning of their lives to the present moment, they had truly fooled nobody. They had lived lives of illusion without wonder, for always they could explain how things were done—all their magic was performed by silent, subservient, electronic demiurges.

"Turn to the last card in your decks," I said. "Show me who is King."

On every one of their decks, the King of Hearts was inscribed with two names. They held the cards out simultaneously. Each Negative carried a card bearing his or her name, and in larger letters, RODERICK ESCHER.

The fibers seemed to give a mighty heave. Roderick came forward, and I saw the fibers fleeing from his legs, his suit, his face and skin.

The Negatives turned to each other in confusion. Cant giggled. They compared their decks, searched them. "They're made of matter," Wont said. "They aren't false—"

"Tricks," Shant said.

"Can *you* do them?" Wont asked.

"In an instant," Shant said. Cards fluttered down around him, twisted, formed a tall mannequin, and danced around us all. The fibers withdrew from around him as if singed by flames.

"Not the point," Roderick said, free of fibers now. "You can do anything you want, but you *subscribe.* Cardino does these things by himself, alone."

The fibers bunched around my feet. Shant made his cards and the mannequin vanish. "How?" he asked, shrugging.

"Skill," Roderick said.

"Skill of the body," Shant said haughtily. "Who needs that?"

"Self-discipline, training, years of concentrated effort," Roderick said. "Isn't that right, Cardino?"

"Yes," I said, the confidence of my performance fading. I was caught in a game whose rules I could not understand. Roderick was using me, and I did not know why.

"Nothing any of us can experience compares to what this man does all by himself," Roderick continued.

The five froze in place for a moment. I could see some change in their structure, a momentary fluctuation in their illusory solid shapes.

Roderick lifted his arms and stared at his body. "I'm free!" he said to me in an undertone, as if confiding to a priest.

"What's all this about?" I asked.

"It's about skill and friendship and death," Roderick said.

The five began to move again. The fibers touched my shoes, the hem of my pants. Instinctively, I kicked at them, sending glowing bits scattering like sparks. They recoiled, toughened, pushed in more insistently.

"My time is ending," Roderick said. "I've done all I can, experienced all I can."

The five smiled and circled around me. "*They* favor you," Cant said, and she bent to push a wave of growing fibers toward my legs. I backed off, kicked again without effect, shouted to Roderick,

"What do they want?"

"You," Roderick said. "My time is done. Maja is dead; I go to follow her."

I turned and ran from the room, sliding on the clumps of fibers, falling. The fibers lightly touched my face, felt at my cheeks, prodded my lips as if to push into my mouth, but I jumped to my feet and ran through the door. Roderick followed, and behind him a surge of fibers clogged the door.

Wherever I ran in the house, eager fibers grew from the walls, the floor, fell from the ceiling, like webs trying to ensnare me. Cant appeared in a twisted hallway ahead. I fell to my hands and knees, staring as the floor twisted into a corkscrew, afraid I would pitch forward into the architectural madness.

Dr. Ont appeared, shoulders dipped in failure, hands beseeching to explain. "Roderick, do not—"

"It is done!" Roderick cried.

A cold wind flowed down the hall, conveying a low moan of endless agony. Roderick helped me to my feet, his thin fingers cold even through the fabric of my suit.

"Can you feel it?" he whispered to me. "King Nerve has released me. I'm dying, Robert!" He turned to Dr. Ont. "I'm dying, and there's nothing you can do! I know all the permutations! I've experienced it all, and *I am bored. Let me die!*"

Dr. Ont stared at Roderick with an expression of infinite pity. "Your sister—"

Roderick gripped my shoulders. "We are walled in like prisoners by the laziness of gods, all desires sated, all refinements exhausted. Let them crown the new master!"

The moaning grew louder. Behind Dr. Ont, Roderick's sister appeared, even more haggard and pale, the feeblest energy of purpose animating a husk, her dry and shrunken mouth trying to speak.

Dr. Ont stood aside as Roderick saw her. "Maja!" Roderick cried, holding up his hands to block out sight of her.

"Still alive," Dr. Ont said. "I was wrong. She cannot die. We have all forgotten how."

The five brushed past Roderick, smiling only at me.

"The House of Escher loses all support," Cant said, touching my arm lightly. "The flow is with you. The world wants you. You will teach them your experience. You will show them what it feels to be *skilled* and to have fleshly talents, to *work* and *touch* in a primal way. Roderick was absolutely correct— you are a marvel!"

I looked at Roderick, frozen in terror, and then at Maja, her eyes like pits sucking in nothing, as isolated as any corpse but still alive.

The walls shuddered around me. The fibers withdrew from the stones, and where they no longer held, cracks appeared, running in crazed patterns over the white-and-yellow surfaces. The tiles of the floor heaved up, the tessellations disrupted, all order scattered.

Cant took my hand and led me through the disintegrating corridors, down the shivering and swaying stairs. Behind me, the stairs buckled and crumbled, and the beams of the ceiling split and jabbed down to the floor like broken elbows. Ahead, a tide of fibers withdrew from the house like sea sucked from a cave, and above the ripping snap of tearing timbers, the rumble and slam of stone blocks falling and shattering, I heard Roderick's high, chicken-cluck shriek, the cry of an avatar driven past desperation into madness:

"No death! *No Death!* King Nerve forever!"

And his bray of laughter at the final jest revealed, all his plans cocked asunder.

The antitheticals blew me through the front door like a wind, and down the walk into the ruined garden, among the twisted and fiber-covered trees, until I was away from the house of Roderick Escher. All of his spreading distractions and entertainments, all of his chambers filled with the world's diversions, the pandering to the commonest denominators of a frozen or disembodied horde . . . the impossible and convoluted towers leaned, shuddered, and collapsed, blowing dust and splinters through the door and the windows of the first floor.

The fibers pushed from the ground, binding my feet, rising up my legs toward my trunk, feeling through my suit, probing for secrets, for solutions. I felt voices and demands in my head, petulant, childish, *Show us. Do for us. Give us.* The fibers burrowed into my flesh, with the pricks of thousands of tiny cold needles.

Cant took my arm. "You are favored," she said.

The voices picked at my thoughts, rudely invaded my memories, making crude and cruel jokes. They seemed to know nothing but expletives, arranged in no sensible order, and they applied them accompanied by demands that went beyond the obscene, demands that echoed again and again; and I saw that this new world was composed not of gods, but of mannerless children who had never faced responsibility or consequences, and whose lives were all secrecy, all privilege, conducted behind thick and impersonal walls.

Tingles shot up my hands and feet and along my spine, and I felt sparks at the very basement of my reason.

Do for us, do everything, live for us, let us feel, all new and all unique, all superlatives and all gladness and joy, and no death no end

My hands jerked out, holding a pack of cards, and I felt a will other than mine—a collective will—move my fingers, attempt to spread the cards into a fan. The fingers jerked and spilled the cards into the dirt, across the creeping fibers. "Get them away from me!" I cried in furious panic.

The blocks and timbers and reduced towers of the House of Escher settled with a final groaning sigh, but I pictured Roderick and Maja buried beneath its timbers, still alive.

The fibers lanced into my tongue. The voices filling my head hissed and slid and insinuated like snakes, like *worms in my living brain*, demanding *tapeworms*, asking numbing questions, prodding, prickling, insatiable.

Cant said, "You must assert yourself. They demand much, but you have so much to give—"

The fibers shoved down my throat, piercing and threading through my tissues as if to connect with every cell of my being. I clawed at my mouth, my throat, my body, trying to tug free, but the fibers were strong as steel wires, though thinner than the strands of a spider's web.

"Newness is a treasure," Musnt said, standing beside Cant. Wont and Shant and Dont joined her.

My legs buckled, but the fibers stiffened and held me like a puppet. I could not speak, could only gag, could hardly hear above the dissonant voices. *Amuse. Give all. Share all. Live all.*

"Hail to the new and masterful," Cant said worshipfully, smiling broadly, simply, innocently. Even in my terror and pain that smile seemed angelic, entrancing.

"A hundred billion people cannot be wrong," Shant said, and touched the crown of my head with his outspread hand.

"We anoint the new Master of King Nerve," the five said as one, and I could breathe, and speak, for myself, no more.

SOLDIER, SAILOR

By Lewis Shiner

Stepping out of the airlock behind Reese, Kane was amazed by the weight & wetness of the air. He could make out the odors of cut grass, honeysuckle & ivy. Martian night was falling outside the dome & he sensed clouds forming above him. Rain on Mars. Evenly spaced houses surrounded him, covered with ivy & separated by rows of elephant ears & ferns. The intricacy of the ecological planning startled him; a bee floated over his head & somewhere a mockingbird whistled.

The sight of the colonists sitting on their porches in the sunset filled him with a mixture of nostalgia & surrealist horror. They smiled & nodded to Kane as if it had been days instead of years since they'd seen a stranger, as if the space program still existed & Reese was once more in uniform.

Reading Ouspensky, he had found the first clue to the strange visions that spun around the lip of his consciousness. "Every separate human life is a moment in the life of some *great being* which lives *in us.*" But when he tried for a more concrete image than ships & shadowy figures rising from the ground, it melted away. From Campbell Kane learned of the Pattern of the Hero, the inexorable circle, the path of exile & return. For an instant the memories—if that was what they were—clarified. Kane saw that he must take it all personally. Then it was gone again.

Eventually Curtis asked how things were on Earth & Reese framed a careful reply. Kane paid little attention to the measured, cautious description of the riots, the famines, the plagues. Instead he examined Curtis, the governor of the colony, with care. The man was soft, pallid, mannered in his speech. Kane asked simple questions—limits to the population, energy sources, chains of command. He found Curtis's answers evasive, dismissive. Kane felt the vast gulf between himself & the Earth as an ache inside him.

• • •

Their first morning on Mars, Reese had taken him to the ruins of the native city. Kane was fascinated by the enigma of the Martian holocaust—the artifacts of intelligence assimilated into the processes of nature.

"Why no bodies?" Kane asked, scuffing through the rings of ash, sand & boiled rock. "They should have mummified when the water went."

Reese shrugged, the motion barely discernible through his bulky suit.

Kane wandered off, trying to picture the city before the disaster. Some of the walls were almost intact, blistered & pitted, but recognizable, while on all sides there was only rubble. The stone, obviously artificial, was indistinguishable from the surrounding rocks. It formed an architecture of intersecting lines, with the Druidic power of Stonehenge.

At dinner he sat across from Curtis's wife, Molly. She was tall, dark, full breasted, with a quality of listless abstraction that Kane found compelling. He desired her in a dark, impersonal way that was nonetheless intense. As for Curtis, Kane found him increasingly officious, dangerously authoritative. He identified Curtis with his uncle; at the thought, the taste of his food turned sour. His mood turned chaotic & violent & he held his fists under the table until the worst of it passed.

"The panel," his uncle said, "is circular, about 35 cm in diameter, studded at irregular but frequent intervals with PROMs." The fluorescent light was harsh & Kane's attention wandered toward the smog & riot-torn streets outside the window. "At least three of these chips are mutants, and are responsible for the power output curves on this chart."

Kane glanced at the chart & away again, despising his uncle, the broad waxed desk, his own poverty & failure. His uncle's life depended on his staying in business; if he failed, his employees would tear him to pieces.

"We have to get those chips into the lab," his uncle said, "or we'll never know why they perform the way they do."

"You say this panel is dangerous."

"In the hands of the colonists, yes. It's been ten years since the space program was terminated. They undoubtedly need resources from Earth, if they're even alive at all. How do they feel about Earth after we cut them off? Can we even hope to understand them? A ship powered by that panel is a weapon pointed at the Earth."

The walls of the office were lined with renderings of yet more offices. Kane sat & allowed himself to be manipulated. Something had gone out of him during his years of student exile. He no longer had the will to resist.

On their second trip to the ruins, Reese took Kane into the central underground complex. The entrance was small, a vivid black hole in the orange glow of the desert. Kane lowered himself after Reese & found himself on a steeply descending ramp. As his eyes adjusted to their flashlights he made out the circular pit to his left. It seemed to have no bottom. The ramp curved around it & he followed, no more than a spectator, just as he had been in grade school, watching on TV as Reese planted the US flag on these same ruins & turned to wave to the cameras.

Now Reese turned off the ramp & moved between tilted slabs of rock to an inner chamber. Reese's hand moved & a door swung open from the wall. Kane followed him inside. The door closed behind them & Kane heard the unmistakable hiss of pressurized air. Inside his helmet a light changed from red to green. Reese took off his helmet & opened an inner door. Light flowed from the walls themselves & Kane turned off his flash.

The walls were made of the same artificial stone as the ruins above, lacking all ornament. Walking into the room, he loosened his helmet & set it on the floor. The chill air stung his cheeks & made him wince. Here there was finally decoration, a low relief that reminded Kane of a printed circuit board. It ran from floor to ceiling with circular protrusions at key points, but no visible dials or meters. He understood the chauvinism of such an expectation. At the far end of the room, where Reese stood, the outlines of a door were etched into solid rock. No handle or indentation marred its surface. Kane pressed his hand to it. He sensed its importance, connected it instinctively to the disappearance of the Martians, but could not guess its function. It did not respond to his touch. He turned to look at Reese. "What does it mean?"

Reese put his helmet back on & started for the door.

• • •

Like a fragment of melody on a tape loop: clear, high voices in a minor key, without a message, offering only coloration, a distortion in his ability to see the world. Or like a flickering at the edges of his vision that seemed to be the curves & angles of fourth-dimensional space. Behind it a sense of alien personality, lurking. The ghosts of the Martian builders?

Kane wandered barefoot through the city under the dome. It was a quiet suburb painted by Magritte, too uniform, too clearly defined, too obviously existing in a vacuum. The grass under his feet was a rich green, round-bladed & moist. The houses were like those in the poverty-level neighborhoods where Kane had grown up, after his father died—vinyl siding, short porches, bushes & trees growing unhindered against the walls.

At the edge of the dome he watched distorted images of dust storms blow past the double wall of yellowing plastic. High CO_2 levels & the peak heat of afternoon made him drowsy & short of breath. Reese & Curtis would be at the ruins all day; he had time for an hour or two of sleep.

Retracing his steps, he saw Curtis's wife, Molly, on the porch of their bungalow.

A chill of prescience went through him. The Presence in his mind sang to him as he climbed the single step & stood in front of her. She was solid, indifferent, languidly sensual. Kane's hands were clenched again.

"Sit down," she said, making it a polite question. Kane sat facing her. He searched her face for information, admiring its clean, symmetrical weight. They had reached the neutrality of afternoon. He could not avoid looking at her breasts, at the wide brown nipples visible through her T-shirt.

"You'd like a drink," she said, standing. Kane heard the power of command she chose not to use. He felt her matriarchal strength, her link with the rich, darkly scented vegetation that surrounded them. He followed her into the gloom of a curtained kitchen, hearing birds cry outside in an eternal, abstracted spring. He stopped Molly at the refrigerator with a light touch on the arm. As she turned to him her eyes lost their focus & became distant, passive. His hands went to her breasts, thumbs touching her nipples as she

298

gripped his elbows. She led him into her bedroom, a dim, fragrant place more personal, more private than her body. Standing across the bed from him she pulled her clothes off as he watched. The aroma of her body drifted to him, heavy, sweet, blatantly sexual. Kane shut his eyes, unwilling for a moment to continue with it: his internal struggles, his helplessness before his own sexual urgings, the climax inevitably empty compared to the ritual preceding it. As their bodies merged, Molly astride him, her hands on his wrists, Kane felt the violence rise within him. With effort he delayed his ejaculation until Molly had satisfied herself; by that time he had become detached from his own passion. He spasmed quickly & they lay together in the heat of the drowning afternoon.

Kane had been amazed by Reese's easy acceptance of his uncle's offer. Clearly Reese had ulterior motives; Kane had no desire to learn them. From this understanding came a kind of mutual respect, or at least silence. Reese did not ask Kane to justify his part in the scenario, a scenario that seemed to point to both their deaths.

Reese claimed to have translated the Martian engravings during the ten years he'd spent on Earth, an involuntary furlough caused by the failure of the space program. Kane eventually began to believe the translations were genuine, but knew Reese was holding something back.

Reese assembled the entire population of the colony in their conference room. Kane sat on the back row with a piece of string, idly weaving cat's cradles.

"Today," Reese said, "I took the preliminary dictionary to the ruins, with Curtis's help. We were able to piece together a long section from one of the engravings."

Kane wondered if Curtis should have been involved. Curtis was clever & authoritarian & the less he knew the better. Kane sensed a primal conflict between himself & Curtis, building toward a violent release.

Reese moved through the translation, pausing frequently to fill in gaps, suggest explanations, grapple with alien concepts. Kane found himself moved, almost against his will, by the story. He gazed out the windows of the auditorium, seeing past the verdant languor of the trees to the desert beyond. Always poor, always dry, feeding a few vastly alien creatures just enough to keep them in perpetual warfare. Reese offered no physical description of the Martians & Kane could only conceive of them in grotesque, cartoon terms.

If anything, he thought, they must have been like Reese. Large, powerful, but carrying an aura of defeat & doom. What culture could have reached the peak that Reese described & left so little behind? A single devastated city, the last refuge of the artists & scientists fleeing the final war. Where they waited for the catastrophe of their own making to wipe the oxygen from the air, boil away the water, lacerate & blister the very stone. The translation made compelling poetry, full of strange pairings & cryptic emphases. In it Kane saw again the equanimity that moved him so strongly in Molly & Reese.

They had given Kane his own house & Molly came to him there. The sexuality of their attraction had withered & Kane had come to see in her the power & competence he saw in Reese. His own nature, prone to extremes of apathy & violence, was in perfect opposition. In the darkness they sat on Kane's bed without touching. As Kane listened, she drew him into the power struggles of the colonists. Without hesitation or encouragement from him she talked of the panel, taking his knowledge of it for granted. He wondered if she took his motives for granted too, or if she even cared.

Curtis wanted the panel to power the generators of the colony, to expand, to solidify. Kane had heard the arguments before, on another world; more or less, they were the same as his uncle's. Plodding, methodical, a denial of impulse or creativity. Molly—& others—wanted the panel to power a ship that could reach Jupiter, Saturn, beyond. Kane listened in silence, allowing Molly to engulf him with her dreams, the way she'd engulfed him earlier with her body. She knew as if by instinct how to reach him, tantalizing him with the inhuman beauty of the outer planets.

Molly & the void of space were linked by the same relationship as Reese & the ruins. In Reese's case it was a destiny of annihilation, the merger of his lost career with the fate of the lost Martians. For Molly it was something more vital, but still a gesture of despair. Both were prisoners, deprived of the frontiers they needed by an accident of time.

After Molly left, Kane took the pistol out of the bottom of his flight bag & stared at it. The voices sang in his mind.

Kane, Molly & Reese went out to the shipyard. Here the remains of the big ships that had brought the colonists from Earth lay in shining disarray. Broken down in orbit, brought piece by piece to the surface in shuttles, converted into furniture, tools, decorations. What was left over stretched for five hundred meters across the pale sand. Kane walked through huge rings of metal, lightly touching them with gloved hands. It was an edited & polished scrap yard, free from the violence of oxygen & rain.

"From this you're going to build a ship?" Kane asked.

"There's still one ship in orbit," Molly said. "Not that we can get to it, of course. But yes, between it and the parts here and the panel, we could build a ship."

"If," Kane said, "Curtis were not governor of this colony."

She didn't answer. Kane thought about Jupiter. Massive, inhuman, constructed on a different principle than Earth or Mars. With moons like worlds, floating under the huge red Eye. He found his breath coming short. His hands tingled & he heard a roaring in his ears. It didn't seem important. Reese called his name. Kane tried to answer but couldn't seem to get his breath.

"Hypoxia," Reese said.

Molly was standing behind him. "Pressure's all right."

"It's the mixture," Reese said. "Look out . . ."

Kane sat down. He was aware that Curtis was trying to kill him, gently & from a distance. Reese disconnected his own tank & traded it for Kane's. In the moment of the exchange, without air for a second or two, Kane had a particularly intense occurrence of the vision.

His mind gradually cleared. Molly was driving them back to the base, Reese lying quietly, living off the air inside his suit. Eyes closed, Reese whispered: "Don't talk about this."

Molly showed Kane where the panel attached to the city power grid, nestled in wiring like a flat egg. Kane had begun to feel the pressure of time & wanted as many pieces of the puzzle within reach as possible. Soon he would have to make his decision.

After sunset Kane sat on his porch & watched the rain. It fell almost hesitantly, without thunder to announce it or wind to carry it. Puddles of light from neighboring windows illuminated the grass & trees.

Reese's suit was missing. Kane did not doubt he'd gone to the ruins. Curtis had noticed as well. Kane felt the wheel turn under him, exposing a new segment of the Circle.

When they stole the ship from Canaveral, with the help of his uncle, Kane had known that Reese was following some elaborate purpose of his own. Without him Kane would have been helpless; Kane himself seemed to make little difference to Reese beyond his ability to provide the ship. Still Reese had taught him to navigate, led him through rigorous physical training, controlled the mission from the first. Now Kane sensed a shift in the power balance. His own time had come, his phase, his moment. Or perhaps Reese had simply diverged, entered the final stage of his own compulsion.

Kane had rejected the idea when it first came to him. But it continued to haunt him. He thought of Reese, out in the ruins, his labors, his feats of courage & strength. He thought of the Circle & the great fourth-dimensional being outside time. Of the salt spray & the shining cup & the others who had come before him. And then he knew.

In the darkness Kane lost sense of his own body. His limbs seemed to shrink & swell as if in a fever dream. Over it all he smelled the stale salt of the sea & high harmonies rang in his ears.

He dressed in darkness & tucked the pistol into his jeans. Out under the dome the rain had ended. The stars were smears of brightness behind the plastic. The lights flickered as Kane switched over to the auxiliary generator, but stayed on. He disconnected the panel with a few precise gestures, hampered by the pressure of the pistol in his waistband.

He sat in the wet grass outside Curtis & Molly's house until the lights went out. Curtis finally emerged & headed for the air lock. Suited up, the panel in one hand, the pistol dangling from the other, Kane followed him across the desert. Taking huge strides in the reduced gravity he slowly gained on Curtis's headlamp, now almost halfway to the ruins.

At night the desert became an ocean. Freckles of white froth sprayed the dune tops. Imaginary ships sailed off its edge. The desert seemed to exist in all dimensionalities, to form a link or stepping stone to the incomprehensible.

"Curtis."

Curtis turned, startled & Kane shot him through the helmet. Curtis's face exploded & a fine spray of blood hissed through shattered glass as the body crumpled to the ground. Kane's hand throbbed slightly from the kick of the gun in the low pressure. He tossed the weapon into the dirt beside Curtis's body. Carrying the panel like a shield in his left arm, he noticed the voices had become quieter.

Once he was into the central pit, he had little trouble finding his way. He went through the airlock & sat down beside Reese.

"How much have you figured out?" Reese asked, not looking around. His hands rested on the carved circles as if they were dials & knobs. Perhaps they were.

"Most of it," Kane said. "I just came to say goodbye."

Reese turned, nodded. "You took the panel. Have you decided what to do with it?"

"Not yet."

The doorframe now surrounded a shimmering, luminous area of force. Rainbow colors ran off it, reminding Kane of an oil slick or a huge fire opal.

"Will you be able to come back?" Kane asked.

"I don't care to, either way," Reese said.

"Good luck." Kane reached up from where he sat & took Reese's hand. He felt the link between them that had never been realized.

Reese nodded & stepped through the shimmering gateway, across billions of miles of nothingness to a new world, just as the last of the Martian builders had, while the city above was pounded into rubble. Kane continued to sit & stare at the shifting pattern. At last he got up & stood beside the opening, hesitating. He stuck one finger into the pulsing glow, felt the summer warmth beyond. And then he turned & walked away from it, the colors fading to chilly stone behind him.

Passing the nadir of descent, Kane felt the insistent tug of the Return, a conceptual rebirth. His pattern nearly finished, he thought of the others who had walked it. Most of all Jason, the obsessed & broken sailor, whose creaking ship & brine-scented voyage had haunted his dreams. Of Percival, the soldier maddened by his realization of the Pattern, ending his days in futile subservience to a nameless God.

Kane knew that each of them, the single being they made up & the single act they performed outside time, would continue. To each of them was a unique moment, a contribution, a change. Kane knew what his had to be.

Molly was asleep & he was relieved that she did not wake up when he entered. His voices silent now, Kane set the panel beside her bed. Her Pattern was yet to come; Kane wondered if Odysseus would sing to her on her voyages.

Kane's point of view had begun to shimmer & bleed, like the gate that Reese had used. Only a force of will held his perceptions together as he suited up & began the walk back to his ship, back to the Earth, back to his kingdom.

THE JACK KEROUAC DISEMBODIED SCHOOL OF POETICS

By Rudy Rucker

I got the tape in Heidelberg. A witch named Karla gave it to me.

I met Karla at Diaconescu's apartment. Diaconescu, a Romanian, was interesting in his own right although, balding, he had a "rope-throw" hairdo. We played chess sometimes in his office, on a marble board with pre-Columbian pieces. I was supposed to be a mathematician and he was supposed to be a physicist. His fantasy was that I would help him develop a computer theory of perception. For my part, I was hoping he had dope. One Sunday I came for tea.

Lots of rolling papers around his place, and lots of what an American would take to be dope-art. But it was only cheap tobacco, only European avant-garde. Wine and tea, tea and Mozart. Oh man. Stuck inside of culture with the freak-out blues again.

Karla had a shiny face, like four foreheads clustered around her basic face-holes. All in all, it occurred to me, men have nine body-holes, women ten. I can't remember if we spoke German or English—English most likely. She was writing a doctoral dissertation on Jack Kerouac.

Jack K. My main man. Those dreary high school years I read *On the Road*, then *Desolation Angels* and *Big Sur* in college, *Mexico City Blues* in grad school and, finally, on the actual airplane to actual Heidelberg, I'd read *Tristessa*: "All of us trembling in our mortality boots, born to die, BORN TO DIE I could write it on the wall and on Walls all over America."

I asked Karla if she had weed. "Well, sure, I mean I will soon," and she gave me her address. Some kind of sex-angle in there too. "We'll talk about the beatniks."

I phoned a few times, and she'd never scored yet. At some point I rode my bike over to her apartment anyway. Going to visit a strange witchy girl alone was something I'd never done since marriage. Ringing Karla's bell felt like reaching in through a waterfall, like passing through an interface.

She had a scuzzy pad, two rooms on either side of a public hall. Coffee in her kitchen and cross the hall to look at books in her bedroom. Dope coming next week maybe.

Well, there we were, her on the bed with four foreheads and ten holes, me cross-legged on the floor looking at this and that. *Heartbeat*, a book by Carolyn Cassady, who married Neal and had Jack for a lover. Xeroxes of letters between Jack and Neal, traces of the long disintegration, both losing their raps, word by word, drink by pill, blank years winding down to boredom, blindness, O. D. death. A long sliding board I'm on too, oh man, oh man, sun in a meat-bag with nine holes.

Karla could see I was real depressed and in no way about to get on that bed with her, hole to hole, hole to hole. To cheer me up she brought out something else: a tape-cassette and a cassette-player. "This is Jack."

"Him doing a reading?"

"No, no. It's really him. This is a very special machine. You know how Neal was involved with the Edgar Cayce people?"

"Yeah, I guess so. I don't know." The tape-player *did* look funny. Instead of the speaker there was a sort of cone-shaped hole. And there were no controls, no fast-forward or reverse, just an on-off switch. I leaned to look at the little tape-cassette. There was a tape in there, but a very fine and silvery sort of tape. For some reason the case was etched all over in patterns like circuit diagrams.

". . . right after death," Karla was saying in her low, hypnotic voice. "Jack's complete software is in here as well as his genetic code. There's only been a few of these made . . . it's more than just science, it's magic." She clicked the tape into the player. "Go on, Alvin, turn Jack on. He'll enjoy meeting you."

I felt dizzy and confused. How long had I been sitting here? How long had she been talking? I reached for the switch, then hesitated. This scene had gotten so unreal so fast. Maybe she'd drugged the coffee?

"Don't be afraid. Turn him on." Karla's voice seemed to come from a long way away. I clicked the switch.

The tape whined on its spools. I could smell something burning. A little puff of smoke floated up from the tape-player's cone, and then there was more smoke, lots of it. The thick plume writhed and folded back on itself, forming layer after layer of intricate haze.

The ghostly figure thickened and drew substance from the player's cone. At some point it was finished. Jack Kerouac was there standing over me with a puzzled frown.

Somehow Karla's coven had caught the Kerouac of 1958, a tough, greasy-faced mind-assassin still years away from his eventual bloat and blood-stomach death.

"I was afraid he'd look like a corpse," I murmured to Karla.

"Well, I feel like a corpse—say a dead horse—what happened?" said Kerouac. He walked over to the window and looked out. "Whooeee, this ain't even Cleveland or the golden tongues of flame. Got any hoocha?" He turned and glared at me with eyes that were dark vortices. Everything about him was right except the eyes.

"Do you have any brandy?" I asked Karla.

"No, but I could begin undressing."

Kerouac and I exchanged a glance of mutual understanding. "Look," I suggested, "Jack and I will go out for a bottle and be right back."

"Oh all right," Karla sighed. "But you have to carry the player with you. And *hang onto it!*"

The soul-player had a carrying strap. As I slung it over my shoulder, Kerouac staggered a bit. "Easy, Jackson," he cautioned.

"My name's Alvin, actually," I said.

"Al von Actually," muttered Kerouac. "Let's rip this joint."

We clattered down the stairs, his feet as loud as mine. Jack seemed a little surprised at the street-scene. I think it was his first time in Germany. I wasn't too well-dressed, and with Jack's rumpled hair and filthy plaid shirt, we made a really scurvy pair of Americans. The passers-by, handsome and nicely dressed, gave us wide berth.

"We can get some brandy down here," I said, jerking my head. "At the candy store. Then let's go sit by the river."

"Twilight of the gods at River Lethe. In the groove, Al, in the gr-gr-oove." He seemed fairly uninterested in talking to me and spoke only in such distracted snatches, spoke like a man playing pinball and talking to a friend over his shoulder. Off and on I had the feeling that if the soul-player were turned off, I'd be the one to disappear. But he was the one with black whirlpools instead of eyes. Kerouac was the ghost, not me.

But not quite ghost either; his grip on the bottle was solid, his drinking was real, and so was mine, of course, as we passed the liter back and forth, sitting on the grassy meadow that slopes down the Neckar River. It was March 12th, basically cold, but with a good strong sun. I was comfortable in my old leather jacket and Jack, Jack was right there with me.

"I like this brandy," I said, feeling it.

"Bee-a-zooze. What do you want from me anyway, Al? Poke a stick in a corpse, get maggots come up on you. Taking a chance, Al, for whyever?"

"Well, I . . . you're my favorite writer. I always wanted to be you. Hitchhike stoned and buy whores in Mexico. I missed all that, I mean I did it, but differently. I guess I want the next kids to like me like I like you."

"Lot of like, it's all nothing. Pain and death, more death and pain. It took me twenty years to kill myself. You?"

"I'm just starting. I figure if I trade some of the drinking off for weed, I can stretch it out longer. If I don't shoot myself. I can't believe you're really here. Jack Kerouac."

He drained the rest of the bottle and pitched it out into the river. A cloud was in front of the sun now and the water was grey. It was, all at once, hard to think of any good reason for living. At least I had a son.

"Look in my eyes," Jack was saying. "Look in there."

I didn't want to, but he leaned in front of me to stare. His face was hard and bitter. I realized I was playing way out of my league.

The eyes. Like I said before, they were spinning dark holes, empty sockets forever draining no place. I thought of Edgar Allen Poe's story about some guys caught for days in a maelstrom, and thinking this, I began to see small figures flailing in the dark spirals, Jack's remembered friends and loved ones maybe, or maybe other dead souls.

The whirlpools fused now to a single dark, huge cyclone, seemingly beneath me. I was scared to breathe, scared to fall, scared even that Kerouac himself might fall into his own eyes.

A dog ran up to us and the spell snapped. "More *trinken*," said Jack. "Go get another bottle, Al. I'll wait here."

"Okay."

"The player," rasped Jack. "You have to leave the soul-player here, too."

"Fine." I set it down on the ground.

"Out on first," said Kerouac. "The pick-off. Tell the bitch leave me alone." With that he snatched up the soul-player and ran down to the river. I let him go.

Well, I figured that was that. It looked like Kerouac turned himself off by carrying the soul-player into the river and shorting it out . . . which was fine with me. Meeting him hadn't been as much fun as I'd expected.

I didn't want to face Karla with the news I'd lost her machine, so I biked over to my office to phone her up. For some reason Diaconescu was there, waiting for me. I was glad to see a human face.

"What's happening, Ray?"

"Karla sent me. She saw you two from her window and phoned me to meet you here. You're really in trouble, Alvin."

"Look, it was her decision to lend me that machine. I'm sorry Kerouac threw it in the river and ruined it, but . . ."

"He didn't ruin the machine, Alvin. That's the point. The machine is waterproof."

"Then where'd he go? I saw him disappear."

"He went underwater, you idiot. To sneak off. It's the most dangerous thing possible to have a dead soul in control of its own player."

"Oh, man. Are you sure you don't have any weed?"

I filled my knapsack up with beer bought at a newsstand—they sell alcohol everywhere in Germany—and pedaled on home. The seven- kilometer bike-ride from my university office to our apartment in the Foreign Scholars Guest House was usually a time when I got into my body and cooled out. But today my mind was boiling. The death and depression coming off Kerouac had been overwhelming. What had that been in his eyes there? The pit of hell, it'd seemed like, a vortex ring sort of, a long twisty thread running through each of his eyes, and whoever was outside in the air here was variable. The thought of *not* being able to die terrified me more than anything I'd ever heard of: for me death had always seemed like sweet oblivion, a back-door to the burrow, a certain escape. But now I had the feeling that the dark vortex was there, full of thin hare screamers, ineluctable whether or not a soul-player was around to reveal it at this level of reality. The only thing worse than death is eternal life.

Back home my wife, Cybele, was folding laundry on our bed. The baby was on the floor crying.

"Thank God you came back early, Alvin. I'm going nuts. You know what the superintendent told me? He said we can't put the dirty Pampers in the garbage, that it's unsanitary. We're supposed to tear them apart and flush the pieces, can you believe that? And he was so *rude*, all red-faced and puffing. Jesus I hate it here, can't you get us back to the States?"

"Cybele, you won't believe what happened today. I met Jack Kerouac. And now he's on the loose."

"I thought he died a long time ago."

"He did, he did. This witch-girl, Karla? I met her over at Diaconescu's?"

"The time you went without me. Left me home with the baby."

"Yeah, yeah. She conjured up his ghost somehow, and I was supposed to keep control of it; keep control of Kerouac's ghost, but we got drunk together and he freaked me out so much I let him get away."

"You're drunk now?"

"I don't know. Sort of. I bought some beer. You want one?"

"Sure. But you sound like you're off your rocker, Alvin. Why don't you just sit down and play with the baby. Maybe there's a cartoon on TV for you two."

Baby Joe was glad to see me. He held out his arms and opened up his mouth wide. I could see the two little teeth on his bottom gum. His diaper was soaked. I changed him, being careful to flush the paper part of the old diaper, as per request. As usual with the baby, I could forget I was alive, which is, after all, the only thing that makes life worth living.

I gave Cybele a beer, opened one for myself, and sat down in front of the TV with the baby. The evening programs were just starting—there's no daytime TV at all in Germany—and, thank God, *Zorro* was on. The month before they'd been showing old Marx Brothers movies, dubbed of course, and now it was *Zorro*, an episode a day. Baby Joe liked it as much as I did.

But there was something fishy today, something very wrong. Zorro didn't look like he was supposed to. No cape, no sword, no pointy mustache. It was vortex-eyed Kerouac there in his place, sniggering and stumbling over his lines. Instead of slashing a "Z" on a wanted poster, he just spit on it. Instead of defending the waitress's honor during the big saloon brawl, he hopped over the bar and stole a fifth of tequila. When he bowed to the police-chief's daughter, he hiccupped and threw up. At the big masquerade ball he jumped on stage and started shouting about Death and Nothingness. When the peasants came to him for help, he asked them for marijuana. And the whole time he had the soul-player's strap slung over his shoulder.

After awhile I thought of calling Cybele.

"Look at this, baby! It's unbelievable. Kerouac's on TV instead of Zorro. I think he can see me, too. He keeps making faces."

Cybele came and stood next to me, tall and sexy. Instantly Kerouac disappeared from the screen, leaving old cape 'n' sword Zorro in his place. She smiled down at me kindly. "My Alvin. He trips out on acid but he still comes home on time. Just take care of Joe while I fix supper, honey. We're having pork stew with sauerkraut."

"But . . ."

"Are you so far gone you don't remember taking it? The Black-Star that Dennis DeMentis sent you last week. I saw you put it in your knapsack this morning. You can't fool me, Alvin."

"But . . ."

She disappeared into our tiny kitchen and Kerouac reappeared on the screen, elbowing past the horses and soldiers to press his face right up to it.

"Hey, Al," said the TV's speaker in Kerouac's voice. "You're going crazy croozy whack-a-doozy."

"Cybele! Come here!"

She came running out of the kitchen, and this time Kerouac wasn't fast enough; she saw him staring out at us like some giant goldfish. He started to withdraw, then changed his mind.

"Are you Al's old lady love do hop his heart on?"

"Really, Cybele," I whispered. "My story's true. That Black-Star's in my desk at school and Kerouac's ghost's inside our TV."

"A beer for blear, dear." The screen wobbled like Jello and Kerouac wriggled out into our living room. He stank of dead fish. In one hand he held that stolen bottle of tequila, and his other hand cradled the soul-player.

"Just don't look in his eyes," I cautioned Cybele. Baby Joe started crying.

"Be pope, ti Josie," crooned Jack. "Dad's in a castle, Ma's wearing a shell, nothing's the matter, black Jack's here from Hell."

I'd only had one sip of my beer, so I just handed it over to him. "Isn't there any way out?" I asked him. "Any way into Nothingness?"

Just then someone started pounding on our door. Cybele went to open it, walking backwards so she could keep an eye on Kerouac. He took a hit of tequila, a pull of beer, and lit one of the reefers the peasants had given him.

"*Black-jack* means *sap*," he said. "That's me."

It was Karla at the door. Karla and Ray Diaconescu. Before Jack could do anything, they'd run across the room and grabbed him. He was clumsy from all the booze, and Karla was able to wrest the soul-player away from him.

"Turn it off now, Alvin," she urged. "You turned it on and you have to be the one to turn it off. It only worked because you know Jack so well."

"How about it, Jack?" I looked over at him. His eyes were swirling worse than ever. You could almost feel a breeze from air rushing into them.

He gave a tight smile and passed me his reefer. "Bee-a-zlast on, brother. They call this Germany? I call it the Land of Nod. Friar Tuck awaits her shadowy pleasure. The cactus-shapes of nowhere night."

"Do you want me to turn it off or what? I can't give the player back to you. You'll drive me nuts. But anything else, man, I mean I know your pain."

Suddenly he threw an arm around my neck and dragged me up against him. Karla, still holding the soul-player, gasped and took a step back. Kerouac's voice was harsh in my ear.

"*I knew a guy who died.* That's what Corso says about me now. Only I didn't. He's keeping me in the whirlpool, you are. Let me in, Al, carry me." I tried to pull back, repelled by his closeness, his smell, but the crook of his arm held my neck like a vise. He was still talking. "Let me in your eyes, man, and I'll keep quiet till you crack up. I'll help you write. And you'll end up in the whirly dark, too. Sweet and low from the foggy dew, corrupting the boys from Kentucky ham-spread dope-rush street sweets."

He drew back then, and we stared into each other's eyes; and I saw the thin hare screamers in the black pit same as before, only this time I jumped in, but really it jumped in me. All at once Jack was gone. I turned Karla's machine off for her, saw her and Ray to the door, then had supper with Cybele and Baby Joe. And that's how I became a writer.

MR. BOY

By James Patrick Kelly

I was already twitching by the time they strapped me down. Nasty pleasure and beautiful pain crackled through me, branching and rebranching like lightning. Extreme feelings are hard to tell apart when you have endorphins spilling across your brain. Another spasm shot down my legs and curled my toes. I moaned. The stiffs wore surgical masks that hid their mouths, but I knew they were smiling. They hated me because my mom could afford to have me stunted. When I really was just a kid I did not understand that. Now I hated them back; it helped me get through the therapy. We had a very clean transaction going here. No secrets between us.

Even though it hurts, getting stunted is still the ultimate flash. As I unlived my life, I overdosed on dying feelings and experiences. My body was not big enough to hold them all; I thought I was going to explode. I must have screamed because I could see the laugh lines crinkling around the stiffs' eyes. You do not have to worry about laugh lines after they twank your genes and reset your mitotic limits. My face was smooth and I was going to be twelve years old forever, or at least as long as Mom kept paying for my rejuvenation.

I giggled as the short one leaned over me and pricked her catheter into my neck. Even through the mask, I could smell her breath. She reeked of dead meat.

Getting stunted always left me wobbly and thick, but this time I felt like last Tuesday's pizza. One of the stiffs had to roll me out of recovery in a wheelchair.

The lobby looked like a furniture showroom. Even the plants had been newly waxed. There was nothing to remind the clients that they were bags of blood and piss. You are all biological machines now, said the lobby, clean as space-station lettuce. A scattering of people sat on the hard chairs. Stennie and Comrade were fidgeting by the elevators. They looked as if they were thinking of rearranging the furniture—like maybe into a pile in the middle of the room. Even before they waved, the stiff seemed to know that they were waiting for me.

Comrade smiled. *"Zdrast'ye."*

"You okay, Mr. Boy?" said Stennie. Stennie was a grapefruit-yellow stenonychosaurus with a brown underbelly. His razor-clawed toes clicked against the slate floor as he walked.

"He's still a little weak," said the stiff, as he set the chair's parking brake. He strained to act nonchalant, not realizing that Stennie enjoys being stared at. "He needs rest. Are you his brother?" he said to Comrade.

Comrade appeared to be a teenaged spike neck with a head of silky black hair that hung to his waist. He wore a window coat on which twenty-three different talking heads chattered. He could pass for human, even though he was really a Panasonic. *"Nyet,"* said Comrade. "I'm just another one of his hallucinations."

The poor stiff gave him a dry nervous cough that might have been meant as a chuckle. He was probably wondering whether Stennie wanted to take me home or eat me for lunch. I always thought that the way Stennie got reshaped was more funny looking than fierce—a python that had rear-ended an ostrich. But even though he was a head shorter than me, he did have enormous eyes and a mouthful of serrated teeth. He stopped next to the wheelchair and rose up to his full height. "I appreciate everything you've done." Stennie offered the stiff his spindly three-fingered hand to shake. "Sorry if he caused any trouble."

The stiff took it gingerly, then shrieked and flew backward. I mean, he jumped almost a meter off the floor. Everyone in the lobby turned, and Stennie opened his hand and waved the joy buzzer. He slapped his tail against the slate in triumph. Stennie's sense of humor was extreme, but then he was only thirteen years old.

Stennie's parents had given him the Nissan Alpha for his twelfth birthday, and we had been customizing it ever since. We installed blue mirror glass, and Stennie painted scenes from the Late Cretaceous on the exterior body armor. We ripped out all the seats, put in a wall-to-wall gel mat and a fridge and a microwave and a screen and a minidish. Comrade had even done an illegal operation on the carbrain so that we could override in an emergency and actually steer the Alpha ourselves with a joystick. It would have been cramped, but we would have lived in Stennie's car if our parents had let us.

"You okay there, Mr. Boy?" said Stennie.

"Mmm." As I watched the trees whoosh past in the rain, I pretended that the car was standing still and the world was passing me by.

"Think of something to do, okay?" Stennie had the car and all and he was fun to play with, but ideas were not his specialty. He was probably smart for a dinosaur. "I'm bored."

"Leave him alone, will you?" Comrade said.

"He hasn't said anything yet." Stennie stretched and nudged me with his foot. "Say something." He had legs like a horse: yellow skin stretched tight over long bones and stringy muscle.

"*Prosrees!* He just had his genes twanked, you jack." Comrade always took good care of me. Or tried to. "Remember what that's like? He's in damage control."

"Maybe I should go to socialization," Stennie said. "Aren't they having a dance this afternoon?"

"You're talking to me?" said the Alpha. "You haven't earned enough learning credits to socialize. You're a quiz behind and forty-five minutes short of E-class. You haven't linked since—"

"Just shut up and drive me over." Stennie and the Alpha did not get along. He thought the car was too strict. "I'll make up the plugging quiz, okay?" He probed a mess of empty juice boxes and snack wrappers with his foot. "Anyone see my comm anywhere?"

Stennie's schoolcomm was wedged behind my cushion. "You know," I said, "I can't take much more of this." I leaned forward, wriggled it free, and handed it over.

"Of what, *poputchik?*" said Comrade. "Joyriding? Listening to the lizard here?"

"Being stunted."

Stennie flipped up the screen of his comm and went online with the school's computer. "You guys help me, okay?" He retracted his claws and tapped at the oversized keyboard.

"It's extreme while you're on the table," I said, "but now I feel empty. Like I've lost myself."

"You'll get over it," said Stennie. "First question: Brand name of the first wiseguys sold for home use?"

"NEC-Bots, of course," said Comrade.

"Geneva? It got nuked, right?"

"*Da.*"

"Haile Selassie was that king of Ethiopia who the Marleys claim is god, right? Name the Cold Wars: Nicaragua, Angola . . . Korea was the first." Typing was hard work for Stennie; he did not have enough fingers for it. "One was something like Venezuela. Or something."

"Sure it wasn't Venice?"

"Or Venus?" I said, but Stennie was not paying attention.

"All right, I know that one. And that. The Sovs built the first space station. Ronald Reagan—he was the president who dropped the bomb?"

Comrade reached inside of his coat and pulled out an envelope. "I got you something, Mr. Boy. A get-well present for your collection."

I opened it and scoped a picture of a naked dead fat man on a stainless-steel table. The print had a DI verification grid on it, which meant this was the real thing, not a composite. Just above the corpse's left eye there was a neat hole. It was rimmed with purple that had faded to bruise blue. He had curly gray hair on his head and chest, skin the color of dried mayonnaise, and a wonderfully complicated penis graft. He looked relieved to be dead. "Who was he?" I liked Comrade's present. It was extreme.

"CEO of Infoline. He had the wife, you know, the one who stole all the money so she could download herself into a computer."

I shivered as I stared at the dead man. I could hear myself breathing and feel the blood squirting through my arteries. "Didn't they turn her off?" I said. This was the kind of stuff we were not even supposed to imagine, much less look at. Too bad they had cleaned him up. "How much did this cost me?"

"You don't want to know."

"Hey!" Stennie thumped his tail against the side of the car. "I'm taking a quiz here, and you guys are drooling over porn. When was the First World Depression?"

"Who cares?" I slipped the picture back into the envelope and grinned at Comrade.

"Well, let me see then." Stennie snatched the envelope. "You know what I think, Mr. Boy? I think this corpse jag you're on is kind of sick. Besides, you're going to get in trouble if you let Comrade keep breaking laws. Isn't this picture private?"

"Privacy is twentieth-century thinking. It's all information, Stennie, and information should be accessible." I held out my hand. "But if *glasnost* bothers you, give it up." I wiggled my fingers.

Comrade snickered. Stennie pulled out the picture, glanced at it, and hissed. "You're scaring me, Mr. Boy."

His schoolcomm beeped as it posted his score on the quiz, and he sailed the envelope back across the car at me. "Not Venezuela, Vietnam. Hey, *Truman* dropped the plugging bomb. Reagan was the one who spent all the money. What's wrong with you dumbscuts? Now I owe school another fifteen minutes."

"Hey, if you don't make it look good, they'll know you had help." Comrade laughed.

"What's with this dance anyway? You don't dance." I picked Comrade's present up and tucked it into my shirt pocket. "You find yourself a cush or something, lizard boy?"

"Maybe." Stennie could not blush, but sometimes when he was embarrassed the loose skin under his jaw quivered. Even though he had been reshaped into a dinosaur, he was still growing up. "Maybe I am getting a little. What's it to you?"

"If you're getting it," I said, "it's got to be microscopic." This was a bad sign. I was losing him to his dick, just like all the other pals. No way I wanted to start over with someone new. I had been alive for twenty-five years now. I was running out of things to say to thirteen-year-olds.

As the Alpha pulled up to the school, I scoped the crowd waiting for the doors to open for third shift. Although there was a handful of stunted kids, a pair of gorilla brothers who were football stars, and Freddy the Teddy—a bear who had furry hands instead of real paws—the majority of students at New Canaan High looked more or less normal. Most working stiffs thought that people who had their genes twanked were freaks.

"Come get me at five-fifteen," Stennie told the Alpha. "In the meantime, take these guys wherever they want to go." He opened the door. "You rest up, Mr. Boy, okay?"

"What?" I was not paying attention. "Sure." I had just seen the most beautiful girl in the world.

She leaned against one of the concrete columns of the portico, chatting with a couple other kids. Her hair was long and nut-colored and the ends twinkled. She was wearing a loose black robe over mirror skintights. Her schoolcomm dangled from a strap around her wrist. She appeared to be seventeen, maybe eighteen. But of course, appearances could be deceiving.

Girls had never interested me much, but I could not help but admire this one. "Wait, Stennie! Who's that?" She saw me point at her. "With the hair?"

"She's new—has one of those names you can't pronounce." He showed me his teeth as he got out. "Hey, Mr. Boy, you're *stunted*. You haven't got what she wants."

He kicked the door shut, lowered his head, and crossed in front of the car. When he walked, he looked like he was trying to squash a bug with each step. His snaky tail curled high behind him for balance, his twiggy little arms dangled. When the new girl saw him, she pointed and smiled. Or maybe she was pointing at me.

"Where to?" said the car.

"I don't know." I sank low into my seat and pulled out Comrade's present again. "Home, I guess."

I was not the only one in my family with twanked genes. My mom was a three-quarter-scale replica of the Statue of Liberty. Originally she wanted to be full-sized, but then she would have been the tallest thing in New Canaan, Connecticut. The town turned her down when she applied for a zoning variance. Her lawyers and their lawyers sued and countersued for almost two years. Mom's claim was that since she was born human, her freedom of form was protected by the Thirtieth Amendment. However, the form she wanted was a curtain of reshaped cells that would hang on a forty-two-meter-high ferroplastic skeleton. Her structure, said the planning board, was clearly subject to building codes and zoning laws. Eventually they reached an out-of-court settlement, which was why Mom was only as tall as an eleven-story building.

She complied with the town's request for a setback of five hundred meters from Route 123. As Stennie's Alpha drove us down the long driveway,

Comrade broadcast the recognition code that told the robot sentries that we were okay. One thing Mom and the town agreed on from the start: no tourists. Sure, she loved publicity, but she was also very fragile. In some places her skin was only a centimeter thick. Chunks of ice falling from her crown could punch holes in her.

The end of our driveway cut straight across the lawn to Mom's granite-paved foundation pad. To the west of the plaza, directly behind her, was a utility building faced in ashlar that housed her support systems. Mom had been bioengineered to be pretty much self-sufficient. She was green not only to match the real Statue of Liberty but also because she was photosynthetic. All she needed was a yearly truckload of fertilizer, water from the well, and 150 kilowatts of electricity a day. Except for emergency surgery, the only time she required maintenance was in the fall, when her outer cells tended to flake off and had to be swept up and carted away.

Stennie's Alpha dropped us off by the doorbone in the right heel and then drove off to do whatever cars do when nobody is using them. Mom's greeter was waiting in the reception area inside the foot.

"Peter." She tried to hug me, but I dodged out of her grasp. "How are you, Peter?"

"Tired." Even though Mom knew I did not like to be called that, I kissed the air near her cheek. Peter Cage was her name for me; I had given it up years ago.

"You poor boy. Here, let me see you." She held me at arm's length and brushed her fingers against my cheek. "You don't look a day over twelve. Oh, they do such good work—don't you think?" She squeezed my shoulder. "Are you happy with it?"

I think my mom meant well, but she never did understand me. Especially when she talked to me with her greeter remote. I wormed out of her grip and fell back onto one of the couches. "What's to eat?"

"Doboys, noodles, fries—whatever you want." She beamed at me and then bent over impulsively and gave me a kiss that I did not want. I never paid much attention to the greeter; she was lighter than air. She was always smiling and asking five questions in a row without waiting for an answer and flitting around the room. It wore me out just watching her. Naturally, everything I said or did was cute, even if I was trying to be obnoxious. It was no fun being cute. Today Mom had her greeter wearing a dark blue dress and a very dumb white apron. The greeter's umbilical was too short to stretch up to the kitchen. So why was she wearing an apron?

"I'm really, really glad you're home," she said.

"I'll take some cinnamon doboys." I kicked off my shoes and rubbed my bare feet through the dense black hair on the floor. "And a beer."

All of Mom's remotes had different personalities. I liked Nanny all right; she was simple, but at least she listened. The lovers were a challenge because they were usually too busy looking into mirrors to notice me. Cook was as pretentious as a four-star menu; the housekeeper had all the charm of a vacuum cleaner. I had always wondered what it would be like to talk directly to Mom's main brain up in the head, because then she would not be filtered through a remote. She would be herself.

"Cook is making you some nice broth to go with your doboys," said the greeter. "Nanny says you shouldn't be eating dessert all the time."

"Hey, did I ask for broth?"

At first Comrade had hung back while the greeter was fussing over me. Then he slid along the wrinkled pink walls of the reception room toward the plug where the greeter's umbilical was attached. When she started in about the broth, I saw him lean against the plug. Carelessly, you know? At the same time he stepped on the greeter's umbilical, crimping the furry black cord. She gasped and the smile flattened horribly on her face, as if her lips were two ropes someone had suddenly yanked taut. Her head jerked toward the umbilical plug.

"E-Excuse me." She was twitching.

"What?" Comrade glanced down at his foot as if it belonged to a stranger. "Oh, sorry." He pushed away from the wall and strolled across the room toward us. Although he seemed apologetic, about half the heads on his window coat were laughing.

The greeter flexed her cheek muscles. "You'd better watch out for your toy, Peter," she said. "It's going to get you in trouble someday."

Mom did not like Comrade much, even though she had given him to me when I was first stunted. She got mad when I snuck him down to Manhattan a couple of years ago to have a chop job done on his behavioral regulators. For a while after the operation, he used to ask me before he broke the law. Now he was on his own. He got caught once, and she warned me he was out of control. But she still threw money at the people until they went away.

"Trouble?" I said. "Sounds like fun." I thought we were too rich for trouble. I was the trust baby of a trust baby; we had vintage money and lots of it. I stood and Comrade picked up my shoes for me. "And he's not a toy; he's my best friend." I put my arms around his shoulder. "Tell Cook I'll eat in my rooms."

I was tired after the long climb up the circular stairs to Mom's chest. When the roombrain sensed I had come in, it turned on all the electronic windows and blinked my message indicator. One reason I still lived in my mom was that she kept out of my rooms. She had promised me total security, and I believed her. Actually I doubted that she cared enough to pry, although she could easily have tapped my windows. I was safe from her remotes up here, even the housekeeper. Comrade did everything for me.

I sent him for supper, perched on the edge of the bed, and cleared the nearest window of army ants foraging for meat through some Angolan jungle. The first message in the queue was from a gray-haired stiff wearing a navy blue corporate uniform. "Hello, Mr. Cage. My name is Weldon Montross and I'm with Datasafe. I'd like to arrange a meeting with you at your convenience. Call my DI number, 408-966-3286. I hope to hear from you soon."

"What the hell is Datasafe?"

The roombrain ran a search. "Datasafe offers services in encryption and information security. It was incorporated in the state of Delaware in 2013. Estimated billings last year were three hundred and forty million dollars. Headquarters are in San Jose, California, with branch offices in White Plains, New York, and Chevy Chase, Maryland. Foreign offices—"

"Are they trying to sell me something or what?"

The room did not offer an answer. "Delete," I said. "Next?"

Weldon Montross was back again, looking exactly as he had before. I wondered if he were using a virtual image. "Hello, Mr. Cage. I've just discovered that you've been admitted to the Thayer Clinic for rejuvenation therapy. Believe me when I say that I very much regret having to bother you during your convalescence, and I would not do so if this were not a matter of importance. Would you please contact the Department of Identification number 408-966-3286 as soon as you're able?"

"You're a pro, Weldon, I'll say that for you." Prying client information out of the Thayer Clinic was not easy, but then the guy was no doubt some kind of op. He was way too polite to be a salesman. What did Datasafe want with me? "Any more messages from him?"

"No," said the roombrain.

"Well, delete this one too, and if he calls back tell him I'm too busy unless he wants to tell me what he's after." I stretched out on my bed. "Next?" The gel mattress shivered as it took my weight.

Happy Lurdane was having a smash party on the twentieth, but Happy was a boring cush and there was a bill from the pet store for the iguanas that I paid and a warning from the SPCA that I deleted and a special offer for preferred customers from my favorite fireworks company that I saved to look at later and my dad was about to ask for another loan when I paused him and deleted and last of all there was a message from Stennie, time-stamped ten minutes ago.

"Hey, Mr. Boy, if you're feeling better I've lined up a VE party for tonight." He did not quite fit into the school's telelink booth; all I could see was his toothy face and the long yellow curve of his neck. "Bunch of us have reserved some time on Playroom. Come in disguise. That new kid said she'd link, so scope her yourself if you're so hot. I found out her name, but it's kind of unpronounceable. Tree-something Joplin. Anyway, it's at seven, meet on channel seventeen, password is *warhead*. Hey, did you send my car back yet? Later." He faded.

"Sounds like fun." Comrade kicked the doorbone open and backed through, balancing a tray loaded with soup and fresh doboys and a mug of cold beer. "Are we going?" He set it onto the nightstand next to my bed.

"Maybe." I yawned. It felt good to be in my own bed. "Flush the damn soup, would you?" I reached over for a doboy and felt something crinkle in my jacket pocket. I pulled out the picture of the dead CEO. About the only thing I did not like about it was that the eyes were shut. You feel dirtier when the corpse stares back. "This is one sweet hunk of meat, Comrade." I propped the picture beside the tray. "How did you get it, anyway? Must have taken some operating."

"Three days' worth. Encryption wasn't all that tough, but there was lots of it." Comrade admired the picture with me as he picked up the bowl of soup. "I ended up buying about ten hours from IBM to crack the file. Kind of pricey, but since you were getting stunted, I had nothing else to do."

"You see the messages from that security op?" I bit into a doboy. "Maybe you were a little sloppy." The hot cinnamon scent tickled my nose.

"*Ya v'rot ego ebal!*" He laughed. "So some stiff is cranky? Plug him if he can't take a joke."

I said nothing. Comrade could be a pain sometimes. Of course I loved the picture, but he really should have been more careful. He had made a mess and left it for me to clean up. Just what I needed. I knew I would only get mad if I thought about it, so I changed the subject. "Well, do you think she's cute?"

"What's-her-face Joplin?" Comrade turned abruptly toward the bathroom. "Sure, for a *perdunya*," he said over his shoulder. "Why not?" Talking about girls made him snippy. I think he was afraid of them.

I brought my army ants back onto the window; they were swarming over a lump with brown fur. Thinking about him hanging on my elbow when I met this Tree-something Joplin made me feel weird. I listened as he poured the soup down the toilet. I was not myself at all. Getting stunted changes you; no one can predict how. I chugged the beer and rolled over to take a nap. It was the first time I had ever thought of leaving Comrade behind.

"VE party, Mr. Boy." Comrade nudged me awake. "Are we going or not?"

"Huh?" My gut still ached from the rejuvenation, and I woke up mean enough to chew glass. "What do you mean *we?*"

"Nothing." Comrade had that blank look he always put on so I would not know what he was thinking. Still, I could tell he was disappointed. "Are you going then?" he said.

I stretched—*ouch!* "Yeah, sure, get my joysuit." My bones felt brittle as candy. "And stop acting sorry for yourself." This nasty mood had momentum; it swept me past any regrets. "No way I'm going to lie here all night watching you pretend you have feelings to hurt."

"*Tak tochno.*" He saluted and went straight to the closet. I got out of bed and hobbled to the bathroom.

"This is a costume party, remember," Comrade called. "What are you wearing?"

"Whatever." Even his efficiency irked me; sometimes he did too much. "You decide." I needed to get away from him for a while.

Playroom was a new virtual-environment service on our local net. If you wanted to throw an electronic party at Versailles or Monticello or San Simeon, all you had to do was link—if you could get a reservation.

I came back to the bedroom and Comrade stepped up behind me, holding the joysuit. I shrugged into it, velcroed the front seam, and eyed myself in the nearest window. He had synthesized some kid-sized armor in the German Gothic style. My favorite. It was made of polished silver, with great fluting and scalloping. He had even programmed a little glow into the image so that on the window I looked like a walking night light. There was an armet helmet with a red ostrich plume; the visor was tipped up so I could see my face. I raised my arm, and the joysuit translated the movement to the window so that my armored image waved back.

"Try a few steps," he said.

Although I could move easily in the lightweight joysuit, the motion interpreter made walking in the video armor seem realistically awkward. Comrade had scored the sound effects, too. Metal hinges rasped, chain mail rattled softly, and there was a satisfying *clunk* whenever my foot hit the floor.

"Great." I clenched my fist in approval. I was awake now and in control of my temper. I wanted to make up, but Comrade was not taking the hint. I could never quite figure out whether he was just acting like a machine or whether he really did not care how I treated him.

"They're starting." All the windows in the room lit up with Playroom's welcome screen. "You want privacy, so I'm leaving. No one will bother you."

"Hey, Comrade, you don't have to go . . ."

But he had already left the room. Playroom prompted me to identify myself. "Mr. Boy," I said, "Department of Identification number 203-966-2445. I'm looking for channel seventeen; the password is *warhead.*"

A brass band started playing "Hail to the Chief" as the title screen lit the windows:

The White House
1600 Pennsylvania Avenue

Washington, DC, USA

® 2096, Playroom Presentations

REPRODUCTION OR REUSE STRICTLY PROHIBITED and then I was looking at a wraparound view of a VE ballroom. A caption bar opened at the top of the windows and a message scrolled across. *This is the famous East Room, the largest room in the main house. It is used for press conferences, public receptions, and entertainments.* I lowered my visor and entered the simulation.

The East Room was decorated in bone white and gold; three chandeliers hung like cut-glass mushrooms above the huge parquet floor. A band played skitter at one end of the room, but no one was dancing yet. The band was Warhead, according to their drum set. I had never heard of them. Someone's disguise? I turned, and the joysuit changed the view on the windows. Just ahead Satan was chatting with a forklift and a rhinoceros. Beyond, some blue cartoons were teasing Johnny America. There was not much furniture in the room, a couple of benches, an ugly piano, and some life-sized paintings of George and Martha. George looked like he had just been peeled off a cash card. I stared at him too long, and the closed-caption bar informed me that the painting had been painted by Gilbert Stuart and was the only White House object dating from the mansion's first occupancy in 1800.

"Hey," I said to a girl who was on fire. "How do I get rid of the plugging tour guide?"

"Can't," she said. "When Playroom found out we were kids, they turned on all their educational crap and there's no override. I kind of don't think they want us back."

"Dumbscuts." I scoped the room for something that might be Stennie. No luck. "I like the way your hair is burning." Now that it was too late, I was sorry I had to make idle party chat.

"Thanks." When she tossed her head, sparks flared and crackled. "My mom helped me program it."

"So, I've never been to the White House. Is there more than this?"

"Sure," she said. "We're supposed to have pretty much the whole first floor. Unless they shorted us. You wouldn't be Stone Kinkaid in there, would you?"

"No, not really." Even though the voice was disguised, I could tell this was Happy Lurdane. I edged away from her. "I'm going to check the other rooms now. Later."

"If you run into Stone, tell him I'm looking for him."

I left the East Room and found myself in a long marble passageway with a red carpet. A dog skeleton trotted toward me. Or maybe it was supposed to be a sheep. I waved and went through a door on the other side.

Everyone in the Red Room was standing on the ceiling; I knew I had found Stennie. Even though what they see is only a simulation, most people lock into the perceptual field of a VE as if it were real. Stand on your head long enough—even if only in your imagination—and you get airsick. It took kilohours of practice to learn to compensate. Upside down was one of Stennie's trademark ways of showing off.

The Red Room is an intimate parlor in the American Empire style of 1815–20 . . .

"Hi," I said. I hopped over the wainscoting and walked up the silk-covered wall to join the three of them.

"You're wearing German armor." When the boy in blue grinned at me, his cheeks dimpled. He was wearing shorts and white knee socks, a navy sweater over a white shirt. "Augsburg?" said Little Boy Blue. Fine blond hair drooped from beneath his tweed cap.

"Try Wolf of Landshut," I said. Stennie and I had spent a lot of time fighting VE wars in full armor. "Nice shorts." Stennie's costume reminded me of Christopher Robin. Terminally cute.

"It's not fair," said the snowman, who I did not recognize. "He says this is what he actually looks like." The snowman was standing in a puddle that was dripping onto the rug below us. Great effect.

"No," said Stennie, "what I said was I *would* look like this if I hadn't done something about it, okay?"

I had not known Stennie before he was a dinosaur. "No wonder you got twanked." I wished I could have saved this image, but Playroom was copy-protected.

"You've been twanked? No joke?" The great horned owl ruffled in alarm. She had a girl's voice. "I know it's none of my business, but I don't understand why anyone would do it. Especially a kid. I mean, what's wrong with good old-fashioned surgery? And you can be whoever you want in a VE." She paused, waiting for someone to agree with her. No help. "Okay, so I don't understand. But when you mess with your genes, you change who you are. I mean, don't you like who you are? I do."

"We're so happy for you." Stennie scowled. "What is this, mental health week?"

"We're rich," I said. "We can afford to hate ourselves."

"This may sound rude"—the owl's big blunt head swiveled from Stennie to me—"but I think that's sad."

"Yeah well, we'll try to work up some tears for you, birdie," Stennie said.

Silence. In the East Room, the band turned the volume up.

"Anyway, I've got to be going." The owl shook herself. "Hanging upside down is fine for bats, but not for me. Later." She let go of her perch and swooped out into the hall. The snowman turned to watch her go.

"You're driving them off, young man." I patted Stennie on the head. "Come on now, be nice."

"Nice makes me puke."

"You *do* have a bit of an edge tonight." I had trouble imagining this dainty little brat as my best friend. "Better watch out you don't cut someone."

The dog skeleton came to the doorway and called up to us. "We're supposed to dance now."

"About time." Stennie fell off the ceiling like a drop of water and splashed headfirst onto the beige Persian rug. His image went all muddy for a moment and then he re-formed, upright and unharmed. "Going to skitter, tin man?"

"I need to talk to you for a moment," the snowman murmured.

"You *need* to?" I said.

"Dance, dance, dance," sang Stennie. "Later." He swerved after the skeleton out of the room.

The snowman said, "It's about a possible theft of information."

Right then was when I should have slammed it into reverse. Caught up with Stennie or maybe faded from Playroom altogether. But all I did was raise my hands over my head. "You got me, snowman; I confess. But society is to blame, too, isn't it? You will tell the judge to go easy on me? I've had a tough life."

"This is serious."

"You're Weldon—what's your name?" Down the hall, I could hear the thud of Warhead's bass line. "Montross."

"I'll come to the point, Peter." The only acknowledgment he made was to drop the kid voice. "The firm I represent provides information security services. Last week someone operated on the protected database of one of our clients. We have reason to believe that a certified photograph was accessed and copied. What can you tell me about this?"

"Not bad, Mr. Montross, sir. But if you were as good as you think you are, you'd know my name isn't Peter. It's Mr. Boy. And since nobody invited you to this party, maybe you'd better tell me now why I shouldn't just go ahead and have you deleted?"

"I know that you were undergoing genetic therapy at the time of the theft, so you could not have been directly responsible. That's in your favor. However, I also know that you can help me clear this matter up. And you need to do that, son, just as quickly as you can. Otherwise there's big trouble coming."

"What are you going to do, tell my mommy?" My blood started to pump; I was coming back to life.

"This is my offer. It's not negotiable. You let me sweep your files for this image. You turn over any hard copies you've made, and you instruct your wiseguy to let me do a spot reprogramming, during which I will erase his memory of this incident. After that, we'll consider the matter closed."

"Why don't I just drop my pants and bend over while I'm at it?"

"Look, you can pretend if you want, but you're not a kid anymore. You're twenty-five years old. I don't believe for a minute that you're as thick as your friends out there. If you think about it, you'll realize that you can't fight us. The fact that I'm here and I know what I know means that all your personal information systems are already tapped. I'm an op, son. I could wipe your files clean any time and I will, if it comes to that. However, my orders are to be thorough. The only way I can be sure I have everything is if you cooperate."

"You're not even real, are you, Montross? I'll bet you're nothing but cheesy old code. I've talked to elevators with more personality."

"The offer is on the table."

"Stick it!"

The owl flew back into the room, braked with outstretched wings, and caught onto the armrest of the Dolley Madison sofa. "Oh, you're still here," she said, noticing us. "I didn't mean to interrupt . . ."

"Wait there," I said. "I'm coming right down."

"I'll be in touch," said the snowman. "Let me know just as soon as you change your mind." He faded.

I flipped backward off the ceiling and landed in front of her; my video armor rang from the impact. "Owl, you just saved the evening." I knew I was showing off, but just then I was willing to forgive myself. "Thanks."

"You're welcome, I guess." She edged away from me, moving with precise little birdlike steps toward the top of the couch. "But all I was trying to do was escape the band."

"Bad?"

"And loud." Her ear tufts flattened. "Do you think shutting the door would help?"

"Sure. Follow me. We can shut lots of doors." When she hesitated, I flapped my arms like silver wings. Actually, Montross had done me a favor; when he threatened me, some inner clock had begun an adrenaline tick. If this was trouble, I wanted more. I felt twisted and dangerous and I did not care what happened next. Maybe that was why the owl flitted after me as I walked into the next room.

The sumptuous State Dining Room can seat about 130 for formal dinners. The white-and-gold decor dates from the administration of Theodore Roosevelt.

The owl glided over to the banquet table. I shut the door behind me. "Better?" Warhead still pounded on the walls.

"A little." She settled on a huge bronze doré centerpiece with a mirrored surface. "I'm going soon anyway."

"Why?"

"The band stinks, I don't know anyone, and I hate these stupid disguises."

"I'm Mr. Boy." I raised my visor and grinned at her. "All right? Now you know someone."

She tucked her wings into place and fixed me with her owlish stare. "I don't like VEs much."

"They take some getting used to."

"Why bother?" she said. "I mean, if anything can happen in a simulation, nothing matters. And I feel dumb standing in a room all alone jumping up and down and flapping my arms. Besides, this joysuit is hot and I'm renting it by the hour."

"The trick is not to look at yourself," I said. "Just watch the screens and use your imagination."

"Reality is less work. You look like a little kid."

"Is that a problem?"

"Mr. Boy? What kind of name is that anyway?"

I wished she would blink. "A made-up name. But then all names are made up, aren't they?"

"Didn't I see you at school Wednesday? You were the one who dropped off the dinosaur."

"My friend Stennie." I pulled out a chair and sat facing her. "Who you probably hate because he's twanked."

"That was him on the ceiling, wasn't it? Listen, I'm sorry about what I said. I'm new here. I'd never met anyone like him before I came to New Canaan. I mean, I'd heard of reshaping and all—getting twanked. But where I used to live, everybody was pretty much the same."

"Where was that, Squirrel Crossing, Nebraska?"

"Close." She laughed. "Elkhart; it's in Indiana."

The reckless ticking in my head slowed. Talking to her made it easy to forget about Montross. "You want to leave the party?" I said. "We could go into discreet."

"Just us?" She sounded doubtful. "Right now?"

"Why not? You said you weren't staying. We could get rid of these disguises. And the music."

She was silent for a moment. Maybe people in Elkhart, Indiana, did not ask one another into discreet unless they had met in Sunday school or the 4-H Club.

"Okay," she said finally, "but I'll enable. What's your DI?"

I gave her my number.

"Be back in a minute."

I cleared Playroom from my screens. The message Enabling Discreet Mode flashed. I decided not to change out of the joysuit; instead I called up my wardrobe menu and chose an image of myself wearing black baggies. The loose folds and padded shoulders helped hide the scrawny little boy's body.

The message changed. DISCREET MODE ENABLED. DO YOU ACCEPT, YES/NO?

"Sure," I said.

She was sitting naked in the middle of a room filled with tropical plants. Her skin was the color of cinnamon. She had freckles on her shoulders and across her breasts. Her hair tumbled down the curve of her spine; the ends glowed like embers in a breeze. She clutched her legs close to her and gave me a curious smile. Teenage still life. We were alone and secure. No one could tap us while we were in discreet. We could say anything we wanted. I was too croggled to speak.

"You *are* a little kid," she said.

I did not tell her that what she was watching was an enhanced image, a virtual me. "Uh . . . well, not really." I was glad Stennie could not see me. Mr. Boy at a loss—a first. "Sometimes I'm not sure what I am. I guess you're not going to like me either. I've been stunted a couple of times. I'm really twenty-five years old."

She frowned. "You keep deciding I won't like people. Why?"

"Most people are against genetic surgery. Probably because they haven't got the money."

"Myself, I wouldn't do it. Still, just because you did doesn't mean I hate you." She gestured for me to sit. "But my parents would probably be horrified. They're realists, you know."

"No fooling?" I could not help but chuckle. "That explains a lot." Like why she had an attitude about twanking. And why she thought VEs were dumb. And why she was naked and did not seem to care. According to hard-core realists, first came clothes, then jewelry, fashion, makeup, plastic surgery, skin tints, and hey, jack! here we are up to our eyeballs in the delusions of 2096. Gene twanking, VE addicts, people downloading themselves into computers—better never to have started. They wanted to turn back to worn-out twentieth-century modes. "But you're no realist," I said. "Look at your hair."

She shook her head and the ends twinkled. "You like it?"

"It's extreme. But realists don't decorate!"

"Then maybe I'm not a realist. My parents let me try lots of stuff they wouldn't do themselves, like buying hairworks or linking to VEs. They're afraid I'd leave otherwise."

"Would you?"

She shrugged. "So what's it like to get stunted? I've heard it hurts."

I told her how sometimes I felt as if there were broken glass in my joints and how my bones ached and—more showing off—about the blood I would find on the toilet paper. Then I mentioned something about Mom. She had heard of Mom, of course. She asked about my dad, and I explained how Mom paid him to stay away but that he kept running out of money. She wanted to know if I was working or still going to school, and I made up some stuff about courses in history I was taking from Yale. Actually I had faded after my first semester. Couple of years ago. I did not have time to link to some boring college; I was too busy playing with Comrade and Stennie. But I still had an account at Yale.

"So that's who I am." I was amazed at how little I had lied. "Who are you?"

She told me that her name was Treemonisha but her friends called her Tree. It was an old family name; her great-great-grandsomething-or-other had been a composer named Scott Joplin. *Treemonisha* was the name of his opera.

I had to force myself not to stare at her breasts when she talked. "You like *opera?*" I said.

"My dad says I'll grow into it." She made a face. "I hope not."

The Joplins were a franchise family; her mom and dad had just been transferred to the Green Dream, a plant shop in the Elm Street Mall. To hear her talk, you would think she had ordered them from the Good Fairy. They had been married for twenty-two years and were still together. She had a brother, Fidel, who was twelve. They all lived in the greenhouse next to the shop where they grew most of their food and where flowers were always in bloom and where everybody loved everyone else. Nice life for a bunch of mall drones. So why was she thinking of leaving?

"You should stop by sometime," she said.

"Sometime," I said. "Sure."

For hours after we faded, I kept remembering things about her I had not realized I had noticed. The fine hair on her legs. The curve of her eyebrows. The way her hands moved when she was excited.

It was Stennie's fault: after the Playroom party he started going to school almost every day. Not just linking to E-class with his comm, but actually showing up. We knew he had more than remedial reading on his mind, but no matter how much we teased, he would not talk about his mysterious new cush. Before he fell in love we used to joyride in his Alpha afternoons. Now Comrade and I had the car all to ourselves. Not as much fun.

We had already dropped Stennie off when I spotted Treemonisha waiting for the bus. I waved, she came over. The next thing I knew we had another passenger on the road to nowhere. Comrade stared vacantly out the window as we pulled onto South Street; he did not seem pleased with the company.

"Have you been out to the reservoir?" I said. "There are some extreme houses out there. Or we could drive over to Greenwich and look at yachts."

"I haven't been anywhere yet, so I don't care," she said. "By the way, you don't go to college." She was not accusing me or even asking—merely stating a fact.

"Why do you say that?" I said.

"Fidel told me."

I wondered how her twelve-year-old brother could know anything at all about me. Rumors maybe, or just guessing. Since she did not seem mad, I decided to tell the truth.

"He's right," I said, "I lied. I have an account at Yale, but I haven't linked for months. Hey, you can't live without telling a few lies. At least I don't discriminate. I'll lie to anyone, even myself."

"You're bad." A smile twitched at the corners of her mouth. "So what *do* you do then?"

"I drive around a lot." I waved at the interior of Stennie's car. "Let's see . . . I go to parties. I buy stuff and use it."

"Fidel says you're rich."

"I'm going to have to meet this Fidel. Does money make a difference?"

When she nodded, her hairworks twinkled. Comrade gave me a knowing glance, but I paid no attention. I was trying to figure out how she could make insults sound like compliments when I realized we were flirting. The idea took me by surprise. *Flirting.*

"Do you have any music?" Treemonisha said.

The Alpha asked what groups she liked, and so we listened to some mindless dance hits as we took the circle route around the Laurel Reservoir.

Treemonisha told me about how she was sick of her parents' store and rude customers and especially the dumb Green Dream uniform. "Back in Elkhart, Daddy used to make me wear it to school. Can you believe that? He said it was good advertising. When we moved, I told him either the khakis went or I did."

She had a yellow-and-orange dashiki over midnight-blue skintights. "I like your clothes," I said. "You have taste."

"Thanks." She bobbed her head in time to the music. "I can't afford much because I can't get an outside job because I have to work for my parents. It makes me mad, sometimes. I mean, franchise life is fine for Mom and Dad; they're happy being tucked in every night by GD, Inc. But I want more. Thrills, chills—you know, adventure. No one has adventures in the mall."

As we drove, I showed her the log castle, the pyramids, the private train that pulled sleeping cars endlessly around a two-mile track, and the marble bunker where Sullivan, the assassinated president, still lived on in computer memory. Comrade kept busy acting bored.

"Can we go see your mom?" said Treemonisha. "All the kids at school tell me she's awesome."

Suddenly Comrade was interested in the conversation. I was not sure what the kids at school were talking about. Probably they wished they had seen Mom, but I had never asked any of them over—except for Stennie.

"Not a good idea." I shook my head. "She's more flimsy than she looks, you know, and she gets real nervous if strangers just drop by. Or even friends."

"I just want to look. I won't get out of the car."

"Well," said Comrade, "if she doesn't get out of the car, who could she hurt?"

I scowled at him. He knew how paranoid Mom was. She was not going to like Treemonisha anyway, but certainly not if I brought her home without warning. "Let me work on her, okay?" I said to Treemonisha. "One of these days. I promise."

She pouted for about five seconds and then laughed at my expression. When I saw Comrade's smirk, I got angry. He was just sitting there watching us. Looking to cause trouble. Later there would be wisecracks. I had had about enough of him and his attitude.

By that time the Alpha was heading up High Ridge Road toward Stamford. "I'm hungry," I said. "Stop at the 7-Eleven up ahead." I pulled a cash card out and flipped it at him. "Go buy us some doboys."

I waited until he disappeared into the store and then ordered Stennie's car to drive on.

"Hey!" Treemonisha twisted in her seat and looked back at the store. "What are you doing?"

"Ditching him."

"Why? Won't he be mad?"

"He's got my card; he'll call a cab."

"But that's mean."

"So?"

Treemonisha thought about it. "He doesn't say much, does he?" She did not seem to know what to make of me—which I suppose was what I wanted. "At first I thought he was kind of like your teddy bear. Have you seen those big ones that keep little kids out of trouble?"

"He's just a wiseguy."

"Have you had him long?"

"Maybe too long."

I could not think of anything to say after that, so we sat quietly listening to the music. Even though he was gone, Comrade was still aggravating me.

"Were you really hungry?" Treemonisha said finally. "Because I was. Think there's something in the fridge?"

I waited for the Alpha to tell us, but it said nothing. I slid across the seat and opened the refrigerator door. Inside was a sheet of paper. "Dear Mr. Boy," it said. "If this was a bomb, you and Comrade would be dead and the problem would be solved. Let's talk soon. Weldon Montross."

"What's that?"

I felt the warm flush that I always got from good corpse porn, and for a moment I could not speak. "Practical joke," I said, crumpling the paper. "Too bad he doesn't have a sense of humor."

Push-ups. Ten, *eleven.*

"Uh-oh. Look at this," said Comrade.

"I'm busy!" *Twelve, thirteen, fourteen, fifteen . . . sixteen . . . seven . . .* Dizzy, I slumped and rested my cheek against the warm floor. I could feel Mom's pulse beneath the tough skin. It was no good. I would never get muscles this way. There was only one fix for my skinny arms and bony shoulders. Grow up, Mr. Boy.

"*Ya yebou!* You really should scope this," said Comrade. "Very spooky."

I pulled myself onto the bed to see why he was bothering me; he had been pretty tame since I had stranded him at the 7-Eleven. Most of the windows showed the usual: army ants next to old war movies next to feeding time from the Bronx Zoo's reptile house. But Firenet, which provided twenty-four-hour coverage of killer fires from around the world, had been replaced with a picture of a morgue. There were three naked bodies, shrouds pulled back for identification: a fat gray-haired CEO with a purple hole over his left eye, Comrade, and me.

"You look kind of dead," said Comrade.

My tongue felt thick. "Where's it coming from?"

"Viruses all over the system," he said. "Probably Montross."

"You know about him?" The image on the window changed back to a *barrida* fire in Lima.

"He's been in touch." Comrade shrugged. "Made his offer."

Crying women watched as the straw walls of their huts peeled into flame and floated away.

"Oh." I did not know what to say. I wanted to reassure him, but this was serious. Montross was invading my life, and I had no idea how to fight back. "Well, don't talk to him anymore."

"Okay." Comrade grinned. "He's dull as a spoon anyway."

"I bet he's a simulation. What else would a company like Datasafe use? You can't trust real people." I was still thinking about what I would look like dead. "Whatever, he's kind of scary." I shivered, worried and aroused at the same time. "He's slick enough to operate on Playroom. And now he's hijacking windows right here in my own mom." I should probably have told Comrade then about the note in the fridge, but we were still not talking about that day.

"He tapped into Playroom?" Comrade fitted input clips to the spikes on his neck, linked, and played back the house files. "*Zayebees.* He was already here then. He piggybacked on with you." Comrade slapped his leg. "I can't understand how he beat my security so easily."

The roombrain flicked the message indicator. "Stennie's calling," it said.

"Pick up," I said.

"Hi, it's that time again." Stennie was alone in his car. "I'm on my way over to give you jacks a thrill." He pushed his triangular snout up to the camera and licked at the lens. "Doing anything?"

"Not really. Sitting around."

"I'll fix that. Five minutes." He faded.

Comrade was staring at nothing.

"Look, Comrade, you did your best," I said. "I'm not mad at you."

"Too plugging easy." He shook his head as if I had missed the point.

"What I don't understand is why Montross is so cranky anyway. It's just a picture of meat."

"Maybe he's not really dead."

"Sure he is," I said. "You can't fake a verification grid."

"No, but you can fake a corpse."

"You know something?"

"If I did I wouldn't tell you," said Comrade. "You have enough problems already. Like how do we explain this to your mom?"

"We don't. Not yet. Let's wait him out. Sooner or later he's got to realize that we're not going to use his picture for anything. I mean, if he's that nervous, I'll even give it back. I don't care anymore. You hear that, Montross, you dumbscut? We're harmless. Get out of our lives!"

"It's more than the picture now," said Comrade. "It's me. I found the way in." He was careful to keep his expression blank.

I did not know what to say to him. No way Montross would be satisfied erasing only the memory of the operation. He would probably reconnect Comrade's regulators to bring him back under control. Turn him to pudding. He would be just another wiseguy, like anyone else could own. I was surprised that Comrade did not ask me to promise not to hand him over. Maybe he just assumed I would stand by him.

We did not hear Stennie coming until he sprang into the room.

"Have fun or die!" He was clutching a plastic gun in his spindly hand, which he aimed at my head.

"Stennie, *no*."

He fired as I rolled across the bed. The jellybee buzzed by me and squished against one of the windows. It was a purple, and immediately I smelled the tang of artificial grape flavor. The splatter on the wrinkled wall pulsed and split in two, emitting a second burst of grapeness. The two halves oozed in opposite directions, shivered, and divided again.

"Fun extremist!" He shot Comrade with a cherry as he dove for the closet. "Dance!"

I bounced up and down on the bed, timing my move. He fired a green at me that missed. Comrade, meanwhile, gathered himself up as zits of red jellybee squirmed across his window coat. He barreled out of the closet into Stennie, knocking him sideways. I sprang on top of them and wrestled the gun away. Stennie was paralyzed with laughter. I had to giggle too, in part because now I could put off talking to Comrade about Montross.

By the time we untangled ourselves, the jellybees had faded. "Set for twelve generations before they all die out," Stennie said as he settled himself on the bed. "So what's this my car tells me, you've been giving free rides? Is this the cush with the name?"

"None of your business. You never tell me about your cush."

"Okay. Her name is Janet Hoyt."

"Is it?" He caught me off-guard again. Twice in one day, a record. "Comrade, let's see this prize."

Comrade linked to the roombrain and ran a search. "Got her." He called Janet Hoyt's DI file to screen, and her face ballooned across an entire window.

She was a tanned, blue-eyed blonde with the kind of off-the-shelf looks that med students slapped onto rabbits in genoplasty courses. Nothing on her face said she was different from any other ornamental moron fresh from the OR—not a dimple or a mole, not even a freckle. "You're ditching me for her?" It took all the imagination of a potato chip to be as pretty as Janet Hoyt. "Stennie, she's generic."

"Now wait a minute," said Stennie. "If we're going to play critic, let's scope your cush, too."

Without asking, Comrade put Tree's DI photo next to Janet's. I realized he was still mad at me because of her; he was only pretending not to care. "She's not my cush," I said, but no one was listening.

Stennie leered at her for a moment. "She's a stiff, isn't she?" he said. "She has that hungry look."

Seeing him standing there in front of the two huge faces on the wall, I felt like I was peeping on a stranger—that I was a stranger, too. I could not imagine how the two of us had come to this: Stennie and Mr. Boy with cushes. We were growing up. A frightening thought. Maybe next Stennie would get himself untwanked and really look like he had on Playroom. Then where would I be?

"Janet wants me to plug her," Stennie said.

"Right, and I'm the queen of Brooklyn."

"I'm old enough, you know." He thumped his tail against the floor.

"You're a dinosaur!"

"Hey, just because I got twanked doesn't mean my dick fell off."

"So do it then."

"I'm going to. I will, okay? But . . . this is no good." Stennie waved impatiently at Comrade. "I can't think with them watching me." He nodded at the windows. "Turn them off already."

"*N'ye pizdi!*" Comrade wiped the two faces from the windows, cleared all the screens in the room to blood red, yanked the input clips from his neck spikes, and left them dangling from the roombrain's terminal. His expression empty, he walked from the room without asking permission or saying anything at all.

"What's his problem?" Stennie said.

"Who knows?" Comrade had left the door open; I shut it. "Maybe he doesn't like girls."

"Look, I want to ask a favor." I could tell Stennie was nervous; his head kept swaying. "This is kind of embarrassing, but . . . okay, do you think maybe your mom would maybe let me practice on her lovers? I don't want Janet to know I've never done it before, and there's some stuff I've got to figure out."

"I don't know," I said. "Ask her."

But I did know. She would be amused.

People claimed my mom did not have a sense of humor. Lovey was huge, an ocean of a woman. Her umbilical was as big around as my thigh. When she walked, waves of flesh heaved and rolled. She had beautiful skin, flawless and moist. It did not take much to make her sweat. Peeling a banana would do it. Lovey was as oral as a baby; she would put anything into her mouth. And when she did not have a mouthful, she would babble on about whatever came into Mom's head. Dear hardly ever talked, although he could moan and growl and laugh. He touched Lovey whenever he could and shot her long smoldering looks. He was not furry, exactly, but he was covered with fine silver hair. Dear was a little guy, about my size. Although he had one of Upjohn's finest penises, elastic and overloaded with neurons, he was one of the least convincing males I had ever met. I doubt Mom herself believed in him all that much.

Big chatty woman; squirrelly, tongue-tied little man. It *was* funny in a bent sort of way to watch the two of them go at each other. Kind of like a tug churning against a supertanker. They did not get the chance that often. It was dangerous; Dear had to worry about getting crushed, and poor Lovey's heart had stopped two or three times. Besides, I think Mom liked building up the pressure. Sometimes, as the days without sex stretched, you could almost feel lust sparkling off them like static electricity.

That was how they were when I brought Stennie up. Their suite took up the entire floor at the hips, Mom's widest part. Lovey was lolling in a tub of warm oil. She liked it flowery and laced with pheromones. Dear was prowling around her with a desperate expression, like he might jam his plug into a wall socket if he did not get taken care of soon. Stennie's timing was perfect.

"Look who's come to visit, Dear," said Lovey. "Peter and Stennie. How nice of you boys to stop by." She let Dear mop her forehead with a towel. "What can we do for you?"

The skin under Stennie's jaw quivered. He glanced at me, then at Dear, and then at the thick red lips that served as the bathroom door. Never even looked at her. He was losing his nerve.

"Oh, my, isn't this exciting, Dear? There's something going on." She sank into the bath until her chin touched the oil. "It's a secret, isn't it, Peter? Share it with Lovey."

"No secret," I said. "He wants to ask a favor." And then I told her.

She giggled and sat up. "I love it." Honey-colored oil ran from her hair and slopped between her breasts. "Were you thinking of both of us, Stennie? Or just me?"

"Well, I . . ." Stennie's tail switched. "Maybe we just ought to forget it."

"No, no." She waved a hand at him "Come here, Stennie. Come close, my pretty little monster."

He hesitated, then approached the tub. She reached for his right leg and touched him just above the heelknob. "You know, I've always wondered what scales would feel like." Her hand climbed; the oil made his yellow hide glisten. His eyes were the size of eggs.

The bedroom was all mattress. Beneath the transparent skin was a screen implant, so that Mom could project images not only on the walls but on the surface of the bed itself. Under the window was a layer of heavily vascular flesh, which could be stiffened with blood or drained until it was as soft as raw steak. A window dome arched over everything and could show slo-mo or thermographic FX across its span. The air was warm and wet and smelled like a chemical engineer's idea of a rose garden.

I settled by the lips. Dear ghosted along the edges of the room, dragging his umbilical like a chain, never coming quite near enough to touch anyone. I heard him humming as he passed me, a low moaning singsong, as if to block out what was happening. Stennie and Lovey were too busy with each other to care. As Lovey knelt in front of Stennie, Dear gave a mocking laugh. I did not understand how he could be jealous. He was with her, part of it. Lovey and Dear were Mom's remotes, two nodes of her nervous system. Yet his pain was as obvious as her pleasure. At last he squatted and rocked back and forth on his heels. I glanced up at the FX dome; yellow scales slid across oily rolls of flushed skin.

I yawned. I had always found sex kind of dull. Besides, this was all on the record. I could have Comrade replay it for me anytime. Lovey stopped breathing—then came four or five shuddering gasps in a row. I wondered where Comrade had gone. I felt sorry for him. Stennie said something to her about rolling over. "Okay?" Feathery skin sounds. A grunt. The soft wet slap of flesh against flesh. I thought of my mother's brain, up there in the head where no one ever went. I had no idea how much attention she was paying. Was she quivering with Lovey and at the same time calculating insolation rates on her chloroplasts? Investing in soy futures on the Chicago Board of

Trade? Fending off Weldon Montross's latest attack? *Plug Montross.* I needed to think about something fun. My collection. I started piling bodies up in my mind. The hangings and the open-casket funerals and the stacks of dead at the camps and all those muddy soldiers. I shivered as I remembered the empty rigid faces. I liked it when their teeth showed. "Oh, oh, *oh!*" My greatest hits dated from the late twentieth century. The dead were everywhere back then, in vids and the news and even on T-shirts. They were not shy. That was what made Comrade's photo worth having; it was hard to find modern stuff that dirty. Dear brushed by me, his erection bobbing in front of him. It was as big around as my wrist. As he passed, I could see Stennie's leg scratch across the mattress skin, which glowed with blood-blue light. Lovey giggled beneath him and her umbilical twitched and suddenly I found myself wondering whether Tree was a virgin.

I came into the mall through the Main Street entrance and hopped the westbound slidewalk headed up Elm Street toward the train station. If I caught the 3:36 to Grand Central, I could eat dinner in Manhattan, far from my problems with Montross and Comrade. Running away had always worked for me before. Let someone else clean up the mess while I was gone.

The slidewalk carried me past a real-estate agency, a flash bar, a jewelry store, and a Baskin-Robbins. I thought about where I wanted to go after New York. San Francisco? Montreal? Maybe I should try Elkhart, Indiana—no one would think to look for me there. Just ahead, between a drugstore and a take-out Russian restaurant, was the wiseguy dealership where Mom had bought Comrade.

I did not want to think about Comrade waiting for me to come home, so I stepped into the drugstore and bought a dose of Carefree for $4.29. Normally I did not bother with drugs. I had been stunted; no over-the-counter flash could compare to that. But the propyl dicarbamates were all right. I fished the cash card out of my pocket and handed it to the stiff behind the counter. He did a double take when he saw the denomination, then carefully inserted the card into the reader to deduct the cost of the Carefree. It had my mom's name on it; he must have expected it would trip some alarm for counterfeit plastic or stolen credit. He stared at me for a moment, as if trying to remember my face so he could describe me to a cop, and then gave the cash card back. The denomination readout said it was still good for $16,381.18.

I picked out a bench in front of a specialty shop called The Happy Hippo, hiked up my shorts, and poked Carefree into the widest part of my thigh. I took a short, dreamy swim in the sea of tranquillity and when I came back to myself, my guilt had been washed away. But so had my energy. I sat for a while and scoped the display of glass hippos and plastic hippos and fuzzy stuffed hippos, hippo vids and sheets and candles. Down the bench from me a homeless woman dozed. It was still pretty early in the season for a weather gypsy to have come this far north. She wore red shorts and droopy red socks with plastic sandals and four long-sleeved shirts, all unbuttoned, over a Funny Honey halter top. Her hair needed vacuuming and she smelled old. All grown-ups smelled that way to me; it was something I had never gotten used to. No perfume or deodorant could cover up the leathery stink of adulthood. Kids could smell bad too, but usually from something they got on them. It did not come from a rotting body. I rubbed a finger in the dampness under my arm, slicked it, and sniffed. There was a sweetness to kid sweat. I touched the drying finger to my tongue. You could even taste it. If I gave up getting stunted, stopped being Mr. Boy, I would smell like the woman at the end of the bench. I would start to die. I had never understood how grown-ups could live with that.

The gypsy woke up, stretched, and smiled at me with gummy teeth. "You left Comrade behind?" she said.

I was startled. "What did you say?"

"You know what this is?" She twitched her sleeve, and a penlight appeared in her hand.

My throat tightened. "I know what it looks like."

She gave me a wicked smile, aimed the penlight, and burned a pinhole through the bench a few centimeters from my leg. "Maybe I could interest you in some free laser surgery?"

I could smell scorched plastic. "You're going to needle me here, in the middle of the Elm Street Mall?" I thought she was bluffing. Probably. I hoped.

"If that's the way you want it. Mr. Montross wants to know when you're delivering the wiseguy to us."

"Get away from me."

"Not until you do what needs to be done."

When I saw Happy Lurdane come out of The Happy Hippo, I waved. A desperation move, but then it was easy to be brave with a head full of Carefree.

"Mr. Boy." She veered over to us. "Hi!"

I scooted farther down the bench to make room for her between me and the gypsy. I knew she would stay to chat. Happy Lurdane was one of those chirpy lightweights who seemed to want lots of friends but did not really try to be one. We tolerated her because she did not mind being snubbed and she threw great parties.

"Where have you been?" She settled beside me. "Haven't seen you in ages." The penlight disappeared, and the gypsy fell back into drowsy character.

"Around."

"Want to see what I just bought?"

I nodded. My heart was hammering.

She opened the bag and took out a fist-sized bundle covered with shipping plastic. She unwrapped a statue of a blue hippopotamus. "Be careful." She handed it to me.

"Cute." The hippo had crude flower designs drawn on its body; it was chipped and cracked.

"Ancient Egyptian. That means it's even *before* antique." She pulled a slip from the bag and read. "Twelfth Dynasty, 19911786 BC Can you believe you can just buy something like that here in the mall? I mean, it must be like a thousand years old or something."

"Try four thousand."

"No wonder it cost so much. He wasn't going to sell it to me, so I had to spend some of next month's allowance." She took it from me and rewrapped it. "It's for the smash party tomorrow. You're coming, aren't you?"

"Maybe."

"Is something wrong?"

I ignored that.

"Hey, where's Comrade? I don't think I've ever seen you two apart before."

I decided to take a chance. "Want to get some doboys?"

"Sure." She glanced at me with delighted astonishment. "Are you sure you're all right?"

I took her arm, maneuvering to keep her between me and the gypsy. If Happy got needled, it would be no great loss to Western Civilization. She babbled on about her party as we stepped onto the westbound slidewalk. I turned to look back. The gypsy waved as she hopped the eastbound.

"Look, Happy," I said, "I'm sorry, but I changed my mind. Later, okay?"

"But . . ."

I did not stop for an argument. I darted off the slidewalk and sprinted through the mall to the station. I went straight to a ticket window, shoved the cash card under the grill, and asked the agent for a one-way to Grand Central. Forty thousand people lived in New Canaan; most of them had heard of me because of my mom. Nine million strangers jammed New York City; it was a good place to disappear. The agent had my ticket in her hand when the reader beeped and spat the card out.

"No!" I slammed my fist on the counter. "Try it again." The cash card was guaranteed by AmEx to be secure. And it had just worked at the drugstore.

She glanced at the card, then slid it back under the grill. "No use." The denomination readout flashed alternating messages: Voided and Bank Recall. "You've got trouble, son."

She was right. As I left the station, I felt the Carefree struggle one last time with my dread—and lose. I did not even have the money to call home. I wandered around for a while, dazed, and then I was standing in front of the flower shop in the Elm Street Mall.

Green Dream
Contemporary and Conventional Plants

I had telelinked with Tree every day since our drive, and every day she had asked me over. But I was not ready to meet her family; I suppose I was still trying to pretend she was not a stiff. I wavered at the door now, breathing the cool scent of damp soil in clay pots. The gypsy could come after me again; I might be putting these people in danger. Using Happy as a shield was one thing, but I liked Tree. A lot. I backed away and peered through a window fringed with sweat and teeming with bizarre plants with flame-colored tongues. Someone wearing khaki moved. I could not tell if it was Tree or not. I thought of what she had said about no one having adventures in the mall.

The front of the showroom was a green cave, darker than I had expected. Baskets dripping with bright flowers hung like stalactites; leathery-leaved understory plants formed stalagmites. As I threaded my way toward the back, I came upon the kid I had seen wearing the Green Dream uniform, a khaki nightmare of pleats and flaps and brass buttons and about six too many pockets. He was misting leaves with a pump bottle filled with blue liquid. I decided he must be the brother.

"Hi," I said. "I'm looking for Treemonisha."

Fidel was shorter than me and darker than his sister. He had a wiry plush of beautiful black hair that I was immediately tempted to touch.

"Are you?" He eyed me as if deciding how hard I would be to beat up, then he smiled. He had crooked teeth. "You don't look like yourself."

"No?"

"What are you, scared? You're whiter than rice, cashman. Don't worry, the stiffs won't hurt you." Laughing, he feinted a punch at my arm; I was not reassured.

"You're Fidel."

"I've seen your DI files," he said. "I asked around, I know about you. So don't be telling my sister any more lies, understand?" He snapped his fingers in my face. "Behave yourself, cashman, and we'll be fine." He still had the boyish excitability I had lost after the first stunting. "She's out back, so first you have to get by the old man."

The rear of the store was brighter; sunlight streamed through the clear krylac roof. There was a counter and behind it a glass-doored refrigerator filled with cut flowers. A side entrance opened to the greenhouse. Mrs. Schlieman, one of Mom's lawyers who had an office in the mall, was deciding what to buy. She was shopping with her wiseguy secretary, who looked like he had just stepped out of a vodka ad.

"Wait." Fidel rested a hand on my shoulder. "I'll tell her you're here."

"But how long will they last?" Mrs. Schlieman sniffed a frilly yellow flower. "I should probably get the duraroses."

"Whatever you want, Mrs. Schlieman. Duraroses are a good product, I sell them by the truckload," said Mr. Joplin with a chuckle. "But these carnations are real flowers, raised here in my greenhouse. So maybe you can't stick them in your dishwasher, but put some where people can touch and smell them and I guarantee you'll get compliments."

"Why, Peter Cage," said Mrs. Schlieman. "Is that you? I haven't seen you since the picnic. How's your mother?" She did not introduce her wiseguy.

"Extreme," I said.

She nodded absently. "That's nice. All right then, Mr. Joplin, give me a dozen of your carnations—and two dozen yellow duraroses."

Mrs. Schlieman chatted politely at me while Tree's father wrapped the order. He was a short, rumpled, balding man who smiled too much. He seemed to like wearing the corporate uniform. Anyone else would have fixed the hair and the wrinkles. Not Mr. Joplin; he was a museum-quality throwback. As he took Mrs. Schlieman's cash card from the wiseguy, he beamed at me over his glasses. Glasses!

When Mrs. Schlieman left, so did the smile. "Peter Cage?" he said. "Is that your name?"

"Mr. Boy is my name, sir."

"You're Tree's new friend." He nodded. "She's told us about you. She's doing chores just now. You know, we have to work for a living here."

Sure, and I knew what he left unsaid: *unlike you, you spoiled little freak.* It was always the same with these stiffs. I walked in the door and already they hated me. At least he was not pretending, like Mrs. Schlieman. I gave him two points for honesty and kept my mouth shut.

"What is it you want here, Peter?"

"Nothing, sir." If he was going to "Peter" me, I was going to "sir" him right back. "I just stopped by to say hello. Treemonisha did invite me, sir, but if you'd rather I left . . ."

"No, no. Tree warned us you might come."

She and Fidel raced into the room as if they were afraid their father and I would already be at each other's throats. "Oh, hi, Mr. Boy," she said.

Her father snorted at the sound of my name.

"Hi." I grinned at her. It was the easiest thing I had done that day.

She was wearing her uniform. When she saw that I had noticed, she blushed. "Well, you asked for it." She tugged self-consciously at the waist of her fatigues. "You want to come in?"

"Just a minute." Mr. Joplin stepped in front of the door, blocking our escape. "You finished E-class?"

"Yes."

"Checked the flats?"

"I'm almost done."

"After that you'd better pick some dinner and get it started. Your mama called and said she wouldn't be home until six-fifteen."

"Sure."

"And you'll take orders for me on line two?"

She leaned against the counter and sighed. "Do I have a choice?"

He backed away and waved us through. "Sorry, sweetheart. I don't know how we would get along without you." He caught her brother by the shirt. "Not you, Fidel. You're misting, remember?"

A short tunnel ran from their mall storefront to the rehabbed furniture warehouse built over the Amtrak rails. Green Dream had installed a krylac roof and fans and a grolighting system; the Joplins squeezed themselves into the leftover spaces not filled with inventory. The air in the greenhouse was heavy and warm and it smelled like rain. No walls, no privacy other than that provided by the plants.

"Here's where I sleep." Tree sat on her unmade bed. Her space was formed by a cinder-block wall painted yellow and a screen of palms. "Chinese fan, bamboo, lady, date, kentia," she said, naming them for me like they were her pets. "I grow them myself for spending money." Her schoolcomm was on top of her dresser. Several drawers hung open; pink skintights trailed from one. Clothes were scattered like piles of leaves across the floor. "I guess I'm kind of a slob," she said as she stripped off the uniform, wadded it, and then banked it off the dresser into the top drawer. I could see her bare back in the mirror plastic taped to the wall. "Take your things off if you want."

I hesitated.

"Or not. But it's kind of muggy to stay dressed. You'll sweat."

I unvelcroed my shirt. I did not at all mind seeing Tree without clothes. But I did not undress for anyone except the stiffs at the clinic. I stepped out of my pants. Being naked somehow had gotten connected with being helpless. I had this puckery feeling in my dick, like it was going to curl up and die. I could imagine the gypsy popping out from behind a palm and laughing at me. No, I was not going to think about *that*. Not here.

"Comfortable?" said Tree.

"Sure." My voice was turning to dust in my throat. "Do all Green Dream employees run around the back room in the nude?"

"I doubt it." She smiled as if the thought tickled her. "We're not exactly your average mall drones. Come help me finish the chores."

I was glad to let her lead so that she was not looking at me, although I could still watch her. I was fascinated by the sweep of her buttocks, the curve of her spine. She strolled, flat-footed and at ease, through her private jungle. At first I scuttled along on the balls of my feet, ready to dart behind a plant if anyone came. But after a while I decided to stop being so skittish. I realized I would probably survive being naked.

Tree stopped in front of a workbench covered with potted seedlings in plastic trays and picked up a hose from the floor.

"What's this stuff?" I kept to the opposite side of the bench, using it to cover myself.

"Greens." She lifted a seedling to check the water level in the tray beneath.

"What are greens?"

"It's too boring." She squirted some water in and replaced the seedling.

"Tell me, I'm interested."

"In greens? You liar." She glanced at me and shook her head. "Okay." She pointed as she said the names. "Lettuce, spinach, bok choi, chard, kale, rocket—got that? And a few tomatoes over there. Peppers, too. GD is trying to break into the food business. They think people will grow more of their own if they find out how easy it is."

"Is it?"

"Greens are." She inspected the next tray. "Just add water."

"Yeah, sure."

"It's because they've been photosynthetically enhanced. Bigger leaves arranged better, low respiration rates. They teach us this stuff at GD Family Camp. It's what we do instead of vacation." She squashed something between her thumb and forefinger. "They mix all these bacteria that make their own fertilizer into the soil—fix nitrogen right out of the air. And then there's this other stuff that sticks to the roots, rhizobacteria and mycorrhizae." She finished the last tray and coiled the hose. "These flats will produce under candlelight in a closet. Bored yet?"

"How do they taste?"

"Pretty bland, most of them. Some stink, like kale and rocket. But we have to eat them for the good of the corporation." She stuck her tongue out. "You want to stay for dinner?"

Mrs. Joplin made me call home before she would feed me; she refused to understand that my mom did not care. So I linked, asked Mom to send a car to the back door at 8:30, and faded. No time to discuss the missing sixteen thousand.

Dinner was from the cookbook Tree had been issued at camp: a bowl of cold bean soup, fresh cornbread, and chard and cheese loaf. She let me help her make it, even though I had never cooked before. I was amazed at how simple cornbread was. Six ingredients: flour, cornmeal, baking powder, milk, oil, and ovobinder. Mix and pour into a greased pan. Bake twenty minutes at 220°C and serve! There is nothing magic or even very mysterious about homemade cornbread, except for the way its smell held me spellbound.

Supper was the Joplins' daily meal together. They ate in front of security windows near the tunnel to the store; when a customer came, someone ran out front. According to contract, they had to stay open twenty-four hours a day. Many of the suburban malls had gone to all-night operation; the competition from New York City was deadly. Mr. Joplin stood duty most of the time, but since they were a franchise family everybody took turns. Even Mrs. Joplin, who also worked part-time as a factfinder at the mall's DataStop.

Tree's mother was plump and graying, and she had a smile that was almost bright enough to distract me from her naked body. She seemed harmless, except that she knew how to ask questions. After all, her job was finding out stuff for DataStop customers. She had this way of locking onto you as you talked; the longer the conversation, the greater her intensity. It was hard to lie to her. Normally that kind of aggressiveness in grown-ups made me jumpy.

No doubt she had run a search on me; I wondered just what she had turned up. Factfinders had to obey the law, so they only accessed public-domain information—unlike Comrade, who would cheerfully operate on whatever I set him to. The Joplins' bank records, for instance. I knew that Mrs. Joplin had made about $11,000 last year at the Infomat in the Elkhart

Mall, that the family borrowed $135,000 at 9.78 percent interest to move to their new franchise, and that they lost $213 in their first two months in New Canaan.

I kept my research a secret, of course, and they acted innocent too. I let them pump me about Mom as we ate. I was used to being asked; after all, Mom was famous. Fidel wanted to know how much it had cost her to get twanked, how big she was, what she looked like on the inside and what she ate, if she got cold in the winter. Stuff like that. The others asked more personal questions. Tree wondered if Mom ever got lonely and whether she was going to be the Statue of Liberty for the rest of her life. Mrs. Joplin was interested in Mom's remotes, of all things. Which ones I got along with, which ones I could not stand, whether I thought any of them was really her. Mr. Joplin asked if she liked being what she was. How was I supposed to know?

After dinner, I helped Fidel clear the table. While we were alone in the kitchen, he complained. "You think they eat this shit at GD headquarters?" He scraped his untouched chard loaf into the composter.

"I kind of liked the cornbread."

"If only he'd buy meat once in a while, but he's too cheap. Or doboys. Tree says you bought her doboys."

I told him to skip school sometime and we would go out for lunch; he thought that was a great idea.

When we came back out, Mr. Joplin actually smiled at me. He had been losing his edge all during dinner. Maybe chard agreed with him. He pulled a pipe from his pocket, began stuffing something into it, and asked me if I followed baseball. I told him no. Paintball? No. Basketball? I said I watched dino fights sometimes.

"His pal is the dinosaur that goes to our school," said Fidel.

"He may look like a dinosaur, but he's really a boy," said Mr. Joplin, as if making an important distinction. "The dinosaurs died out millions of years ago."

"Humans aren't allowed in dino fights," I said, just to keep the conversation going. "Only twanked dogs and horses and elephants."

Silence. Mr. Joplin puffed on his pipe and then passed it to his wife. She watched the glow in the bowl through half-lidded eyes as she inhaled. Fidel caught me staring.

"What's the matter? Don't you get twisted?" He took the pipe in his turn.

I was so croggled I did not know what to say. Even the Marleys had switched to THC inhalers. "But smoking is bad for you." It smelled like a dirty sock had caught fire.

"Hemp is ancient. Natural." Mr. Joplin spoke in a clipped voice as if swallowing his words. "Opens the mind to what's real." When he sighed, smoke poured out of his nose. "We grow it ourselves, you know."

I took the pipe when Tree offered it. Even before I brought the stem to my mouth, the world tilted and I watched myself slide into what seemed very much like a hallucination. Here I was sitting around naked, in the mall, with a bunch of stiffs, smoking antique drugs. And I was enjoying myself. Incredible. I inhaled and immediately the flash hit me; it was as if my brain were an enormous bud, blooming inside my head.

"Good stuff." I laughed smoke and then began coughing.

Fidel refilled my glass with ice water. "Have a sip, cashman."

"Customer." Tree pointed at the window.

"Leave!" Mr. Joplin waved impatiently at him. "Go away." The man on the screen knelt and turned over the price tag on a fern. "Damn." He jerked his uniform from the hook by the door, pulled on the khaki pants, and was slithering into the shirt as he disappeared down the tunnel.

"So is Green Dream trying to break into the flash market too?" I handed the pipe to Mrs. Joplin. There was a fleck of ash on her left breast.

"What we do back here is our business," she said. "We work hard so we can live the way we want." Tree was studying her fingerprints. I realized I had said the wrong thing, so I shut up. Obviously, the Joplins were drifting from the lifestyle taught at Green Dream Family Camp.

Fidel announced he was going to school tomorrow, and Mrs. Joplin told him no, he could link to E-class as usual, and Fidel claimed he could not concentrate at home, and Mrs. Joplin said he was trying to get out of his chores. While they were arguing, Tree nudged my leg and shot me a *let's leave* look. I nodded.

"Excuse us." She pushed back her chair. "Mr. Boy has got to go home soon."

Mrs. Joplin pointed for her to stay. "You wait until your father gets back," she said. "Tell me, Mr. Boy, have you lived in New Canaan long?"

"All my life," I said.

"How old did you say you were?"

"Mama, he's twenty-five," said Tree. "I told you."

"And what do you do for a living?"

"*Mama*, you promised."

"Nothing," I said. "I'm lucky, I guess. I don't need to worry about money. If you didn't need to work, would you?"

"Everybody needs work to do," Mrs. Joplin said. "Work makes us real. Unless you have work to do and people who love you, you don't exist."

Talk about twentieth-century humanist goop! At another time in another place, I probably would have snapped, but now the words would not come. My brain had turned into a flower; all I could think were daisy thoughts. The Joplins were such a strange combination of fast-forward and rewind. I could not tell what they wanted from me.

"Seventeen dollars and ninety-nine cents," said Mr. Joplin, returning from the storefront. "What's going on in here?" He glanced at his wife, and some signal that I did not catch passed between them. He circled the table, came up behind me, and laid his heavy hands on my shoulders. I shuddered; I thought for a moment he meant to strangle me.

"I'm not going to hurt you, Peter," he said. "Before you go, I have something to say."

"*Daddy*."

Tree squirmed in her chair. Fidel looked uncomfortable too, as if he guessed what was coming.

"Sure." I did not have much choice.

The weight on my shoulders eased but did not entirely go away. "You should feel the ache in this boy, Ladonna."

"I know," said Mrs. Joplin.

"Hard as plastic." Mr. Joplin touched the muscles corded along my neck. "You get too hard, you snap." He set his thumbs at the base of my skull and kneaded with an easy circular motion. "Your body isn't some machine that you've downloaded into. It's alive. Real. You have to learn to listen to it. That's why we smoke. Hear these muscles? They're screaming." He let his hand slide down my shoulders. "Now listen." His fingertips probed along my upper spine. "Hear that? Your muscles stay tense because you don't trust anyone. You always have to be ready to take a hit, and you can't tell where it's coming from. You're rigid and angry and scared. Reality . . . your body is speaking to you."

His voice was as big and warm as his hands. Tree was giving him a look that could boil water, but the way he touched me made too much sense to resist.

"We don't mind helping you ease the strain. That's the way Mrs. Joplin and I are. That's the way we brought the kids up. But first you have to admit you're hurting. And then you have to respect us enough to take what we have to give. I don't feel that in you, Peter. You're not ready to give up your pain. You just want us poor stiffs to admire how hard it's made you. We haven't got time for that kind of shit, okay? You learn to listen to yourself and you'll be welcome around here. We'll even call you Mr. Boy, even though it's a damn stupid name."

No one spoke for a moment.

"Sorry, Tree," he said. "We've embarrassed you again. But we love you, so you're stuck with us." I could feel it in his hands when he chuckled. "I suppose I do get carried away sometimes."

"*Sometimes?*" said Fidel. Tree just smoldered.

"It's late," said Mrs. Joplin. "Let him go now, Jamaal. His mama's sending a car over."

Mr. Joplin stepped back, and I almost fell off my chair from leaning against him. I stood, shakily. "Thanks for dinner."

Tree stalked through the greenhouse to the rear exit, her hairworks glittering against her bare back. I had to trot to keep up with her. There was no car in sight, so we waited at the doorway and I put on my clothes.

"I can't take much more of this." She stared through the little wire-glass window in the door, like a prisoner plotting her escape. "I mean, he's not a psychologist or a great philosopher or whatever the hell he thinks he is. He's just a pompous mall drone."

"He's not that bad." Actually, I understood what her father had said to me; it was scary. "I like your family."

"You don't have to live with them!" She kept watching at the door. "They promised they'd behave with you; I should have known better. This happens every time I bring someone home." She puffed an imaginary pipe, imitating her father. "Think what you're doing to yourself, you poor fool, and say, isn't it just too bad about modern life? Love, love, love—*fuck*!" She turned to me. "I'm sick of it. People are going to think I'm as sappy and thickheaded as my parents."

"I don't."

"You're lucky. You're rich and your mom leaves you alone. You're New Canaan. My folks are Elkhart, Indiana."

"Being New Canaan is nothing to brag about. So what are you?"

"Not a Joplin." She shook her head. "Not much longer, anyway; I'm eighteen in February. I think your car's here." She held out her arms and hugged me good-bye. "Sorry you had to sit through that. Don't drop me, okay? I like you, Mr. Boy." She did not let go for a while.

Dropping her had never occurred to me; I was not thinking of anything at all except the silkiness of her skin, the warmth of her body. Her breath whispered through my hair and her nipples brushed my ribs and then she kissed me. Just on the cheek, but the damage was done. I was stunted. I was not supposed to feel this way about anyone.

Comrade was waiting in the backseat. We rode home in silence; I had nothing to say to him. He would not understand—none of my friends would. They would warn me that all she wanted was to spend some of my money. Or they would make bad jokes about the nudity or the Joplins' mushy realism. No way I could explain the innocence of the way they touched one another. *The old man did what to you?* Yeah, and if I wanted a hug at home who was I supposed to ask? Comrade? Lovey? The greeter? Was I supposed to climb up to the head and fall asleep against Mom's doorbone, waiting for it to open, like I used to do when I was really a kid?

The greeter was her usual nonstick self when I got home. She was so glad to see me and she wanted to know where I had been and if I had a good time and if I wanted Cook to make me a snack? Around. Yes. No.

She said the bank had called about some problem with one of the cash cards she had given me, a security glitch that they had taken care of and were very sorry about. Did I know about it and did I need a new card and would twenty thousand be enough? Yes. Please. Thanks.

And that was it. I found myself resenting Mom because she did not have to care about losing sixteen or twenty or fifty thousand dollars. And she had reminded me of my problems when all I wanted to think of was Tree. She was no help to me, never had been. I had things so twisted around that I almost told her about Montross myself, just to get a reaction. Here some guy had tapped our files and threatened my life, and she asked if I wanted a snack.

Why keep me around if she was going to pay so little attention? I wanted to shock her, to make her take me seriously.

But I did not know how.

The roombrain woke me. "Stennie's calling."

"Mmm."

"Talk to me, Mr. Party Boy." A window opened; he was in his car. "You dead or alive?"

"Asleep." I rolled over. "Time is it?"

"Ten-thirty and I'm bored. Want me to come get you now, or should I meet you there?"

"Wha . . . ?"

"Happy's. Don't tell me you forgot. They're doing a *piano*."

"Who cares?" I crawled out of bed and slouched into the bathroom.

"She says she's asking Tree Joplin," Stennie called after me.

"Asking her what?" I came out.

"To the party."

"Is she going?"

"She's your cush." He gave me a toothy smile. "Call back when you're ready. Later." He faded.

"She left a message," said the roombrain. "Half-hour ago."

"Tree? You got me up for Stennie and not for her?"

"He's on the list, she's not. Happy called, too."

"Comrade should've told you. Where is he?" Now I was grouchy. "She's on the list, okay? Give me playback."

Tree seemed pleased with herself. "Hi, this is me. I got myself invited to a smash party this afternoon. You want to go?" She faded.

"That's all? Call her!"

"Both her numbers are busy; I'll set redial. I found Comrade; he's on another line. You want Happy's message?"

"No. Yes."

"You promised, Mr. Boy." Happy giggled. "Look, you really, really don't want to miss this. Stennie's coming, and he said I should ask Joplin if I wanted you here. So you've got no excuse."

Someone tugged at her. "Stop that! Sorry, I'm being molested by a thick . . ." She batted at her assailant. "Mr. Boy, did I tell you that this Japanese reporter is coming to shoot a vid? What?" She turned off camera. "Sure, just like on the Nature Channel. *Wildlife of America.* We're all going to be famous. In Japan! This is history, Mr. Boy. And you're . . ."

Her face froze as the redial program finally linked to the Green Dream. The roombrain brought Tree up in a new window. "Oh, hi," she said. "You rich boys sleep late."

"What's this about Happy's?"

"She invited me." Tree was recharging her hairworks with a red brush. "I said yes. Something wrong?"

Comrade slipped into the room; I shushed him. "You sure you want to go to a smash party? Sometimes they get a little crazy."

She aimed the brush at me. "You've been to smash parties before. You survived."

"Sure, but . . ."

"Well, I haven't. All I know is that everybody at school is talking about this one, and I want to see what it's about."

"You tell your parents you're going?"

"Are you kidding? They'd just say it was too dangerous. What's the matter, Mr. Boy, are you scared? Come on, it'll be extreme."

"She's right. You *should* go," said Comrade.

"Is that Comrade?" Tree said. "You tell him, Comrade!"

I glared at him. "Okay, okay, I guess I'm outnumbered. Stennie said he'd drive. You want us to pick you up?"

She did.

I flew at Comrade as soon as Tree faded. "Don't you ever do that again!" I shoved him, and he bumped up against the wall. "I ought to throw you to Montross."

"You know, I just finished chatting with him." Comrade stayed calm and made no move to defend himself. "He wants to meet—the three of us, face to face. He suggested Happy's."

"He suggested . . . I told you not to talk to him."

"I know." He shrugged. "Anyway, I think we should do it."

"Who gave you permission to think?"

"You did. What if we give him the picture back and open our files and then I grovel, say I'm sorry, it'll never happen again, *blah, blah, blah*. Maybe we can even buy him off. What have we got to lose?"

"You can't bribe software. And what if he decides to snatch us?" I told Comrade about the gypsy with the penlight. "You want Tree mixed up in this?"

All the expression drained from his face. He did not say anything at first, but I had watched his subroutines long enough to know that when he looked this blank, he was shaken. "So we take a risk, maybe we can get it over with," he said. "He's not interested in Tree, and I won't let anything happen to you. Why do you think your mom bought me?"

Happy Lurdane lived on the former estate of Philip Johnson, a notorious twentieth-century architect. In his will Johnson had arranged to turn his compound into the Philip Johnson Memorial Museum, but after he died his work went out of fashion. The glass skyscrapers in the cities did not age well; they started to fall apart or were torn down because they wasted energy. Nobody visited the museum, and it went bankrupt. The Lurdanes had bought the property and made some changes.

Johnson had designed all the odd little buildings on the estate himself. The main house was a shoebox of glass with no inside walls; near it stood a windowless brick guest house. On a pond below was a dock that looked like a Greek temple. Past the circular swimming pool near the houses were two galleries that had once held Johnson's art collection, long since sold off. In Johnson's day, the scattered buildings had been connected only by paths, which made the compound impossible in the frosty Connecticut winters. The Lurdanes had enclosed the paths in clear tubes and commuted in a golf cart. Stennie told his Alpha not to wait, since the lot was already full and cars were parked well down the driveway. Five of us squeezed out of the car: me, Tree, Comrade, Stennie, and Janet Hoyt. Janet wore a Yankees jersey over pinstriped shorts, Tree was a little overdressed in her silver jaunts, I had on baggies padded to make me seem bigger, and Comrade wore his usual window coat. Stennie lugged a box with his swag for the party.

Freddy the Teddy let us in. "Stennie and Mr. Boy!" He reared back on his hindquarters and roared. "Glad I'm not going to be the only beastie here. Hi,

Janet. Hi, I'm Freddy," he said to Tree. His pink tongue lolled. "Come in, this way. Fun starts right here. Some kids are swimming, and there's sex in the guest house. Everybody else is with Happy having lunch in the sculpture gallery."

The interior of the Glass House was bright and hard. Dark woodblock floor, some unfriendly furniture, huge panes of glass framed in black-painted steel. The few kids in the kitchen were passing an inhaler around and watching a microwave fill up with popcorn.

"I'm hot." Janet stuck the inhaler into her face and pressed. "Anybody want to swim? Tree?"

"Okay." Tree breathed in a polite dose and breathed out a giggle. "You?" she asked me.

"I don't think so." I was too nervous: I kept expecting someone to jump out and throw a net over me. "I'll watch."

"I'd swim with you," said Stennie, "but I promised Happy I'd bring her these party favors as soon as I arrived." He nudged the box with his foot. "Can you wait a few minutes?"

"Comrade and I will take them over." I grabbed the box and headed for the door, glad for the excuse to leave Tree behind while I went to find Montross. "Meet you at the pool."

The golf cart was gone, so we walked through the tube toward the sculpture gallery. "You have the picture?" I said.

Comrade patted the pocket of his window coat.

The tube was not air-conditioned, and the afternoon sun pounded us through the optical plastic. There was no sound inside; even our footsteps were swallowed by the AstroTurf. The box got heavier. We passed the entrance to the old painting gallery, which looked like a bomb shelter. Finally I had to break the silence. "I feel strange, being here," I said. "Not just because of the thing with Montross. I really think I lost myself last time I got stunted. Not sure who I am anymore, but I don't think I belong with these kids."

"People change, *tovarisch*," said Comrade. "Even you."

"Have I changed?"

He smiled. "Now that you've got a cush, your own mother wouldn't recognize you."

"You know what your problem is?" I grinned and bumped up against him on purpose. "You're jealous of Tree."

"Shouldn't I be?"

"Oh, I don't know. I can't tell if Tree likes who I was or who I might be. She's changing, too. She's so hot to break away from her parents, become part of this town. Except that what she's headed for probably isn't worth the trip. I feel like I should protect her, but that means guarding her from people like me, except I don't think I'm Mom's Mr. Boy anymore. Does that make sense?"

"Sure." He gazed straight ahead, but all the heads on his window coat were scoping me. "Maybe when you're finished changing, you won't need me."

The thought had occurred to me. For years he had been the only one I could talk to, but as we closed on the gallery, I did not know what to say. I shook my head. "I just feel strange."

And then we arrived. The sculpture gallery was designed for show-offs: short flights of steps and a series of stagy balconies descended around the white-brick exterior walls to the central exhibition area. The space was open so you could chat with your little knot of friends and, at the same time, spy on everyone else. About thirty kids were eating pizza and Crispix off paper plates. At the bottom of the stairs, as advertised, was a black upright piano. Piled beside it was the rest of the swag. A Boston rocker, a case of green Coke bottles, a Virgin Mary in half a blue bathtub, a huge conch shell, china and crystal and assorted smaller treasures, including a four-thousand-year-old ceramic hippo. There were real animals too, in cages near the gun rack: a turkey, some stray dogs and cats, turtles, frogs, assorted rodents.

I was threading my way across the first balcony when I was stopped by the Japanese reporter, who was wearing microcam eyes.

"Excuse me, please," he said, "I am Matsuo Shikibu, and I will be recording this event today for Nippon Hoso Kyokai. Public telelink of Japan." He smiled and bowed. When his head came up, the red light between his lenses was on. "You are . . . ?"

"Raskolnikov," said Comrade, edging between me and the camera. "Rodeo Raskolnikov." He took Shikibu's hand and pumped it. "And my associate here, Mr. Peter Pan." He turned as if to introduce me, but we had long since choreographed this dodge. As I sidestepped past, he kept shielding me from the reporter with his body. "We're friends of the bride," Comrade said, "and we're really excited to be making new friends in your country. Banzai, Nippon!"

I slipped by them and scooted downstairs. Happy was basking by the piano; she spotted me as I reached the middle landing.

"Mr. Boy!" It was not so much a greeting as an announcement. She was wearing a body mike, and her voice boomed over the sound system. "You made it."

The stream of conversation rippled momentarily, a few heads turned, and then the party flowed on. Shikibu rushed to the edge of the upper balcony and caught me with a long shot.

I set the box on the Steinway. "Stennie brought this."

She opened it eagerly. "Look, everyone!" She held up a stack of square cardboard albums, about thirty centimeters on a side. There were pictures of musicians on the front, words on the back. "What are they?" she asked me.

"Phonograph records," said the kid next to Happy. "It's how they used to play music before digital."

"Erroll Garner, *Soliloquy*," she read aloud. "What's this? D-j-a-n-g-o Reinhardt and the American Jazz Giants. Sounds scary." She giggled as she pawed quickly through the other albums. Handy, Ellington, Hawkins, Parker, three Armstrongs. One was *Piano Rags by Scott Joplin*. Stennie's bent idea of a joke? Maybe the lizard was smarter than he looked. Happy pulled a black plastic record out of one sleeve and scratched a fingernail across little ridges. "Oh, a nonslip surface."

The party had a limited attention span. When she realized she had lost her audience, she shut off the mike and put the box with the rest of the swag. "We have to start at four, no matter what. There's so much stuff." The kid who knew about records wormed into our conversation; Happy put her hand on his shoulder. "Mr. Boy, do you know my friend Weldon?" she said. "He's new."

Montross grinned. "We met on Playroom."

"Where *is* Stennie, anyway?" said Happy.

"Swimming," I said. Montross appeared to be in his late teens. Bigger than me—everyone was bigger than me. He wore green shorts and a window shirt of surfers at Waimea. He looked like everybody; there was nothing about him to remember. I considered bashing the smirk off his face, but it was a bad idea. If he was software, he could not feel anything and I would probably break my hand on his temporary chassis. "Got to go. I promised Stennie I'd meet him back at the pool. Hey, Weldon, want to tag along?"

"You come right back," said Happy. "We're starting at four. Tell everyone."

We avoided the tube and cut across the lawn for privacy. Comrade handed Montross the envelope. He slid the photograph out, and I had one last glimpse. This time the dead man left me cold. In fact, I was embarrassed. Although he kept a straight face, I knew what Montross was thinking about me. Maybe he was right. I wished he would put the picture away. He was not one of us; he could not understand. I wondered if Tree had come far enough yet to appreciate corpse porn.

"It's the only copy," Comrade said.

"All right." Finally Montross crammed it into the pocket of his shorts.

"You tapped our files; you know it's true."

"So?"

"So enough!" I said. "You have what you wanted."

"I've already explained." Montross was being patient. "Getting this back doesn't close the case. I have to take preventive measures."

"Meaning you turn Comrade into a carrot."

"Meaning I repair him. You're the one who took him to the chop shop. Deregulated wiseguys are dangerous. Maybe not to you, but certainly to property and probably to other people. It's a straightforward procedure. He'll be fully functional afterward."

"Plug your procedure, jack. We're leaving."

Both wiseguys stopped. "I thought you agreed," said Montross.

"Let's go, Comrade." I grabbed his arm, but he shook me off.

"Where?" he said.

"Anywhere! Just so I never have to listen to this again." I pulled again, angry at Comrade for stalling. Your wiseguy is supposed to anticipate your needs, do whatever you want.

"But we haven't even tried to—"

"Forget it then. I give up." I pushed him toward Montross. "You want to chat, fine, go right ahead. Let him rip the top of your head off while you're at it, but I'm not sticking around to watch."

I checked the pool, but Tree, Stennie, and Janet had already gone. I went through the Glass House and caught up with them in the tube to the sculpture gallery.

"Can I talk to you?" I put my arm around Tree's waist, just like I had seen grown-ups do. "In private." I could tell she was annoyed to be separated from Janet. "We'll catch up." I waved Stennie on. "See you over there."

She waited until they were gone. "What?" Her hair, slick from swimming, left dark spots where it brushed her silver jaunts.

"I want to leave. We'll call my mom's car." She did not look happy. "I'll take you anywhere you want to go."

"But we just got here. Give it a chance."

"I've been to too many of these things."

"Then you shouldn't have come."

Silence. I wanted to tell her about Montross—everything—but not here. Anyone could come along and the tube was so hot. I was desperate to get her away, so I lied. "Believe me, you're not going to like this. I know." I tugged at her waist. "Sometimes even I think smash parties are too much."

"We've had this discussion before," she said. "Obviously you weren't listening. I don't need you to decide for me whether I'm going to like something, Mr. Boy. I have two parents too many; I don't need another." She stepped away from me. "Hey, I'm sorry if you're having a bad time. But do you really need to spoil it for me?" She turned and strode down the tube toward the gallery, her beautiful hair slapping against her back. I watched her go.

"But I'm in trouble," I muttered to the empty tube—and then was disgusted with myself because I did not have the guts to say it to Tree. I was too scared she would not care. I stood there, sweating. For a moment the stink of doubt filled my nostrils. Then I followed her in. I could not abandon her to the extremists.

The gallery was jammed now; maybe a hundred kids swarmed across the balconies and down the stairs. Some perched along the edges, their feet scuffing the white brick. Happy had turned up the volume.

". . . according to *Guinness*, was set at the University of Oklahoma in Norman, Oklahoma, in 2012. Three minutes and fourteen seconds." The crowd rumbled in disbelief. "The challenge states each piece must be small enough to pass through a hole thirty centimeters in diameter."

I worked my way to an opening beside a rubber tree. Happy posed on the keyboard of the piano. Freddy the Teddy and the gorilla brothers, Mike and Bubba, lined up beside her. "No mechanical tools are allowed." She gestured at an armory of axes, sledgehammers, spikes, and crowbars laid out on the floor. A paper plate spun across the room. I could not see Tree.

"This piano is over two hundred years old," Happy continued, "which means the white keys are ivory." She plunked a note. "Dead elephants!" Everybody heaved a sympathetic *aumrw*. "The blacks are ebony, hacked from the rain forest." Another note, less reaction. "It deserves to die."

Applause. Comrade and I spotted each other at almost the same time. He and Montross stood toward the rear of the lower balcony. He gestured for me to come down; I ignored him.

"Do you boys have anything to say?" Happy said.

"Yeah." Freddy hefted an ax. "Let's make landfill."

I ducked around the rubber tree and heard the *crack* of splitting wood, the iron groan of a piano frame yielding its last music. The spectators hooted approval. As I bumped past kids, searching for Tree, the instrument's death cry made me think of taking a hammer to Montross. If fights broke out, no one would care if Comrade and I dragged him outside. I wanted to beat him until he shuddered and came unstrung and his works glinted in the thudding August light. It would make me feel extreme again. *Crunch!* Kids shrieked, "Go, go, go!" The party was lifting off and taking me with it.

"You are Mr. Boy Cage." Abruptly Shikibu's microcam eyes were in my face. "We know your famous mother." He had to shout to be heard. "I have a question."

"Go away."

"*Thirty seconds.*" A girl's voice boomed over the speakers.

"US and Japan are very different, yes?" He pressed closer. "We honor ancestors, our past. You seem to hate so much." He gestured at the gallery. "Why?"

"Maybe we're spoiled." I barged past him.

I saw Freddy swing a sledgehammer at the exposed frame. *Clang!* A chunk of twisted iron clattered across the brick floor, trailing broken strings. Happy scooped the mess up and shoved it through a thirty-centimeter hole drilled in an upright sheet of particle board.

The timekeeper called out again. *"One minute."* I had come far enough around the curve of the stairs to see her.

"Treemonisha!"

She glanced up, her face alight with pleasure, and waved. I was frightened for her. She was climbing into the same box I needed to break out of. So I rushed down the stairs to rescue her—little boy knight in shining armor—and ran right into Comrade's arms.

"I've decided," he said. *"Mnye vcyaw ostoyeblo."*

"Great." I had to get to Tree. "Later, okay?" When I tried to go by, he picked me up. I started thrashing. It was the first fight of the afternoon and I lost. He carried me over to Montross. The gallery was in an uproar.

"All set," said Montross. "I'll have to borrow him for a while. I'll drop him off tonight at your mom. Then we're done."

"Done?" I kept trying to get free, but Comrade crushed me against him.

"It's what you want." His body was so hard. "And what your mom wants."

"Mom? She doesn't even know."

"She knows everything," Comrade said. "She watches you constantly. What else does she have to do all day?" He let me go. "Remember you said I was sloppy getting the picture? I wasn't; it was a clean operation. Only someone tipped Datasafe off."

"But she promised. Besides, that makes no—"

"Two minutes," Tree called.

". . . But he threatened me," I said. "He was going to blow me up. Needle me in the mall."

"We wouldn't do that." Montross spread his hands innocently. "It's against the law."

"Yeah? Well, then, drop dead, jack." I poked a finger at him. "Deal's off."

"No, it's not," said Comrade. "It's too late. This isn't about the picture anymore, Mr. Boy; it's about you. You weren't supposed to change, but you did. Maybe they botched the last stunting, maybe it's Treemonisha. Whatever, you've outgrown me, the way I am now. So I have to change too, or else I'll keep getting in your way."

He always had everything under control; it made me crazy. He was too good at running my life. "You should have told me Mom turned you in." *Crash!* I felt like the crowd was inside my head, screaming.

"You could've figured it out, if you wanted to. Besides, if I had said anything, your mom wouldn't have bothered to be subtle. She would've squashed me. She still might, even though I'm being fixed. Only by then I won't care. *Rosproyebi tvayou mat!*"

I heard Tree finishing the count. ". . . *twelve, thirteen, fourteen!*" No record today. Some kids began to boo, others laughed. "Time's up, you losers!"

I glared at the two wiseguys. Montross was busy emulating sincerity. Comrade found a way to grin for me, the same smirk he always wore when he tortured the greeter. "It's easier this way."

Easier. My life was too plugging easy. I had never done anything important by myself. Not even grow up. I wanted to smash something.

"Okay," I said. "You asked for it."

Comrade turned to Montross and they shook hands. I thought next they might clap one another on the shoulder and whistle as they strolled off into the sunset together. I felt like puking. "Have fun," said Comrade. "*Da svedanya.*"

"Sure." Betraying Comrade, my best friend, brought me both pain and pleasure at once—but not enough to satisfy the shrieking wildness within me. The party was just starting.

Happy stood beaming beside the ruins of the Steinway. Although nothing of what was left was more than half a meter tall, Freddy, Mike, and Bubba had given up now that the challenge was lost. Kids were already surging down the stairs to claim their share of the swag. I went along with them.

"Don't worry," announced Happy. "Plenty for everyone. Come take what you like. Remember, guns and animals outside, if you want to hunt. The safeties won't release unless you go through the door. Watch out for one another, people, we don't want anyone shot."

A bunch of kids were wrestling over the turkey cage; one of them staggered backward and knocked into me. "Gobble, gobble," she said. I shoved her back.

"Mr. Boy! Over here." Tree, Stennie, and Janet were waiting on the far side of the gallery. As I crossed to them, Happy gave the sign and Stone Kinkaid hurled the four-thousand-year-old ceramic hippo against the wall. It shattered. Everybody cheered.

In the upper balconies, they were playing catch with a frog.

"You see who kept time?" said Janet.

"Didn't need to see," I said. "I could hear. They probably heard in Elkhart. So you like it, Tree?"

"It's about what I expected: dumb but fun. I don't think they . . ." The frog sailed from the top balcony and splatted at our feet. Its legs twitched and guts spilled from its open mouth. I watched Tree's smile turn brittle. She seemed slightly embarrassed, as if she had just been told the price of something she could not afford.

"This is going to be a war zone soon," Stennie said.

"Yeah, let's fade." Janet towed Stennie to the stairs, swerving around the three boys lugging Our Lady of the Bathtub out to the firing range.

"Wait." I blocked Tree. "You're here, so you have to destroy something. Get with the program."

"I have to?" She seemed doubtful. "Oh, all right—but no animals."

A hail of antique Coke bottles crashed around Happy as she directed traffic at the dwindling swag heap. "Hey, people, please be very careful where you throw things." Her amplified voice blasted us as we approached. The first floor was a graveyard of broken glass and piano bones and bloody feathers. Most of the good stuff was already gone.

"Any records left?" I said.

Happy wobbled closer to me. "What?" She seemed punchy, as if stunned by the success of her own party.

"The box I gave you. From Stennie." She pointed; I spotted it under some cages and grabbed it. Tree and the others were on the stairs. Outside I could hear the crackle of small-arms fire. I caught up.

"Sir! Mr. Dinosaur, please." The press still lurked on the upper balcony. "Matsuo Shikibu, Japanese telelink NHK. Could I speak with you for a moment?"

"Excuse me, but this jack and I have some unfinished business." I handed Stennie the records and cut in front. He swayed and lashed his tail upward to counterbalance their weight.

"Remember me?" I bowed to Shikibu.

"My apologies if I offended . . ."

"Hey, Matsuo—can I call you Matsuo? This is your first smash party, right? Please, eyes on me. I want to explain why I was rude before. Help you understand the local customs. You see, we're kind of self-conscious here in the US. We don't like it when someone just watches while we play. You either join in or you're not one of us."

My little speech drew a crowd. "What's he talking about?" said Janet. She was shushed.

"So if you drop by our party and don't have fun, people resent you," I told him. "No one came here today to put on a show. This is who we are. What we believe in."

"Yeah!" Stennie was cheerleading for the extreme Mr. Boy of old. "Tell him." Too bad he did not realize it was his final appearance. What was Mr. Boy without his Comrade? "Make him feel some pain."

I snatched an album from the top of the stack, slipped the record out, and held it close to Shikibu's microcam eyes. "What does this say?"

He craned his neck to read the label. "John Coltrane, *Giant Steps*."

"Very good." I grasped the record with both hands and raised it over my head for all to see. "We're not picky, Matsuo. We welcome everyone. Therefore today it is my honor to initiate you—and the home audience back on NHK. If you're still watching, you're part of this too." I broke the record over his head.

He yelped and staggered backward and almost tripped over a dead cat. Stone Kinkaid caught him and propped him up. "Congratulations," said Stennie, as he waved his claws at Japan. "You're all extremists now."

Shikibu gaped at me, his microcam eyes askew. A couple of kids clapped.

"There's someone else here who has not yet joined us." I turned on Tree. "Another spectator." Her smile faded.

"You leave her alone," said Janet. "What are you, crazy?"

"I'm not going to touch her." I held up empty hands. "No, I just want her to ruin something. That's why you came, isn't it, Tree? To get a taste?" I rifled through the box until I found what I wanted. "How about this?" I thrust it at her.

"Oh, yeah," said Stennie, "I meant to tell you . . ."

She took the record and scoped it briefly. When she glanced up at me, I almost lost my nerve.

"Matsuo Shikibu, meet Treemonisha Joplin." I clasped my hands behind my back so no one could see me tremble. "The great-great-great-granddaughter of the famous American composer, Scott Joplin. Yes, Japan, we're all celebrities here in New Canaan. Now please observe." I read the record for him. "*Piano

Rags by Scott Joplin*, Volume III. Who knows, this might be the last copy. We can only hope. So, what are you waiting for, Tree? You don't want to be a Joplin anymore? Just wait until your folks get a peek at this. We'll even send GD a copy. Go ahead, enjoy."

"Smash it!" The kids around us took up the chant. "Smash it!" Shikibu adjusted his lenses.

"You think I won't?" Tree pulled out the disk and threw the sleeve off the balcony. "This is a piece of junk, Mr. Boy." She laughed and then shattered the album against the wall. She held on to a shard. "It doesn't mean anything to me."

I heard Janet whisper. "What's going on?"

"I think they're having an argument."

"You want me to be your little dream cush." Tree tucked the piece of broken plastic into the pocket of my baggies. "The stiff from nowhere who knows nobody and does nothing without Mr. Boy. So you try to scare me off. You tell me you're so rich, you can afford to hate yourself. Stay home, you say, it's too dangerous, we're all crazy. Well, if you're so sure this is poison, how come you've still got your wiseguy and your cash cards? Are you going to move out of your mom, leave town, stop getting stunted? You're not giving it up, Mr. Boy, so why should I?"

Shikibu turned his camera eyes on me. No one spoke.

"You're right," I said. "She's right." I could not save anyone until I saved myself. I felt the wildness lifting me to it. I leapt onto the balcony wall and shouted for everyone to hear. "Shut up and listen, everybody! You're all invited to my place, okay?"

There was one last thing to smash.

"Stop this, Peter." The greeter no longer thought I was cute. "What're you doing?" She trembled as if the kids spilling into her were an infection.

"I thought you'd like to meet my friends," I said. A few had stayed behind with Happy, who had decided to sulk after I hijacked her guests. The rest had followed me home in a caravan so I could warn off the sentry robots.

It was already a hall-of-fame bash. "Treemonisha Joplin, this is my mom. Sort of."

"Hi," Tree held out her hand uncertainly.

The greeter was no longer the human doormat. "Get them out of me." She was too jumpy to be polite. "Right now!"

Someone turned up a boombox. Skitter music filled the room like a siren. Tree said something I could not hear. When I put a hand to my ear, she leaned close and said, "Don't be so mean, Mr. Boy. I think she's really frightened."

I grinned and nodded. "I'll tell Cook to make us some snacks."

Bubba and Mike carried boxes filled with the last of the swag and set them on the coffee table. Kids fanned out, running their hands along her wrinkled blood-hot walls, bouncing on the furniture. Stennie waved at me as he led a bunch upstairs for a tour. A leftover cat had gotten loose and was hissing and scratching underfoot. Some twisted kids had already stripped and were rolling in the floor hair, getting ready to have sex.

"Get dressed, you." The greeter kicked at them as she coiled her umbilical to keep it from being trampled. She retreated to her wall plug. "You're *hurting* me." Although her voice rose to a scream, only half a dozen kids heard her. She went limp and sagged to the floor.

The whole room seemed to throb, as if to some great heartbeat, and the lights went out. It took a while for someone to kill the sound on the boombox. "What's wrong?" Voices called out. "Mr. Boy? Lights."

Both doorbones swung open, and I saw a bughead silhouetted against the twilit sky. Shikibu in his microcams. "Party's over," Mom said over her speaker system. There was nervous laughter. "Leave before I call the cops. Peter, go to your room right now. I want to speak to you."

As the stampede began, I found Tree's hand. "Wait for me?" I pulled her close. "I'll only be a minute."

"What are you going to do?" She sounded frightened. It felt good to be taken so seriously.

"I'm moving out, chucking all this. I'm going to be a working stiff." I chuckled. "Think your dad would give me a job?"

"Look out, dumbscut! Hey, *hey*. Don't push!"

Tree dragged me out of the way. "You're crazy."

"I know. That's why I have to get out of Mom."

"Listen," she said, "you've never been poor, you have no idea . . . Only a rich kid would think it's easy being a stiff. Just go up, apologize, tell her it won't happen again. Then change things later on, if you want. Believe me, life will be a lot simpler if you hang on to the money."

"I can't. Will you wait?"

"You want me to tell you it's okay to be stupid, is that it? Well, I've *been* poor, Mr. Boy, and still am, and I don't recommend it. So don't expect me to stand around and clap while you throw away something I've always wanted." She spun away from me, and I lost her in the darkness. I wanted to catch up with her, but I knew I had to do Mom now or I would lose my nerve.

As I was fumbling my way upstairs, I heard stragglers coming down. "On your right," I called. Bodies nudged by me.

"Mr. Boy, is that you?" I recognized Stennie's voice.

"He's gone," I said.

Seven flights up, the lights were on. Nanny waited on the landing outside my rooms, her umbilical stretched nearly to its limit. She was the only remote that was physically able to get to my floor, and this was as close as she could come.

It had been a while since I had seen her; Mom did not use her much anymore and I rarely visited, even though the nursery was only one flight down. But this was the remote who used to pick me up when I cried and who had changed my diapers and who taught me how to turn on my roombrain. She had skin so pale you could almost see veins and long black hair piled high on her head. I never thought of her as having a body because she always wore dark turtlenecks and long woolen skirts and silky pantyhose. Nanny was a smile and warm hands and the smell of fresh pillowcases. Once upon a time, I thought her the most beautiful creature in the world. Back then I would have done anything she said.

She was not smiling now. "I don't know how you expect me to trust you anymore, Peter." Nanny had never been a very good scold. "Those brats were out of control. I can't let you put me in danger this way."

"If you wanted someone to trust, maybe you shouldn't have had me stunted. You got exactly what you ordered, the never-ending kid. Well, kids don't have to be responsible."

"What do you mean, what I ordered? It's what you wanted, too."

"Is it? Did you ever ask? I was only ten, the first time, too young to know better. For a long time I did it to please you. Getting stunted was the only thing I did that seemed important to you. But *you* never explained. You never sat me down and said, 'This is the life you'll have and this is what you'll miss and this is how you'll feel about it.'"

"You want to grow up, is that it?" She was trying to threaten me. "You want to work and worry and get old and die someday?" She had no idea what we were talking about.

"I can't live this way anymore, Nanny."

At first she acted stunned, as if I had spoken in Albanian. Then her expression hardened when she realized she had lost her hold on me. She was ugly when she was angry. "They put you up to this." Her gaze narrowed in accusation. "That little black cush you've been seeing. Those realists!"

I had always managed to hide my anger from Mom. Right up until then. "How do you know about her?" I had never told her about Tree.

"Peter, they live in a mall!"

Comrade was right. "You've been spying on me." When she did not deny it, I went berserk. "You liar." I slammed my fist into her belly. "You said you wouldn't watch." She staggered and fell onto her umbilical, crimping it. As she twitched on the floor, I pounced. "You promised." I slapped her face. "Promised." I hit her again. Her hair had come undone and her eyes rolled back in their sockets and her face was slack. She made no effort to protect herself. Mom was retreating from this remote too, but I was not going to let her get away.

"Mom!" I rolled off Nanny. "I'm coming up, Mom! You hear? Get ready." I was crying; it had been a long time since I had cried. Not something Mr. Boy did.

I scrambled up to the long landing at the shoulders. At one end another circular stairway wound up into the torch; in the middle, four steps led into the neck. It was the only doorbone I had never seen open; I had no idea how to get through.

"Mom, I'm here." I pounded. "Mom! You hear me?"

Silence.

"Let me in, Mom." I smashed myself against the doorbone. Pain branched through my shoulder like lightning, but it felt great because Mom shuddered from the impact. I backed up and, in a frenzy, hurled myself again. Something warm dripped on my cheek. She was bleeding from the hinges. I aimed a vicious kick at the doorbone, and it banged open. I went through.

For years I had imagined that if only I could get into the head I could meet my real mother. Touch her. I had always wondered what she looked like; she got reshaped just after I was born. When I was little I used to think of her as a magic princess glowing with fairy light. Later I pictured her as one or another of my friends' moms, only better dressed. After I had started getting twanked, I was afraid she might be just a brain floating in nutrient solution, like in some pricey memory bank. All wrong.

The interior of the head was dark and absolutely freezing.

There was no sound except for the hum of refrigeration units. "Mom?" My voice echoed in the empty space. I stumbled and caught myself against a smooth wall. Not skin, like everywhere else in Mom—metal. The tears froze on my face.

"There's nothing for you here," she said. "This is a clean room. You're compromising it. You must leave immediately."

Sterile environment, metal walls, the bitter cold that superconductors needed. I did not need to see. No one lived here. It had never occurred to me that there was no Mom to touch. She had downloaded, become an electron ghost tripping icy logic gates. "How long have you been dead?"

"This isn't where you belong," she said.

I shivered. "How long?"

"Go away," she said.

So I did. I had to. I could not stay very long in her secret place, or I would die of the cold.

As I reeled down the stairs, Mom herself seemed to shift beneath my feet and I saw her as if she were a stranger. Dead—and I had been living in a tomb. I ran past Nanny; she still sprawled where I had left her. All those years I had loved her, I had been in love with death. Mom had been sucking life from me the way her refrigerators stole the warmth from my body.

Now I knew there was no way I could stay, no matter what anyone said. I knew it was not going to be easy leaving, and not just because of the money. For a long time Mom had been my entire world. But I could not let her use me to pretend she was alive, or I would end up like her.

I realized now that the door had always stayed locked because Mom had to hide what she had become. If I wanted, I could have destroyed her. Downloaded intelligences have no more rights than cars or wiseguys. Mom was legally dead and I was her only heir. I could have had her shut off, her body razed. But somehow it was enough to go, to walk away from my inheritance. I was scared, and yet with every step I felt lighter. Happier. Extremely free.

I had not expected to find Tree waiting at the doorbone, chatting with Comrade as if nothing had happened. "I just had to see if you were really the biggest fool in the world," she said.

"Out." I pulled her through the door. "Before I change my mind."

Comrade started to follow us. "No, not you." I turned and stared back at the heads on his window coat. I had not intended to see him again; I had wanted to be gone before Montross returned him. "Look, I'm giving you back to Mom. She needs you more than I do."

If he had argued, I might have given in. The old unregulated Comrade would have said something. But he just slumped a little and nodded and I knew that he was dead, too. The thing in front of me was another ghost. He and Mom were two of a kind. "Pretend you're her kid, maybe she'll like that." I patted his shoulder.

"*Prekrassnaya ideya*," he said. "*Spaceba.*"

"You're welcome," I said. *Tree and I trotted together down the long driveway. Robot sentries crossed the lawn and turned their spotlights on us. I wanted to tell her she was right. I had probably just done the single most irresponsible thing of my life— and I had high standards. Still, I could not imagine how being poor could be worse than being rich and hating yourself. I had seen enough of what it was like to be dead. It was time to try living. "Are we going someplace, Mr. Boy?" Tree squeezed my hand. "Or are we just wandering around in the dark?"*

"Mr. Boy is a damn stupid name, don't you think?" I laughed. "Call me Pete." I felt like a kid again.

WOLVES OF THE PLATEAU

By John Shirley

Nine A.M., and Jerome-X wanted a smoke. He didn't smoke, but he wanted one in here, and he could see how people went into prison non-smokers and came out doing two packs a day. Maybe had to get their brains rewired to get off it. Which was ugly, he'd been rewired once to get off Sink, synthetic cocaine, and he'd felt like a processor with a glitch for a month after that.

He pictured his thoughts like a little train, zipping around the cigarette-burnt graffiti: "YOU FUCKED NOW" and "GASMAN WUZZERE" and "GASMAN IS AN IDIOT-MO." The words were stippled on the dull pink ceiling in umber burn spots. Jerome wondered who GASMAN was and what they'd put him in prison for.

He yawned. He hadn't slept much the night before. It took a long time to learn to sleep in prison. He wished he'd upgraded his chip so he could use it to activate his sleep endorphins. But that was a grade above what he'd been able to afford—and way above the kind of brain chips he'd been dealing. He wished he could turn off the light panel, but it was sealed in.

There was a toilet and a broken water fountain in the cell. There were also a few bunks, but he was alone in this static place of watery blue light and faint pink distances. The walls were salmon-colored garbage blocks. The words singed into the ceiling were blurred and impotent.

Almost noon, his stomach rumbling, Jerome was still lying on his back on the top bunk when the trashcan said, "Eric Wexler, re-ma-a-in on your bunk while the ne-ew prisoner ente-e-ers the cell!"

Wexler? Oh, yeah. They thought his name was Wexler. The fake ID program.

He heard the cell door slide open; he looked over, saw the trashcan ushering a stocky Chicano guy into lockup. The robot everyone called "the trashcan" was a stumpy metal cylinder with a group of camera lenses, a retractable plastic arm, and a gun muzzle that could fire a Taser charge, rubber bullets, tear-gas pellets, or .45-caliber rounds. It was supposed to use the .45 only in extreme situations, but the robot was battered, it whined when it moved, its digital voice was warped. When they got like that, Jerome had heard, you didn't fuck with them; they'd mix up the rubber bullets with the .45-caliber, Russian Roulette style.

The door sucked itself shut, the trashcan whined away down the hall, its rubber wheels squeaking once with every revolution. Jerome heard a tinny cymbal crash as someone, maybe trying to get it to shoot at a guy in the next cell, threw a tray at it; followed by some echoey human shouting and a distorted admonishment from the trashcan. The Chicano was still standing by the plexigate, hands shoved in his pockets, staring at Jerome, looking like he was trying to place him.

"'Sappenin'," Jerome said, sitting up on the bed. He was grateful for the break in the monotony.

"*Que pasa?* You like the top bunk, huh? Tha's good."

"I can read the ceiling better from up here. About ten seconds' worth of reading matter. It's all I got. You can have the lower bunk."

"You fuckin'-A I can." But there was no real aggression in his tone. Jerome thought about turning on his chip, checking the guy's subliminals, his somatic signals, going for a model of probable-aggression index; or maybe project for deception. He could be an undercover cop: Jerome hadn't given them his dealer, hadn't bargained at all.

But he decided against switching the chip on. Some jails had scanners for unauthorized chip output. Better not use it unless he had to. And his gut told him this guy was only a threat if he felt threatened. His gut was right almost as often as his brain chip.

The Chicano was maybe five foot six, a good five inches shorter than Jerome but probably outweighing him by fifty pounds. His face had Indian angles and small jet eyes. He was wearing printout gray-blue prison jams, #6631; they'd let him keep his hairnet. Jerome had never understood the Chicano hairnet, never had the balls to ask about it.

Jerome was pleased. He liked to be recognized, except by people who could arrest him.

"You put your hands in the pockets of those paper pants, they'll rip, and in LA County they don't give you any more for three days," Jerome advised him.

"Yeah? Shit." The Chicano took his hands carefully out of his pockets. "I don't want my cojones hanging out, people think I'm advertising—they some big fucking cojones too. You not a faggot, right?"

"Nope."

"Good. How come I know you? When I *don't* know you."

Jerome grinned. "From television. You saw my tag. Jerome-X. I mean—I do some music too. I had that song, 'Six Kinds of Darkness'—"

"I don't know that, bro—oh wait, Jerome-X. The tag—I saw that. Your face-tag. You got one of those little transers? Interrupt the transmissions with your own shit?"

"Had. They confiscated it."

"That why you here? Video graffiti?"

"I wish. I'd be out in a couple months. No. Illegal augs."

"Hey, man! Me too!"

"You?" Jerome couldn't conceal his surprise. You didn't see a lot of barrio dudes doing illegal augmentation. They generally didn't like people tinkering in their brains.

"What, you think a guy from East LA can't use augs?"

"No, no. I know lots of Latino guys that use it," Jerome lied.

"Ooooh, he says *Latino*, that gotta nice sound." Overtones of danger.

Jerome hastily changed the direction of the conversation. "You never been in the big lockups where they use these fuckin' paper jammies?"

"No, just the city jail once. They didn't have those motherfucking screw machines either. Hey, you're Jerome—my name's Jessie. Actually, it Jesus"— he pronounced it "hay-soo"—"but people they, you know . . . You got any smokes? No? Shit. Okay, I adjust. I get used to it. Shit. No smokes. Fuck."

He sat on the edge of the bed, to one side of Jerome's dangling legs, and tilted his head forward. He reached under his hairnet, and under what turned out to be a hairpiece, and pulled a chip from a jack unit set into the base of his skull.

Jerome stared. "Goddamn, their probes really are busted."

Jessie frowned over the chip. There was a little blood on it. The jack unit was leaking. Cheap installation. "No, they ain't busted, there's a guy working on the probe, he's paid off, he's letting everyone through for a couple of days because of some Russian mob guys coming in, he don't know which ones they are. Some of them Russian mob guys got the augments."

"I thought sure they were going to find my unit," Jerome said. "The strip search didn't find it, but I thought the prison probes would and that'd be another year on my sentence. But they didn't."

Neither one of them thinking of throwing away the chips. It'd be like cutting out an eye.

"Same story here, bro. We both lucky."

Jessie put the microprocessing chip in his mouth, the way people did with their contact lenses, to clean it, lubricate it. Of course, bacterially speaking, it came out dirtier than it went in.

"Does the jack hurt?" Jerome asked.

Jessie took the chip out, looked at it a moment on his fingertips. It was smaller than a contact lens, a sliver of silicon and non-osmotic gallium arsenide and transparent interface-membrane, with, probably, 800,000,000 nanotransistors of engineered protein molecules sunk into it, maybe more. "No, it don't hurt yet. But if it's leaking, it fuckin' *will* hurt, man." He said something else in Spanish, shaking his head. He slipped the chip back into his jack-in unit and tapped it with the thumbnail of his right hand. So that was where the activation mouse was: under the thumbnail. Jerome's was in a knuckle.

Jessie rocked slightly, just once, sitting up on his bunk, which meant the chip had engaged and he was getting a readout. They tended to feed back into your nervous system a little at first, make you twitch once or twice; if they weren't properly insulated, they could make you crap your pants.

"That's okay," Jessie said, relaxing. "That's better." The chip inducing his brain to secrete vasopressin, contract the veins, simulate the effect of nicotine. It worked for a while, till you could get cigarettes. High-grade chip could do some numbing if you were hung up on Sim, synthetic morphine, and couldn't get any. But that was Big Scary. You could turn yourself off for good that way. You better be doing some damn fine adjusting.

Jerome thought about the hypothetical chip scanners. Maybe he should object to the guy using his chip here. But what the Chicano was doing wouldn't make for much leakage.

"What you got?" Jerome asked.

"I got an Apple NanoMind II. Big gigas. What you got?"

"You got the Mercedes, I got the Toyota. I got a Seso Picante Mark I. One of those Argentine things." (How had this guy scored an ANM II?)

"Yeah, what you got, they kinda basic, but they do most what you need. Hey, our names, they both start with J. And we both here for illegal augs. What else we got in common. What's your sign?"

"Uh—" What was it, anyway? He always forgot. "Pisces I think."

"No shit! I can relate to Pisces. I ran an astrology program, figured out who I should hang with. Pisces is okay. But Aquarius is—I'm a Scorpio, like— Aquarius, *que bueno*."

What did he mean exactly, *hang with*, Jerome wondered. Scoping me about am I a faggot, maybe that was something defensive.

But he meant something else. "You know somethin', Jerome, you got your chip too, we could do a link and maybe get over on that trashcan."

Break out? Jerome felt a chilled thrill go through him. "Link with that thing? Control it? I don't think the two of us would be enough."

"We need some more guys maybe, but I got news, Jerome, there's more comin'. Maybe their names all start with J. You know, I mean—in a way."

In quick succession, the trashcan brought their cell three more guests: a fortyish beach bum named Eddie; a cadaverous black dude named Bones; a queen called Swish, whose real name, according to the trashcan, was Paul Torino.

"This place smells like it's comin' apart," Eddie said. He had a surfer's greasy blond topknot and all the usual Surf Punk tattoos. Meaningless now, Jerome thought; the pollution-derived oxidation of the offshore had pretty much ended surfing. The anaerobics had taken over the surf, in North America, thriving in the toxic waters like a gelatinous Sargasso. If you surfed you did it with an antitoxin suit and a gas mask. "Smells in here like somethin' died and didn't go to heaven. Stinks worse'n Malibu."

"It's those landfill blocks," Bones said. He was missing three front teeth, and his sunken face was like something out of a zombie video. But he was an energetic zombie, pacing back and forth as he spoke. "Compressed garbage," he told Eddie. "Organic stuff mixed with the polymers, the plastics, whatever was in the trash heap, make 'em into bricks 'cause they run outta landfill, but after a while, if the contractor didn't get 'em to set right, y'know, they start to rot. It's hot outside is why you're gettin' it now. Use garbage to cage garbage, they say. Fucking assholes."

● ● ●

The trashcan pushed a rack of trays up to the Plexiglas bars and whirred their lunch to them, tray by tray. The robot gave them an extra tray. It was screwing up.

They ate their chicken patties—the chicken was almost greaseless, gristleless, which meant it was vat chicken, genetically engineered fleshstuff— and between bites they bitched about the food and indulged the usual paranoid speculation about mind-control chemicals in the coffee.

Jerome looked around at the others, thinking: at least they're not ass-kickers.

They were crammed here because of the illegal augs sweep, some political drive to clean up the clinics, maybe to see to it that the legal augmentation companies kept their pit bull grip on the industry. So there wasn't anybody in for homicide, for gang torture, or anything. No major psychopaths. Not a bad cell to be in.

"You Jerome-X, really?" Swish fluted. She (Jerome always thought of a queen as she and her, out of respect for the tilt of her consciousness) was probably Filipino; had her face girled up at a cheap clinic. Cheeks built up for a heart shape, eyes rounded, lips filled out, tits looking like there were a couple of tin funnels under her jammies. Some of the collagen they'd injected to fill out her lips had shifted its bulk so her lower lip was lopsided. One cheekbone was a little higher than the other. A karmic revenge on at least some of malekind, Jerome thought, for forcing women into girdles and footbinding and anorexia. What did this creature use her chip for, besides getting high?

"Oooh, Jerome-X! I saw your tag before on the TV. The one when your face kind of floated around the President's head and some printout words came out of your mouth and blocked her face out. God, she's such a *cunt*."

"What words did he block her out with?" Eddie asked.

"I think . . . 'Would you know a liar if you heard one anymore?' That's what it was!" Swish said. "It was sooo perfect, because that cunt wanted that war to go on forever, you *know* she did. And she lies about it, ooh *God* she lies."

"You just think she's a cunt because you *want* one," Eddie said, dropping his pants to use the toilet. He talked loudly to cover up the noise of it. "You want one and you can't afford it. I think the Prez was right, the fucking Mexican People's Republic is jammin' our borders, sending commie agents in—"

Swish said, "Oh, God, he's a Surf Nazi—but God yes, I want one—I want *her* cunt. That bitch doesn't know how to use it anyway. Honey, I know how I'd use that thing—" Swish stopped abruptly and shivered, hugged herself. Using her long purple nails, she reached up and pried loose a flap of skin behind her ear, plucked out her chip. She wet it, adjusted its feed mode, put it back in, tapping it with the activation mouse under a nail. She pressed the flap shut. Her eyes glazed as she adjusted. She could get high on the chip-impulses for maybe twenty-four hours and then it'd kill her. She'd have to go cold turkey or die. Or get out. And maybe she'd been doing it for a while now . . .

None of them would be allowed to post bail. They'd each get the two years mandatory minimum sentence. Illegal augs, the feds thought, were getting out of hand. Black-market chip implants were good for playing havoc with the state database lottery; used by bookies of all kinds; used to keep accounts where the IRS couldn't find them unless they cornered you physically and broke your code; the aug chips were used to out-think banking computers, and for spiking cash machines; used to milk the body, prod the brain into authorizing the secretion of betaendorphins and ACTH and adrenaline and testosterone and other biochemical toys; used to figure the odds at casinos; used to compute the specs for homemade designer drugs; used by the mob's street dons to play strategy and tactics; used by the kid gangs for the same reasons; used for illegal congregations on the Plateau.

It was the Plateau, Jerome thought, that really scared the shit out of the feds. It had possibilities.

It was way beyond the fucking Internet; it was past the Deep Internet; it was even beyond the Grid.

The trashcan dragged in a cot for the extra man, shoved it folded under the door, and blared, "Lights out, all inmates are required to be i-i-in their bu-unks-s-s . . ." Its voice was failing.

After the trashcan and the light had gone, they climbed off their bunks and sat hunkered in a circle on the floor.

They were on chips, but not transmission-linked to one another. Jacked-up on the chips, they communicated in a spoken shorthand.

"Bull," Bones was saying. "Door." He was a voice in the darkness; a scarecrow of shadow.

"Time," Jessie said.

"Compatibility? Know?" Eddie said.

Jerome said, "Noshee!" Snorts of laughter from the others.

"Link check," Bones said.

"Models?" Jessie said.

Then they joined in an incantation of numbers.

It was a fifteen-minute conversation in less than a minute.

Translated, the foregoing conversation went: "It's bullshit, you get past the trashcan, there's human guards, you can't reprogram them."

"But at certain hours," Jessie told him, "there's only one on duty. They're used to seeing the can bring people in and out. They won't question it till they try to confirm it. By then we'll be on their ass."

"We might not be compatible," Eddie had pointed out. "You understand, compatible?"

"Oh, hey, man, I *think* we can comprehend that," Jerome said, making the others snort with laughter. Eddie wasn't liked much.

Then Bones had said, "The only way to see if we're compatible is to do a systems link. We got the links, we got the thinks, like the man says. It's either the chain that holds us in, or it's the chain that pulls us out."

Jerome's scalp tightened. A systems link. A mini-Plateau. Sharing minds. Brutal intimacy. Maybe some fallout from the Plateau. He wasn't ready for it.

If it went sour, he could get time tacked onto his sentence for attempted jailbreak. And somebody might get dusted. They might have to kill a human guard. Jerome had once punched a dealer in the nose, and the spurt of blood had made him sick. He couldn't kill anyone. But . . . he had shit for alternatives. He knew he wouldn't make it through two years anyway, when they sent him up to the Big One.

The Big One'd grind him up for sure. They'd find his chip there, and it'd piss them off. They'd let the bulls rape him and give him the New Virus; he'd flip out from being locked in and chipless, and they'd put him under Aversion Rehab and burn him out.

Jerome savaged a thumbnail with his incisors. *Sent to the Big One.*

He'd been trying not to think about it. Making himself take it one day at a time. But now he had to look at the alternatives. His stomach twisted itself to punish him for being so stupid. For getting into dealing augments so he could finance a big transer. *Why?* A transer didn't get him anything but his face pirated onto local TV for maybe twenty seconds. He'd thrown himself away trying to get it . . .

Why was it so fucking important? his stomach demanded, wringing itself vindictively.

"Thing is," Bones said, "we could all be cruisin' into a setup. Some kind of sting thing. Maybe it's a little too weird how the police prober let us all through."

(Someone listening would have heard him say, "Sting, funny luck.")

Jessie snorted. "I tol' you, man. The prober is paid off. They letting them all through because some of them are mob. I know that, because I'm part of the thing. We deal wid the Russians. Okay?"

("Probe greased, fa-me.")

"You with the mob?" Bones asked.

("You'm?")

"You got it. Just a dealer. But I know where a half million Newbux wortha augshit is, so they going to get me out if I do my part. The way the system is set up, the prober had to let everyone through. His boss thinks we got our chips taken out when they arraigned us; sometimes they do it that way. This time it was supposed to be the jail surgeon. By the time they catch up their own red tape, we get outta here. Now listen—we can't do the trashcan without we all get into it, because we haven't got enough K otherwise. So who's in, for fuck's sake?"

He'd said, "Low, half mill, bluff surgeon, there here, twip, all-none, *who* yuh fucks?"

Something in his voice skittered with claws behind smoked glass: he was getting testy, irritable from the chip adjustments for his nicotine habit, maybe other adjustments: the side effects of liberal cerebral self-modulating burning through a threadbare nervous system.

The rest of the meeting, translated . . .

"I dunno," Eddie said. "I thought I'd do my time, 'cause if it goes sour—"

"Hey man," Jessie said, "I can *take* your fuckin' chip. And be out before they notice your ass don't move no more."

"The man's right," Swish said. Her pain-suppression system was unraveling, axon by axon, and she was running out of adjust. "Let's just do it, okay? Please? Okay? I gotta get out. I feel like I wish I was dogshit so I could be something better."

"I can't handle two years in the Big, Eddie, and I'll do what I gotta, dudeski," Jerome heard himself say, realizing he was helping Jessie threaten Eddie. Amazed at himself. Not his style.

"It's all of us or nobody, Eddie," Bones said.

Eddie was quiet for a while.

Jerome had turned off his chip, because it was thinking endlessly about Jessie's plan, and all it came up with was an ugly model of the risks. You had to know when to go with intuition.

Jerome was committed. And he was standing on the brink of link. The time was now, starting with Jessie.

Jessie was *operator*. He picked the order. First Eddie, to make sure about him. Then Jerome. Maybe because he had Jerome scoped for a refugee from the middle class, an anomaly here, and Jerome might try and raise the Heat on his chip, make a deal. Once they had him linked in, he was locked up.

After Jerome, it'd be Bones and then Swish.

They held hands, so that the link signal, transmitted from the chip using the electric field generated by the brain, would be carried with the optimum fidelity.

He heard them exchange frequency designates, numbers strung like beads in the darkness, and heard the hiss of suddenly indrawn breaths as Jessie and Eddie linked in. And he heard, "Let's go, Jerome."

Jerome's eyes had adjusted to the dark, the night giving up some of its buried light, and Jerome could just make a crude outline of Jessie's features like a charcoal rubbing from an Aztec carving.

Jerome reached to the back of his own head, found the glue-tufted hairs that marked his flap, and pulled the skin away from the chip's jack unit. He tapped the chip. It didn't take. He tapped it again, and this time he felt the shift in his bioelectricity; felt it hum between his teeth.

Jerome's chip communicated with his brain via an interface of nano-print configured rhodopsin protein; the ribosomes borrowing neurohumoral transmitters from the brain's blood supply, reordering the transmitters so that they carried a programmed pattern of ion releases for transmission across synaptic gaps to the brain's neuronal dendrites; the chip using magnetic resonance holography to collate with brain-stored memories and psychological trends. Declaiming to itself the mythology of the brain; reenacting on its silicon stage the Legends of his subjective world history.

Jerome closed his eyes and looked into the back of his eyelids. The digital read-out was printed in luminous green across the darkness. He focused on the cursor, concentrated so it moved up to ACCESS. He subverbalized, "Open frequency." The chip heard his practiced subverbalization, and numbers appeared on the back of his eyelids: 63391212.70. He read them out to the others and they picked up his frequency. Almost choking on the word, knowing what it would bring, he told the chip: "Open."

It opened to the link. He'd only done it once before. It was illegal, and he was secretly glad it was illegal because it scared him. "They're holding the Plateau back," his brain-chip wholesaler had told him, "because they're scared of what worldwide electronic telepathy might bring down on them. Like, everyone will collate information, use it to see through the bastards' game, throw the assbites out of office."

Maybe that was the real reason. It was something the power brokers couldn't control. But there were other reasons.

Reasons like a strikingly legitimate fear of people going mad.

All Jerome and the others wanted was a sharing of processing capabilities. Collaborative calculation. But the chips weren't designed to filter out the irrelevant input before it reached the user's cognition level. Before the chip had done its filtering, the two poles of the link—Jerome and Jessie—would each see the swarming hive of the other's total consciousness. Would see how the other perceived themselves to be, and then objectively, as they really were.

He saw Jessie as a grid and as a holographic entity. He braced himself and the holograph came at him, an abstract tarantula of computer-generated color and line, scrambling down over him . . . and for an instant it crouched in the seat of his consciousness: Jessie. Jesus Chaco.

Jessie was a family man. He was a patriarch, a protector of his wife and six kids (six kids!) and his widowed sister's four kids and of the poor children of his barrio. He was a muddied painting of his father, who had fled the social forest fire of Mexico's civil war between the drug cartels and the government, spiriting his capital to Los Angeles where he'd sown it into the black market. Jessie's father had been killed defending territory from the Russian-American mob; Jessie compromised with the mob to save his father's business, and loathed himself for it. Wanted to kill their bosses; had to work side by side with them. Perceived his wife as a functional pet, an object of adoration who was the very apotheosis of her fixed role. To imagine her doing other than child-rearing and keeping house would be to imagine the sun become a snowball, the moon become a monkey. Jessie's family insistently clung to the old, outdated roles.

And Jerome glimpsed Jessie's undersides; Jesus Chaco's self-image with its outsized penis and impossibly spreading shoulders, sitting in a perfect and shining cherry automobile, always the newest and most luxurious model, the automotive throne from which he surveyed his kingdom. Jerome saw guns emerging from the grill of the car to splash Jessie's enemies apart with his unceasing ammunition . . . It was a Robert Williams cartoon capering at the heart of Jessie's unconscious . . . Jessie saw himself as Jerome saw him; the electronic mirrors reflecting one another. Jessie cringed.

Jerome saw himself then, reflected back from Jessie.

He saw Jerome-X on a video screen with lousy vertical hold; wobbling, trying to arrange its pixels firmly and losing them. A figure of mewling inconsequence; a brief flow of electrons that might diverge left or right like spray from a water hose depressed with the thumb. Raised in a high-security condo village, protected by cameras and computer lines to private security thugs; raised in a media-windowed womb, with PCs and VCRs and a thousand varieties of video games; shaped by cable TV and fantasy rental; sexuality imprinted by sneaking his parents' badly hidden cache of brainsex files. And in stations from around the world, seeing the same StarFaces appear on channel after channel as the star's fame spread like a stain across the frequency bands. Seeing the Star's World Self crystallizing; the media figure coming into definition against the backdrop of media competition, becoming real in this electronic collective unconscious.

Becoming real, himself, in his own mind, simply because he'd appeared on a few thousand TV screens, through video tagging, transer graffiti. Growing up with a sense that media events were real and personal events were not. Anything that didn't happen on the Grid didn't happen. Even as he hated conventional programming, even as he regarded it as the cud of ruminants, still the net and tv and di-vees defined his sense of personal unreality; and left him unfinished.

Jerome saw Jerome: perceiving himself unreal. Jerome: scamming a transer, creating a presence via video graffiti. Thinking he was doing it for reasons of radical statement. Seeing, now, that he was doing it to make himself feel substantial, to superimpose himself on the Media Grid . . .

And then Eddie's link was there, Eddie's computer model sliding down over Jerome like a mudslide. Eddie seeing himself as a Legendary Wanderer, a rebel, a homemade mystic; his fantasy parting to reveal an anal-expulsive sociopath; a whiner perpetually scanning for someone to blame for his sour luck.

Suddenly Bones tumbled into the link; a complex worldview that was a sort of streetside sociobiology, mitigated by a loyalty to friends, a mystical faith in brain chips and amphetamines. His underside a masochistic dwarf, the troll of self-doubt, lacerating itself with guilt.

And then Swish, a woman with an unsightly growth, errant glands that were like tumors in her, something other people called "testicles." Perpetually hungry for the means to dampen the pain of an infinite self-derision that mimicked her father's utter rejection of her. A mystical faith in synthetic morphine.

. . . Jerome mentally reeling with disorientation, seeing the others as a network of distorted self-images, caricatures of grotesque ambitions. Beyond them he glimpsed another realm through a break in the psychic clouds: the Plateau, the whispering plane of brain chips linked on forbidden frequencies, an electronic haven for doing deals unseen by cops; a Plateau prowled only by the exquisitely ruthless; a vista of enormous challenges and inconceivable risks and always the potential for getting lost, for madness. A place roamed by the wolves of wetware.

There was a siren quiver from that place, a soundless howling, pulling at them . . . drawing them in . . .

"*Uh-uh*, wolflost, pross," Bones said, maybe aloud or maybe through the chips. Translated from chip shorthand, those two syllables meant. "Stay away from the Plateau, or we get sucked into it, we lose our focus. Concentrate on parallel processing function."

Jerome looked behind his eyelids, sorted through the files. He moved the cursor down . . .

Suddenly, it was there. The group-thinking capacity looming above them, a sentient skyscraper. They all felt a rush of megalomaniacal pleasure in identifying with it; with a towering edifice of Mind. Five chips became One.

They were ready. Jessie transmitted the bait.

Alerted to an illegal use of implant chips, the trashcan was squeaking down the hall, scanning to precisely locate the source. It came to a sudden stop, rocking on its wheels in front of their cell. Jessie reached through the bars and touched its input jack.

The machine froze with a *clack* midway through a turn, and hummed as it processed what they fed it. Would the robot bite?

Bones had a program for the IBM Cyberguard Fourteens, with all the protocol and a range of sample entry codes. Parallel processing from samples took less than two seconds to decrypt the trashcan's access code. Then—

They were in. The hard part was the reprogramming.

Jerome found the way. He told the trashcan that he wasn't Eric Wexler, because the DNA code was all wrong, if you looked close enough; what we have here is a case of mistaken identity.

Since this information *seemed* to be coming from authorized sources—the decrypted access code made them authorized—the trashcan fell for the gag and opened the cage.

The trashcan took the five Eric Wexlers down the hall—that was Jessie's doing, showing them how to make it think of five as one, something his people had learned from the immigration computers. It escorted them through the plastiflex door, through the steel door, and into Receiving. The human guard was heaping sugar into his antique Ronald McDonald coffee mug and watching *The Mutilated* on his wallet TV. Bones and Jessie were in the room and moving in on him before he broke free of the television and went for the button. Bones's long left arm spiked out and his stiffened fingers hit a nerve cluster below the guy's left ear, and he went down, the sugar dispenser in one hand swishing a white fan onto the floor.

Jerome's chip had cross-referenced Bones's attack style. Bones was trained by commandos, the chip said. Military elite. Was he a plant? Bones smiled at him and tilted his head, which Jerome's chip read as: *No. I'm trained by the Underground. Radics.*

Jessie was at the console, deactivating the trashcan, killing the cameras, opening the outer doors. Jessie and Swish led the way out, Swish whining softly and biting her lip. There were two more guards at the gate, one of them asleep. Jessie had taken the gun from the guy Bones had put under, so the first guard at the gate was dead before he could hit an alarm. The catnapping guy woke and yelled with hoarse terror, and then Jessie shot him in the throat.

Watching the guard fall, spinning, blood making its own slow-motion spiral in the air, Jerome felt a perfect mingling of sickness, fear, and self-disgust. The guard was young, wearing a cheap wedding ring, probably had a young family. So Jerome stepped over the dying man and made an adjustment; used his chip, chilled himself out with adrenaline. Had to—he was committed now. And he knew with a bland certainty that they had reached the Plateau after all.

He would live on the Plateau now. He belonged there, now that he was one of the wolves.

THE NOSTALGIST

By Daniel H. Wilson

He was an old man who lived in a modest gonfab, and over the last eighty hours his Eyes™ and Ears™ had begun to fail. In the first forty hours, he had ignored the increasingly strident sounds of the city of Vanille and focused on teaching the boy who lived with him. But after another forty hours the old man could no longer stand the Doppler-affected murmur of travelers on the slidewalks outside, and the sight of the boy's familiar deformities became overwhelming. It made the boy sad to see the old man's stifled revulsion, so he busied himself by sliding the hanging plastic sheets of the inflatable dwelling into layers that dampened the street noise. The semitransparent veils were stiff with grime and they hung still and useless like furled, ruined sails.

The old man was gnarled and bent, and his tendons were like taut cords beneath the skin of his arms. He wore a soiled white undershirt and his sagging chest bristled with gray hairs. A smooth patch of pink skin occupied a hollow under his left collarbone, marking the place where a rifle slug had passed cleanly through many decades before. He had been a father, an engineer, and a war-fighter, but for many years now he had lived peacefully with the boy.

Everything about the old man was natural and wrinkled except for his Eyes™ and Ears™, thick glasses resting on the creased bridge of his nose and two flesh-colored buds nestled in his ears. They were battered technological artifacts that captured sights and sounds and sanitized every visual and auditory experience. The old man sometimes wondered whether he could bear to live without these artifacts. He did not think so.

"Grandpa," the boy said as he arranged the yellowed plastic curtains. "Today I will visit Vanille City and buy you new Eyes™ and Ears™."

The old man had raised the boy and healed him when he was sick, and the boy loved him.

"No, no," replied the old man. "The people there are cruel. I can go myself."

"Then I will visit the metro fab and bring you some lunch."

"Very well," said the old man, and he pulled on his woolen coat.

A faded photo of the boy, blond and smiling and happy, hung next to the door of the gonfab. They passed by the photo, pushed the door flaps aside, and walked together into the brilliant dome light. A refreshing breeze ruffled the boy's hair. He faced into it as he headed for the slidewalk at the end of the path. A scrolling gallery of pedestrians passed steadily by. Sometimes the fleeting pedestrians made odd faces at the boy, but he was not angry. Other pedestrians, the older ones, looked at him and were afraid or sad, but tried not to show it. Instead, they stepped politely onto faster slidestrips further away from the stained gonfab.

"I will meet you back here in one hour," said the old man.

"See you," replied the boy, and the old man winced. His failing Ears™ had let through some of the grating quality of the boy's true voice, and it unsettled him. But his Ears™ crackled back online and, as the slidestrips pulled them away in separate directions, he chose only to wave goodbye.

The boy did not wear Eyes™ or Ears™. Near the time of the boy's birth, he had undergone direct sensory augmentation. The old man had seen to it himself. When the boy squinted in just the right way, he could see the velocity trajectories of objects hovering in the air. When he closed his eyes entirely, he could watch the maximum probability version of the world continue to unfold around him. He was thankful for his gift and did not complain about his lessons or cry out when the old man made adjustments or improvements to the devices.

The city is unsafe and I must protect the old man, thought the boy. *He will probably visit the taudi quarter for used gear. Mark his trajectory well*, he told himself. *Remember to be alert to the present and to the future.*

The boy expertly skipped across decelerating slidestrips until his direction changed. Other passengers shied away in disgust, but again the boy did not mind. He walked directly to the center strip and was accelerated to top speed. A vanilla-smelling breeze pushed thin blond hair from his disfigured, smiling face.

• • •

The old man smiled as he cruised along the slidewalk. The systematic flow of identical people was beautiful. The men wore dark blue suits and red ties. Some of them carried briefcases or wore hats. The women wore dark blue skirts and white blouses with red neckerchiefs. The men and women walked in lockstep and were either silent or extremely polite. There was a glow of friendly recognition between the pedestrians, and it made the old man feel very glad, and also very cautious.

I must hurry to the taudi quarter and be careful, he thought. *The rigs there have all been stolen or taken from the dead, but I have no choice.*

The old man made his way to the decelerator strip, but a dark-suited businessman blocked his path. He gingerly tapped the man on his padded shoulder. The businessman in the neatly pressed suit spun around and grabbed the old man by his coat.

"Don't touch me," he spat.

For a split second the clean-cut businessman transformed into a gaunt and dirty vagrant. A writhing tattoo snaked down half of his stubbled face and curled around his neck. The old man blinked hard, and the dark-suited man reappeared, smiling. The old man hastily tore himself from the man's grasp and pushed to the exit and the taudi quarter beyond.

Bright yellow dome light glistened from towering, monolithic buildings in the taudi quarter. It reflected off of polished sidewalks in front of stalls and gonfabs that were filled with neatly arranged goods laid out on plastic blankets. The old man tapped his malfunctioning Ears™ and listened to the shouts of people trading goods in dozens of languages. He caught the trickling sound of flowing refuse and the harsh sucking sound of neatly dressed people walking through filth. He looked at his shoes and they were clean. The smell of the street was almost unbearable.

The old man approached a squat wooden stall and waited. A large man wearing a flamboyant, filthy pink shirt soon appeared. The man shook his great head and wiped his calloused hands on a soiled rag. "What can I do for you, Drew?" he said.

"LaMarco," said the old man, "I need a used Immersion System. Late model with audiovisual. No olfactory." He tapped his Eyes™. "Mine are beyond repair, even for me."

LaMarco ran a hand through his hair. "You're not still living with that . . . thing, are you?"

Receiving no reply, LaMarco rummaged below the flimsy wooden counter. He dropped a bundle of eyeglasses and ear buds onto the table. One lens was smeared with dried blood.

"These came from a guy got zipped by the militia last week," said LaMarco. "Almost perfect condition, but the ID isn't wiped. You'll have to take care of that."

The old man placed a plastic card on the table. LaMarco swiped the card, crossed his arms, and stood, waiting.

After a pause, the old man resignedly removed his glasses and ear buds and handed them to LaMarco. He shuddered at the sudden sights and sounds of a thriving slum.

"For parts," he coaxed.

LaMarco took the equipment and turned it over delicately with his large fingers. He nodded, and the transaction was complete. The old man picked up his new Immersion System and wiped the lenses with his coat. He slid the glasses onto his face and inserted the flesh-colored buds into his ears. Cleanliness and order returned to the slums.

"Look," said LaMarco, "I didn't mean anything by—"

He was interrupted by the violent roar of airship turbines. Immediately, the old man heard the smack-smack of nearby stalls being broken down. Gonfabs began to deflate, sending a stale breeze into the air. Shouts echoed from windowless buildings. The old man turned to the street. Merchants and customers clutched briefcases and ran hard, their chiseled faces contorted with strange, fierce smiles.

"Go," hissed LaMarco.

The whine of turbines grew stronger. Dust devils swirled across the promenade. LaMarco flipped the wooden countertop over, picked up the equipment-filled crate, and cradled it in his powerful arms.

"Another raid," he huffed, and lumbered off through a dark gap between two buildings.

The old man felt wary but calm. When a massive, dead-black sheet of cloth unfurled impossibly from the sky, he was not surprised. He turned and another sheet dropped. A swirling black confusion of sackcloth walls surrounded him. He looked straight up and saw that the convulsing walls stretched for miles up into the atmosphere. A small oval of dome light floated high above. The old man heard faint laughter.

The militia are here with their ImmerSyst censors, he observed.

Two black-clad militiamen strode through the twisting fabric like ghosts. Both wore lightly actuated lower-extremity exoskeletons, the word LEEX stenciled down the side of each leg. Seeing the old man standing alone, they advanced and spread out, predatorily.

A familiar insignia on the nearest officer's chest stood out: a lightning bolt striking a link of chain. This man was a veteran light-mechanized infantryman of the Auton Conflicts. Six symmetric scars stood out on the veteran's cheeks and forehead like fleshy spot welds.

A stumper attached its thorax to this man's face some time ago, thought the old man. *The machine must have been lanced before its abdomen could detonate.*

"This your shack?" asked the scarred veteran.

He walked toward the old man, his stiff black boots crunching through a thick crust of mud mixed with Styrofoam, paper, and shards of plastic and glass.

"No."

"Where'd you get that ImmerSyst?" asked the other officer.

The old man said nothing. The veteran and the young officer looked at each other and smiled.

"Give it here," said the veteran.

"Please," said the old man, "I can't." He clawed the Immersion System from his face. The flowing black censor walls disappeared instantly. He blinked apprehensively at the scarred veteran, shoved the devices deep into his coat pockets, and ran toward the alley.

The veteran groaned theatrically and pulled a stubby impact baton from his belt.

"Fine," he said. "Let's make this easy." He flicked his wrist and the dull black instrument clacked out to its full length. With an easy trot, he came up behind the old man and swung the baton low, so that it connected with the back of his knees. The impact baton convulsed and delivered a searing electric shock that buckled the old man's legs. He collapsed onto his stomach and was still.

Then he began to crawl with his elbows.

Have to make it out of this alive, he thought. *For the boy.*

The veteran pinned the old man with a heavy boot between the shoulder blades. He lifted his baton again.

A sharp, alien sound rang out—low and metallic and with the tinny ring of mechanical gears meshing. It was not a human voice.

"Stop!" it said, although the word was barely recognizable.

The boy strode into the clearing. The old man, without his Eyes™ or Ears™, noticed that the boy's legs were not quite the same length. He abruptly remembered cobbling them together from carbon fiber scavenged from a downed military UAV. Each movement of the boy's limbs generated a wheezing sigh of pneumatically driven gases. The boy reeked of a familiar oil and hot battery smell that the old man had not noticed in years.

The veteran locked eyes with the small boy and his armored body began to quake. He unconsciously fingered the scars on his face with one hand as he lifted his boot from the old man's back.

The old man rolled over and grunted, "Run, boy!"

But the boy did not run.

"What's this?" asked the younger officer, unfazed. "Your Dutch wife?" The officer popped his impact baton to full length and stood towering over the boy. He leaned down and looked directly into the boy's eye cameras.

"Hey there, toaster oven," said the officer quietly. "Think you're human?"

These words confused the boy, who said nothing.

"Watch out!" came a strangled cry from the veteran. He stood with his knees bent and his left palm extended defensively. His other elbow jutted out awkwardly as he fumbled for his gun. "That is unspecked hardware!" he shouted hoarsely. "Could be anything. Could be military grade. Back away from it!"

The younger officer looked at the veteran uncertainly.

The boy took a hesitant step forward. "What did you say to me?" he asked. His voice was the low, tortured croak of a rusty gate. He reached for the officer with a trembling, three-fingered hand. "Hey," he said.

The officer turned and instinctively swung his impact baton. It thumped against the boy's chest and discharged like a crack of lightning. The blow charred the boy's tee shirt and tore a chunk out of his polyurethane chestpiece, revealing a metal ribcage frame riddled with slots for hardware and housing a large, warm, rectangular battery. The boy sat heavily on the ground, puzzled.

Looking around in a daze, he saw that the old man was horrified. The boy mustered a servo-driven smile that pulled open a yawning hole in his cheek. The old man took a shuddering breath and buried his face in the crook of his elbow.

And the boy suddenly understood.

He looked down at his mangled body. A single vertiginous bit of information lurched through his consciousness and upended all knowledge and memory: *Not a boy.* He remembered the frightened looks of the slidewalk pedestrians. He remembered long hours spent playing cards with the old man. And finally he came to remember the photograph of the blond boy that hung on a plastic hook near the door of the gonfab. At this memory, the boy felt deeply ashamed.

No, no, no, no. I cannot think of these things, he told himself. *I must be calm and brave now.*

The boy rose unsteadily to his feet and adopted a frozen stance. Standing perfectly still removed uncertainty. It made mentals in physical space simpler, more accurate, and much, much faster. The old man had taught the boy how to do this, and they had practiced it together many times.

Ignoring the commands of his veteran partner, the young officer swung his impact baton again. The sparking cudgel followed a simple, visible trajectory. The boy watched a blue rotational vector emerge from the man's actuated hip, and neatly stepped around his stationary leg. The officer realized what had happened, but it was too late: the boy already stood behind him. *The man's hair smells like cigarettes,* thought the boy; and then he shoved hard between the officer's shoulder blades.

The officer pitched forward lightly, but the LEEX resisted and jerked reflexively backward to maintain its balance. The force of this recoil snapped the officer's spine somewhere in his lower back. Sickeningly, the actuated legs walked away, dragging the unconscious top half of the officer behind them, his limp hands scraping furrows in the dirt.

The boy heard a whimpering noise and saw the veteran standing with his gun drawn. A line visible only to the boy extended from the veteran's right eye, along the barrel of the pistol, and to a spot on the boy's chest over his pneumatic heart.

Carefully, the boy rotated sideways to minimize the surface area of his body available to the veteran's weapon. *Calm and brave.*

A pull trajectory on the veteran's trigger finger announced an incoming bullet. Motors squealed and the boy's body violently jerked a precise distance in space. The bullet passed by harmlessly, following its predicted trajectory. An echoing blast resounded from the blank-walled buildings. The veteran stood for a moment, clutched his sweating face with his free hand, turned, and fled.

"Grandpa!" said the boy, and rushed over to help.

But the old man would not look at him or take his hand; his face was filled with disgust and fear and desperation. Blindly, the old man shoved the boy away and began scrabbling in his pockets, trying frantically to put his new Eyes™ and Ears™ back on. The boy tried to speak, but stopped when he heard his own coarse noise. Uncertain, he reached out, as if to touch the old man on the shoulder, but did not. After a few long seconds, the boy turned and hobbled away, alone.

The old man grasped the cool, black handrail of the slidewalk with his right hand. He curled his left hand under his chin, pulling his woolen coat tight. Finally, he limped to the decelerator strip and stepped off. He had to pause and breathe slowly three times before he reached the house.

Inside the dim gonfab, he hung his coat on a transparent plastic hook. He wet his rough hands from a suspended water bag and placed cool palms over his weathered face.

Without opening his Eyes™, he said "You may come out."

Metal rings supporting a curtained partition screeched apart and the boy emerged into a shaft of yellow dome light. The ragged wound in his cosmetic chest carapace gaped obscenely. His dilated mechanical irises audibly spiraled down to the size of two pinpricks, and the muted light illuminated a few blond hairs clinging anemone-like to his scalded plastic scalp. He was clutching the photograph of the blond boy and crying and had been for some time, but there was no sign of this on his crudely sculpted face.

The old man saw the photograph.

"I am sorry," he said, and embraced the boy. He felt an electrical actuator poking rudely through the child's tee shirt, like a compound fracture.

"Please," he whispered. "I will make things the way they were before."

But the boy shook his head. He looked up into the old man's watery blue

Eyes™. The room was silent except for the whirring of a fan. Then, very deliberately, the boy slid the glasses from the old man's face, leaving the Ears™.

The old man looked at the small, damaged machine with tired eyes full of love and sadness. When the thing spoke, the shocking hole opened in its cheek again and the old man heard the clear, piping voice of a long-dead little boy.

"I love you, Grandpa," it said.

And these words were as true as sunlight.

With deft fingers, the boy-thing reached up and pressed a button at the base of its own knobbed metal spine. There was a winding-down noise as all the day's realization and shame and understanding faded away into nothingness.

The boy blinked slowly and his hands settled down to his sides. He could not remember arriving, and he looked around in wonder. The gonfab was silent. The boy saw that he was holding a photograph of himself. And then the boy noticed the old man.

"Grandpa?" asked the boy, very concerned. "Have you been crying?"

The old man did not answer. Instead, he closed his eyes and turned away.

LIFE IN THE ANTHROPOCENE

By Paul Di Filippo

*This story is indebted to Gaia Vince and her article in
New Scientist, "Surviving in a Warmer World."*

1. SOLAR GIRDLE EMERGENCY

Aurobindo Bandjalang got the emergency twing through his vib on the morning of August 8, 2121, while still at home in his expansive bachelor's digs. At 1LDK, his living space was three times larger than most unmarried individuals enjoyed, but his high-status job as a Power Jockey for New Perthpatna earned him extra perks.

While a short-lived infinitesimal flock of beard clippers grazed his face, A.B. had been showering and vibbing the weather feed for Reboot City Twelve: the more formal name for New Perthpatna.

Sharing his shower stall but untouched by the water, beautiful weather idol Midori Mimosa delivered the feed.

"Sunrise occurred this morning at three-oh-two A.M. Max temp projected to be a comfortable, shirtsleeves thirty degrees by noon. Sunset at ten-twenty-nine P.M. this evening. Cee-oh-two at four-hundred-and-fifty parts per million, a significant drop from levels at this time last year. Good work, Rebooters!"

The new tweet/twinge/ping interrupted both the weather and A.B.'s ablutions. His vision greyed out for a few milliseconds as if a sheet of smoked glass had been slid in front of his MEMS contacts, and both his left palm and the sole of his left foot itched: Attention Demand 5.

A.B.'s boss, Jeetu Kissoon, replaced Midori Mimosa under the sparsely downfalling water: a dismaying and disinvigorating substitution. But A.B.'s virt-in-body operating system allowed for no squelching of twings tagged AD4 and up. Departmental policy.

Kissoon grinned and said, "Scrub faster, A.B. We need you here yesterday. I've got news of face-to-face magnitude."

"What's the basic quench?"

"Power transmission from the French farms is down by one percent. Sat photos show some kind of strange dust accumulation on a portion of the collectors. The on-site kybes can't respond to the stuff with any positive remediation. Where's it from, why now, and how do we stop it? We've got to send a human team down there, and you're heading it."

Busy listening intently to the bad news, A.B. had neglected to rinse properly. Now the water from the low-flow showerhead ceased, its legally mandated interval over. He'd get no more from that particular spigot till the evening. Kissoon disappeared from A.B.'s augmented reality, chuckling.

A.B. cursed with mild vehemence and stepped out of the stall. He had to use a sponge at the sink to finish rinsing, and then he had no sink water left for brushing his teeth. Such a hygienic practice was extremely old-fashioned, given self-replenishing colonies of germ-policing mouth microbes, but A.B. relished the fresh taste of toothpaste and the sense of righteous manual self-improvement. Something of a twentieth-century recreationist, Aurobindo. But not this morning.

Outside A.B.'s 1LDK: his home corridor, part of a well-planned, spacious, senses-delighting labyrinth featuring several public spaces, constituting the one-hundred-and-fiftieth floor of his urbmon.

His urbmon, affectionately dubbed "The Big Stink": one of over a hundred colossal, densely situated high-rise habitats that amalgamated into New Perthpatna.

New Perthpatna: one of over a hundred such Reboot Cities sited across the habitable zone of Earth, about twenty-five percent of the planet's landmass, collectively home to nine billion souls.

A.B. immediately ran into one of those half-million souls of the Big Stink: Zulqamain Safranski.

Zulqamain Safranski was the last person A.B. wanted to see.

Six months ago, A.B. had logged an ASBO against the man.

Safranski was a parkour. Harmless hobby—if conducted in the approved sports areas of the urbmon. But Safranski blithely parkour'd his ass all over the common spaces, often bumping into or startling people as he ricocheted from ledge to bench. After a bruising encounter with the aggressive urban bounder, A.B. had filed his protest, attaching AD tags to already filed but overlooked video footage of the offenses. Not altogether improbably, A.B.'s complaint had been the one to tip the scales against Safranski, sending him via police trundlebug to the nearest Sin Bin, for a punitively educational stay.

But now, all too undeniably, Safranski was back in New Perthpatna, and instantly in A.B.'s chance-met (?) face.

The buff, choleric, but laughably diminutive fellow glared at A.B., then said, spraying spittle upward, "You just better watch your ass night and day, Bang-a-gong, or you might find yourself doing a *lâché* from the roof without really meaning to."

A.B. tapped his ear and, implicity, his implanted vib audio pickup. "Threats go from your lips to the ears of the wrathful Ekh Dagina—and to the ASBO Squad as well."

Safranski glared with wild-eyed malice at A.B., then stalked off, his planar butt muscles, outlined beneath the tight fabric of his mango-colored plugsuit, somehow conveying further ire by their natural contortions.

A.B. smiled. Amazing how often people still forgot the panopticon nature of life nowadays, even after a century of increasing immersion in and extension of null-privacy. Familiarity bred forgetfulness. But it was best to always recall, at least subliminally, that everyone heard and saw everything equally these days. Just part of the Reboot Charter, allowing a society to function in which people could feel universally violated, universally empowered.

At the elevator banks closest to home, A.B. rode up to the two-hundred-and-first floor, home to the assigned space for the urbmon's Power Administration Corps. Past the big active mural depicting drowned Perth, fishes swimming round the BHP Tower. Tags in the air led him to the workpod that Jeetu Kissoon had chosen for the time being.

Kissoon looked good for ninety-seven years old: he could have passed for A.B.'s slightly older brother, but not his father. Coffee-bean skin, snowy temples, laugh lines cut deep, only slightly counterbalanced by somber eyes.

When Kissoon had been born, all the old cities still existed, and many, many animals other than goats and chickens flourished. Kissoon had seen the cities abandoned, and the Big Biota Crash, as well as the whole Reboot. Hard for young A.B. to conceive. The man was a walking history lesson. A.B. tried to honor that.

But Kissoon's next actions soon evoked a yawp of disrespectful protest from the younger man.

"Here are the two other Jocks I've assigned to accompany you."

Interactive dossiers hung before A.B.'s gaze. He two-fingered through them swiftly, growing more stunned by the second. Finally he burst out: "You're giving me a furry and a keek as helpers?"

"Tigerishka and Gershon Thales. They're the best available. Live with them, and fix this glitch."

Kissoon stabbed A.B. with a piercing stare, and A.B. realized this meatspace proximity had been demanded precisely to convey the intensity of Kissoon's next words.

"Without power, we're doomed."

2. 45TH PARALLEL BLUES

Jet-assisted flight was globally interdicted. Not enough resources left to support regular commercial or recreational aviation. No military anywhere with a need to muster its own air force. Jet engines too harmful to a stressed atmosphere.

And besides, why travel?

Everywhere was the same. Vib served fine for most needs.

The habitable zone of Earth consisted of those lands—both historically familiar and newly disclosed from beneath vanished icepack—above the 45th parallel north, and below the 45th parallel south. The rest of the Earth's landmass had been desertified or drowned: sand or surf.

The immemorial ecosystems of the remaining climactically tolerable territories had been devastated by Greenhouse change, then, ultimately and purposefully, wiped clean. Die-offs, migratory invaders, a fast-forward churn culminating in an engineered ecosphere. The new conditions supported no animals larger than mice, and only a monoculture of GM plants.

Giant aggressive hissing cockroaches, of course, still thrived.

A portion of humanity's reduced domain hosted forests specially designed for maximum carbon uptake and sequestration. These fast-growing, long-lived hybrid trees blended the genomes of eucalyptus, loblolly pine, and poplar, and had been dubbed "eulollypops."

The bulk of the rest of the land was devoted to the crops necessary and sufficient to feed nine billion people: mainly quinoa, kale, and soy, fertilized by human wastes. Sugarbeet plantations provided feedstock for bio-polymer production.

And then, on their compact footprints, the hundred-plus Reboot Cities, ringed by small but efficient goat and chicken farms.

Not a world conducive to sightseeing Grand Tours.

On each continent, a simple network of maglev trains, deliberately held to a sparse schedule, linked the Reboot Cities (except for the Sin Bins, which were sanitarily excluded from easy access to the network). Slow but luxurious aerostats serviced officials and businessmen. Travel between continents occurred on SkySail-equipped water ships. All travel was predicated on state-certified need.

And when anyone had to deviate from standard routes—such as a trio of Power Jockeys following the superconducting transmission lines south to France—they employed a trundlebug.

Peugeot had designed the first trundlebugs over a century ago, the Ozones. Picture a large rolling drum fashioned of electrochromic biopoly, featuring slight catenaries in the lines of its body from end to end. A barrel-shaped compartment suspended between two enormous wheels large as the cabin itself. Solid-state battery packs channeled power to separate electric motors. A curving door spanned the entire width of the vehicle, sliding upward.

Inside, three seats in a row, the center one commanding the failsafe manual controls. Storage behind the seats.

And in those seats:

Aurobindo Bandjalang working the joystick with primitive recreationist glee and vigor, rather than vibbing the trundlebug.

Tigerishka on his right and Gershon Thales on his left.

A tense silence reigned.

Tigerishka exuded a bored professionalism only slightly belied by a gently twitching tailtip and alertly cocked tufted ears. Her tigrine pelt poked out from the edges of her plugsuit, pretty furred face and graceful neck the largest bare expanse.

A.B. thought she smelled like a sexy stuffed toy. Disturbing.

She turned her slit-pupiled eyes away from the monotonous racing landscape for a while to gnaw delicately with sharp teeth at a wayward cuticle around one claw.

Furries chose to express non-inheritable parts of the genome of various extinct species within their own bodies, as a simultaneous expiation of guilt and celebration of lost diversity. Although the Vaults at Reboot City Twenty-nine (formerly Svalbard, Norway) safely held samples of all the vanished species that had been foolish enough to compete with humanity during this Anthropocene Age, their non-human genomes awaiting some far-off day of re-instantiation, that sterile custody did not sit well with some. The furries wanted other species to walk the earth again, if only by partial proxy.

In contrast to Tigerishka's stolid boredom, Gershon Thales manifested a frenetic desire to maximize demands on his attention. Judging by the swallow-flight motions of his hands, he had half a dozen virtual windows open, upon what landscapes of information A.B. could only conjecture. (He had tried vibbing into Gershon's eyes, but had encountered a pirate privacy wall. Hard to build team camaraderie with that barrier in place, but A.B. had chosen not to call out the man on the matter just yet.)

No doubt Gershon was hanging out on keek fora. The keeks loved to indulge in endless talk.

Originally calling themselves the "punctuated equilibriumists," the cult had swiftly shortened their awkward name to the "punk eeks," and then to the "keeks."

The keeks believed that after a long period of stasis, the human species had reached one of those pivotal Darwinian climacterics that would launch the race along exciting if unpredictable new vectors. What everyone else viewed as a grand tragedy—implacable and deadly climate change leading to the Big Biota Crash—they interpreted as a useful kick in humanity's collective pants. They discussed a thousand, thousand schemes intended to further this leap, most of them just so much mad vaporware.

A.B. clucked his tongue softly as he drove. Such were the assistants he had been handed, to solve a crisis of unknown magnitude.

Tigerishka suddenly spoke, her voice a velvet growl. "Can't you push this bug any faster? The cabin's starting to stink like simians already."

New Perthpatna occupied the site that had once hosted the Russian city of Arkhangelsk, torn down during the Reboot. The closest malfunctioning solar collectors in what had once been France loomed 2800 kilometers distant. Mission transit time: an estimated thirty-six hours, including overnight rest.

"No, I can't. As it is, we're going to have to camp at least eight hours for the batteries to recharge. The faster I push us, the more power we expend, and the longer we'll have to sit idle. It's a calculated tradeoff. Look at the math."

A.B. vibbed Tigerishka a presentation. She studied it, then growled in frustration.

"I need to run! I can't sit cooped up in a smelly can like this for hours at a stretch! At home, I hit the track every hour."

A.B. wanted to say, *I'm not the one who stuck those big-cat codons in you, so don't yell at me!* But instead he notched up the cabin's HVAC and chose a polite response. "Right now, all I can do is save your nose some grief. We'll stop for lunch, and you can get some exercise then. Can't you vib out like old Gershon there?"

Gerson Thales stopped his air haptics to glare at A.B. His lugubrious voice resembled wet cement plopping from a trough. "What's that comment supposed to imply? That I'm wasting my time? Well, I'm not. I'm engaged in posthuman dialectics at Saltation Central. Very stimulating. You two should try to expand your minds in a similar fashion."

Tigerishka hissed. A.B. ran an app that counted to ten for him using gently breaking waves to time the calming sequence.

"As mission leader, I don't really care how anyone passes the travel time. Just so long as you all perform when it matters. Now how about letting me enjoy the drive."

The "road" actually required little of A.B.'s attention. A wide border of rammed earth, kept free of weeds by cousins to A.B.'s beard removers, the road paralleled the surprisingly dainty superconducting transmission line that powered a whole city. It ran straight as modern justice toward the solar collectors that fed it. Shade from the rows of eulollypops planted alongside cut down any glare and added coolness to their passage.

Coolness was a desideratum. The further south they traveled, the hotter things would get. Until, finally, temperatures would approach fifty degrees at many points of the Solar Girdle. Only their plugsuits would allow the Power Jockeys to function outside under those conditions.

A.B. tried to enjoy the sensations of driving, a recreationist pastime he seldom got to indulge. Most of his work day consisted of indoor maintenance and monitoring, optimization of supply and demand, the occasional high-level debugging. Humans possessed a fluidity of response and insight no kybes could yet match. A field expedition marked a welcome change of pace from this indoor work. Or would have, with comrades more congenial.

A.B. sighed, and kicked up their speed just a notch.

After traveling for nearly five hours, they stopped for lunch, just a bit north of where Moscow had once loomed. No Reboot City had ever been erected in its place, more northerly locations being preferred.

As soon as the wide door slid upward, Tigerishka bolted from the cabin. She raced laterally off into the endless eulollypop forest, faster than a baseline human. Thirty seconds later, a rich, resonant, hair-raising caterwaul of triumph made both A.B. and Gershon Thales jump.

Thales said drily, "Caught a mouse, I suppose."

A.B. laughed. Maybe Thales wasn't such a stiff.

A.B. jacked the trundlebug into one of the convenient stepdown charging nodes in the transmission cable designed for just such a purpose. Even an hour's topping up would help. Then he broke out sandwiches of curried goat salad. He and Thales ate companionably. Tigerishka returned with a dab of overlooked murine blood at the corner of her lips, and declined any human food.

Back in the moving vehicle, Thales and Tigerishka reclined their seats and settled down to a nap after lunch, and their drowsiness soon infected A.B. He put the trundlebug on autopilot, reclined his own seat, and soon was fast asleep as well.

Awaking several hours later, A.B. discovered their location to be nearly atop the 54th parallel, in the vicinity of pre-Crash Minsk.

The temperature outside their cozy cab registered a sizzling thirty-five, despite the declining sun.

"We'll push on toward Old Warsaw, then call it a day. That'll leave just a little over eleven hundred klicks to cover tomorrow."

Thales objected. "We'll get to the farms late in the day tomorrow—too late for any useful investigation. Why not run all night on autopilot?"

"I want us to get a good night's rest without jouncing around. And besides, all it would take is a tree freshly down across the road, or a new sinkhole to ruin us. The autopilot's not infallible."

Tigerishka's sultry purr sent tingles through A.B.'s scrotum. "I need to work out some kinks myself."

Night halted the trundlebug. When the door slid up, furnace air blasted the trio, automatically activating their plugsuits. Sad old fevered planet. They pulled up their cowls and felt relief.

Three personal homeostatic pods were decanted, and popped open upon vibbed command beneath the allée. They crawled inside separately to eat and drop off quickly to sleep.

Stimulating caresses awakened A.B. Hazily uncertain what hour this was that witnessed Tigerishka's trespass upon his homeopod, or whether she had visited Thales first, he could decisively report in the morning, had such a report been required by Jeetu Kissoon and the Power Administration Corps, that she retained enough energy to wear him out.

3. THE SANDS OF PARIS

The vast, forbidding, globe-encircling desert south of the 45th parallel depressed everyone in the trundlebug. A.B. ran his tongue around lips that felt impossibly cracked and parched, no matter how much water he sucked from his plugsuit's kamelbak.

All greenery gone, the uniform trackless, and silent wastes baking under the implacable sun brought to mind some alien world that had never known human tread. No signs of the mighty cities that had once reared their proud towers remained, nor any traces of the sprawling suburbs, the surging highways. What had not been disassembled for reuse elsewhere had been buried.

On and on the trundlebug rolled, following the superconductor line, its enormous wheels operating as well on loose sand as on rammed earth.

A.B. felt anew the grievous historical impact of humanity's folly upon the planet, and he did not relish the emotions. He generally devoted little thought to that sad topic.

An utterly modern product of his age, a hardcore Rebooter through and through, Aurobindo Bandjalang was generally happy with his civilization. Its contorted features, its limitations and constraints, its precariousness, and its default settings he accepted implicitly, just as a child of trolls believes its troll mother to be utterly beautiful.

He knew pride in how the human race had managed to build a hundred new cities from scratch and shift billions of people north and south in only half a century, outracing the spreading blight and killer weather. He enjoyed the hybrid multicultural mélange that had replaced old divisions and rivalries, the new blended mankind. The nostalgic stories told by Jeetu Kissoon and others of his generation were entertaining fairy tales, not the chronicle of any lost Golden Age. He could not lament what he had never known. He was too busy keeping the delicate structures of the present day up and running, and happy to be so occupied.

Trying to express these sentiments and lift the spirits of his comrades, A.B. found that his evaluation of Reboot civilization was not universal.

"Every human of this fallen Anthropocene age is shadowed by the myriad ghosts of all the other creatures they drove extinct," said Tigerishka, in a surprisingly poetic and somber manner, given her usual blunt and unsentimental earthiness. "Whales and dolphins, cats and dogs, cows and horses—they all peer into and out of our sinful souls. Our only shot at redemption is that someday, when the planet is restored, our coevolved partners might be re-embodied."

Thales uttered a scoffing grunt. "Good riddance to all that nonsapient genetic trash! Homo sapiens is the only desirable endpoint of all evolutionary lines. But right now, the dictatorial Reboot has our species locked down in a dead end. We can't make the final leap to our next level until we get rid of the chaff."

Tigerishka spat, and made a taunting feint toward her coworker across A.B.'s chest, causing A.B. to swerve the car and Thales to recoil. When the keek realized he hadn't actually been hurt, he grinned with a sickly superciliousness.

"Hold on one minute," said A.B. "Do you mean that you and the other keeks want to see another Crash?"

"It's more complex than that. You see—"

But A.B.'s attention was diverted that moment from Thales's explanation. His vib interrupted with a Demand Four call from his apartment.

Vib nodes dotted the power transmission network, keeping people online just like at home. Plenty of dead zones existed elsewhere, but not here, adjacent to the line.

A.B. had just enough time to place the trundlebug on autopilot before his vision was overlaid with a feed from home.

The security system on his apartment had registered an unauthorized entry.

Inside his 1LDK, an optical distortion the size of a small human moved around, spraying something similar to used cooking oil on A.B.s furniture. The hands holding the sprayer disappeared inside the whorl of distortion.

A.B. vibbed his avatar into his home system. "Hey, you! What the fuck are you doing?!"

The person wearing the invisibility cape laughed, and A.B. recognized the distinctive crude chortle of Zulqamain Safranski.

"Safranski! Your ass is grass! The ASBOs are on their way!"

Unable to stand the sight of his lovely apartment being desecrated, frustrated by his inability to take direct action himself, A.B. vibbed off.

Tigerishka and Thales had shared the feed, and commiserated with their fellow Power Jock. But the experience soured the rest of the trip for A.B., and he stewed silently until they reached the first of the extensive constructions upon which the Reboot Cities relied for their very existence.

The Solar Girdle featured a tripartite setup, for the sake of security of supply.

First came the extensive farms of solar updraft towers: giant chimneys that fostered wind flow from base to top, thus powering their turbines.

Then came parabolic mirrored troughs that followed the sun and pumped heat into special sinks, lakes of molten salts, which in turn ran different turbines after sunset.

Finally, serried ranks of photovoltaic panels generated electricity directly. These structures, in principle the simplest and least likely to fail, were the ones experiencing difficulties from some kind of dust accretion.

Vibbing GPS coordinates for the troublespot, A.B. brought the trundlebug up to the infected photovoltaics. Paradoxically, the steady omnipresent whine of the car's motors registered on his attention only when he had powered them down.

Outside the vehicle's polarized plastic shell, the sinking sun glared like the malign orb of a cyclops bent on mankind's destruction.

When the bug-wide door slid up, dragon's breath assailed the Power Jocks. Their plugsuits strained to shield them from the hostile environment.

Surprisingly, a subdued and pensive Tigerishka volunteered for camp duty. As dusk descended, she attended to erecting their intelligent shelters and getting a meal ready: chicken croquettes with roasted edamame.

A.B. and Thales sluffed through the sand for a dozen yards to the nearest infected solarcell platform. The keek held his pocket lab in gloved hand.

A little maintenance kybe, scuffed and scorched, perched on the high trellis, valiantly but fruitlessly chipping with its multitool at a hard siliceous shell irregularly encrusting the photovoltaic surface.

Thales caught a few flakes of the unknown substance as they fell, and inserted them into the analysis chamber of the pocket lab.

"We should have a complete readout of the composition of this stuff by morning."

"No sooner?"

"Well, actually, by midnight. But I don't intend to stay up. I've done nothing except sit on my ass for two days, yet I'm still exhausted. It's this oppressive place—"

"Okay," A.B. replied. The first stars had begun to prinkle the sky. "Let's call it a day."

They ate in the bug, in a silent atmosphere of forced companionability, then retired to their separate shelters.

A.B. hoped with mild lust for another nocturnal visit from a prowling Tigerishka, but was not greatly disappointed when she never showed to interrupt his intermittent drowsing. Truly, the desert sands of Paris sapped all his usual joie de vivre.

Finally falling fast asleep, he dreamed of the ghostly waters of the vanished Seine, impossibly flowing deep beneath his tent. Somehow, Zulqamain Safranski was diverting them to flood A.B.'s apartment . . .

4. THE RED QUEEN'S TRIATHLON

In the morning, after breakfast, A.B. approached Gershon Thales, who stood apart near the trundlebug. Already the sun thundered down its oppressive cargo of photons, so necessary for the survival of the Reboot Cities, yet, conversely, just one more burden for the overstressed Greenhouse ecosphere. Feeling irritable and impatient, anxious to be back home, A.B. dispensed with pleasantries.

"I've tried vibbing your pocket lab for the results, but you've got it offline, behind that pirate software you're running. Open up, now."

The keek stared at A.B. with mournful stolidity. "One minute, I need something from my pod."

Thales ducked into his tent. A.B. turned to Tigerishka. "What do you make—"

Blinding light shattered A.B.'s vision for a millisecond in a painful nova, before his MEMS contacts could react protectively by going opaque. Tigerishka vented a stifled yelp of surprise and shock, showing she had gotten the same actinic eyekick.

A.B. immediately thought of vib malfunction, some misdirected feed from a solar observatory, say. But then, as his lenses de-opaqued, he realized the stimulus had to have been external.

When he could see again, he confronted Gershon Thales holding a pain gun whose wide bell muzzle covered both of the keek's fellow Power Jocks. At the feet of the keek rested an exploded spaser grenade.

A.B. tried to vib, but got nowhere.

"Yes," Thales said, "we're in a dead zone now. I fried all the optical circuits of the vib nodes with the grenade."

A large enough burst of surface plasmons could do that? Who knew? "But why?"

With his free hand, keeping the pain gun unwavering, Thales reached into a plugsuit pocket and took out his lab. "These results. They're only the divine sign we've been waiting for. Reboot civilization is on the way out now. I couldn't let anyone in the PAC find out. The longer they stay in the dark, the more irreversible the changes will be."

"You're claiming this creeping crud is that dangerous?"

"Did you ever hear of ADRECS?"

A.B. instinctively tried to vib for the info and hit the blank, frustrating walls of the newly created dead zone. Trapped in the twentieth century! Recreationist passions only went so far. Where was the panopticon when you needed it!?!

"Aerially Delivered Re-forestation and Erosion Control System," continued Thales. "A package of geoengineering schemes meant to stabilize the spread of deserts. Abandoned decades ago. But apparently, one scheme's come alive again on its own. Mutant instruction drift is my best guess. Or Darwin's invisible hand."

"What's come alive then?"

"Nanosand. Meant to catalyze the formation of macroscale walls that would block the flow of normal sands."

"And that's the stuff afflicting the solarcells?"

"Absolutely. Has an affinity for bonding with the surface of the cells and can't be removed with destroying them. Self-replicating. Best estimates are that the nanosand will take out thirty percent of production in just a month, if left unchecked. Might start to affect the turbines too."

Tigerishka asked, in an intellectually curious tone of voice that A.B. found disconcerting, "But what good does going offline do? When PAC can't vib us, they'll just send another crew."

"I'll wait here and put them out of commission too. I only have to hang in for a month."

"What about food?" said Tigerishka. "We don't have enough provisions for a month, even for one person."

"I'll raid the fish farms on the coast. Desalinate my drinking water. It's just a short round trip by bug."

A.B. could hardly contain his disgust. "You're fucking crazy, Thales. Dropping the power supply by thirty percent won't kill the cities."

"Oh, but we keeks think it will. You see, Reboot civilization is a wobbly three-legged stool, hammered together in a mad rush. We're not in the Red Queen's Race, but the Red Queen's Triathlon. Power, food, and social networks. Take out any one leg, and it all goes down. And we're sawing at the other two legs as well. Look at that guy who vandalized your apartment. Behavior like that is on the rise. The urbmons are driving people crazy. Humans weren't meant to live in hives."

Tigerishka stepped forward, and Thales swung the gun more toward her unprotected face. A blast of high-intensity microwaves would leave her screaming, writhing, and puking on the sands.

"I want in," she said, and A.B.'s heart sank through his boots. "The only way other species will ever get to share this planet is when most of mankind is gone."

Regarding the furry speculatively and clinically, Thales said, "I could use your help. But you'll have to prove yourself. First, tie up Bandjalang."

Tigerishka grinned vilely at A.B. "Sorry, apeboy."

Using biopoly cords from the bug, she soon had A.B. trussed with circulation-deadening bonds, and stashed in his homeopod.

What were they doing out there!?! A.B. squirmed futilely. He banged around so much, he began to fear he was damaging the life-preserving tent, and he stopped. Wiped out after hours of struggle, he fell into a stupor made more ennervating by the suddenly less-than-ideal heat inside the homeopod, whose compromised systems strained to deal with the desert conditions. He began to hallucinate about the subterranean Seine again, and realized he was very, very thirsty. His kamelbak was dry when he sipped at its straw.

At some point, Tigerishka appeared and gave him some water. Or did she? Maybe it was all just another dream.

Outside the smart tent, night came down. A.B. heard wolves howling, just like they did on archived documentaries. Wolves? No wolves existed. But someone was howling.

Tigerishka having sex. Sex with Thales. Bastard. Bad guy not only won the battle, but got the girl as well . . .

A.B. awoke to the pins and needles of returning circulation: discomfort of a magnitude unfelt by anyone before or after the Lilliputians tethered Gulliver.

Tigerishka was bending over him, freeing him.

"Sorry again, apeboy, that took longer than I thought. He even kept his hand on the gun right up until he climaxed."

Something warm was dripping on A.B.'s face. Was his rescuer crying? Her voice belied any such emotion. A.B. raised a hand that felt like a block of wood to his own face, and clumsily smeared the liquid around, until some entered his mouth.

He imagined that this forbidden taste was equally as satisfying to Tigerishka as mouse fluids.

Heading north, the trundlebug seemed much more spacious with just two passengers. The corpse of Gershon Thales had been left behind, for eventual recovery by experts. Desication and cooking would make it a fine mummy.

Once out of the dead zone, A.B. vibbed everything back to Jeetu Kissoon, and got a shared commendation that made Tigerishka purr. Then he turned his attention to his personal queue of messages.

The ASBO Squad had bagged Safranski. But they apologized for some delay in his sentencing hearing. Their caseload was enormous these days.

Way down at the bottom of his queue was an agricultural newsfeed. An unprecedented kind of black rot fungus had made inroads into the kale crop on the farms supplying Reboot City Twelve.

Calories would be tight in New Perthpatna, but only for a while.

Or so they hoped.

WHEN SYSADMINS RULED THE EARTH

By Cory Doctorow

When Felix's special phone rang at two in the morning, Kelly rolled over and punched him in the shoulder and hissed, "Why didn't you turn that fucking thing off before bed?"

"Because I'm on call," he said.

"You're not a fucking doctor," she said, kicking him as he sat on the bed's edge, pulling on the pants he'd left on the floor before turning in. "You're a goddamned *systems administrator*."

"It's my job," he said.

"They work you like a government mule," she said. "You know I'm right. For Christ's sake, you're a father now, you can't go running off in the middle of the night every time someone's porn supply goes down. Don't answer that phone."

He knew she was right. He answered the phone.

"Main routers not responding, BGP not responding." The mechanical voice of the systems monitor didn't care if he cursed at it, so he did, and it made him feel a little better.

"Maybe I can fix it from here," he said. He could log in to the UPS for the cage and reboot the routers. The UPS was in a different netblock, with its own independent routers on their own uninterruptible power supplies.

Kelly was sitting up in bed now, an indistinct shape against the headboard. "In five years of marriage, you have never once been able to fix anything from here." This time she was wrong—he fixed stuff from home all the time, but he did it discreetly and didn't make a fuss, so she didn't remember it. And she was right, too—he had logs that showed that after 1:00 AM, nothing could ever be fixed without driving out to the cage. Law of Infinite Universal Perversity—AKA Felix's Law.

Five minutes later Felix was behind the wheel. He hadn't been able to fix it from home. The independent routers' netblock was offline, too. The last time that had happened, some dumbfuck construction worker had driven a ditch-witch through the main conduit into the data-center and Felix had joined a cadre of fifty enraged sysadmins who'd stood atop the resulting pit for a week, screaming abuse at the poor bastards who labored 24-7 to splice ten thousand wires back together.

His phone went off twice more in the car and he let it override the stereo and play the mechanical status reports through the big, bassy speakers of more critical network infrastructure offline. Then Kelly called.

"Hi," he said.

"Don't cringe, I can hear the cringe in your voice."

He smiled involuntarily. "Check, no cringing."

"I love you, Felix," she said.

"I'm totally bonkers for you, Kelly. Go back to bed."

"2.0's awake," she said. The baby had been Beta Test when he was in her womb, and when her water broke, he got the call and dashed out of the office, shouting, '*The Gold Master just shipped!*' They'd started calling him 2.0 before he'd finished his first cry. "This little bastard was born to suck tit."

"I'm sorry I woke you," he said. He was almost at the data-center. No traffic at 2 AM. He slowed down and pulled over before the entrance to the garage. He didn't want to lose Kelly's call underground.

"It's not waking me," she said. "You've been there for seven years. You have three juniors reporting to you. Give them the phone. You've paid your dues."

"I don't like asking my reports to do anything I wouldn't do," he said.

"You've done it," she said. "Please? I hate waking up alone in the night. I miss you most at night."

"Kelly—"

"I'm over being angry. I just miss you is all. You give me sweet dreams."

"Okay," he said. "Simple as that?"

"Exactly. Simple as that. Can't have you having bad dreams, and I've paid my dues. From now on, I'm only going on night call to cover holidays."

She laughed. "Sysadmins don't take holidays."

"This one will," he said. "Promise."

"You're wonderful," she said. "Oh, gross. 2.0 just dumped core all over my bathrobe."

"That's my boy," he said.

"Oh that he is," she said. She hung up, and he piloted the car into the data-center lot, badging in and peeling up a bleary eyelid to let the retinal scanner get a good look at his sleep-depped eyeball.

He stopped at the machine to get himself a guarana/medafonil power-bar and a cup of lethal robot-coffee in a spill-proof clean-room sippy-cup. He wolfed down the bar and sipped the coffee, then let the inner door read his hand-geometry and size him up for a moment. It sighed open and gusted the airlock's load of positively pressurized air over him as he passed finally to the inner sanctum.

It was bedlam. The cages were designed to let two or three sysadmins maneuver around them at a time. Every other inch of cubic space was given over to humming racks of servers and routers and drives. Jammed among them were no fewer than twenty other sysadmins. It was a regular convention of black tee shirts with inexplicable slogans, bellies overlapping belts with phones and multitools.

Normally it was practically freezing in the cage, but all those bodies were overheating the small, enclosed space. Five or six looked up and grimaced when he came through. Two greeted him by name. He threaded his belly through the press and the cages, toward the Ardent racks in the back of the room.

"Felix." It was Van, who wasn't on call that night.

"What are you doing here?" he asked. "No need for both of us to be wrecked tomorrow."

"What? Oh. My personal box is over there. It went down around 1:30 and I got woken up by my process-monitor. I should have called you and told you I was coming down—spared you the trip."

Felix's own server—a box he shared with five other friends—was in a rack one floor down. He wondered if it was offline too.

"What's the story?"

"Massive flashworm attack. Some jackass with a zero-day exploit has got every Windows box on the net running Monte Carlo probes on every IP block, including IPv6. The big Ciscos all run administrative interfaces over v6, and they all fall over if they get more than ten simultaneous probes, which means that just about every interchange has gone down, DNS is screwy, too—like maybe someone poisoned the zone transfer last night. Oh, and there's an email and IM component that sends pretty lifelike messages to everyone in your address book, barfing up Eliza-dialog that keys off of your logged email and messages to get you to open a trojan."

"Jesus."

"Yeah." Van was a type-two sysadmin, over six feet tall, long ponytail, bobbing Adam's apple. Over his toast-rack chest, his tee said CHOOSE YOUR WEAPON and featured a row of polyhedral RPG dice.

Felix was a type-one admin, with an extra seventy or eighty pounds all around the middle, and a neat but full beard that he wore over his extra chins. His tee said HELLO CTHULHU and featured a cute, mouthless, Hello Kitty–style Cthulhu. They'd known each other for fifteen years, having met on Usenet, then f2f at Toronto Freenet beer sessions, a Star Trek convention or two, and eventually Felix had hired Van to work under him at Ardent. Van was reliable and methodical. Trained as an electrical engineer, he kept a procession of spiral notebooks filled with the details of every step he'd ever taken, with time and date.

"Not even PEBKAC this time," Van said. Problem Exists Between Keyboard And Chair. Email trojans fell into that category—if people were smart enough not to open suspect attachments, email trojans would be a thing of the past. But worms that ate Cisco routers weren't a problem with the lusers—they were the fault of incompetent engineers.

"No, it's Microsoft's fault," Felix said. "Any time I'm at work at 2 AM, it's either PEBKAC or Microsloth."

They ended up just unplugging the frigging routers from the Internet. Not Felix, of course, though he was itching to do it and get them rebooted after shutting down their IPv6 interfaces. It was done by a couple bull-goose Bastard Operators From Hell who had to turn two keys at once to get access to their cage—like guards in a Minuteman silo. Ninety-five percent of the long-distance traffic in Canada went through this building. It had *better* security than most Minuteman silos.

Felix and Van got the Ardent boxes back online one at a time. They were being pounded by worm-probes—putting the routers back online just exposed the downstream cages to the attack. Every box on the Internet was drowning in worms, or creating worm-attacks, or both. Felix managed to get through to NIST and Bugtraq after about a hundred timeouts, and download some kernel patches that should reduce the load the worms put on the machines in his care. It was 10 AM, and he was hungry enough to eat the ass out of a dead bear, but he recompiled his kernels and brought the machines back online. Van's long fingers flew over the administrative keyboard, his tongue protruding as he ran load-stats on each one.

"I had two hundred days of uptime on Greedo," Van said. Greedo was the oldest server in the rack, from the days when they'd named the boxes after *Star Wars* characters. Now they were all named after Smurfs, and they were running out of Smurfs and had started in on McDonaldland characters, starting with Van's laptop, Mayor McCheese.

"Greedo will rise again," Felix said. "I've got a 486 downstairs with over five years of uptime. It's going to break my heart to reboot it."

"What the everlasting shit do you use a 486 for?"

"Nothing. But who shuts down a machine with five years' uptime? That's like euthanizing your grandmother."

"I wanna eat," Van said.

"Tell you what," Felix said. "We'll get your box up, then mine, then I'll take you to the Lakeview Lunch for breakfast pizzas and you can have the rest of the day off."

"You're on," Van said. "Man, you're too good to us grunts. You should keep us in a pit and beat us like all the other bosses. It's all we deserve."

"It's your phone," Van said. Felix extracted himself from the guts of the 486, which had refused to power up at all. He had cadged a spare power supply from some guys who ran a spam operation and was trying to get it fitted. He let Van hand him the phone, which had fallen off his belt while he was twisting to get at the back of the machine.

"Hey, Kel," he said. There was an odd, snuffling noise in the background. Static, maybe? 2.0 splashing in the bath? "Kelly?"

The line went dead. He tried to call back, but didn't get anything—no ring nor voicemail. His phone finally timed out and said NETWORK ERROR.

"Dammit," he said, mildly. He clipped the phone to his belt. Kelly wanted to know when he was coming home, or wanted him to pick something up for the family. She'd leave voicemail.

He was testing the power supply when his phone rang again. He snatched it up and answered it. "Kelly, hey, what's up?" He worked to keep anything like irritation out of his voice. He felt guilty: technically speaking, he had discharged his obligations to Ardent Financial LLC once the Ardent servers were back online. The past three hours had been purely personal—even if he planned on billing them to the company.

There was sobbing on the line.

"Kelly?" He felt the blood draining from his face and his toes were numb.

"Felix," she said, barely comprehensible through the sobbing. "He's dead, oh Jesus, he's dead."

"Who? *Who,* Kelly?"

"Will," she said.

Will? he thought. *Who the fuck is*— He dropped to his knees. William was the name they'd written on the birth certificate, though they'd called him 2.0 all along. Felix made an anguished sound, like a sick bark.

"I'm sick," she said, "I can't even stand anymore. Oh, Felix. I love you so much."

"Kelly? What's going on?"

"Everyone, everyone—" she said. "Only two channels left on the tube. Christ, Felix, it looks like *Dawn of the Dead* out the window—" He heard her retch. The phone started to break up, washing her puke-noises back like an echoplex.

"Stay there, Kelly," he shouted as the line died. He punched 911, but the phone went NETWORK ERROR again as soon as he hit SEND.

He grabbed Mayor McCheese from Van and plugged it into the 486's network cable and launched Firefox off the command line and Googled for the Metro Police site. Quickly, but not frantically, he searched for an online contact form. Felix didn't lose his head, ever. He solved problems and freaking out didn't solve problems.

He located an online form and wrote out the details of his conversation with Kelly like he was filing a bug report, his fingers fast, his description complete, and then he hit SUBMIT.

Van had read over his shoulder. "Felix—" he began.

"God," Felix said. He was sitting on the floor of the cage and he slowly pulled himself upright. Van took the laptop and tried some news sites, but they were all timing out. Impossible to say if it was because something terrible was happening or because the network was limping under the superworm.

"I need to get home," Felix said.

"I'll drive you," Van said. "You can keep calling your wife."

They made their way to the elevators. One of the building's few windows was there, a thick, shielded porthole. They peered through it as they waited for the elevator. Not much traffic for a Wednesday. Were there more police cars than usual?

"*Oh my God*—" Van pointed.

The CN Tower, a giant white-elephant needle of a building, loomed to the east of them. It was askew, like a branch stuck in wet sand. Was it moving? It was. It was heeling over, slowly, but gaining speed, falling northeast toward the financial district. In a second, it slid over the tipping point and crashed down. They felt the shock, then heard it, the whole building rocking from the impact. A cloud of dust rose from the wreckage, and there was more thunder as the world's tallest freestanding structure crashed through building after building.

"The Broadcast Centre's coming down," Van said. It was—the CBC's towering building was collapsing in slow motion. People ran every way, were crushed by falling masonry. Seen through the porthole, it was like watching a neat CGI trick downloaded from a file-sharing site.

Sysadmins were clustering around them now, jostling to see the destruction.

"What happened?" one of them asked.

"The CN Tower fell down," Felix said. He sounded far away in his own ears. "Was it the virus?"

"The worm? What?" Felix focused on the guy, who was a young admin with just a little type-two flab around the middle.

"Not the worm," the guy said. "I got an email that the whole city's quarantined because of some virus. Bioweapon, they say." He handed Felix his Blackberry.

Felix was so engrossed in the report—purportedly forwarded from Health Canada—that he didn't even notice that all the lights had gone out. Then he did, and he pressed the Blackberry back into its owner's hand, and let out one small sob.

The generators kicked in a minute later. Sysadmins stampeded for the stairs. Felix grabbed Van by the arm, pulled him back.

"Maybe we should wait this out in the cage," he said.

"What about Kelly?" Van said.

Felix felt like he was going to throw up. "We should get into the cage, now." The cage had microparticulate air filters.

They ran upstairs to the big cage. Felix opened the door and then let it hiss shut behind him.

"Felix, you need to get home—"

"It's a bioweapon," Felix said. "Superbug. We'll be okay in here, I think, so long as the filters hold out."

"What?"

"Get on IRC," he said.

They did. Van had Mayor McCheese and Felix used Smurfette. They skipped around the chat channels until they found one with some familiar handles.

> pentagons gone/white house too

> MY NEIGHBORS BARFING BLOOD OFF HIS BALCONY IN SAN DIEGO

> Someone knocked over the Gherkin. Bankers are fleeing the City like rats.

> I heard that the Ginza's on fire

Felix typed: I'm in Toronto. We just saw the CN Tower fall. I've heard reports of bioweapons, something very fast.

Van read this and said, "You don't know how fast it is, Felix. Maybe we were all exposed three days ago."

Felix closed his eyes. "If that were so we'd be feeling some symptoms, I think."

> Looks like an EMP took out Hong Kong and maybe Paris—realtime sat footage shows them completely dark, and all netblocks there aren't routing

> You're in Toronto?

It was an unfamiliar handle.

> Yes—on Front Street

> my sisters at UofT and i cnt reach her—can you call her?

> No phone service

Felix typed, staring at NETWORK PROBLEMS.

"I have a soft phone on Mayor McCheese," Van said, launching his voice-over-ip app. "I just remembered."

Felix took the laptop from him and punched in his home number. It rang once, then there was a flat, blatting sound like an ambulance siren in an Italian movie.

> No phone service

Felix typed again.

He looked up at Van, and saw that his skinny shoulders were shaking. Van said, "Holy motherfucking shit. The world is ending."

Felix pried himself off of IRC an hour later. Atlanta had burned. Manhattan was hot—radioactive enough to screw up the webcams looking out over Lincoln Plaza. Everyone blamed Islam until it became clear that Mecca was a smoking pit and the Saudi royals had been hanged before their palaces.

His hands were shaking, and Van was quietly weeping in the far corner of the cage. He tried calling home again, and then the police. It didn't work any better than it had the last twenty times.

He sshed into his box downstairs and grabbed his mail. Spam, spam, spam. More spam. Automated messages. There—an urgent message from the intrusion detection system in the Ardent cage.

He opened it and read quickly. Someone was crudely, repeatedly probing his routers. It didn't match a worm's signature, either. He followed the traceroute and discovered that the attack had originated in the same building as him, a system in a cage one floor below.

He had procedures for this. He portscanned his attacker and found that port 1337 was open—1337 was "leet" or "elite" in hacker number/letter substitution code. That was the kind of port that a worm left open to slither in and out of. He Googled known sploits that left a listener on port 1337, narrowed this down based on the fingerprinted operating system of the compromised server, and then he had it.

It was an ancient worm, one that every box should have been patched against years before. No mind. He had the client for it, and he used it to create a root account for himself on the box, which he then logged into, and took a look around.

There was one other user logged in, "scaredy," and he checked the process monitor and saw that scaredy had spawned all the hundreds of processes that were probing him and plenty of other boxen.

He opened a chat:

> Stop probing my server

He expected bluster, guilt, denial. He was surprised.

> Are you in the Front Street data center?

> Yes

> Christ I thought I was the last one alive. I'm on the fourth floor. I think there's a bioweapon attack outside. I don't want to leave the clean room.

Felix whooshed out a breath.

> You were probing me to get me to trace back to you?

> Yeah

> That was smart

Clever bastard.

> I'm on the sixth floor, I've got one more with me.

> What do you know?

Felix pasted in the IRC log and waited while the other guy digested it. Van stood up and paced. His eyes were glazed over.

"Van? Pal?"

"I have to pee," he said.

"No opening the door," Felix said. "I saw an empty Mountain Dew bottle in the trash there."

"Right," Van said. He walked like a zombie to the trash can and pulled out the empty magnum. He turned his back.

> I'm Felix

> Will

Felix's stomach did a slow somersault as he thought about 2.0.

"Felix, I think I need to go outside," Van said. He was moving toward the airlock door. Felix dropped his keyboard and struggled to his feet and ran headlong to Van, tackling him before he reached the door.

"Van," he said, looking into his friend's glazed, unfocused eyes. "Look at me, Van."

"I need to go," Van said. "I need to get home and feed the cats."

"There's something out there, something fast acting and lethal. Maybe it will blow away with the wind. Maybe it's already gone. But we're going to sit here until we know for sure or until we have no choice. Sit down, Van. Sit."

"I'm cold, Felix."

It was freezing. Felix's arms were broken out in gooseflesh and his feet felt like blocks of ice.

"Sit against the servers, by the vents. Get the exhaust heat." He found a rack and nestled up against it.

> Are you there?
> Still here—sorting out some logistics
> How long until we can go out?
> I have no idea

No one typed anything for quite some time then.

Felix had to use the Mountain Dew bottle twice. Then Van used it again. Felix tried calling Kelly again. The Metro Police site was down.

Finally, he slid back against the servers and wrapped his arms around his knees and wept like a baby.

After a minute, Van came over and sat beside him, with his arm around Felix's shoulder.

"They're dead, Van," Felix said. "Kelly and my s—son. My family is gone."

"You don't know for sure," Van said.

"I'm sure enough," Felix said. "Christ, it's all over, isn't it?"

"We'll gut it out a few more hours and then head out. Things should be getting back to normal soon. The fire department will fix it. They'll mobilize the army. It'll be okay."

Felix's ribs hurt. He hadn't cried since—Since 2.0 was born. He hugged his knees harder.

Then the doors opened.

The two sysadmins who entered were wild-eyed. One had a tee that said TALK NERDY TO ME and the other one was wearing an Electronic Frontiers Canada shirt.

"Come on," TALK NERDY said. "We're all getting together on the top floor. Take the stairs."

Felix found he was holding his breath.

"If there's a bioagent in the building, we're all infected," TALK NERDY said. "Just go, we'll meet you there."

"There's one on the sixth floor," Felix said, as he climbed to his feet.

"Will, yeah, we got him. He's up there."

TALK NERDY was one of the Bastard Operators From Hell who'd unplugged the big routers. Felix and Van climbed the stairs slowly, their steps echoing in the deserted shaft. After the frigid air of the cage, the stairwell felt like a sauna.

There was a cafeteria on the top floor, with working toilets, water and coffee and vending machine food. There was an uneasy queue of sysadmins before each. No one met anyone's eye. Felix wondered which one was Will and then he joined the vending machine queue.

He got a couple more energy bars and a gigantic cup of vanilla coffee before running out of change. Van had scored them some table space and Felix set the stuff down before him and got in the toilet line. "Just save some for me," he said, tossing an energy bar in front of Van.

By the time they were all settled in, thoroughly evacuated, and eating, TALK NERDY and his friend had returned again. They cleared off the cash register at the end of the food-prep area and TALK NERDY got up on it. Slowly the conversation died down.

"I'm Uri Popovich, this is Diego Rosenbaum. Thank you all for coming up here. Here's what we know for sure: the building's been on generators for three hours now. Visual observation indicates that we're the only building in central Toronto with working power—which should hold out for three more days. There is a bioagent of unknown origin loose beyond our doors. It kills quickly, within hours, and it is aerosolized. You get it from breathing bad air. No one has opened any of the exterior doors to this building since five this morning. No one will open the doors until I give the go-ahead.

"Attacks on major cities all over the world have left emergency responders in chaos. The attacks are electronic, biological, nuclear and conventional explosives, and they are very widespread. I'm a security engineer, and where I come from, attacks in this kind of cluster are usually viewed as opportunistic: group B blows up a bridge because everyone is off taking care of group A's dirty nuke event. It's smart. An Aum Shinrikyo cell in Seoul gassed the subways there about 2 AM Eastern—that's the earliest event we can locate, so it may have been the Archduke that broke the camel's back. We're pretty sure that Aum Shinrikyo couldn't be behind this kind of mayhem: they have no history of infowar and have never shown the kind of organizational acumen necessary to take out so many targets at once. Basically, they're not smart enough.

"We're holing up here for the foreseeable future, at least until the bioweapon has been identified and dispersed. We're going to staff the racks and keep the networks up. This is critical infrastructure, and it's our job to make sure it's got five nines of uptime. In times of national emergency, our responsibility to do that doubles."

One sysadmin put up his hand. He was very daring in a green Incredible Hulk ring-tee, and he was at the young end of the scale.

"Who died and made you king?"

"I have controls for the main security system, keys to every cage, and passcodes for the exterior doors—they're all locked now, by the way. I'm the one who got everyone up here first and called the meeting. I don't care if someone else wants this job, it's a shitty one. But someone needs to have this job."

"You're right," the kid said. "And I can do it every bit as well as you. My name's Will Sario."

Popovich looked down his nose at the kid. "Well, if you'll let me finish talking, maybe I'll hand things over to you when I'm done."

"Finish, by all means." Sario turned his back on him and walked to the window. He stared out of it intensely. Felix's gaze was drawn to it, and he saw that there were several oily smoke plumes rising up from the city.

Popovich's momentum was broken. "So that's what we're going to do," he said.

The kid looked around after a stretched moment of silence. "Oh, is it my turn now?"

There was a round of good-natured chuckling.

"Here's what I think: the world is going to shit. There are coordinated attacks on every critical piece of infrastructure. There's only one way that those attacks could be so well-coordinated: via the Internet. Even if you buy the thesis that the attacks are all opportunistic, we need to ask how an opportunistic attack could be organized in minutes: the Internet."

"So you think we should shut down the Internet?" Popovich laughed a little, but stopped when Sario said nothing.

"We saw an attack last night that nearly killed the Internet. A little DoS on the critical routers, a little DNS-foo, and down it goes like a preacher's daughter. Cops and the military are a bunch of technophobic lusers, they hardly rely on the 'Net at all. If we take the Internet down, we'll disproportionately disadvantage the attackers, while only inconveniencing the defenders. When the time comes, we can rebuild it."

"You're shitting me," Popovich said. His jaw literally hung open.

"It's logical," Sario said. "Lots of people don't like coping with logic when it dictates hard decisions. That's a problem with people, not logic."

There was a buzz of conversation that quickly turned into a roar.

"Shut up!" Popovich hollered. The conversation dimmed by one watt. Popovich yelled again, stamping his foot on the countertop. Finally there was a semblance of order. "One at a time," he said. He was flushed red, his hands in his pockets.

One sysadmin was for staying. Another for going. They should hide in the cages. They should inventory their supplies and appoint a quartermaster. They should go outside and find the police, or volunteer at hospitals. They should appoint defenders to keep the front door secure.

Felix found to his surprise that he had his hand in the air. Popovich called on him.

"My name is Felix Tremont," he said, getting up on one of the tables, drawing out his PDA. "I want to read you something.

"'Governments of the Industrial World, you weary giants of flesh and steel, I come from Cyberspace, the new home of Mind. On behalf of the future, I ask you of the past to leave us alone. You are not welcome among us. You have no sovereignty where we gather.

"'We have no elected government, nor are we likely to have one, so I address you with no greater authority than that with which liberty itself always speaks. I declare the global social space we are building to be naturally independent of the tyrannies you seek to impose on us. You have no moral right to rule us nor do you possess any methods of enforcement we have true reason to fear.

"'Governments derive their just powers from the consent of the governed. You have neither solicited nor received ours. We did not invite you. You do not know us, nor do you know our world. Cyberspace does not lie within your borders. Do not think that you can build it, as though it were a public construction project. You cannot. It is an act of nature and it grows itself through our collective actions.'

"That's from the Declaration of Independence of Cyberspace. It was written twelve years ago. I thought it was one of the most beautiful things I'd ever read. I wanted my kid to grow up in a world where cyberspace was free—and where that freedom infected the real world, so meatspace got freer too."

He swallowed hard and scrubbed at his eyes with the back of his hand. Van awkwardly patted him on the shoe.

"My beautiful son and my beautiful wife died today. Millions more, too. The city is literally in flames. Whole cities have disappeared from the map."

He coughed up a sob and swallowed it again.

"All around the world, people like us are gathered in buildings like this. They were trying to recover from last night's worm when disaster struck. We have independent power. Food. Water.

"We have the network, that the bad guys use so well and that the good guys have never figured out.

"We have a shared love of liberty that comes from caring about and caring for the network. We are in charge of the most important organizational and governmental tool the world has ever seen. We are the closest thing to a government the world has right now. Geneva is a crater. The East River is on fire and the UN is evacuated.

"The Distributed Republic of Cyberspace weathered this storm basically unscathed. We are the custodians of a deathless, monstrous, wonderful machine, one with the potential to rebuild a better world.

"I have nothing to live for but that."

There were tears in Van's eyes. He wasn't the only one. They didn't applaud him, but they did one better. They maintained respectful, total silence for seconds that stretched to a minute.

"How do we do it?" Popovich said, without a trace of sarcasm.

The newsgroups were filling up fast. They'd announced them in news. admin, net-abuse.email, where all the spamfighters hung out, and where there was a tight culture of camaraderie in the face of full-out attack. The new group was alt.novembers-disaster.recovery, with .recovery.goverance, .recovery.finance, .recovery.logistics and .recovery.defense hanging off of it. Bless the wooly alt. hierarchy and all those who sail in her.

The sysadmins came out of the woodwork. The Googleplex was online, with the stalwart Queen Kong bossing a gang of rollerbladed grunts who wheeled through the gigantic data center swapping out dead boxen and hitting reboot switches. The Internet Archive was offline in the Presidio, but the mirror in Amsterdam was live and they'd redirected the DNS so that you'd hardly know the difference. Amazon was down. PayPal was up. Blogger, TypePad, and Live Journal were all up, and filling with millions of posts from scared survivors huddling together for electronic warmth.

The Flickr photostreams were horrific. Felix had to unsubscribe from them after he caught a photo of a woman and a baby, dead in a kitchen, twisted into an agonized hieroglyph by the bioagent. They didn't look like Kelly and 2.0, but they didn't have to. He started shaking and couldn't stop.

Wikipedia was up, but limping under load. The spam poured in as though nothing had changed. Worms roamed the network.

.recovery.logistics was where most of the action was.

> We can use the newsgroup voting mechanism to hold regional
> elections

Felix knew that this would work. Usenet newsgroup votes had been running for more than twenty years without a substantial hitch.

> We'll elect regional representatives and they'll pick a Prime
> Minister.

The Americans insisted on President, which Felix didn't like. Seemed too partisan. His future wouldn't be the American future. The American future had gone up with the White House. He was building a bigger tent than that.

There were French sysadmins online from France Telecom. The EBU's data center had been spared in the attacks that hammered Geneva, and it was filled with wry Germans whose English was better than Felix's. They got on well with the remains of the BBC team in Canary Wharf.

They spoke polyglot English in .recovery.logistics, and Felix had momentum on his side. Some of the admins were cooling out the inevitable stupid flamewars with the practice of long years. Some were chipping in useful suggestions.

Surprisingly few thought that Felix was off his rocker.

> I think we should hold elections as soon as possible. Tomorrow
> at the latest. We can't rule justly without the consent of the
> governed.

Within seconds the reply landed in his inbox.

> You can't be serious. Consent of the governed? Unless I miss my
> guess, most of the people you're proposing to govern are puking
> their guts out, hiding under their desks, or wandering
> shell-shocked through the city streets. When do THEY get a vote?

Felix had to admit she had a point. Queen Kong was sharp. Not many women sysadmins, and that was a genuine tragedy. Women like Queen Kong were too good to exclude from the field. He'd have to hack a solution to get women balanced out in his new government. Require each region to elect one woman and one man?

He happily clattered into argument with her. The elections would be the next day; he'd see to it.

"Prime Minister of Cyberspace? Why not call yourself the Grand Poobah of the Global Data Network? It's more dignified, sounds cooler, and it'll get you just as far." Will had the sleeping spot next to him, up in the cafeteria, with Van on the other side. The room smelled like a dingleberry: twenty-five sysadmins who hadn't washed in at least a day all crammed into the same room. For some of them, it had been much, much longer than a day.

"Shut up, Will," Van said. "You wanted to try to knock the Internet offline."

"Correction: I *want* to knock the Internet offline. Present tense."

Felix cracked one eye. He was so tired, it was like lifting weights.

"Look, Sario—if you don't like my platform, put one of your own forward. There are plenty of people who think I'm full of shit and I respect them for that, since they're all running opposite me or backing someone who is. That's your choice. What's not on the menu is nagging and complaining. Bedtime now, or get up and post your platform."

Sario sat up slowly, unrolling the jacket he had been using for a pillow and putting it on. "Screw you guys, I'm out of here."

"I thought he'd never leave," Felix said, and turned over, lying awake a long time, thinking about the election.

There were other people in the running. Some of them weren't even sysadmins. A US senator on retreat at his summer place in Wyoming had generator power and a satellite phone. Somehow he'd found the right newsgroup and thrown his hat into the ring. Some anarchist hackers in Italy strafed the group all night long, posting broken-English screeds about the political bankruptcy of "governance" in the new world. Felix looked at their netblock and determined that they were probably holed up in a small Interaction Design institute near Turin. Italy had been hit very bad, but out in the small town, this cell of anarchists had taken up residence.

A surprising number were running on a platform of shutting down the Internet. Felix had his doubts about whether this was even possible, but he thought he understood the impulse to finish the work and the world. Why not? From every indication, it seemed that the work to date had been a cascade of disasters, attacks, and opportunism, all of it adding up to *Gotterdammerung*. A terrorist attack here, a lethal counteroffensive there from an overreactive government . . . Before long, they'd made short work of the world.

He fell asleep thinking about the logistics of shutting down the Internet, and dreamed bad dreams in which he was the network's sole defender.

He woke to a papery, itchy sound. He rolled over and saw that Van was sitting up, his jacket balled up in his lap, vigorously scratching his skinny arms. They'd gone the color of corned beef, and had a scaly look. In the light streaming through the cafeteria windows, skin motes floated and danced in great clouds.

"What are you doing?" Felix sat up. Watching Van's fingernails rip into his skin made him itch in sympathy. It had been three days since he'd last washed his hair and his scalp sometimes felt like there were little egg-laying insects picking their way through it. He'd adjusted his glasses the night before and had touched the backs of his ears; his fingers came away shining with thick sebum. He got blackheads in the backs of his ears when he didn't shower for a couple days, and sometimes gigantic, deep boils that Kelly finally popped with sick relish.

"Scratching," Van said. He went to work on his head, sending a cloud of dandruff-crud into the sky, there to join the scurf that he'd already eliminated from his extremities. "Christ, I itch all over."

Felix took Mayor McCheese from Van's backpack and plugged it into one of the Ethernet cables that snaked all over the floor. He Googled everything he could think of that could be related to this. "Itchy" yielded 40,600,000 links. He tried compound queries and got slightly more discriminating links.

"I think it's stress-related eczema," Felix said, finally.

"I don't get eczema," Van said.

Felix showed him some lurid photos of red, angry skin flaked with white. "Stress-related eczema," he said, reading the caption.

Van examined his arms. "I have eczema," he said.

"Says here to keep it moisturized and to try cortisone cream. You might try the first-aid kit in the second-floor toilets. I think I saw some there." Like all of the sysadmins, Felix had had a bit of a rummage around the offices, bathrooms, kitchen, and storerooms, squirreling away a roll of toilet paper in his shoulder bag along with three or four power bars. They were sharing out the food in the caf by unspoken agreement, every sysadmin watching every other for signs of gluttony and hoarding. All were convinced that there was hoarding and gluttony going on out of eyeshot, because all were guilty of it themselves when no one else was watching.

Van got up and when his face hove into the light, Felix saw how puffed his eyes were. "I'll post to the mailing list for some antihistamine," Felix said. There had been four mailing lists and three wikis for the survivors in the building within hours of the first meeting's close, and in the intervening days they'd settled on just one. Felix was still on a little mailing list with five of his most trusted friends, two of whom were trapped in cages in other countries. He suspected that the rest of the sysadmins were doing the same.

Van stumbled off. "Good luck on the elections," he said, patting Felix on the shoulder.

Felix stood and paced, stopping to stare out the grubby windows. The fires still burned in Toronto, more than before. He'd tried to find mailing lists or blogs that Torontonians were posting to, but the only ones he'd found were being run by other geeks in other data centers. It was possible—likely, even—that there were survivors out there who had more pressing priorities than posting to the Internet. His home phone still worked about half the time but he'd stopped calling it after the second day, when hearing Kelly's voice on the voicemail for the fiftieth time had made him cry in the middle of a planning meeting. He wasn't the only one.

Election day. Time to face the music.

> Are you nervous?

> Nope, Felix typed.

> I don't much care if I win, to be honest. I'm just glad we're doing this. The alternative was sitting around with our thumbs up our ass, waiting for someone to crack up and open the door.

The cursor hung. Queen Kong was very high latency as she bossed her gang of Googloids around the Googleplex, doing everything she could to keep her data center online. Three of the offshore cages had gone offline and two of their six redundant network links were smoked. Lucky for her, queries-per-second were way down.

> There's still China,

she typed. Queen Kong had a big board with a map of the world colored in Googlequeries-per-second, and could do magic with it, showing the drop-off overtime in colorful charts. She'd uploaded lots of video clips showing how the plague and the bombs had swept the world: the initial upswell of queries from people wanting to find out what was going on, then the grim, precipitous shelving off as the plagues took hold.

> China's still running about ninety percent nominal.

Felix shook his head.

> You can't think that they're responsible

> No

she typed, but then she started to key something and then stopped.

> No of course not. I believe the Popovich Hypothesis. Every asshole in the world is using the other assholes for cover. But China put them down harder and faster than anyone else. Maybe we've finally found a use for totalitarian states.

Felix couldn't resist. He typed:

> You're lucky your boss can't see you type that. You guys were pretty enthusiastic participants in the Great Firewall of China.

> Wasn't my idea, she typed.

> And my boss is dead. They're probably all dead. The whole Bay Area got hit hard, and then there was the quake.

They'd watched the USGS's automated data stream from the 6.9 that trashed northern Cal from Gilroy to Sebastopol. Soma webcams revealed the scope of the damage—gas-main explosions, seismically retrofitted buildings crumpling like piles of children's blocks after a good kicking. The Googleplex, floating on a series of gigantic steel springs, had shook like a plateful of Jell-O, but the racks had stayed in place and the worst injury they'd had was a badly bruised eye on a sysadmin who'd caught a flying cable-crimper in the face.

> Sorry. I forgot.

> It's okay. We all lost people, right?

> Yeah. Yeah. Anyway, I'm not worried about the election. Whoever wins, at least we're doing SOMETHING

> Not if they vote for one of the fuckrags

Fuckrag was the epithet that some of the sysadmins were using to describe the contingent that wanted to shut down the Internet. Queen Kong had coined it—apparently it had started life as a catch-all term to describe clueless IT managers that she'd chewed up through her career.

> They won't. They're just tired and sad is all. Your endorsement will carry the day.

The Googloids were one of the largest and most powerful blocs left behind, along with the satellite uplink crews and the remaining transoceanic crews. Queen Kong's endorsement had come as a surprise and he'd sent her an email that she'd replied to tersely: "Can't have the fuckrags in charge."

> gtg

she typed and then her connection dropped. He fired up a browser and called up Google.com. The browser timed out. He hit reload, and then again, and then the Google front page came back up; whatever had hit Queen Kong's workplace—power failure, worms, another quake—she had fixed it. He snorted when he saw that they'd replaced the O's in the Google logo with little planet Earths with mushroom clouds rising from them.

"Got anything to eat?" Van said to him. It was midafternoon, not that time particularly passed in the data center. Felix patted his pockets. They'd put a quartermaster in charge, but not before everyone had snagged some chow out of the machines. He'd had a dozen power bars and some apples. He'd taken a couple sandwiches but had wisely eaten them first before they got stale.

"One power bar left," he said. He'd noticed a certain looseness in his waistline that morning and had briefly relished it. Then he'd remembered Kelly's teasing about his weight and he'd cried some. Then he'd eaten two power bars, leaving him with just one left.

"Oh," Van said. His face was hollower than ever, his shoulders sloping in on his toast-rack chest.

"Here," Felix said. "Vote Felix."

Van took the power bar from him and then put it down on the table, "Okay, I want to give this back to you and say, 'No, I couldn't,' but I'm fucking *hungry*, so I'm just going to take it and eat it, okay?"

"That's fine by me," Felix said. "Enjoy."

"How are the elections coming?" Van said, once he'd licked the wrapper clean.

"Dunno," Felix said. "Haven't checked in a while." He'd been winning by a slim margin a few hours before. Not having his laptop was a major handicap when it came to stuff like this. Up in the cages, there were a dozen more like him, poor bastards who'd left the house on Der Tag without thinking to snag something Wi-Fi-enabled.

"You're going to get smoked," Sario said, sliding in next to them. He'd become famous in the center for never sleeping, for eavesdropping, for picking fights in RL that had the ill-considered heat of a Usenet flamewar. "The winner will be someone who understands a couple of fundamental facts." He held up a fist, then ticked off his bullet points by raising one finger at a time. "Point: The terrorists are using the Internet to destroy the world, and we need to destroy the Internet first. Point: Even if I'm wrong, the whole thing is a joke. We'll run out of generator fuel soon enough. Point: Or if we don't, it will be because the old world will be back and running, and it won't give a crap about your new world. Point: We're gonna run out of food before we run out of shit to argue about or reasons not to go outside. We have the chance to do something to help the world recover— we can kill the 'Net and cut it off as a tool for bad guys. Or we can rearrange some more deck chairs on the bridge of your personal *Titanic* in the service of some sweet dream about an 'independent cyberspace.'"

The thing was that Sario was right. They would be out of fuel in two days—intermittent power from the grid had stretched their generator lifespan. And if you bought his hypothesis that the Internet was primarily being used as a tool to organize more mayhem, shutting it down would be the right thing to do.

But Felix's son and his wife were dead. He didn't want to rebuild the old world. He wanted a new one. The old world was one that didn't have any place for him. Not anymore.

Van scratched his raw, flaking skin. Puffs of dander and scurf swirled in the musty, greasy air. Sario curled a lip at him. "That is disgusting. We're breathing recycled air, you know. Whatever leprosy is eating you, aerosolizing it into the air supply is pretty antisocial."

"You're the world's leading authority on antisocial, Sario," Van said. "Go away or I'll multitool you to death." He stopped scratching and patted his sheathed multi-pliers like a gunslinger.

"Yeah, I'm antisocial. I've got Asperger's and I haven't taken any meds in four days. What's your fucking excuse."

Van scratched some more. "I'm sorry," he said. "I didn't know."

Sario cracked up. "Oh, you are priceless. I'd bet that three-quarters of this bunch is borderline autistic. Me, I'm just an asshole. But I'm one who isn't afraid to tell the truth, and that makes me better than you, dickweed."

"Fuckrag," Felix said, "fuck off." They had less than a day's worth of fuel when Felix was elected the first ever Prime Minister of Cyberspace. The first count was spoiled by a bot that spammed the voting process and they lost a critical day while they added up the votes a second time.

But by then, it was all seeming like more of a joke. Half the data centers had gone dark. Queen Kong's net-maps of Google queries were looking grimmer and grimmer as more of the world went offline, though she maintained a leaderboard of new and rising queries—largely related to health, shelter, sanitation, and self-defense.

Worm-load slowed. Power was going off to many home PC users, and staying off, so their compromised PCs were going dark. The backbones were still lit up and blinking, but the missives from those data centers were looking more and more desperate. Felix hadn't eaten in a day and neither had anyone in a satellite Earth-station of transoceanic head-end.

Water was running short, too.

Popovich and Rosenbaum came and got him before he could do more than answer a few congratulatory messages and post a canned acceptance speech to newsgroups.

"We're going to open the doors," Popovich said. Like all of them, he'd lost weight and waxed scruffy and oily. His BO was like a cloud coming off trash bags behind a fish market on a sunny day. Felix was quite sure he smelled no better.

"You're going to go for a reccy? Get more fuel? We can charter a working group for it—great idea."

Rosenbaum shook his head sadly. "We're going to go find our families. Whatever is out there has burned itself out. Or it hasn't. Either way, there's no future in here."

"What about network maintenance?" Felix said, though he knew the answers. "Who'll keep the routers up?"

"We'll give you the root passwords to everything," Popovich said. His hands were shaking and his eyes were bleary. Like many of the smokers stuck in the data center, he'd gone cold turkey this week. They'd run out of caffeine products two days earlier, too. The smokers had it rough.

"And I'll just stay here and keep everything online?"

"You and anyone else who cares anymore."

Felix knew that he'd squandered his opportunity. The election had seemed noble and brave, but in hindsight all it had been was an excuse for infighting when they should have been figuring out what to do next. The problem was that there was nothing to do next.

"I can't make you stay," he said.

"Yeah, you can't." Popovich turned on his heel and walked out. Rosenbaum watched him go, then he gripped Felix's shoulder and squeezed it.

"Thank you, Felix. It was a beautiful dream. It still is. Maybe we'll find something to eat and some fuel and come back."

Rosenbaum had a sister whom he'd been in contact with over IM for the first days after the crisis broke. Then she'd stopped answering. The sysadmins were split among those who'd had a chance to say goodbye and those who hadn't. Each was sure the other had it better.

They posted about it on the internal newsgroup—they were still geeks, after all, and there was a little honor guard on the ground floor, geeks who watched them pass toward the double doors. They manipulated the keypads and the steel shutters lifted, then the first set of doors opened. They stepped into the vestibule and pulled the doors shut behind them. The front doors opened.

It was very bright and sunny outside, and apart from how empty it was, it looked very normal. Heartbreakingly so.

The two took a tentative step out into the world. Then another. They turned to wave at the assembled masses. Then they both grabbed their throats and began to jerk and twitch, crumpling in a heap on the ground.

"Shiii—!" was all Felix managed to choke out before they both dusted themselves off and stood up, laughing so hard they were clutching their sides. They waved once more and turned on their heels.

"Man, those guys are sick," Van said. He scratched his arms, which had long, bloody scratches on them. His clothes were so covered in scurf they looked like they'd been dusted with icing sugar.

"I thought it was pretty funny," Felix said.

"Christ, I'm hungry," Van said, conversationally.

"Lucky for you, we've got all the packets we can eat," Felix said.

"You're too good to us grunts, Mr. President," Van said.

"Prime Minister," he said. "And you're no grunt, you're the Deputy Prime Minister. You're my designated ribbon-cutter and hander-out of oversized novelty checks."

It buoyed both of their spirits. Watching Popovich and Rosenbaum go, it buoyed them up. Felix knew then that they'd all be going soon. That had been preordained by the fuel supply, but who wanted to wait for the fuel to run out, anyway?

> half my crew split this morning,

Queen Kong typed. Google was holding up pretty good anyway, of course. The load on the servers was a lot lighter than it had been since the days when Google fit on a bunch of hand-built PCs under a desk at Stanford.

> we're down to a quarter Felix typed back. It was only a day since Popovich and Rosenbaum left, but the traffic on the newsgroups had fallen down to near zero. He and Van hadn't had much time to play Republic of Cyberspace. They'd been too busy learning the systems that Popovich had turned over to them, the big, big routers that had gone on acting as the major interchange for all the network backbones in Canada.

Still, someone posted to the newsgroups every now and again, generally to say goodbye. The old flamewars about who would be PM, or whether they would shut down the network, or who took too much food—it was all gone.

He reloaded the newsgroup. There was a typical message.

> Runaway processes on Solaris TK

>

> Uh, hi. I'm just a lightweight MSCE but I'm the only one awake here and four of the DSLAMS just went down. Looks like there's some custom accounting code that's trying to figure out how much to bill our corporate customers and it's spawned ten thousand threads and it's eating all the swap. I just want to kill it but I can't seem to do that. Is there some magic invocation I need to do to get this goddamned weenix box to kill this shit? I mean, it's not as if any of our customers are ever going to pay us again. I'd ask the guy who wrote this code, but he's pretty much dead as far as anyone can work out.

He reloaded. There was a response. It was short, authoritative, and helpful—just the sort of thing you almost never saw in a high-caliber newsgroup when a noob posted a dumb question. The apocalypse had awoken the spirit of patient helpfulness in the world's sysop community.

Van shoulder-surfed him. "Holy shit, who knew he had it in him?"

He looked at the message again. It was from Will Sario.

He dropped into his chat window.

> sario i thought you wanted the network dead why are you helping msces fix their boxen?

> [sheepish grin] Gee Mr PM, maybe I just can't bear to watch a computer suffer at the hands of an amateur.

He flipped to the channel with Queen Kong in it.

> How long?

> Since I slept? Two days. Until we run out of fuel? Three days. Since we ran out of food? Two days.

> Jeez. I didn't sleep last night either. We're a little short-handed around here.

> asl? Im monica and I live in pasadena and Im bored with my homework. Would you like to download my pic???

The trojan bots were all over IRC these days, jumping to every channel that had any traffic on it. Sometimes you caught five or six flirting with each other.

It was pretty weird to watch a piece of malware try to con another instance of itself into downloading a trojan.

They both kicked the bot off the channel simultaneously. He had a script for it now. The spam hadn't even tailed off a little.

> How come the spam isn't reducing? Half the goddamned data centers have gone dark

Queen Kong paused a long time before typing. As had become automatic when she went high-latency, he reloaded the Google homepage. Sure enough, it was down.

> Sario, you got any food?

> You won't miss a couple more meals, Your Excellency

Van had gone back to Mayor McCheese but he was in the same channel. "What a dick. You're looking pretty buff, though, dude."

Van didn't look so good. He looked like you could knock him over with a stiff breeze and he had a phlegmy, weak quality to his speech.

> hey kong everything okay?

> everything's fine just had to go kick some ass

"How's the traffic, Van?"

"Down 25 percent from this morning," he said. There were a bunch of nodes whose connections routed through them. Presumably most of these were home or commercial customers in places where the power was still on and the phone company's COS were still alive.

Every once in a while, Felix would wiretap the connections to see if he could find a person who had news of the wide world. Almost all of it was automated traffic, though: network backups, status updates. Spam. Lots of spam.

> Spam's still up because the services that stop spam are failing faster than the services that create it. All the anti-worm stuff is centralized in a couple places. The bad stuff is on a million zombie computers. If only the lusers had had the good sense to turn off their home PC s before keeling over or taking off.

> at the rate were going well be routing nothing but spam by dinnertime

Van cleared his throat, a painful sound. "About that," he said. "I think it's going to hit sooner than that. Felix, I don't think anyone would notice if we just walked away from here."

Felix looked at him, his skin the color of corned beef and streaked with long, angry scabs. His fingers trembled.

"You drinking enough water?"

Van nodded. "All frigging day, every ten seconds. Anything to keep my belly full." He pointed to a refilled Pepsi Max bottle full of water by his side.

"Let's have a meeting," he said.

There had been forty-three of them on D-Day. Now there were fifteen. Six had responded to the call for a meeting by simply leaving. Everyone knew without having to be told what the meeting was about.

"So that's it, you're going to let it all fall apart?" Sario was the only one with the energy left to get properly angry. He'd go angry to his grave. The veins on his throat and forehead stood out angrily. His fists shook angrily. All the other geeks went lids-down at the site of him, looking up in unison for once at the discussion, not keeping one eye on a chat-log or a tailed service log.

"Sario, you've got to be shitting me," Felix said. "You wanted to pull the goddamned plug!"

"I wanted it to go *clean*," he shouted. "I didn't want it to bleed out and keel over in little gasps and pukes forever. I wanted it to be an act of will by the global community of its caretakers. I wanted it to be an affirmative act by human hands. Not entropy and bad code and worms winning out. Fuck that, that's just what's happened out there."

Up in the top-floor cafeteria, there were windows all around, hardened and light-bending, and by custom, they were all blinds-down. Now Sario ran around the room, yanking down the blinds. *How the hell can he get the energy to run?* Felix wondered. He could barely walk up the stairs to the meeting room.

Harsh daylight flooded in. It was a fine sunny day out there, but everywhere you looked across that commanding view of Toronto's skyline, there were rising plumes of smoke. The TD Tower, a gigantic black modernist glass brick, was gouting flame to the sky. "It's all falling apart, the way everything does.

"Listen, listen. If we leave the network to fall over slowly, parts of it will stay online for months. Maybe years. And what will run on it? Malware. Worms. Spam. System processes. Zone transfers. The things we use fall apart and require constant maintenance. The things we abandon don't get used and they last forever. We're going to leave the network behind like a lime pit filled with industrial waste. That will be our fucking legacy—the legacy of every keystroke you and I and anyone, anywhere ever typed. You understand? We're going to leave it to die slow like a wounded dog, instead of giving it one clean shot through the head."

Van scratched his cheeks, then Felix saw that he was wiping away tears.

"Sario, you're not wrong, but you're not right either," he said. "Leaving it up to limp along is right. We're going to all be limping for a long time, and maybe it will be some use to someone. If there's one packet being routed from any user to any other user, anywhere in the world, it's doing its job."

"If you want a clean kill, you can do that," Felix said. "I'm the PM and I say so. I'm giving you root. All of you." He turned to the whiteboard where the cafeteria workers used to scrawl the day's specials. Now it was covered with the remnants of heated technical debates that the sysadmins had engaged in over the days since the day.

He scrubbed away a clean spot with his sleeve and began to write out long, complicated alphanumeric passwords salted with punctuation. Felix had a gift for remembering that kind of password. He doubted it would do him much good, ever again.

> Were going, kong. Fuels almost out anyway

> yeah well thats right then, it was an honor, mr prime minister

> you going to be okay?

> ive commandeered a young sysadmin to see to my feminine needs and weve found another cache of food thatll last us a coupel weeks now that were down to fifteen admins—im in hog heaven pal

> youre amazing, Queen Kong, seriously. Dont be a hero though. When you need to go go. Theres got to be something out there

> be safe felix, seriously—btw did i tell you queries are up in Romania? maybe theyre getting back on their feet .

> really?

> yeah, really, we're hard to kill—like fucking roaches

Her connection died. He dropped to Firefox and reloaded Google and it was down. He hit reload and hit reload and hit reload, but it didn't come up. He closed his eyes and listened to Van scratch his legs and then heard Van type a little.

"They're back up," he said.

Felix whooshed out a breath. He sent the message to the newsgroup, one that he'd run through five drafts before settling on, "Take care of the place, okay? We'll be back, someday."

Everyone was going except Sario. Sario wouldn't leave. He came down to see them off, though.

The sysadmins gathered in the lobby and Felix made the safety door go up, and the light rushed in.

Sario stuck his hand out.

"Good luck," he said.

"You too," Felix said. He had a firm grip, Sario, stronger than he had any right to be. "Maybe you were right," he said.

"Maybe," he said.

"You going to pull the plug?"

Sario looked up at the drop-ceiling, seeming to peer through the reinforced floors at the humming racks above. "Who knows?" he said at last.

Van scratched and a flurry of white motes danced in the sunlight.

"Let's go find you a pharmacy," Felix said. He walked to the door and the other sysadmins followed.

They waited for the interior doors to close behind them and then Felix opened the exterior doors. The air smelled and tasted like mown grass, like the first drops of rain, like the lake and the sky, like the outdoors and the world, an old friend not heard from in an eternity.

"Bye, Felix," the other sysadmins said. They were drifting away while he stood transfixed at the top of the short concrete staircase. The light hurt his eyes and made them water.

"I think there's a Shopper's Drug Mart on King Street," he said to Van. 'We'll throw a brick through the window and get you some cortisone, okay?"

"You're the Prime Minister," Van said. "Lead on."

They didn't see a single soul on the fifteen-minute walk. There wasn't a single sound except for some bird noises and some distant groans, and the wind in the electric cables overhead. It was like walking on the surface of the moon.

"Bet they have chocolate bars at the Shopper's," Van said.

Felix's stomach lurched. Food. "Wow," he said, around a mouthful of saliva.

They walked past a little hatchback, and in the front seat was the dried body of a woman holding the dried body of a baby, and his mouth filled with sour bile, even though the smell was faint through the rolled-up windows.

He hadn't thought of Kelly or 2.0 in days. He dropped to his knees and retched again. Out here in the real world, his family was dead. Everyone he knew was dead. He just wanted to lie down on the sidewalk and wait to die, too.

Van's rough hands slipped under his armpits and hauled weakly at him. "Not now," he said. "Once we're safe inside somewhere and we've eaten something, then you can do this, but not now. Understand me, Felix? Not fucking now."

The profanity got through to him. He got to his feet. His knees were trembling.

"Just a block more," Van said, and slipped Felix's arm around his shoulders and led him along.

"Thank you, Van. I'm sorry."

"No sweat," he said. "You need a shower, bad. No offense."

"None taken."

The Shopper's had a metal security gate, but it had been torn away from the front windows, which had been rudely smashed. Felix and Van squeezed through the gap and stepped into the dim drugstore. A few of the displays were knocked over, but other than that, it looked okay. By the cash registers, Felix spotted the racks of candy bars at the same instant that Van saw them, and they hurried over and grabbed a handful each, stuffing their faces.

"You two eat like pigs."

They both whirled at the sound of the woman's voice. She was holding a fire axe that was nearly as big as she was. She wore a lab coat and comfortable shoes.

"You take what you need and go, okay? No sense in there being any trouble." Her chin was pointy and her eyes were sharp. She looked to be in her forties. She looked nothing like Kelly, which was good, because Felix felt like running and giving her a hug as it was. Another person alive!

"Are you a doctor?" Felix said. She was wearing scrubs under the coat, he saw.

"You going to go?" She brandished the axe.

Felix held his hands up. "Seriously, are you a doctor? A pharmacist?"

"I used to be an RN, ten years ago. I'm mostly a Web designer."

"You're shitting me," Felix said.

"Haven't you ever met a girl who knew about computers?"

"Actually, a friend of mine who runs Google's data center is a girl. A woman, I mean."

"You're shitting me," she said. "A woman ran Google's data center?"

"Runs," Felix said. "It's still online."

"NFW," she said. She let the axe lower.

"Way. Have you got any cortisone cream? I can tell you the story. My name's Felix and this is Van, who needs any antihistamines you can spare."

"I can spare? Felix old pal, I have enough dope here to last a hundred years. This stuff's going to expire long before it runs out. But are you telling me that the 'Net's still up?"

"It's still up," he said. "Kind of. That's what we've been doing all week. Keeping it online. It might not last much longer, though."

"No," she said. "I don't suppose it would." She set the axe down. "Have you got anything to trade? I don't need much, but I've been trying to keep my spirits up by trading with the neighbors. It's like playing civilization."

"You have neighbors?"

"At least ten," she said. "The people in the restaurant across the way make a pretty good soup, even if most of the veg is canned. They cleaned me out of Sterno, though."

"You've got neighbors and you trade with them?"

"Well, nominally. It'd be pretty lonely without them. I've taken care of whatever sniffles I could. Set a bone—broken wrist. Listen, do you want some Wonder Bread and peanut butter? I have a ton of it. Your friend looks like he could use a meal."

"Yes please," Van said. "We don't have anything to trade, but we're both committed workaholics looking to learn a trade. Could you use some assistants?"

"Not really." She spun her axe on its head. "But I wouldn't mind some company."

They ate the sandwiches and then some soup. The restaurant people brought it over and made their manners at them, though Felix saw their noses wrinkle up and ascertained that there was working plumbing in the back room. Van went in to take a sponge bath and then he followed.

"None of us know what to do," the woman said. Her name was Rosa, and she had found them a bottle of wine and some disposable plastic cups from the housewares aisle. "I thought we'd have helicopters or tanks or even looters, but it's just quiet."

"You seem to have kept pretty quiet yourself," Felix said.

"Didn't want to attract the wrong kind of attention."

"You ever think that maybe there's a lot of people out there doing the same thing? Maybe if we all get together we'll come up with something to do."

"Or maybe they'll cut our throats," she said.

Van nodded. "She's got a point."

Felix was on his feet. "No way, we can't think like that. Lady, we're at a critical juncture here. We can go down through negligence, dwindling away in our hiding holes, or we can try to build something better."

"Better?" She made a rude noise.

"Okay, not better. Something though. Building something new is better than letting it dwindle away. Christ, what are you going to do when you've read all the magazines and eaten all the potato chips here?"

Rosa shook her head. "Pretty talk," she said. "But what the hell are we going to do, anyway?"

"Something," Felix said. "We're going to do something. Something is better than nothing. We're going to take this patch of the world where people are talking to each other, and we're going to expand it. We're going to find everyone we can and we're going to take care of them and they're going to take care of us. We'll probably fuck it up. We'll probably fail. I'd rather fail than give up, though."

Van laughed. "Felix, you are crazier than Sario, you know it?"

"We're going to go and drag him out, first thing tomorrow. He's going to be a part of this, too. Everyone will. Screw the end of the world. The world doesn't end. Humans aren't the kind of things that have endings."

Rosa shook her head again, but she was smiling a little now. "And you'll be what, the Pope-Emperor of the World?"

"He prefers Prime Minister," Van said in a stagey whisper. The antihistamines had worked miracles on his skin, and it had faded from angry red to a fine pink.

"You want to be Minister of Health, Rosa?" he said.

"Boys," she said. "Playing games. Howa bout this. I'll help out however I can provided you never ask me to call you Prime Minister and you never call me the Minister of Health?"

"It's a deal, he said.

Van refilled their glasses, upending the wine bottle to get the last few drops out.

They raised their glasses. "To the world," Felix said. "To humanity." He thought hard. "To rebuilding."

"To anything," Van said.

"To anything," Felix said. "To everything."

"To everything," Rosa said.

They drank. He wanted to go see the house—see Kelly and 2.0, though his stomach churned at the thought of what he might find there. But the next day, they started to rebuild. And months later, they started over again, when disagreements drove apart the fragile little group they'd pulled together. And a year after that, they started over again. And five years later, they started again.

It was nearly six months before he went home. Van helped him along, riding cover behind him on the bicycles they used to get around town. The further north they rode, the stronger the smell of burnt wood became. There were lots of burnt-out houses. Sometimes marauders burnt the houses they'd looted, but more often it was just nature, the kinds of fires you got in forests and on mountains. There were six choking, burnt blocks where every house was burnt before they reached home.

But Felix's old housing development was still standing, an oasis of eerily pristine buildings that looked like maybe their somewhat neglectful owners had merely stepped out to buy some paint and fresh lawnmower blades to bring their old homes back up to their neat, groomed selves.

That was worse, somehow. He got off the bike at the entry of the subdivision and they walked the bikes together in silence, listening to the sough of the wind in the trees. Winter was coming late that year, but it was coming, and as the sweat dried in the wind, Felix started to shiver.

He didn't have his keys anymore. They were at the data-center, months and worlds away. He tried the door-handle, but it didn't turn. He applied his shoulder to the door and it ripped away from its wet, rotted jamb with a loud, splintering sound. The house was rotting from the inside.

The door splashed when it landed. The house was full of stagnant water, four inches of stinking pond-scummed water in the living room. He splashed carefully through it, feeling the floorboards sag spongily beneath each step.

Up the stairs, his nose full of that terrible green mildewy stench. Into the bedroom, the furniture familiar as a childhood friend.

Kelly was in the bed with 2.0. The way they both lay, it was clear they hadn't gone easy—they were twisted double, Kelly curled around 2.0. Their skin was bloated, making them almost unrecognizable. The smell— God, the smell.

Felix's head spun. He thought he would fall over and clutched at the dresser. An emotion he couldn't name—rage, anger, sorrow?—made him breathe hard, gulp for air like he was drowning.

And then it was over. The world was over. Kelly and 2.0—over. And he had a job to do. He folded the blanket over them—Van helped, solemnly. They went into the front yard and took turns digging, using the shovel from the garage that Kelly had used for gardening. They had lots of experience digging graves by then. Lots of experience handling the dead. They dug, and wary dogs watched them from the tall grass on the neighboring lawns, but they were also good at chasing off dogs with well-thrown stones.

When the grave was dug, they laid Felix's wife and son to rest in it. Felix quested after words to say over the mound, but none came. He'd dug so many graves for so many men's wives and so many women's husbands and so many children—the words were long gone.

Felix dug ditches and salvaged cans and buried the dead. He planted and harvested. He fixed some cars and learned to make biodiesel. Finally he fetched up in a data center for a little government—little governments came and went, but this one was smart enough to want to keep records and needed someone to keep everything running, and Van went with him.

They spent a lot of time in chat rooms and sometimes they happened upon old friends from the strange time they'd spent running the Distributed Republic of Cyberspace, geeks who insisted on calling him PM, though no one in the real world ever called him that anymore.

It wasn't a good life, most of the time. Felix's wounds never healed, and neither did most other people's. There were lingering sicknesses and sudden ones. Tragedy on tragedy.

But Felix liked his data center. There in the humming of the racks, he never felt like it was the first days of a better nation, but he never felt like it was the last days of one, either.

> gotobed,felix
> soon, kong, soon—almost got this backup running
> youre a junkie, dude.
> look whos talking.

He reloaded the Google homepage. Queen Kong had had it online for a couple years now. The Os in Google changed all the time, whenever she got the urge. Today they were little cartoon globes, one smiling the other frowning.

He looked at it for a long time and propped back into a terminal to check his backup. It was running clean, for a change. The little government's records were safe.

> okay night night

> take care

Van waved at him as he creaked to the door, stretching out his back with a long series of pops.

"Sleep well, boss," he said.

"Don't stick around here all night again," Felix said. "You need your sleep, too."

"You're too good to us grunts," Van said, and went back to typing.

Felix went to the door and walked out into the night. Behind him, the biodiesel generator hummed and made its acrid fumes. The harvest moon was up, which he loved. Tomorrow, he'd go back and fix another computer and fight off entropy again. And why not?

It was what he did. He was a sysadmin.